TO A DARKER SHORE

LEANNE SCHWARTZ

PAGE STREET YA

PAGE STREET YA

First published in 2024 by
Page Street Publishing Co.
27 Congress Street, Suite 1511
Salem, MA 01970
www.pagestreetpublishing.com

Distributed by Macmillan, sales in Canada by The Canadian Manda Group.

28   27   26   25   24   1   2   3   4   5

ISBN-13: 978-1-64567-840-3
ISBN-10: 1-64567-840-7

Library of Congress Control Number: 2023907226

Cover and book design by Rosie Stewart for Page Street Publishing Co.
Cover illustration © Flora Kirk

Printed and bound in China

FOR DAVID

Manuscript Content Warnings

Light gore and body horror. Some bullying/sizeist body talk, and conflict with a parent over masking autism (internalized but ultimately rejected by the main characters). Societal/parental homophobia (with happy outcomes). Claustrophobic panic attacks. Implied suicidal ideation. Illness, loss, grief.

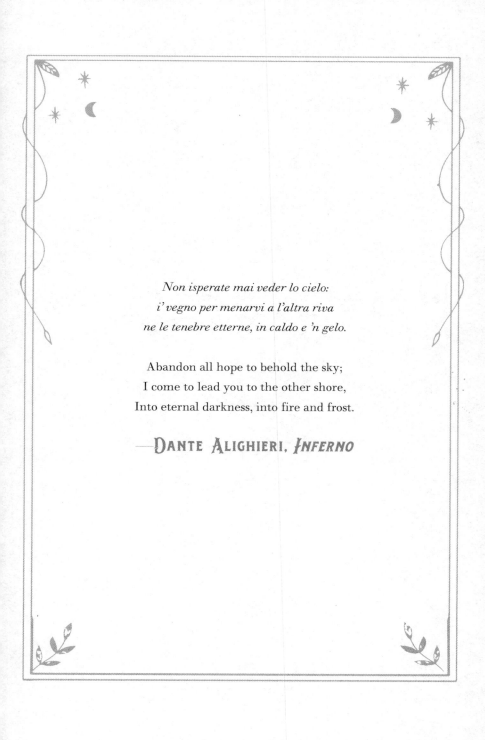

Non isperate mai veder lo cielo:
i' vegno per menarvi a l'altra riva
ne le tenebre etterne, in caldo e 'n gelo.

Abandon all hope to behold the sky;
I come to lead you to the other shore,
Into eternal darkness, into fire and frost.

—DANTE ALIGHIERI, *INFERNO*

Part One

PARADISO

An Unholy Hunger

Alesta expected monsters.

She grew distracted only a moment, watching the terns soar over the bright blue sea, wondering how their wings kept them aloft. The birds pulled her gaze along the coast and to the sky.

That's when the branzono must have crept over the low cliff and rocky dunes.

It drew up as tall as Alesta on its two legs, wicked fins jutting from its calves and back, skin pulled taut over wide, boney shoulders and too-long arms—green like the headland, but the visceral wrongness of it here in Soladisa's garden paradise turned the warm salt air on her tongue to an acid tang of fear.

The monster shambled nearer the grassy stretch of grazing land Alesta's flock was abandoning with violent bleats, more strident warning than the bells up at the Towers. Shaken from her reverie, Alesta dodged sheep, spooked and scattering and heedless of any bellwether. She raced for the branzono.

Herder's staff in hand, skirts flying, she cursed herself for having taken her eyes off the ground. Branzonos were a common enough threat, especially on this side of the island, facing the monster's rock, where the sea was full of them—and worse. She and Nonnina couldn't afford to lose a single sheep to a monster's spiny teeth.

Wariness of the hunger of monsters lived deep in Alesta's bones. Wasn't it the appetite of the greatest devil of them all out on that cursed rock that was devouring Alesta's hope for any real future?

With a swell of frustration at that reality coursing through her limbs, she cracked her staff against the monster's side before it could reach its claws toward any of the panicked animals. "Oh, no you *don't.*"

It gave a strangled scream and clutched at the staff, dragging Alesta off-balance. Not easy, considering her sturdy build—this thing was strong. She took advantage, letting it pull her and throwing all of her weight into the staff, driving the creature back on its webbed feet. They both toppled over, her crook trumbling from their grasps. Alesta reached for the knife at her belt as she rolled. She twisted over the beast to thrust the blade down, aiming for the monster's shriveled heart.

The branzono grabbed her wrist. Against her tan skin, the webbing between its long white claws shimmered like seaweed, like most of its slimy body. But hell burned in the devil even as it yet dripped with seawater; the leathery hide over its upper arms and shoulders blistered and peeled away from seeping, deeper layers of skin, even muscle, in black-crusted folds. The unholy steam coming off them seared her skin as she strained against the branzono's hold. The monster stared up at Alesta, pale eyes cast with terrible longing, vast and vacant as the sky.

Just hunger. And she was no one's meal. Not yet. Not today.

Alesta drove her elbow down into the branzono's chest. It gave a startling crack. The creature swiped out at her wildly with its free hand. Its claws missed her eye, thank Hektorus, but tore through her hair. Its knuckles bashed against her cheekbone with that monstrous strength. She shouted. But the branzono, in greater pain, loosened its grip. Alesta pushed the rest of her outrage into her final blow, wrapping both hands about her knife's simple wooden hilt and plunging its blade deep through monster skin and sinew and muscle.

She shoved herself back, but dark blood spurted from the wound, and the wind off the sea carried a mist of it into her face. With a grimace, Alesta let herself fall fully into the damp grass, chest heaving against her leather bodice's laces, mangled hair sticking to her face with sweat and blood.

Which was the perfect moment, of course, for the future king of Soladisa to find her.

His low voice, out of breath and raked through with concern, came from just behind her. "You all right?"

She tilted her chin to squint up at him. His tall silhouette was nearly lost in the afternoon sun's sharp beams. "Never better."

He strode to her side, careful to avoid where the branzono still twitched, and threw out a hand to help her up.

She wiped her bloody palm on her overskirt—already stained with grass and dark with sandy earth—before accepting. For a moment, her insides pinched with worry that she'd be too heavy for the boy to pull her to her feet without a struggle. Then she was up, looking straight into Kyr's eyes. Holding his hand.

She dropped it and wiped her hair from her face, trying to

smooth it down. The vanity of it made her feel foolish, though, so she played it off, and with the affectation of a lady of the Towers, said, "By Hektorus' breath, you do meet all sorts out here on the headland."

His concerned face broke into a slight smile. "I hope I'm a more welcome sight than a branzono." One dimple flickered into existence. "You perfect calamity."

She scrunched her face as if considering his glossy, dark curls kissed with golden highlights, his long straight nose, his strong jaw and sharp cheekbones. Her heart twitched a little, like the monster at her feet, but she shrugged, acting unimpressed. "At least you don't try to eat my sheep."

His smile—that wide, full mouth—turned wry. "Unless Nonnina's invited me to dinner." The light in his brown eyes dimmed a little. His voice went flat, like it always did when he was being serious. "You need to go to the Arbor at once to be absolved." His thumb scraped back and forth over the worn embossing of the book he held.

She sighed and crouched beside the monster to pull her knife from its stilled chest. One more reason she hated the things. Now she had to trudge up to the Towers and submit to the ministrations of an albero, to cleanse her of the killing, when she was already so short on time, still desperate to think up an invention to present at this year's Festival of Virtues. Though, as long as she *had* killed this one—"Look at the gills." She tilted her head and used the tip of her knife to pull one set apart to better see where the skin turned pale and sieve-like. "I wonder if the structure could have applications for cleansing water in the aqueducts? And this webbing . . ." She prodded at the skin with her own finger.

It stretched easily over her nail. Kyr made a disgusted sound in the back of his throat. "It's actually translucent, but still strong."

"Alesta."

That stopped her. She lifted her gaze from the carcass to Kyr, now backlit by the glittering sea like the fractured glass worked into the murals in the Towers' courtyard walls.

"Within the hour of a devil's dispatching—" he recited at her. His hand left off the book to worry one of the shining buttons on his colorful, embroidered jacket.

She sucked her teeth. "If I try to haul this home or get cleaned up before going to the Towers, you're just going to get twitchier, aren't you?"

He screwed up his face the same considering way she had, then nodded emphatically. "My twitchiest."

Always such a stickler. She slapped her palm to a thigh and blew out a breath as she rose. "Fine. But you're coming with me." She sheathed her knife.

"Of course. I was on my way to spend the afternoon with you. Here or there." He shrugged, as if it made no difference to him.

She knew he was avoiding the Towers, though, even more than usual. It was a tithing moon.

Normally they didn't pretend with each other, not about anything important. But Kyr never wanted to talk about the tithing. He swallowed and held the book out to her. "Brought this for you."

A kindness. Even if he couldn't admit it aloud, they were both aware what was coming in mere weeks, and how the threat of each season's tithing weighed upon some more than others. How frantic Alesta had been growing to prove herself at the festival before this particular axe could fall. Warmth flooded her insides as she took the volume—old enough for Kyr to be passing on to his poor tenant friend, so it wasn't as if her smudged hands could hurt its cracked leather binding.

And when she asked him about it, as they set off, she got to see Kyr's face light up, eyes rounding, tan skin aglow. With great sweeps of his hands he told her about the story writ in verse, his words coming so fast, sometimes they stuttered from his mouth. He paused only when they passed Alesta's neighbor, brought off his field by the commotion of fleeing sheep. Vittore offered to gather and pen them for Alesta while she was absolved. They'd traded favors since she and her grandmother were left to run their farm on their own—Vittore and his children helping with the harvest, Alesta fixing his plow and remaking his olive press to be more effective. Not to mention killing branzonos before they could make their way further inland and onto his fields.

Kyr fidgeted with a stray thread at the elbow of his jacket until Alesta got moving again. Through rolling green hills and along the edges of orchards, they filled their hike up to the city with talk of monster slaying, or the wingspan of terns, or the latest landscape Kyr had finished painting.

As they passed through the cobblestone streets of the city, winding closer to the Towers, Kyr grew straighter-spined and more reserved. No more animated explanations or questions to Alesta. His hands no longer flew about like birds but trapped one another at the small of his back. Tradespeople nodded to him, and he nodded back with precision.

The city made its demands upon everyone in its own way.

Too soon, the front entrance to the Towers loomed before them—an intimidating expanse of granite steps Kyr didn't hesitate striding up. Alesta forced herself to match his pace. Inside the Towers' stately halls, she wanted to walk to one side, off the plush rugs with their elaborate weaves and out of the way of courtiers in their billowing, elegant dresses. Yet Kyr walked straight down their center, and she stuck beside him.

He was used to the place, but Alesta's eyes roved hungrily over the swooping reliefs decorating the stone halls, the glittering lamps aglow with eternal-burning kharis. Each carving was like a toehold for her to climb, each glint a blade sharpening her ambition. Someday she'd belong here as much as any of these courtiers, whose faces beamed as Kyr passed, who bowed and curtsied and exchanged brief pleasantries with him as he ushered Alesta through the network of corridors and staircases and courtyards.

"My lord Kyrian!" one dark-haired girl sang out. She waved her fan and elbow in a sinuous greeting.

Kyr bowed in return. "My lady Rina."

He made as if to continue down the hall, but Rina swished her skirts in front of him and launched into a gleeful recitation of courtly gossip, barely stopping for breath. "It's been ages; you've missed so much. And when, pray tell, are you finally going to paint my portrait? Our lord Silvio's recently had his done, and the court is all abuzz about it—"

"Anytime you wish, my lady. Only just now—"

"—though you *must* allow me to tell you what was said about it at our lady Francesca's dinner last night—" Rina rushed on, black eyes twinkling. The daughter of the most powerful clairvoyant of Soladisa and the admiral of its royal fleet, Rina looked like she belonged in these halls, where every surface and structure had been made into art. Her hair was bound in complex braids, with strings of pearls winding through her tresses. Tiny jewels dotted each of her clean, polished nails. No calluses marred her silky brown skin. Her full, melon-colored skirts fell all the way past her dainty, embroidered slippers to the floor, because she only ever walked the clean-swept marble tiles and spotless rugs of the Towers. Alesta tugged at her own stained skirts that came to her calves, feeling like a child instead of a grown girl of seventeen—one who would not reach eighteen unless she got moving and let the alberos berate and shrive her.

Kyr had completed his transformation. As he murmured vague responses to Rina's litany of minor scandals, he matched the other courtiers' posture, mirrored their cultivated gestures, mimicked their dulcet inflection. He was always one of the Towers set, really, but living down the island at his mother's villa, he had spent more time running wild with Alesta than with them.

Then King Enzo's only son was killed by a branzono two years ago, and everyone assumed the king would name his eldest nephew his new heir. Kyr's mother sent him regularly to study alongside his younger cousins living in the noble apartments at the Towers, and Kyr had taken it upon himself to learn everything he would need someday to be a proper king.

Alesta shifted uncomfortably beside him and Rina. A much different fate awaited her, if she didn't watch out sharp for herself. Earning a place here at the Towers—the seat of Soladisa's government, religion and, most importantly, university—was the surest alternative, but right now, feeling frumpish and mussed, she wished she were far away. Or invisible.

Perhaps Rina had begun Seeing like her mother, because she seemed to pick up on Alesta's embarrassment at that very moment.

"Lessie! It's such—a pleasure to see you." Her enthusiastic words slowed the further she got in her greeting, as if she were a mechanical doll winding down. Her courtly manners faltered as her eyes roamed over Alesta's face and clothes.

Alesta was used to searching looks, even when she wasn't covered in branzono blood and dirt. Not the appreciative glances some might enjoy, but arrested stares. Like she was an abomination and not a girl.

Whispers often followed, behind her back, from certain other youths after weekly chapel—her body showed gluttony and laziness, her face could scare monsters away. Always couched in tones of righteous concern for her and her immortal spirit. As if being pretty was a chore Alesta had foolishly neglected. She couldn't even bash the whisperers with her herding staff unless she wanted the alberos piling more sins at her feet. After all, those youths were only echoing the Arbor's stories of Hektorus blighting those who strayed too near the devil—who shirked their duty to the Arbor and its absolution—and blessing the virtuous with beauty that shone like their goodness, making them in his image.

She preferred the way most people pretended they didn't see her at all.

It was for the best, because, just as Kyr had a side of himself he hid at the Towers, around most people Alesta went silent. Like now. Kyr cleared his throat. "We're just off to the Arbor."

Rina's eyes lit with understanding. She snapped her fan and smiled at Alesta. "Oh, of course. So good of you to protect the kingdom—" Her delighted expression collapsed, the recollection of tithing month falling like a shadow. "In a manner I hope you may continue for some time."

Alesta managed a grim smile. At least Rina acted like she cared.

Suddenly the girl's face again became a mask of jollity, as her gaze darted down the hall. "There's my mother coming now." She let out a loud, thin laugh and leaned near, tapping her fan against Kyr's chest. "She'll scold you for staying away so long, and only coming when she's dreadfully busy preparing for the ceremony."

Kyr blinked. "I'm afraid you'll have to offer my apologies for me. We should get to the alberos." He gripped Alesta's elbow and steered her away. Rina nodded and curtsied a goodbye as he hurried Alesta down the corridor, in the opposite direction from Rina's mother the Seer. Davina Bianca performed the tithing selection every season, and in her purple robes stark against her pale skin she seemed to Alesta like an approaching omen of doom, harrying at their backs. "This could not possibly be worse timing," Kyr muttered.

He didn't need to tell her. She wasn't the one getting distracted by beautiful girls. Her stomach pinched like Kyr's long fingers on her arm. Not that Alesta cared about beauty, or catching anyone's attention with it. Only the fact that her lack of any meant she was that much more at risk.

A few weeks before tithing was a poor moment to let sins stack up, but she still had time to be absolved, just as she still had time to devise something to share at the festival. Snatch up some virtues to make up for the vices.

Kyr's steps slowed and his hold loosened. They were nearing the tithing chamber, in the final tower before the Arbor. Wide archways revealed an artificial forest filling the high-vaulted room, a brazier in its center. Hundreds of slender boughs, some fresh and green, some gone gray, were set about in small clay stands. Kyr sped his shiny boots again, angling his face away, but Alesta's eyes locked on one stand, one bough, the exact shape and angle of it branded into her memory since her name was carved upon the wood on her thirteenth birthday, like all Soladisans, and it was added to the tithing chamber. So many times she'd insisted on attending the ceremony here. All in the kingdom were welcome to observe the ritual, but most didn't bother—or couldn't stand to—while some attended with morbid fascination every cycle. Alesta usually let Kyr try to distract her on tithing days, far from the Towers, but whenever her worry grew too large and loud, she came and stood among anxious tradespeople with children at risk and courtiers with time to kill, watching Davina Bianca kneel before the brazier, ignite the incense infused with magical kharis, and call upon it to reveal Hektorus' will and judgment.

Then even Kyr's hand squeezing her own couldn't distract Alesta if the divinely-guided smoke stretched closer to that part of the room where the little branch waited for fate to choose it or pass it by, sending dread brushing down her spine.

Somewhere a bough bore Kyr's full name, too, but the kharis smoke never went near it. It judged each Soladisan's spirit by the seven virtues and seven sins, and Kyr was a shining example of too many of the former, too careful to fall into any of the latter.

Last season the smoke had chosen a farm boy from the eastern side of the island, wrapping itself around and around his bough, a strangling snake, until the branch was lost in the thick haze of augury. When the davinas had read the carved name, and Alesta's tense shoulders had relaxed, she'd hated herself for it. She did all she could to guard against the smoke—every moment lost in the workings of wings or helping with olive presses or improving her reading was to that end. The ceremony was the one time when she had no control, no further say. One day—maybe at the tithing in a few weeks—the sacred smoke might point to her name, and she wouldn't attend university here or even protect sheep from branzonos. Worst of all, she wouldn't be able to care for Nonnina any longer. She'd do nothing but sail across the poison sea to Orroccio, the monster's rock. She'd do nothing but be chained to its cliffside and left as a meal for the monster holding their kingdom hostage, threatening to rain ash over the island, send tides of monsters against their shores. She'd do nothing but die.

Nearly three years yet of tithing to endure before her jubilee birthday, at twenty, the age when each Soladisan's bough was removed, and she would be safe. A chance every three months the smoke would target her, barely enough time to breathe easily before the next season's ceremony menaced. While scholars, Seers, and nobles were rarely, if ever, tithed, farmhands and trade workers' children made up the bulk of sacrifices. She didn't need to be as skilled at mathematics as she was to know her odds were not good.

Alesta turned away from the forest of children's lives waiting to be snapped off and stomped out through the great central courtyard of the Arbor. Here at the heart of Soladisa grew the source of kharis—the glorious Lia tree. Alesta shot past it, past the alberos tending it, past the large mural of Hektorus gifting the tree to the first king of Soladisa and his new wife. The handsome god, wrought in colored glass, glimmered in the air above the two slender figures on either side of the Lia's tall, graceful trunk, all worked in shards of tile. Every fragment seemed to sliver reminders into Alesta's skin of the thousand ways she fell short of Hektorus' expectations for the people of his favored isle, of how the god might see her greatest usefulness as a forfeit to buy more safe and sunny days for those more deserving than her.

She sped past the glass of the atrium behind the Lia, avoiding the sight of her reflection, and practically leaped up the steps on the far side of the yard that led to the alberos' offices and apartments. Kyr, lagging behind her now, was right; she needed to hurry to be absolved of the killing—necessary, sanctioned by the Arbor, but a stain on her spirit, which already threatened to tip into damnation.

As Albero Paolo was always far too eager to remind her. The priest lifted his eyes from his book with a sharp look when she entered the sanctuary and snapped the volume shut. When Kyr appeared at her side, the albero's expression softened, his thin lips pulling into a smile.

"Alesta killed a branzono," Kyr announced, taking his own book back from her. "She needs absolving."

Albero Paolo nodded, his bushy white brows rising like caterpillars inching their way along. "My lord Kyrian, so good of you to usher her to our care. What an attentive shepherd you will be for our people someday."

Kyr smiled blandly. Alesta didn't miss his thumbnail dragging itself over and over the beading stitched along the bottom of his jacket. Any relief he felt at being safe from tithing was burdened by the knowledge he'd one day rule a kingdom whose survival depended on the continued sacrifice of its own people.

Albero Paolo had no kind words for the *actual* shepherdess who had prevented a monster from encroaching into the kingdom not an hour past. He merely led Alesta behind the confessional screen, bid her kneel on the unforgiving stone floor, and anointed her brow with three swipes of kharis oil, arcing upward in the shape of the holy tree, toward Hektorus' beneficence. He daubed the oil onto her raised palms and stepped back to wipe his own hands upon a white cloth kept neatly folded on the wooden altar. "For penance, recite the seven virtues and seven sins."

He watched to make sure she didn't peek past the screens at where the words swooped in golden lettering across the sanctuary wall, within two frames erupting at the corners in ornate swirls— gusts of holy breath and zephyrs molded in the wood.

As if the same words didn't hang in every assembly chamber and home across Soladisa, including above the little altar in Alesta and Nonnina's cottage. Always in pairs, like Hektorus' balanced, golden scales.

As if her mind didn't cycle through them at least once a day, like poking at a bruise, or a tongue prodding a loose tooth. Feeling out how she didn't measure up. Calculating how she fell decidedly, as the alberos had told her since she could remember, on the side of sin.

Alesta closed her eyes to shut out Albero Paolo's stern look and the overwhelming scent and the tingle of the oil, so she could run through the virtues. *Creation, harmony, civility, utility, chastity, discipline, beauty.* Her voice turned husky as she proceeded through the sins. *Destruction, discord, violence, sloth, lust, gluttony, aberrancy.* She cracked open an eye to see Albero Paolo staring at her expectantly.

"Hektorus and his sacred covenants guard you against taking these steps to Teras," he said. "If even other monsters, such as the one that made it to our shore today, attempt to escape that devil's rock, we must understand it to be a very bad place indeed."

"Indeed," she said, because the alberos seemed to dislike it when she simply stared back.

"While it is everyone's duty to submit to the ceremonies for their seven years, you would not want to invite tithing and annihilation in the jaws of that diabolic beast. The creeping evil of the devil must be guarded against always."

Alesta cleared her throat and nodded in the exact solemn way the alberos always nodded. That was why she needed him to get on with it and let her go finish her chores and hopefully figure out some creation to earn Hektorus' grace.

Still he withheld the closing prayer of absolution. "Have you any of those other sins to confess?" He folded his hands before his green robes. "Gluttony? Sloth? It is good to be in harmony with Hektorus and the virtues he extolled after defeating the monsters' god and coming to bless our isle."

She dropped her hands and bunched fistfuls of her skirts under his stare. The alberos spoke of those sins but seemed actually to rebuke her fatness, ignoring how she never had any of the tiny artful confections served during the nightly hours-long dinners at the Towers Kyr complained of, and did not lie about like a courtier with a dozen servants, not when the animals needed tending before sunrise. Even if she did, more like Vittore's wife, who had been unable to walk much since the birth of their youngest daughter—what did it matter to the alberos? Especially when the most exalted themselves stayed inside reading all day? And shouldn't everyone enjoy the bounty of Hektorus' blessed isle the alberos were always praising?

Alesta exhaled slowly through her nose; she could not argue over the sins, not when the tithing smoke waited to put an end to any such debate, but the Arbor's admonishments seemed at times aimed more to make farmers willingly work harder and yield up the designated portions of their crops to their landlords. She ate enough to give herself the energy she needed to haul water and carry stubborn sheep. She could not help her fatness, or her face. If Hektorus loved beauty so much, he should have blessed her with some.

But someone had to feed Teras.

Albero Paolo pressed, "Hektorus gifted us a living piece of his divinity, anchored to our land, and we must make ourselves worthy of it. This kharis from the Lia's holy fruit is precious and not to be wasted on half-hearted devotion." The priest's voice sounded almost triumphant, though his words were those of frustration.

Frustrated herself, as well as confused, Alesta offered, "I'm sorry to disappoint you, Albero. I've been so busy working the farm and helping my neighbors I haven't had time to sin." Or invent anything new.

The albero's eyes widened. Another misstep. She'd thought if she exposed her thoughts like turning out her pockets, everything would sort itself, but somehow, explaining never worked. Whatever reprimand he might have uttered was cut off at the sound of Kyr snorting behind the screen. Albero Paolo squashed his lips in a line. "The grace of our god and the action of penance purge your sin from your spirit, as Hektorus breathes. May he return to purify us of all sin and rid our world of monsters forevermore."

Alesta was on her feet and turning for the door as soon as the prayer left his lips. She heard Kyr thanking the albero as she returned to the sunlight of the courtyard and plopped down onto the steps. Brimstone butterflies sailed above the stone planters spilling over with flowers, around the Lia's slender trunk rising high as another tower, and up into the reaches of the tree's silvery-green leaves.

When he reached her side, Kyr sat and bashed his shoulder into hers. "You can't speak to him like that."

She shoved him in return. "I was only explaining." It was useless talking to most people. Unless there was a catechism of *hello, yes, the weather is fine today like every day, thanks be to Hektorus, here is your wool.* Like smooth ruts in the road for the cart of conversation to roll along.

"They don't want explanation." He handed her back the book. "Only devotion."

She scowled, wrinkling her nose and watching the alberos, in their white smocks cultivating the Lia, or kneeling for the Perpetual Adoration of that living offshoot of Hektorus' power, which Albero Paolo thought her so unworthy of. People were so complicated. Requiring so much puzzling out. Once you knew all their rules, though, you could use them to get what you needed. "I'm absolved, at least."

Kyr's shoulder relaxed against hers. She and Kyr were different—in the same way. Maybe that was why, more than growing up the same age on the same end of the island, they had become and stayed friends. She was better at figuring out the rules and patterns, and he better at fitting himself to them. Underneath, though—the same. Like Lia—branch or kharis oil or seed or root, used for fuel or medicine or other magics—all of the same tree. Both she and Kyr were inclined to their own way of thinking and seeing and being.

The alberos would call her a heretic for comparing herself to the holy Lia. She cleared the worry from her throat. "Whatever good it will do at the solstice." The tithing ceremony was the day after the festival, when invitations to the university were made each year.

Kyr murmured, "Until the monsters chase me back."

When they were nine—before Alesta understood Kyr never faced any actual risk—she'd vowed that she wouldn't let him be taken. She ranted as they lay in the late summer grass, having heard the older youths talking all week of the impending ceremony. She'd propped herself on one elbow and told Kyr, "They'd have to drag me off the ship."

Kyr, swiping his thumb down a seedhead's bristles, had considered this seriously, then with a grin, one-upped her. "I'd jump into the cove and swim after you until the monsters chased me back."

They recited these reassurances like one of the sacred covenants, whenever the shadow of tithing loomed too near. Now Kyr grabbed her hand and gave it a tug. "Let's get out of here."

Anyone else, and this would have sparked enough gossip to keep Rina busy until the fall tithing, though Kyr dropped her hand again immediately.

In this one way, Alesta was perfectly safe.

No one sent her cutting glances for walking alongside the presumed heir, past courtiers strolling among the stands and pavilions and stages already half-assembled for the festival. It was a celebration of the seven virtues, with demonstrations of art and inventions. A chance to share her work where the university's artificers would see.

Utility. She could not make herself beautiful, but she could make herself useful. She only needed something more impressive than an olive press to show everyone how.

And soon. She almost growled, "I'd bargain my pinkie toes for a decent idea at this point."

Kyr snorted. "What would Hektorus do with your toes?" He shook his head. "I wish I held any real sway with the university." His fingers tapped against his thigh, setting the jewels on his rings winking. "What's the point of being next in line for the throne if you can't change what you want? If all it means is——" His hand drew into a fist.

She frowned at where a pulse feathered in his jaw. Normally he was so focused on meeting the demands of his role, he never questioned them. She understood rules and limits, though. That was just reality. A sheep only gave so much wool.

Even the king couldn't prevent someone's tithing. No one could. The ancient deal Teras forced upon the first king was an infernal perversion of the sacred covenants Hektorus bestowed on the worthy, the alberos said, but just as unbreakable, and Hektorus' judgment through the Lia of who most deserved to pay the price for the kingdom must be respected.

Every hundred years or so, the stories told, some hero would show up in a ship blessed by the god of a far-flung isle and declare his intention to free them of the dreadful monster Teras. He'd sail off through the poison sea and never be heard from again.

And as the moon waxed after the next equinox or solstice, Teras would again part a safe path through the sea, and another youth's life would be due by the time the moon grew full.

She shook off the thought. "But my lord Kyrian, surely *you* are eager for the festival."

Kyr put on his most avid smile. "With dancing and music and crowds!"

She laughed at the wild flare of his eyes and his false enthusiasm. "And shouting. Don't forget all the shouting."

He nodded. "Shouting's my favorite."

Someone shouted for him then as they neared the royal tower, a group of courtiers stopping Kyr to invite him and his mother to dine with them, to hint at desired favors, to casually work mentions of their beautiful daughters into the conversation. Without the excuse of going to the Arbor, Kyr was left to smile and trade jests with perfect politeness. This place wore on him, she knew, but at least it wanted him. Alesta needed to find the correct rule to invoke, the right lever to pull, to make it want her more than Teras did. To tip the balance of the scales of virtues and sins. So she, too, could stay.

Just then she really should have headed home on her own. She had chores and needed to scrape something together for the festival. Instead, she lingered as the sun angled closer over the swooping stone rooftops, as Kyr was sought out, his regard a prize, even among all the courtiers in dresses with puff sleeves that were actually birdcages housing little mechanical birds; wide-brimmed straw hats secured by extravagant amounts of imported, painted silk, draping all the way down to their hems; jackets in elaborate cuts of brocade with fragments of mirror or feathers or shells worked into their weave.

Hugging the book to herself, Alesta let a courtier shoulder between her and Kyr, let Soladisa's cherished son draw all the attention, like always. Sunlight played through his curls and bathed his throat as he threw back his head in laughter.

Kyr drew up straight, though, when the king, surrounded by counselors and attendants, emerged from the stone archway of the royal tower and strode his way. King Enzo resembled Kyr, but older, with gray streaking through his dark hair—more and more since his son Ciro's death. All the men of the royal family shared a likeness with each other and to the depictions of the first king in murals and engravings and ancient inked texts. Like Kyr's cousin Mico, trailing the king and in conversation with one of his advisers.

The faint lines etched in King Enzo's face drew themselves deeper as he beamed at Kyr and clapped him on the back in greeting. Kyr bowed his head. "It's good to see you, my boy." The king asked after Kyr's studies, and his work in the studio he kept at the Towers. "We've been discussing plans for the royal pavilion at the festival. Presentations of art—" He inclined his crowned head toward Kyr. "And performances. And anything new and interesting from Molissa, if the ships make it back in time."

"If they make it back at all."

Skirts rustled and jewelry clinked as the courtiers nearest Alesta drew back.

Oh no. Had she said that aloud?

Thank Hektorus she was far enough away the king hadn't heard her. But Mico, hands clasped tightly before his jacket woven through with copper strands, cut his gaze her way, and other eyes painted with bright blues and greens widened, mouths with dark berry shades dropped open. Behind one fan or another someone whispered, "By the boughs, manners as ugly as the rest of her."

The alberos and artists of the Towers said that truth was beauty, but so often when Alesta spoke it, the truth only seemed to put her out of harmony with everyone.

Apparently even truth, on her tongue, twisted into something harsh and ugly.

And it *was* true that communication with other kingdoms was difficult—the sea treacherous, demanding an almost scandalous amount of Lia magic to traverse its boiling, poisonous waters, its strange currents, its sharp rocks and sinkholes, its branzonos and leviathans. Even to the east, away from Orroccio, for a good distance, wide patches of poison frothed and unmappable vortexes threatened to pull ships to the monster-filled depths. The davinas burned through stores of kharis to induce visions and help the captains chart the safest course before each journey. If they managed to avoid where the waves erupted into flame, the more caustic water would still burn anything submerged too long without holy protection. Three cargo ships, their hulls coated thickly with Lia tar, were sent across only once a year for news and trade, and some years only one returned. Or none.

Thankfully all the courtiers were soon distracted again, as Kyr loudly joked about spending his entire annual allowance on whatever books the trade ships brought—and Alesta suddenly didn't care if they were laughing at him or her because something beautiful was unfolding inside her thoughts, like those fans opening and closing, their silk lit through with sunshine—like that monstrous green webbing, light but strong. The book cut into Alesta's clutching fingers as inspiration and images flooded through her: The zigzagging wings of terns. Molissa. The trade ships. Her mind, sharp and pointed as a needle, began stitching together an idea.

She dragged her bottom lip under her teeth and thought, barely seeing the king glance around at his audience, eyes squinting with a touch of mischief. "I know one reason this season's festival is sure to offer excitement." His smile landed on Kyr. "Perhaps a long-awaited declaration at last."

Fans snapped. Brows lifted like terns' wings. Gazes pinned themselves again to Kyr. He was meticulously courteous in his reply. Probably only Alesta recognized the tension in his stillness—how his fingers clawed at the hem of his jacket. Ciro had been like an older brother to Kyr, and Alesta knew he worried about being a good enough replacement as heir.

The king told him, "You must stay and dine with me tonight."

Kyr bowed again in acquiescence before the king strode off alongside his counselors. Surrounded by courtiers drawing him along in the king's wake, Kyr turned and threw Alesta an apologetic look.

She swallowed down her excitement to share her idea with him and shrugged back. It was always going to go like this, sooner or later. Even if she avoided being chosen for Teras, Kyr's fate would take him away from her as surely as tithing.

As he disappeared through the archway leading to the royal apartments, she looked to the university tower, solid and straight against the bruising sky prickling with early stars, where professors and artificers studied and wrote and experimented and built. Field laborers were most commonly called as offerings. But she would make herself into something different. That would be how she saved herself.

Kharis light sparkled through the giant hanging globes to battle the shadows growing in the courtyards and cloisters. Alesta slipped the book into her skirt's large pocket and started back through the city, hurrying to reach the coast before the full fall of dark, alone. She had work to begin, with little time left to complete it.

And Alesta intended to survive.

GOLDEN MASKS

K yrian could find no escape.

In the glittering dining room of the royal tower, his every sense battled an onslaught of clattering silverware, scents of seafood and cheeses mingling, kharis light catching in ladies' jewels and flaring along the gold-rimmed plates. He'd gone to his chambers first and let the attendants change him into a formal jacket, with seams that felt like the fish fork he was holding stabbing his side. His fingers clenched white around the utensil, and he smiled across the table at Davina Bianca.

"I suspected it would not be long before we saw you," the davina said knowingly.

Kyrian trained his eyes on her left earring, close enough to look politely attentive while avoiding her unsettling stare. He knew the davinas relied on kharis to induce their divine visions, but their leader always left him feeling as if she might pluck all the secrets from his heart whenever she wanted anyway. "Impossible to deny oneself the pleasure of such company for long."

"But we know you're doing such marvelous work with your painting." The davina sipped her wine and peered at him over her glass. "What have you been hiding away laboring over? Someone's portrait?"

"A landscape."

Davina Bianca nodded approvingly. "Capturing Hektorus' blessed isle."

Kyrian speared his fork through the boney fish he had no intention of eating, not bothering to explain how the piece was an experiment with form and texture, barely recognizable as Soladisa. More an attempt to explore the play of Hektorus' blessed light across the grass and sheep's wool and clouds. This wasn't the time to ramble on about his process or techniques, even though the urge prodded from within his ribcage like a hungry animal.

And this wasn't what Davina Bianca was truly asking. Her gaze slid along the table to where her daughter sat. "I hear you've promised to capture our Rina's likeness. It will be so nice for you both to enjoy the pleasure of one other's company a little more."

Conversation at the Towers was like fencing, or a dance, one Kyrian often felt he was performing blindfolded, but he'd memorized a thousand moves, vague answers and civil questions. Rules as ingrained in him now as the seven virtues. Words must be considered, your voice easy—never rough or sharp. Keep your eyes on faces, or at least pretend to. No letting them stray out the wide windows to the soft black and reaching stars. No closing them when the Tower bells' hourly tolling made it impossible to take in anything else. His hands were worst—unruly, always wanting to move, to shake with excitement about that painting or tear away this itchy collar or plug his ears against the courtiers' chewing, only finally free when holding a brush, working paint over canvas.

Kyrian pushed his food around his plate and told the davina, "I would be delighted, though I can't hope to do the original justice."

The courtier to the other side of Davina Bianca, landlord of half the northern coast, leaned nearer and cut in, "My sweet-hearted Jovia was telling me at our lady Francesca's dinner last night how she longs for you"—the man dabbed his napkin to his lips—"to paint her portrait." He angled his head toward his golden-haired daughter a few places down, speaking avidly with Mico.

Kyrian's gaze dipped to his plate, where his dinner's glassy eye stared back at him. Careful, careful—the wrong word or look could leave someone feeling slighted. Kyrian shoved down his anxiety he'd say the wrong thing and let only gentle interest play over his face as he answered, "Of course, once I've completed my work for the Festival of Virtues." When his uncle clearly intended to seal his fate. He resigned himself to the idea that once Enzo made his announcement, his studio time would be booked out for months for making technically boring pieces of every young lady in the Towers. Just one more thing he loved being pried away from him. He should be used to it by now. "The morning light would, I think, complement our lady Jovia best. And afternoons for our lady Rina." He nodded respectfully to Davina Bianca, letting out a slow breath of relief that both parents seemed appeased—and that one of the attendants was taking his uneaten fish away without anyone having said a word. "Thank you," he murmured to the servant, who returned a small smile.

Scarcely three years left before the farce of his inclusion in the tithing ceremonies was over and a different ceremony threatened.

Then the rules and fakery would follow him even outside these dinners and meetings and festivals and balls, to his vanishing free moments when he could be alone or with Alesta and try to remember the version of himself he might have been if Ciro had not died and left him the likeliest heir. To his private chambers. *To his bed.* Nausea unrelated to the lingering odor of the fish course roiled through him.

He shoved down the thought. Shove it all down: the worries and wanting and surely sinful weaknesses. The frustration he didn't deserve to feel, as servants brought out another course and placed the food before him. Bury all the feelings, all the parts of himself that didn't fit. Let it all out later upon a canvas.

He didn't even know what he'd share at the festival, but he had plenty of time there yet—maybe he could slip away to the studio tower after dinner and get a few hours of painting in. Guilt tugged at him as he recalled Alesta struggling for both an idea and time to work on it.

Those thoughts were interrupted, like most here, by a new piece of gossip swirling around the table—one that Kyrian was slightly horrified to note involved himself.

Jovia was nodding excitedly, upswept mass of golden hair wobbling. "I heard our lord Kyrian did!" Several sets of eyes shot his way from around the table.

"Oh dear," he said, putting on an arch, playful air, "what have I done now?"

Davina Bianca slipped a smile between them. "After what occurred today, I would feel Rina was quite safe with you even if she went to your studio at the villa."

She'd be more subtle if she'd pushed Rina into his lap when

they'd taken their places at the table. Under his grin, Kyrian's mind was still racing. What *had* he done? He'd finally given the book to Alesta—

Jovia's father offered, "When you killed the branzono?"

"Oh, that was—" That was wrong. That was Alesta—the terror of seeing her facing down the sea monster rushed over him, at the same time his mother's voice in his head reminded him not to directly contradict the courtier. Harmony. Civility. Discipline.

Before he could devise an answer, Mico raised his glass to him. "Quite the hero."

Well, he couldn't let that stand. "Hardly. I'm afraid I cannot claim any such glory." Not like Alesta handling that creature, no holding back. All Kyrian did was sit in shining rooms and hold his tongue, never employing even the fencing skills he was made to practice daily. All the while, wanting to somehow do more than dodge those seeking power and favors. Not simply used, but useful.

The courtier's brows drew together. "We heard you'd been to the Arbor for absolving?"

"I was only helping A—a friend." Again the thought struck him that he hadn't done enough, merely making sure she got herself absolved. It also occurred to him that this conversation might be painful for his uncle. While reports of branzonos weren't rare, it had only been a couple years since they'd lost Ciro.

Kyrian turned to the head of the table, where King Enzo's face was caught in a pensive look. His memories of his own father, who'd passed when he was very young, were muddled together with Enzo, who'd stepped in through his childhood and encouraged Ciro to include him in gatherings and games the rare times his mother brought him to the Towers. More guilt washed through Kyrian; he missed his cousin, and it was a small sacrifice, giving up not even his actual life, only the one he could have experienced had his cousin lived, to be able to serve Enzo in return, and all of Soladisa.

The king noticed Kyrian's concerned look, and a warm smile spread over his face. "Your friend was lucky to have you near." Kyrian swallowed; he wasn't sure about claiming that either, but definitely wasn't about to directly contradict the king.

Albero Paolo leaned closer from his seat beside Enzo. "So modest. I was just saying what care our lord Kyrian shows the people of Soladisa." Before haranguing Alesta of all people about sin. If the albero knew the vices Kyrian was hiding, he wouldn't continue heaping credit upon him. Not even to curry favor with the next king the Arbor would share charge of the Lia tree with.

Enzo's eyes crinkled as he said, "It makes me confident in both my announcement at the festival and how gladly it will be taken." Bare weeks until the festival, and the tithing. Dread and hunger bloomed through Kyrian's stomach.

Surely there was something more he could do, even if it wasn't slaying sea beasts, to have a real impact. To use his unsought position for some good. Ignoring the spiced ragu before him, spinning one of his rings, he hazarded, "Speaking of the festival—"

The king and several others at this end of the table waited, listening, and Kyrian stilled his hand, concentrating hard. How something was said among the court mattered as much or more as what was said, as inane as he found that. "I wondered if there might be improvements to be implemented in how university invitations are made, rather than based solely on demonstrations there."

Mico tilted his head thoughtfully. "How else would you suggest talent be found?"

"Well, there may be someone talented—many talented people, that is—who lack the time or materials to prepare a full demonstration. If they've been busy with other work, or don't have the money for supplies." The servant refilling his wine cast a supportive look at him, and Kyrian went on, "It hardly seems fair. But perhaps the artificers might fashion a practical examination that could be completed at the festival? So no person's gifts go to waste. I know the artificers prize the independence with which they run the university"—their debates with the Arbor each year over what texts to procure from abroad could get fierce—"but surely they'd consider the suggestion, if it meant finding more worthy applicants to fill their ranks and support their work."

Albero Paolo smiled kindly, and for a moment, Kyrian thought he'd succeeded, that he'd made a small contribution to Soladisa. A gift Alesta might accept, when she'd refused anything beyond a used book or trifling painting, otherwise insisting on making a bargain of extra yarn for his mother if he so much as brought a basket from the villa's kitchen stores. The albero's smile didn't waver as he asked, "And what of those who do put in the time and effort to properly prepare? To honor Hektorus?" The sounds of clinking glasses and swallowing grew more intolerable, and Kyrian struggled not to shift in his seat. "What wouldn't be fair, my boy, would be making exceptions while others faithfully save and devote themselves to their studies—endangering the harmony of all Soladisans." The albero snaked his fingers together, bobbing his interwoven hands once for emphasis.

Cold crawled over Kyrian's skin like a thousand insects.

Everyone was staring. Like in his nightmares, where they all saw the truth of him he hid and turned away in horror, even Alesta. "I just thought—" Except he hadn't, blurting out his idea, rather than considering the teachings of the Arbor first. Or of his tutors, who'd emphasized while the king held the greatest authority in Soladisa, ruling on taxes, imports, landowners' inheritances, and petitions regarding crop portions and the like, he did so with the spiritual advice of the alberos and davinas. Kyrian couldn't very well argue against one of the virtues.

That just showed how much he needed their guidance. After a childhood spent always at a loss, never knowing the right things to say or do around anyone but Alesta—baffling the servants, exasperating his mother, disappointing tutors—the Arbor had saved Kyrian. Its clear tenets were the tools he'd used to fix his failings, the pillars he'd used to prop up the façade fooling everyone. He knew better by now, had learned all the games of this place, had faithfully devoted himself to studying, for years, how to get this right. It could only be the sin growing all that time in him as well that led him to make this mistake in front of the king and court. To risk everyone's confidence that he could do this—not merely managing social-climbing courtiers but handling these kinds of important policies and decisions. The very serious duty of leading a kingdom that sent its people to die to keep the rest alive. Where any error on his part would always be balanced against the monstrous power of Teras.

Shit.

Mico, staring along with everyone, quirked his mouth and said, "Indeed, I'm interested to know what you think"—he spun his fork through his dinner—"of this newly proposed guild for textile workers the king's been deliberating." He neatly took a bite and raised his brows encouragingly.

Bless him, moving the conversation on to a new topic. Like when Kyrian had covered for Alesta down on the courtyard, with his clumsy comment about buying too many books. How was Mico so good at this, without any sign of wanting to fidget or hide under the table? Not that Kyrian had been considering resorting to that.

His cousin swallowed and smiled. "Surely our lord Kyrian can help with our uncle's decision about their request."

Surely Kyrian could, if he hadn't given in to his weaknesses and stayed near the villa so long, meaning he'd heard nothing about this proposal. Mind racing through what he knew of the island's weavers and the merchants who imported luxury materials on the trade ships, he wanted to ask about the likely impact on those most in need. But he'd learned his lesson. Stick to the rules. Let the virtues guide him. "Working together in harmony, as a guild, could foster sharing of techniques and advancements in artistry, bolstering the beauty of Soladisa's creations. But no change in policy should be made that could disrupt the harmony between the aspiring artisans and merchants already engaged in providing such goods for Soladisa, as Albero Paolo reminds us."

The albero preened. Enzo nodded thoughtfully. Mico stabbed another bite and chewed with vigor. Kyrian had managed to say nothing at all, and of course somehow that was when he found success. The façade he'd constructed hid an emptiness, only echoing with the words of others from some farther room he could never seem to reach.

Davina Bianca began telling the king of the concerns about import quotas raised by the merchants awaiting her husband the admiral's return, and the servants brought out servings of farro that Kyrian could finally eat. He made himself take measured bites between keeping up conversation with Jovia's father about how the crops were looking this year and trying to ignore the times he heard his name down the table, as people leaned their faces gilt in kharis light near to each other, whispering that he'd still not been seen spending time with any particular girl or another. Because, of course, Alesta didn't count. Everyone knew they'd been friends since they were small. She would fight her way through branzonos and into university without any help of his, and he would take the role handed to him; she would do incredible things, and if he was very lucky, he would get to see them, while hopefully not mis-managing the kingdom and causing Teras to smite them or make Soladisa fall into the sea.

As the meal progressed to dessert, the night sky's hardening black sharpening the stars, Davina Bianca roped him into a prom-ise to breakfast with her and Rina. But Kyrian begged off Mico's invitation to the game court the next afternoon, saying he'd have to return to the villa to see to his mother, who in truth probably wished he'd stay away at the Towers every night.

Soon enough he'd have to, and spend each morning, afternoon, and evening with people wanting only the shiny, false Kyrian. He almost regretted coming here today and getting stuck, even to help Alesta, the one person who never tried to use him or asked any-thing of him. At all.

Alesta was absolved; she was safe, and of course he was glad.

But Kyrian was also trapped.

Chapter Three

CHIAROSCURO

"I cannot believe you dragged that thing back here."

Alesta sliced her knife through the branzono's hide. "This thing ruined my favorite blouse, it owes me."

Kyr tilted his head back from his canvas and sighed. "Alesta, it smells."

"You smell." Of pine resin from his paints and heather from the fields on the way here to the old barn. Not that she'd tell Kyr so. With the entire court fawning over him yesterday, he hardly needed more compliments.

Even when he plucked at the old tunic he wore to paint in and gave it a sniff.

She grinned as she peeled away the monster's slippery skin and lifted it to the tanning frame. Once it was in place, she wiped her hands and knife and sheathed it in her tool belt slung about her hips. Then she returned to her work spread out over an old plank pulled from a stall and laid across two barrels—notes and drawings and calculations.

She'd made flying contraptions before, but only small pieces.

Now she was thinking bigger. How to reach all the way to Molissa. What materials could withstand the elements through the journey. If the flier might carry only letters, or bear greater cargo.

She plucked an old project from the table and gave its heart— the gears and string that brought it to life—a twist. They unwound to set its spiral paper wing fluttering up through the dust motes toward the empty hayloft.

Traveling through the sea Teras ruled demanded untold kharis, but if someone created a way to send messages—perhaps goods— and even people—through the air? That was Hektorus' domain.

The journey would still be demanding. Paper wings wouldn't withstand the possible rain sent by the goddess Pelagia—always in gentle showers upon the favored island, but in fierce storms at times on the horizon—or the attention of seabirds. Even the sun would bleach the strength out of some materials.

She stole a glance at Kyr sitting at his easel, where the sun fell between the wide barn doors. He was always talking about the light he needed, how he worked not in paint but in light. How he tried to capture it at different times of day and in different weather.

He dabbed a brush now at a piece with light nearly bursting from one section of the scraped bark he painted on here, sur- rounded by a sea of black. *Chiaroscuro*, he'd told her. His painting masters up at the Towers taught him all the proper techniques and styles, and Kyr excelled at them. He preferred to experiment, though, and the work that was too strange for sharing with the court, or even with his mother at the villa, decorated the barn along with Alesta's inventions and abandoned or failed experi- ments, leaning against the old stalls or nailed to the frame of the loft. Muscular swirls that might be waves or clouds, faces falling apart over the wood, landscapes with towers twisting up to bloated stars. Paintings that ignored the rules his masters gave him for the artistic unities, for attaining harmony and beauty. Whenever Alesta couldn't solve an issue with an invention, she'd lie out across the barn's packed dirt floor and stare up at his paintings until they jogged her creativity and gave her a new idea to try.

Kyr sat back from his work, frowning. He rolled his broad shoulders under the soft drape of his white tunic. A golden beetle landed atop the brush he held aloft. He set it gently on top of the painting, where it crawled along, glinting in the afternoon sun.

Chiaroscuro. That was Kyr. His dark curls painted golden by hours sitting here in the sun. Like he'd soaked up the light he loved so much.

The toy flier sank back to the ground with a dying thrum.

Alesta snapped her attention back to her work.

Just as they'd made this place into a safe harbor for all their projects, she and Kyr had collaborated on pieces for previous festivals. Automatons that depicted sea battles, or crops growing and towers springing up from Soladisa, the sun and moon chasing each other around and around over the isle. Kyr brought Alesta's moving panels and cut-outs to life with his painting, and anything he presented received abundant attention, at celebrations honoring the king's birthday or betrothals among nobles or Hektorus' long-ago visit to the isle, when the first king showed such hospitality that the god blessed Soladisa forever. Alesta had wanted none of the attention for herself, only for her creations. Not when it meant speaking in front of those crowds.

But she was old enough for university now; for the upcoming festival, she needed to produce something of her own, something spectacular. Something the artificers would marvel over, that would make them beg her to study with them. That would make clear she could offer the kingdom so much more alive than as a monster's ransom.

That she could be so much more than what everyone saw.

She sketched out more concepts with a charcoal pencil. The branzono skin could provide the lightweight yet durable material necessary to fulfill her vision. She still needed to devise a frame and wing design.

And a power source that wouldn't unwind in mere minutes. Alesta bit her lip and stared at the fallen flier. Counterweights were out. Any combustive fuel would somehow have to be protected from the elements without smothering its flame, and would be too heavy besides—

Except for eternal-burning kharis.

Lia wood soaked in kharis, the sacred oil from the tree's fruit, provided a magical amount of power and light. But while the Lia delivered a miraculous bounty—bark that regrew swiftly, fruit and flowers blessing its boughs all through the year—no fragment of the precious tree was ever let go to waste, or given to farmers beyond the leaf scraps used to enhance fertilizer and mulch to protect the crops. She lifted her head to see Kyr cleaning brushes in a bucket of water atop the empty trough. "You have kharis lamps in your royal apartments, don't you?" Rooms were kept for him and his mother at the Towers.

His gaze cut over to her and her work. His eyes narrowed. "Granted by the king for that use."

She spread her palms atop her papers and stared him down. "Kyr."

He waggled his head back at her. "Alesta."

"Come on," she said, drawing out the words to last as she walked over. "I only need one little piece, and you can return it after, and the king and court will be so thrilled to improve correspondence with Molissa they won't even care, and I'll do *anything*—"

Kyr's stern look softened, his mouth falling open a little as he inhaled. He almost always gave in to her plans. Even if half the time they ended in spectacular failures. She could convince him. She grabbed the brush from his hands and scrubbed the paint from it.

"Anything you want. For one tiny piece of kharis no one will even miss."

He swallowed and set the washed brushes in a line to dry. "Teach me to fight."

"What?" She scrunched her nose. "You know how to fight." All courtiers practiced fencing, their highly stylized movements almost like dancing.

"Like you." Kyr's eyes flashed. "I saw you take out that branzono yesterday. Laid it out before I could reach you. *Come on*," he said in a perfect imitation of her own plea. "You've killed how many of them by now? You can't be scared of fighting me." He grinned, tip of his tongue to his canine tooth, and flicked the bristles of the brush she held, sending a spatter of dirty water into her face.

She half-laughed, half-roared at him, and gave his chest a shove. They grappled a moment. Alesta dropped the brush and smacked her palm to Kyr's shoulder. "I don't know what I'd teach you, it's just—you do what you have to. You fight. It's survival."

He flung his head back with a sigh. "Then help me practice dancing." He stopped wrestling her away, instead whirling her around.

She laughed again, letting him drag her about. "You know how to dance, too."

"Well enough," he grumbled, "but everyone is going to be staring at me at this festival's ball."

"More than usual?" He gave her a pointed look. King Enzo's impending announcement did mean all eyes would be on Kyr. "Everyone is going to want you to dance with them, or their daughters, even if you step on all their toes." Like she almost did to him now as he steered them around under the painted clouds and stars. "You don't have to worry about being perfect."

His mouth tensed in a wry line. "I do, though."

She knew. How he felt all the approval at court was conditional and tenuous. How hard he'd worked to fit in. He never allowed himself failures, outside this barn and the frames of his paintings. His mother had let him mostly avoid the Towers, but the last two years had insisted on all sorts of training. Not only the fencing, but singing lessons to help draw out his voice, which used to go flat when he was around most others. Dancing lessons, to master the steps Alesta was barely keeping up with. Days spent studying with his cousins, where his mother told him to concentrate on mimicking their manners and holding eye contact. Tamping down the lingering fits that he'd fallen into almost daily when he was small. Like Alesta back then, too, when she couldn't seem to make anyone understand her.

She'd seen it eating at him lately. Just as in those old days when he'd grow more and more on edge, until he snapped and began shouting. Until Alesta noticed it happened the worst when he wore his shirt with the high collar embroidered by his mother in a pattern of green vines, and Alesta had pinned him down and cut it off him with the shearing scissors.

There was no easy way out of his impending royal duties, though. Kyr turned them about again and blew out a breath. "And once Enzo makes it official, that's it. Those apartments up at the Towers will be home." His fingers clenched, into her back, around her own.

He was so anxious about meeting everyone's expectations. So she reassured him, with a smirk, "You should worry more about courtiers mobbing you at the ball than disappointing anyone." And, because something pinched in her gut, like the crunch of misaligned gears, the snap of over-taut wire, she teased, "Hektorus knows why, but they must see something in you they like."

Kyr grimaced. "A crown, I suppose." His steps slowed. "They are quite determined."

"Very well." She twisted around, trapping his arm behind his back. "I'll teach you to fight, in case you need to fend the most vicious of them off."

"You—perfect calamity!" He broke from her hold and spun to pin her arms to her sides. She writhed to get free, but he held her fast.

Her eagerness for the kharis and to get on with her work was smothered by Kyr's arms wrapped around her, muscles evident through only his paint shirt, still warm from the sun. That scent of pine and honey. Even as their scuffling slowed, her pulse sped. She was sure Kyr could feel the way her heart thumped against his own chest.

His face was near. One brow flicked up and the corners of his mouth curled in the hint of a question.

One too dangerous to answer.

It was a threat greater than a sea monster's teeth, that the knowledge might slip between them, bleed from her to him. Calamity.

They'd been best friends for years. Since before Alesta's parents died, when her mother and Nonnina would send Alesta to the villa with bundles of yarn and thread they'd spun for Kyr's mother. Something had begun changing recently, though. Something growing inside her like the reaching branches of a sapling. Something shifting beneath her like the treacherously sandy headland cliffside.

She could never let on. She could not allow something she might feel for him, that he could never return, ruin their friendship. Kyr was the one person who truly understood her. He was the one who knew, when she was chewing her lip raw, to drop a hand to her thigh, a quiet reminder. Or the one to bash into her shoulder and interrupt whatever spiral of thought she'd been trapped in.

She knew she'd lose him eventually, to days spent meeting with royal advisers. Nights spent dining and dancing with courtiers at festival balls, fingers crusted with jewels and faces painted gold. He'd marry a gorgeous girl like Rina and have beautiful children and never worry about tithing taking away anything he loved.

She would not hasten that loss by making things between them uncomfortable now. She was not after a crown or safety from him. The thought was ridiculous. She only wanted to keep her friend as long as she could.

And that also meant staving off tithing. Focusing on the flier. And teaching Kyr crude fighting, if that got her the kharis.

He moved to brush something from her cheek—paint spatter or charcoal smudge—and, freed, she hauled him over, all the way to the ground.

"Thank Hektorus I don't care for you like that," she said, "or else I might be the one in danger from ambitious courtiers." She forced a laugh as hollow and polished as armor.

He groaned and pushed himself to his knees. "Brutal."

"You literally asked for that." She nudged him with her toe. "Now, let's get to work."

Nonnina was still spinning by the dying light, near the cottage's one little window. Alesta shoved the door closed to keep out the creeping chill and any ill wind blowing from the west. She'd done the evening chores already and penned the sheep Vittore's daughter had watched for her that afternoon, on the nearer grazing land. Now Alesta pulled the late pomegranates she'd brought from her pocket. She left them on the table for after supper, beside the one flickering lamp casting weak light up to the beams and walls where dried herbs and curing garlic and a small painting of Kyr's hung. She checked on the stew bubbling on the stove, her spoon automaton powered by its steam stirring away.

Then she checked on her grandmother, quietly singing an old work song about a fair maiden choosing whom to bestow her kiss to, once her tithing years had all wheeled past and she could marry. On days of good health, Nonnina would keep spinning until all the stars were out. Alesta wasn't sure how strong her eyes were any longer, but a lifetime guided her hands at their work.

Alesta accepted her grandmother's kiss and knelt beside her. She took some wool waiting in one of the woven baskets nestled near the spinning wheel to run through the carding drums she'd built, so the batt would be ready for Nonnina the next morning.

As she turned the crank, Alesta recalled a similar invention she'd seen at the last Festival of Virtues, with nails that plucked not fiber but a sweet, whimsical melody when the drum turned. A different tune captured by each drum. She wondered if the volume might be magnified somehow—if music might play like that at the ball during the upcoming festival, while Kyr danced with a golden face. With all those eager courtiers.

The spikes nearly caught her fingers as she fed the wool too quickly. She finished and left the carded wool in another basket. "If we had kharis for lamps we could work more easily," she said, when the maiden in Nonnina's song had considered a dozen willing boys and chosen the handsomest. "Make more money." And Alesta could work on her barely started flier into the late hours. Finishing it before the festival would be tight.

Nonnina's foot pressed evenly on the treadle. Her palsy wasn't bad today. "It's fine." Her thinned hair was drawn back in a low knot. Lines carved paths deep through her face, and spots kissed by Hektorus' sun dotted her there and over her arms and hands. She had taken care of Alesta, after her parents were carried off by the devil fever that the unholy wind from Orroccio inflicted on some every year—those lacking in moral fortitude, the alberos said. Even left with a palsy from the fever brought by the devil's breath, Nonnina kept their little farm running and Alesta fed. She'd daubed lanolin on Alesta's chapped and bleeding lips like her mother used to, when Alesta worried her teeth over them too much.

Alesta gently pulled her grandmother's hands from the wheel. "I'll have us both living up at the glittering Towers—" She swiped a finger into the pot of lanolin infused with herbs from the garden and massaged it into Nonnina's gnarled hands. "Closer to the sun and all that kharis, before too many more winters." She worked the balm gently over each knotty joint and strained muscle. "As soon as I prove my worth to the kingdom." As long as she wasn't tithed first. She couldn't be, not with Nonnina's good days growing fewer, her need for Alesta's help greater.

"You're a good girl, Alesta. Who cares what anyone up there says?"

What they said, at every catechism lesson or absolution or weekly worship at the villa's chapel, was Alesta was as good as damned for being the way she was. She pressed her lips together hard, but kept her touch and voice light. "I do."

Nonnina clasped one hand atop Alesta's. A gleam brewed in her cloudy eyes. "Cara. When you grow as old as me, you stop caring what anyone else thinks of you."

A pretty sentiment. If only it were as easy to sweep others' opinions from your life as when Hektorus long ago breezed through Soladisa after killing the monsters' god. But even then, the defeated god laid a dying curse, and his children grew more powerful, until the greatest, Teras, extended its infernal sway over the kingdom. People could pray all they wanted for Hektorus to return and wipe out the nest of vipers again, but until then, tithings had to be made.

Alesta wiped her hands on her skirt and guided Nonnina to the table—or started to, before Nonnina brushed her help away with a snort. Alesta went to finish preparing supper. The truth was what others thought of her did matter, because powerful people's opinions determined her reality. She needed the court to think her worthy of that place at university. She'd figured the odds of tithing. Orphan, farm worker, girl. All more commonly tithed. And she was reaching the most likely age. Not to mention the way she was different—differences equaled tithings, too often. She needed to be a scholar who built things for the king to make up for it all. Reality didn't care how you felt—the winter didn't care that those were your parents, sickening and dead just when they all thought they'd made it through to spring. The tithing smoke didn't care that you were full of dreams and hopes—

Some more realistic than others.

She crouched to toast the ends of that morning's bread under the fire and caught sight of her blurred and distorted face in the side of the stove pot. With the back of her hand, she scrubbed away the paint speckling her round cheek, over a bruise from the branzono yesterday and among the spots from her own bout with the fever that had scarred over without expensive Lia salves to treat them. The ache felt right. Escaping to the sky in flight was more likely than Kyr ever looking at her as more than his friend, as a safe place free of the judgments and gossip of court. If anyone knew she wanted more—shame ruddied her cheek. She stood and portioned out the thin stew. She had to be just as realistic about those feelings. They meant nothing.

Alesta wasn't a girl with a dozen boys aching for her kiss. She was more like the man in another song of Nonnina's, who climbed a sunbeam—or a rainbow, if Kyr was reading the story out of one of his books—to beg a boon from Hektorus, medicine for his child or a beautiful wife, depending on the telling. Hektorus made him a sacred covenant that if the man crafted a thousand masks for the gods' carnival, he would have what he asked. The man worked until his fingers bled but finished the thousandth mask just in time. Hektorus was bound to keep his pledge and invited the man to dance with the gods—Cressa the mother, Velio the messenger with his thousand eyes, weeping Pelagia, Fucina, daughter of the forge, and the whole pantheon—and they gave the man their food to take home to heal his child, or their beautiful demigoddess daughter as a bride.

Alesta liked that. Deals offered by Hektorus or Teras at least made their rules clear. If you were clever and hardworking enough, you could craft the outcome you desired, even if the rest of life felt unfair and impossible.

She turned, bowls in hand, to find Nonnina peeling open a pomegranate and plucking free the gemlike seeds. Alesta set the stew down and reached for the fruit. "Nonnina, those are for later—"

Nonnina rapped Alesta's fingers with her wooden spoon. "When you grow as old as me, you might not have any more later." She popped another ruby seed into her mouth. "May as well enjoy the sweetness in front of you."

Alesta rubbed at her knuckles and sat down to eat. She'd be fortunate to grow as old as Nonnina, whose brother had been tithed many seasons ago. She'd have to be lucky to have any later at all. And quick and industrious and smart.

Rainbows didn't last. She had to grab hold of any opportunity when she caught sight of it. She had to understand the world the way it was, and work it like any other mechanism to survive.

She had to do whatever it took.

Chapter Four

A Breath Above

The Towers were singing.

A good wind from the east wound like a ribbon through the spires and the bridges strung between them, with their knife-like slats, all arranged to work Hektorus' breath into a haunting melody. The song floated above the hum—and yes, shouting—of the festival-goers, Soladisans from all over the island mixed with more refined city folk and courtiers.

Alesta fought her way up the final throng-filled streets, judging that the lively breeze would make for a successful demonstration. She looked to the studio tower, where Kyr should have everything ready for the flier. Beyond it rose the university tower, full of spacious workrooms and book-crammed libraries and possibility, slicing into the blue.

Today she would claim a piece of that sky for herself.

"Hello, Lessie!" The daughter of a tailor Alesta sold thread to waved and popped a corn cake speckled with rosemary into her mouth. Alesta nodded back and walked on, past a group of girls and boys from down the island who were watching the end of the same pageant performed at every festival, depicting the long-ago war between the gods, those who favored the fledgling humans pitted against those protecting monsters. Masked players had already acted out how monsters carried away Hektorus' demi-goddess daughter, sparking the conflict. One danced in a feathered costume as Velio, bringing the tragic word to Hektorus, and Alesta came to a stop as another player showed Fucina pulling a breast-plate and arm guards from her forge to outfit him for the war. The Arbor didn't teach much about the minor gods, but Alesta had always liked the old work songs about the daughter of the forge, who made herself from melted scraps, springing from her caul-dron to create armor for Soladisa's protector.

Then shining Hektorus flew into battle against Orroccio and battled its god, weakening only when the monsters drew him down from his airy domain to touch the earth. He shook them off, leaving the monsters strewn across the stage with satin ribbons for blood tossed from their hands as they fell, and slew their master—but not before the dying god uttered his final curse. It was fulfilled after Hektorus flew away, as three actors rose twined together as Teras, emerging from the pit of lava from which all monsters were born, threatening with smoke and ash, demanding the first tith-ing. The Arbor always had this story told, even at the Festival of Virtues, to remind Soladisans to be ever wary of taking any sinful steps toward Teras.

As if Alesta ever forgot. She moved off before the performers could sing the praise song to the Lia tree they always ended with.

"It'll be her turn, I'm sure," one girl said to the boy next to her, in the back of the gathered audience.

"Yes, send Lessie!" The youths were peering at her as she went by, speaking as if she couldn't hear or understand them simply because she never said anything back. "Shouldn't she count for two tithings?"

Laughter. "She'll glut the beast!"

Alesta rushed on, tamping down her feelings like plants she never wanted to see reach the sun. All that mattered was the judgment of the Lia's smoke. All that mattered was earning the chance to prove she was more than monster food.

Around her, the streets and then the courtyards of the Towers were a blur of Soladisans at tents and booths and stages. Displaying glasswork, tapestries, and paintings. Performing dances in swirling, ribbon-heavy skirts and more pageants of gods and heroes, faces behind shining silver masks. Selling honey cakes shaped into spirals or decorated with interlocking diamonds of edible gold and purple petals. Jangling purses and spilling oval coins, each embossed with a delicate Lia tree, into merchants' hands. Taking in all the festival's wonders, eating squash blossoms stuffed with cheese, and calling out to each other.

Demonstrating improvements to farm equipment and fishing gear and even some philosophical experiments.

Alesta's feet stopped short when she spotted some of the artificers from the university observing the meticulous glass tubes and scales at one booth. It was simple to see the aim of this work, even standing too far away to hear the presenter's explanation to the artificers. They nodded between the apparatus and its inventor, a woman with rosy cheeks, doe eyes, hair styled with pearl combs, and a fine green dress fitting snug to her slender form.

The artificers' eagerness to listen to this woman, clearly as skilled as she was beautiful, stirred a particular, familiar ache in

Alesta's chest. Even if you were good, people would simply prefer to uplift those who were good and lovely. Who looked like they deserved the chance to be somebody, like Hektorus had molded them with his beneficent hand for that purpose.

Just wait until she caught their attention, with work too brilliant to deny, even coming from her. Alesta hiked her skirts and hurried on. The noise and excitement around her seemed to build toward a crescendo that would carry her to triumph.

She passed Rina, wearing a spectacular gown unfolding like golden petals around her lithe form, poised as ever but with eyes distracted and hunting as she walked the other way down the cloister. No one else tore their attention from all the wonders of the festival to give Alesta a passing glance, either, until she reached the courtyard wedged behind the tower full of studios kept by artists or their patrons. The open back expanse of the courtyard was blocked off by a ring of screens Kyr had painted in canonical style—scenes of Soladisa's towers meeting rays of sunlight at a perfect angle, Hektorus with a golden nimbus welcoming the viewer of the painting to his airy domain, and the island of Molissa spreading wide in the distance.

Kyr had made Hektorus like every illuminated page in his books or the icons in the sanctuary and chapel. Muscular and beaming. Staring at those images while the albero lectured every week was what sparked Alesta's interest in flight in the first place, a little after her covenant birthday, when her bough was added to the tithing chamber. Her parents were gone, and she'd been filled with the vague but certain knowledge that if she survived, she faced a lonely future, eventually.

She'd begun harboring a secret conviction that—even if no one

else would be there for her, even if no one else could love her—
if she were only good enough, Hektorus would. She became
enamored with the idea of pleasing him with her fliers. But years
of the alberos pointing out how Hektorus would judge her on his
scales of virtues and sins had robbed the dream of its softness, if
not its ambition.

When the flier launched, wings driven by kharis, tethered
by the cable by which Alesta manipulated the controls, it would
appear to soar over the painted sea. She'd tested it yesterday in
the fields, after rushed days of planning and building and obsess-
ing. Days of talking out her problems to Kyr as he painted, of
begging off from going swimming in one of the sheltered coves
when he was done, of talking to herself as she worked for hours
after. The festival stalked closer on the heavy padded feet of one
of the creatures Kyr painted from descriptions in his books, from
lands unblessed by Hektorus, where animals as large as branzonos
filled the fields and forests. Like Teras' three beasts, which fetched
offerings down to hell. The tithing ceremony was tomorrow. But
university invitations would be offered today, and she was ready.

Kyr ducked from behind a screen he was adjusting. "Have you
come to confess?" Alesta only managed to stare before Kyr waggled his brows and pitched his voice in perfect imitation of Albero
Paolo. "It has been far too long since your last confession. Surely
this week you must have eaten some babies—"

She snorted.

"—or at least worn a shirt that clashed with your skirt."

She clutched her hand to her chest with a gasp. "Never that!"

"Straight to Teras!" He hauled her inside and finished pushing
the screens together.

They stopped laughing long enough to prepare for the demonstration. Alesta positioned the flier as Kyr checked over the tether's anchor. She towed the craft, with its frame almost as big as herself and wingspan wide as Kyr was tall, until it lined up before the opening between two screens where the courtyard overlooked another below, full of festival-goers. Alesta dragged her lip under her teeth and stroked a finger along one wing. "Once they all see this, and grant more kharis, I can scale it up to carry a rider."

Kyr tugged at his knot. "Would you fly it?"

She shrugged. "If I need to." She tilted her cheeks to catch the sun and flung her arms out. "Straight to the heavenly fields. Only way I'm reaching them." Like the man who had climbed the sky to Hektorus.

Kyr didn't laugh at her bleak joke like she had his, just worried the beaded tassel at one elbow as if lost in thought.

Maybe his moodiness was to be expected. It was his last day before everything changed for good.

Voices interrupted from outside the screens, Kyr's mother's among them. He stood and brushed at his breeches where he'd been kneeling before slipping out between the paintings.

"What masterful work, my lord Kyrian!" Albero Paolo. Alesta shifted so she could see a slice of the group taking in the festival together. Alberos and davinas and courtiers. Some of Kyr's cousins, as well as his mother.

Kyr clasped his hands behind his back and greeted the albero with perfect politeness and no hint he'd been mimicking him minutes ago.

Albero Paolo gushed on. "I would love for you to paint something for the Arbor to feature. Perhaps a new confessional stand, if King Enzo might be persuaded to sponsor the replacement we've been needing."

"I will be sure to mention it to His Majesty." From this angle, Alesta could see Kyr twisting a ring with his thumb, around and around.

Davina Bianca, golden hair piled high atop her head, jutted her chin at him. "Have you seen my Rina about? You don't have her hidden away in there, do you?" She arched a brow like she was suspicious of Kyr, but her mouth pursed in a pleased smile.

Alesta pushed from between the screens, the compulsion to give the information bubbling up in her. "I saw her heading toward the food stalls not long ago."

Davina Bianca folded her hands together, before her ombre white and purple robes. "Thank you." She didn't meet Alesta's eyes. The rest of the group either pretended she wasn't there, as well, or whispered behind fans.

Alesta set her shoulders back. This was why she didn't mind how people's eyes slid right past her most of the time. She couldn't stand being the subject of people's ridicule—or worse, pity. She didn't want their sympathy. If she had to shed her invisibility to stay on Soladisa, she wanted to make them see her as someone to respect. Love was out of the question, but esteem—gratitude— awe, even—these shimmered in possibility like a gown she might slip over herself, that could fit her perfectly.

Kyr's cousin Mico made a slight bow to Bianca, his dark hair falling gently forward. "I'll fetch her for you, Davina."

Davina Bianca's smile spread and reached her chestnut eyes. As Mico strode away, she turned, gratified, and marveled to Kyr's mother about the demonstration Mico had made that morning of the weapons he'd forged infused with Lia rosin, to stay perpetually sharp.

"I should get back to my own——" Kyr began, taking half a step back.

His mother took hold of him, though, straightening his jacket. "Caro." She dropped her voice low. "*Your* work is now here, spending time with the court." She slapped his hand away from where it tugged on one of his gold and pearl earrings like teardrops. "You must do as expected."

Alesta thought he might beg off. She was already late, having had to finish chores on the farm first thing that morning.

But Kyr stood there as the conversation moved on to how everyone was sharing their artistry at the festival for the glory of Hektorus. Kyr's mother wore a gown with skirts that her embroidery made look like the froth of waves brushed by the god's hand, its darts picked out with golden thread like sunbeams, and her shawl's swirls of stitches evoking his blessed zephyrs. Another courtier had blown glass into trees with boughs pulled into the air in a rainbow of colors, or sea corals with branches as delicate as frost upon a winter window. He spoke of another exhibitor who had projected light through lenses oiled with kharis and set in swiveling stands, to cast moving colored illuminations against a tower wall like a pageant. Alesta, waiting still for Kyr's help to launch the flier, fought the urge to search out this invention and quiz the creator about its specifications. The king had stood rapt observing that for an hour, Kyr's mother said.

Davina Bianca told her, gazing admiringly at her shawl, "Rina's wearing her art as well. You all simply must see."

A courtier asked, "And has Rina begun to See yet?"

The davina's smile didn't change. At all. "Rina is young still. We're welcoming her into the Sight-summonings. Hektorus will bless her at the time his wisdom affirms."

Sympathetic murmurs. Nearly as devastating as how they whispered about their lord Kyrian's odd, unfortunate friend. But no one could argue outright with a woman who could See the future.

In the awkward hush, Kyr said, crafting an affable manner as carefully as any sculpture or textile, "I haven't the Sight, but I can tell you all that if you wait in the courtyard below, you will very shortly behold something much more wonderful than these paintings."

They all exclaimed and moved away, graceful and unburdened, light as Hektorus' steps skimming a breath above the earth when he'd visited Soladisa.

Alesta met Kyr, turning back to where she stood before the screens, with hands fisted and a voice burning with determination. "Let's fly."

She didn't wait for him to answer, but dove back into work. Everything was nearly ready. Alesta plucked the eternal-burning kharis from the box in which Kyr had given it to her, lit its charred end, and set it into the heart of the machine. A mere sliver of Lia wood, soaked in kharis oil, would propel the flier like a roaring furnace. Already her carefully worked gears were coming alive, the wings waking and testing the air. Alesta had also contrived the long, narrow frame to funnel the kharis' holy power into amplifying the lift she'd crafted into the design.

She and Kyr shoved the flier on its oiled runners along the polished planks laid out leading to the balcony. The sun's light throbbed through the translucent wings. Excitement raked down her skin at the gears' turning, the lines running to the wings snapping taut and slack in turn. Everything slotting into place, one thing leading to the next, each part serving its purpose. It was exquisite—a kind of beauty she could create. Inside she felt *right*, felt something slotting into place within herself, felt in harmony with the rest of the world for once.

Like an odd piece of smudged glass set singing in tune with the reverberations of the greater world. Or maybe *she* was the something great. Maybe the world was smudged glass, and she had transformed at least one small part of it into a vibrant hymn.

The flier rushed forward—up—and shot out over the balcony's edge and into the sky.

The tether snaked over the stones and chased the craft into the air, then pulled straight. Alesta walked backward, eyes on the flier, to where she could reach the cords running along the rope that controlled the mechanisms. But out past the screens swelled astonished cries and exclamations of admiration. A symphony of wonder.

She called out instructions, and Kyr took hold of the tether's leather grip a length ahead of her, to help hold it steady, and to pull the flier back if it should fail.

But it wouldn't fail. Its wings skimmed upon Hektorus' holy wind. Alesta pulled the controls to make it weave back and forth through the air, over the festival, above the sounds of awe rising.

Kyr grinned over his shoulder. His smile grew wider when he saw her look of victory. "Sorry that fuss delayed this even one minute."

Triumph ran through her like music. She imagined the group of courtiers walking below and seeing her accomplishment.

University artificers lifting their gazes to her invention. The king, even, wandering through the festival's offerings until it captured his attention. Nothing could spoil this, so she gave a shrug. "Everyone wants a moment with the almost-heir."

The wind dragged Kyr's curls back from his brow. He rolled his eyes. "Everyone wants to use the almost-heir."

"Of course they do. That's how this place works." She adjusted the controls to make the flier bank and return from its arc to the left. "But you just use them right back. None of the rest of it matters." She let the words sear into her like a brand. She was engineering her future for herself, creating something no one could take away. She'd have to ignore anything else she was denied or subjected to.

Kyr's lips thinned. "It means more than that. It's going to be my entire life. The Arbor gives guidance and comfort."

She gave him a look, raising one brow. It was always obvious when he quoted a book or an albero.

He spun about, one arm hanging from the grip. "I have to believe it's not terrible to know the right thing to do."

The flier dragged the tether hard to the right. She fought with the controls to guide it back. "Yes, it's easy to accept the Arbor's idea of right and wrong when it says you're right, everything about you is right and good." And everything about her was wrong or lacking.

"Not everything." Eyes still on Alesta, Kyr pulled the grip with both hands to keep the tether centered. The rope creaked. "You know it's not that simple. It helps—"

"Only because it first convinced you something about you needed helping." The line strung between them vibrated with a wild tension. "That something was wrong about the way you are."

Something passed through Kyr's eyes, a shadow like a bruise. "It's clear at least about what it wants."

She could only gape back. She didn't understand. And she always understood Kyr. It was so uncomfortable a sensation, sending tingles of anxiety down her limbs, she didn't notice at first how the controls had slackened just like her hands.

She shot her gaze to the flier. The sun pierced through its wings. It reared strangely, dipping lower, stirring nausea through Alesta's belly.

She shouted. Kyr twisted back to see the flier fall through the blue. The wind that had borne it up now shredded its tattering wings.

They ran forward, hauling back the tether, fist after fist. But they'd been distracted. They were too late. The flier plummeted. The rope fought back, pulling down. Friction bit Alesta's palms. The crowd beyond the balcony's brink cried out now in horror. Courtiers shoved away as the flier swung low.

There was nothing Alesta could do to prevent its fall as her invention crashed into a screaming girl, dressed like a golden flower.

Perfect calamity.

Chapter Five

AFTER THE FALL

Staring down at where the flier shattered to pieces against the flagstones, Alesta felt as if she were the one falling, falling still, falling forever.

Falling through the screams that carried upward from the crowd. From Davina Bianca, who shrieked as she shoved forward toward Rina's splayed form.

Rina. Face ashen. Mouth open and silent, like a fish.

Alesta teetered dangerously where she stood, half-obscured by the screens. Kyr crashed his palms to his ears. She reached for him, gripped his forearm. "What have I done?" she said. "What have I done?"

The only answer was a blossom of flame at one end of the destroyed machine. The kharis fire, crushed under the frame but not so easily smothered, traveled now along the skeletal remains of the flier.

The tailor's girl, Lor, rushed from the mob to pull Rina back by her shoulders, her pale hair falling over her face as she stooped. Rina loosed a wail of pain. Alesta's shame swelled as she realized she was grateful for the proof the girl was still alive. Lor ran her hands over Rina, checking for hurts, as her mother fretted over them.

Alesta's mind cut through her guilt and cycled faster than kharis-powered gears. No one would ever allow her to step foot in the university tower now. She'd have no shield of any virtue before the solstice tithing and all the others waiting in her path, only the weight of this sin against her, seeming already to press heavily on her chest, making it impossible to breathe.

This was it for her.

She realized she was muttering some of this aloud as Lor pulled off her own sash, worked with fancy pleating, to loop around Rina's shoulder. "I think her arm is broken."

Davina Bianca heaved another shuddering moan. "My poor girl."

Alesta's blood lashed in her ears. Destruction. Violence. Against another person—beyond careful sparring—nearly unheard of, except in Kyr's books. A breath away from murder, an act unknown on the isle. Farmers' and butchers' tools received a special dispensation from the Arbor. Even ending a monster's life required extraordinary absolution.

"She is injured!" Davina Bianca cried, as a physician reached Rina and others moved to tamp out the fire. "She might have been *maimed!*"

Alesta's voice rasped, dry and brittle as a sun-bleached bone. "What am I going to do?" She needed to find the right mechanism to make everything all right again. The right lever to pull or gear to wind. But there wasn't one. "I'm dead."

Kyr had been squinting, barely seeming to see her, until this. Now he dropped one hand to clamp it over hers. His palm was warm against her own cold, trembling fingers.

Another voice broke into the chaos below. "That was my lord Kyrian's contraption!"

Alesta's gaze snapped up to meet Kyr's. There was one device that might serve to free her of this catastrophe she'd made. One pattern to rely on. "No noble has ever been tithed in anyone's memory," she whispered. The nearest was an advisor's son the alberos caught kissing another boy—the Arbor's warnings against how such acts were an abomination to Hektorus and sure steps to Teras were one more reason the place chafed Alesta. Differences equaled tithing. "Let the Lia judge me as it will, but without another chance at the university, even if I survive this selection somehow, I won't make it. Not through three years yet." This was only logic, and her voice fell into the familiar comfort of its flow. There'd be no real harm to Kyr, and one desperate hope to save her life.

Still he remained silent. Not unusual for him when he was thinking. "You wouldn't be risking your immortal spirit," Alesta insisted, "only their opinion of you." And everyone favored Kyr so; it would be no time at all before they were falling over themselves to forgive and forget. Nothing more than an unfortunate accident. And she could still try for the university. She would still stand a chance—a scrap of one, but she had to reach for it, cling to it, as long as it lasted. "Kyr. Please."

Kyr's brows flexed, as if in pain. But Rina was the one hurt, and Alesta the one doomed.

He pried her hand from his arm and walked away. He left her alone, ringed by his paintings' blank backs.

It was too much to ask that he break the meticulous façade he'd constructed, just for her.

Alesta slowly spun back to see people stomping on the charred frame of her beautiful flier. She'd have to face what she'd done.

She ran through the halls, reaching the lower courtyard to see Kyr striding ahead of her. Suddenly knowing what he intended, she wanted to stop him, but there were so many people out there— her voice burrowed down deep inside her.

He walked into the center of the yard. His back was straight, but he bore none of his usual charm he normally put on at court. He knelt beside Rina, opposite Davina Bianca, and pronounced clearly, "I apologize. By Hektorus' breath, I am most sincerely sorry my design caused this injury."

Alesta fought the urge to sink to the ground as well. She slumped against the archway to the courtyard, limp with relief and heavy with horror at once.

The outcry over the flier and Rina had died down a little, but at this a resurgence of talk grew, though after a burst of shock its tone seemed to soften, blunted by everyone's love for Kyr. As he murmured something to a blanched but calmer Rina, his mother stood among her cousins and courtiers, tall and still as one of the statues lining the royal tower's antechamber.

Like the crowd's exclamations, the fire resisted the attempts to snuff it out completely. Albero Paolo peered into the wreckage. Light and shadow parried over his face as he crouched near and pulled the stubbornly burning thorn free.

"You used kharis?" The albero stood, staring at the flier's broken wings. "And this—is this—" He raised his eyes to Kyr. "Branzono skin?"

"No!" Kyr's mother took a jolting step forward. She shook her head at her son. "You don't make things like this." She turned wide eyes to Albero Paolo. "Some mechanicals, yes, but nothing—experimental—like this."

Kyr shifted back on his heels. His voice was gravelly as he answered. "Go to the old barn on the edge of our land and our tenants'. You'll see plenty of my work I've never shown you."

"This is a desecration," Albero Paolo hissed. "Monstrosity mixed with Hektorus' holiest blessing." He gaped, disbelieving, at Kyr.

The air seemed to go taut, like a weapon drawn. Courtiers murmuring how *accidents do happen* stopped and cast hardening stares Kyr's way and whispered into each other's ears.

Alesta was about to run forward, to explain it was no sacrilege, only two different substances she had found a new way to put together. Even if it meant explaining it hadn't been Kyr at all. But a royal attendant blocked her, forcing her to the wall, as King Enzo swept into the courtyard.

"My king—" Albero Paolo and Davina Bianca wasted no time informing the king of what had occurred. The lines upon his brow and around his mouth furrowed deeper.

"Of course, the Arbor will make the best Lia teas and salves available to her for healing," the king said. He cast a considering gaze about the scene, dark eyes lit with sadness, and raised his voice. "It seems a blessing no greater injury was done. These are grave transgressions, even in recklessness." He turned to Kyr, face again severe. "Attend me in the royal tower. After you see that our lady is cared for."

Kyr's mother followed the king and his attendants closely as they left, looking ready to burst with things to say to the king. When they cleared away, Alesta made at last toward Kyr.

He was speaking with Rina and the physician, and the broken

flier waited in her path. The wings she'd wrought were mere skeletons, the last pieces flaking away. "I don't understand," she mumbled to herself, disappointment and frustration twisting together in her belly. "Why did the hide degrade like this? It's strong, strong enough to withstand the poison sea, it—"

"It is monstrous," Albero Paolo said sharply, standing nearer than she'd realized. "It is nothing good and falls easily to corruption." He skirted around her, bearing the kharis nearly as high as his nose. "Hektorus keep us from such evil."

The physician and Kyr helped Rina to her feet, but Davina Bianca quickly inserted herself between her daughter and Kyr, her back to him.

Kyr retreated a few steps. Alesta joined him, where he dragged a ring to one knuckle and back with his thumb. "The way they're looking at me."

He would rub the skin raw. She closed her hands over his. "Thank y—"

He flung her off him. His hands flapped in the air, and he caught them together, tight against his stomach. He muttered, almost to himself, "This is my nightmare."

She couldn't see the problem. "You don't even want to be king." What more could his uncle do than refuse to name him heir? But the king would forgive him, and no matter how Albero Paolo scolded, the choice of successor was completely King Enzo's.

Several young courtiers crushed around Rina as the physician helped her from the courtyard. "Your wonderful dress is ruined," one girl said in sympathy.

Rina ran her fingers over the pleated fabric binding her arm to her side. "My seamstress is so clever; she can fix it." Her wavering voice took on more of its customary enthusiasm. "And perhaps fashion me a beautiful sash like this." The aquilegia petals stuck over her lashes flared as her eyes widened. "One to match each dress—"

Elaborate sashes would be slung around every young lady's bodice before autumn, Alesta predicted. "I'm glad Rina will be all right," she told Kyr, still feeling the vise of guilt—and a nauseous stir of confusion about if Kyr was angry with her. Even though he'd gone ahead and helped her.

"And so will you." He nodded to her, sunlight turning his dark eyes to amber, something unreadable caught in them, and went to follow the king toward the royal tower. Arms hanging stiffly at his sides, his hands fell so she could see red welts burned across his palms.

He passed Mico, who was examining the crumbling ash of the wreck thoughtfully. The courtier lifted his eyes to Alesta, gaze as keen as the dagger at his belt.

Kyrian left the chaos and noise and judgment of the courtyard behind as he entered the royal tower. The throne room's antechamber with its muraled walls and damask drapes was a sanctuary of hush and shadow—until his mother emerged from speaking with the king. A flash of the golden room behind her was eclipsed by the great wooden doors thundering shut, and she rushed toward him, the look on her face shifting from indignant worry to aggravation, the carefully embroidered waves of her skirts like a tide coming to drag him out to sea. "What were you *thinking?*" she demanded in a low voice when she drew close.

"I—" He swallowed. "M—" His childhood stutter only reemerged at the worst times. But there was nothing he could explain anyway.

"How could you? I know you know better than this. We've worked so hard to make sure."

He hid his face against one raised fist. He did know. All the rules. Allow yourself no mistakes. Bury yourself deep, not like a seed but something foul to be forgotten.

It hadn't mattered, weighed against Alesta facing tithing. Not that his lie could shield her from the kharis smoke that sniffed out every secret sin, only those who might make it harder for her to avoid its doom, who would have barred her from the university. This could all be for nothing. He felt his control slipping again and knocked his fist against his head.

"Kyrian, *no*, not here." His mother grabbed his wrist. She let out a distressed sound, eyes widening.

His hand. A rope burn shredded across his palm.

His mother folded his hand within her own. Hers was smaller than his now, not covering it fully, and she squeezed her other hand around it, too. "I only want to see you safe."

But that was never the issue. He was perfectly safe. It was the only thing he was perfect at.

He'd have a long, long life to pretend his way through.

His mother's mouth pulled into an uncertain line, her eyes pooling with regret. "I wish—" She gave a tiny shake of her head. "No matter. Clearly, we need to be doing more to prepare you for your future. So you're accepted in your position. Whatever it ends up being," she added darkly. "You need to focus on learning how to survive here, making more friends among the nobility. No more sneaking off to your"—she huffed—"little friend, or barns—honestly, Kyrian, do you want people associating you with *animals?* You belong here. Assuming the king doesn't banish you from the Towers. He's disappointed and his planned announcement is spoiled." She pressed his hand to his side and smoothed down his hair. "Go in there and apologize. Properly."

The attendants swung the doors for Kyrian open like the jaws of some leviathan unhinging, and he started down the long, bright hall, past all the mirrors reflecting light from high windows over and over, like courtiers whispering gossip along, under masterpieces of glasswork shining with kharis, to where Enzo waited upon his throne cast in gold. Where Kyrian was meant to sit one day. He didn't take in any of the elaborate craftmanship that had always entranced him as a child visiting the king, the sunbursts framing his head, the arms and legs wrought like tree boughs; he focused on not withering under Enzo's scorching stare like a relentless sun.

The king let it sear into Kyrian for a long moment before speaking. "Explain how you allowed this to happen."

Kyrian clasped his hands behind his back and inhaled slowly. "Insufficient testing," he got out. He'd tried to tell them, there wasn't enough time for everyone to prepare for the festival.

"And the mixture of materials? Albero Paolo is claiming sacrilege." Enzo shifted, adjusting his royal medallion upon his silk and velvet jacket. "I don't need to be at war with the Arbor over supplying the royal tower with the kharis everyone relies upon."

"I—" Kyrian twisted his ring. Only Alesta could have thought to pair the kharis and monster parts, and for a moment, it had been glorious. But some things were never meant to come together.

Pretending otherwise only resulted in disaster. "I have no excuse. I'll accept any punishment as deserved penance." Readily. He just wanted to get this over with. The burning shame. He hated this. Hated himself.

Enzo sighed. "We'll have to delay the declaration. This is not the time. You should keep to your rooms for now, until Rina's recovered somewhat; skip the ball tonight." Kyrian blinked. Was that all? His uncle's mouth pressed into a resigned curl. "I haven't been eager to lay all this responsibility on you, I hope you know. Only, the court likes to see an heir in place. I suppose there was time yet for a youthful indiscretion before taking it up."

Kyrian's surprise was matched only by his certainty that punishment would not have slid away so easily from Alesta as a mere indiscretion. But Kyrian was like one of these mirrors, bouncing the blame right off himself. Shining and imitative and blank. "I promise not to make such a mistake again."

Enzo sat back in his throne, hands kneading at the golden boughs, exhaling another long breath. "None of us are faultless, my boy."

No, that was certainly true. Although Kyrian caught sight of himself in the mirror to one side of the king, and no one would ever know, looking at that straight-backed, solemn-faced person, the mess of emotions inside him—a tsunami of relief with an undertow of unease and a biting wind of impatience to finally get to his rooms and be alone.

Maybe Enzo suspected something, though, because he raised a brow, saying, "And don't be too disheartened if the davina is vexed with you over Rina. There are plenty of other girls who'd like someday to be queen."

But only one Kyrian wished wanted him in that way.

His hands twisted behind him like he could wring the feelings out. It would be so much easier to be free of them. What had been kindling within him would never matter, with Enzo and his mother reminding him constantly of his royal duty and Alesta herself reminding him more than a dozen times—because he'd counted—they were friends and nothing else.

There was no question, though—if someone could see past the surface inside Kyrian, they'd see—he'd taken the blame for her today primarily for one selfish, reckless, despicable reason. He would give up his time outside the Towers, his space to paint what he pleased, any sense of himself apart from the role he would play, but in that moment out on the courtyard, after their fight and the flier, something deep down inside Kyrian had finally refused to let go of what was most precious to him, had growled and snapped and clawed back at the idea of Alesta actually being taken away.

He would never tell Enzo or anyone the truth of the accident, like he couldn't tell Alesta why he'd shielded her from the blame, beyond the friendship that meant of course he cared for her well-being. Certainly not now, when she might think he meant to bargain with the favor he'd done her. He repeated his apologies to the king, and made his way to his apartments at last, where his mother launched into her refrain of disappointment until he fidgeted so much she waved her hands and retired to her chamber, like she couldn't stand to look at him any longer. And he tried not to recall Alesta's desperate, despairing face or his own confused and surely monstrous hurt—that she had finally asked something of him freely, and it had only been to make use of his position— chafing like his palms.

Chapter Six
UNTIL THE MONSTERS

Kyrian knew the tithing ceremony was always performed in the morning. He preferred spending these days out in the fields with Alesta, pretending they were the only two people in the world, that nothing threatened to spoil their idyllic hours talking or reading or sprawling in the grass in comfortable silence. Sometimes when she was most anxious or angry, she wanted to go watch the davinas' ritual, and what could he do but accompany her and hope and hope? They always got through tithing day together, though.

Today he was sitting with his mother in the receiving room of their apartments, staring at the same paragraph in a book over and over while she picked perfect stitches through the linen stretched across her embroidery hoop. His worry prickled at him, that Alesta should have received an invitation to university, an entry to the life she wanted, to safety, and instead, nothing stood between her and this morning's kharis smoke, and what if she wasn't given another chance—

His thoughts broke off at his mother's gasp. Kyrian looked up to see what was the matter, where she sat near the window, and saw red blooming across her circle of fabric. She'd stuck herself with the needle, badly. He thought she'd startled at her accident—then noticed, as the hoop and bloody threads fell to her lap, she was looking with horror not at her hands at all but past him.

Kyrian twisted in his chair to find a dozen alberos crowded into the doorway. Solemn faced, their long green robes a lie of life when their task today was to deliver the tithing to their death. Him. They were here for him. "Oh."

Behind him, his mother began screaming.

Kyrian stood, even as the marble floor seemed to drop out from under his feet. He knew he should be panicking, but felt strangely calm. Like in this actual moment of disaster all his practice was kicking in, and he could follow expectations as perfectly as she'd always hoped. He allowed the alberos to take him by the shoulders while one recited to his mother—held back now from Kyrian by two more priests, held up from collapsing—how tithings were allowed gifts from their families before being taken to the Arbor, and then the ship. The rock. Teras.

She couldn't have heard, still crying out that they couldn't, it was a mistake, call the king, *no*. Her tear-bright eyes were the last thing Kyrian saw before the priests ushered him out.

Vaguely he was aware of people stopping in the halls as they passed. Surprised faces. Whispers catching and increasing like the bonfire at the autumn festival—which he would not attend this year, it occurred to him. Or ever again.

That mundane thought snapped him out of his shock, and it hit him like a punch to the gut—*Alesta*. He staggered, the alberos bearing him up and hustling him along to their small private sanctuary in the Arbor, where Albero Paolo greeted him with a reserved, mournful look. "I do wish there were anything to be done."

Kyrian knew this was one of those things people uttered simply to say something, to ease an awkward moment and express concern, but he grasped at the offer, blurting, "Can you make sure—" He swallowed. "Alesta. Send for her. Please." Surely she'd come anyway, when Kyrian failed to appear like every tithing morning, but just to be certain.

Albero Paolo folded his hands together grimly and nodded, almost to himself, before slipping out. Kyrian crossed his arms, pulling threads loose from his jacket sleeves. The albero probably felt Kyrian ought to be praying, meditating on the sin that led him here or his sacrifice for Soladisa, rather than his selfish desires, but he didn't care, only that he'd see Alesta once they took him out to the dock. He'd see her once more at least, like they'd always promised one another, he told himself, over and over, as he waited and gradually became aware of an argument going on somewhere beyond the locked door. Enzo's voice. Alberos speaking of the kharis' infallibility. The kingdom's reliance on honoring its judgment, even of the king's nephew. The covenant that could not be broken.

Kyrian's reeling mind grasped onto this litany, reciting now the delicate balance of power between throne and Arbor, memorized at all those lessons he'd faithfully attended with Mico—the king oversaw the keeping of his subjects and mandated the tithings to protect everyone and their land, while the Arbor tended to the Lia and the spirits of Soladisans, cultivating kharis from the tree and virtues among the people.

And culling them.

There was no argument to be made. Tithing selections were sacrosanct, entirely under control of Hektorus and the Arbor's divinely guided rituals. Sacrosanct, absolute, and deserved.

Even if everyone here believed it was for the violence of the failed flier rather than his true sin.

The king at last insisted they anoint Kyrian before departing. An obscene amount of holy oil spread over his brow, bare chest, arms, and hands. The fabric of Kyrian's shirt sticking to the kharis made it difficult to focus when the king came to stand before him and spoke, voice heavy with regret. "I am so sorry, my boy. You should have been my heir. I seem fated to lose you all." Enzo blinked, and his chest, under his brocade jacket and royal medallion, rose and fell with a sigh. "This is the least I may do for you, in hope that this sacred kharis will allow you to pass from that dark place to the heavenly fields."

More empty words. Teras trapped the sinful spirits of the tithed deep in the burning depths of Orroccio, forever mere shades. The Arbor taught that. Kyrian had learned so carefully.

He knew nothing could help him as they took hold of him again, grips hard, and walked him from the Arbor, and the Towers, down toward the cove. Tithing days were always somber, and the late-afternoon streets were emptier than normal, what people were out turning surprised and watchful faces his way. Kyrian couldn't spare a thought for how they were all learning of his sinfulness; he only searched the scattered crowds for Alesta. All the way to the water, to the royal dock. Because they'd promised. This was the way it was supposed to happen—neither of them really expected it to be him, but if it ever came to this, they would be together until the last moment. Until the alberos dragged them apart.

Until the monsters.

He knew she would not let him go without a goodbye. At the very least.

They led him onto the tithing ship, footsteps hollow upon the deck, and Kyrian was too busy watching for Alesta still and wondering what he might dare to say to her to pay much mind to the alberos closing shackles around his wrists, securing him to the bulwark. He noticed distantly they had to hold his shaking, blistered hands still to fit the irons.

She would come, he knew. He'd risked everything for her, she would let him risk a few words finally. Any moment now, Kyrian told himself. The whole time as the alberos prepared the ship. Even as they shoved away from Soladisa, he was convinced. He searched the shoreline for her figure.

He was so sure.

Soladisa slipped away, smaller and smaller, receding like his hope. They cut out through the poison sea. The ship rocked, nothing to how everything within him was falling off its axis.

She had not come.

The wind had shifted, off the sea to the south, cooling Alesta's sunburned cheeks as she finished her early morning chores and making her hope her luck might change too. She'd waited all afternoon outside the royal tower after Kyr had disappeared inside, lonely, even surrounded by so many people still taking in the pleasures of the festival. Preparations had begun for the evening's ball, Alesta's evening chores had beckoned, and Kyr still hadn't reappeared. She'd hoped he wasn't in too much trouble on her account.

Then she'd come home to find Nonnina having one of her worst days yet, and spent the night and next day preparing poultices to ease her pain, plucking herbs from where they hung overhead, and slipping spoonfuls of broth between Nonnina's lips; tithing day passed in a blur, Alesta's worry growing over how her grandmother wasn't improving and how Kyr had not arrived to spend it together as he always did. How he was possibly still being kept at home as punishment. How perhaps he was avoiding her by his own choice.

How, instead of his fastidious figure, the robed alberos might crest the rolling hills, to take her to Teras, despite everything.

Her only distractions were chores and filling Nonnina's next sleepless night telling the saddest tales her grandmother loved best, of Pelagia searching for her stolen lover, fooled into flooding Orroccio where the trickster god told her he was hidden away, and of the Soladisan peasant and demigoddess who fell in love but were cast apart by a jealous god.

Now Nonnina was resting, and Alesta was going to go apologize to Kyr.

She shut the sheepfold gate, its wood rough against her hands. Taking the blame had been too great to ask of him. However reasonable her assessment of the risks, she'd failed to consider how it would feel for him to damage his reputation at court. She'd pressured him into trading its unmarred gleam for her like it was nothing. Alesta shoved her own feelings aside so often, it was a habit not to question it. She'd seen how to remake the situation as she saw best and pushed.

Alesta knew she was a lot. She was too much—her thoughts

unspooling constantly and sometimes spilling from her unguarded mouth. Her body. Her ambitions. And now it had all been too much, even for Kyr.

She hurried across the fields toward the villa, wishing she could outpace her guilt. She'd apologize. And teach him more fighting. And clean his brushes for the next month. Year.

But at the villa, the servants told her their lord Kyrian and his mother had not yet returned from the Towers. No word had come of when they might be expected back.

Alesta steeled herself to face him on her hike up to the city, through dew-heavy fields and sleepy streets, on into the Towers. Where she'd reached too far, and all her hopes were dashed.

Worry coiled in her gut. Kyr may have covered for her with the alberos and artificers, and she'd survived the day, but there was no hiding her sin from Hektorus and his kharis smoke, when in a mere three months Davina Bianca again sat down at her brazier and bid it point to the next season's tithing. Alesta forced herself to focus on what she could control—if she somehow survived the next few tithings, she needed to think of something else she could do to appeal to the university. The talk of Mico's Lia-forged weapons had her pondering what might be useful to the fishers and farmers she sometimes saw along the coast driving sea monsters away with their longbows.

Her mind was deep in considerations of tension and draw weight as she crossed the royal courtyard, cast in cool shadows and reaching sunlight.

She thought it was Kyr at first, when a boy rose from his seat on a wide ledge, where he'd been leaning against a cobalt-blue planter and sketching or writing in a book. Her hopeful heart raced on a moment even as she realized it wasn't.

Mico. His black hair a bit straighter, his shoulders a stretch broader. Nearly the same age as Kyr.

He jumped down, landing on soft leather boots and not bothering to button his linen jacket, patterned with trumpet vines and laced at the sides with green ribbons. "Kyrian's friend, right?"

"Right." She'd never spoken with Mico before, and her anxiety fluttering inside her today sent all the proper words scattering out of her grasp, along with any guess why he was addressing her now. "I need to see him."

His face pinched, brows drawing together. "I'm sorry," he said stiffly.

She was bungling everything again. Etiquette. Manners. The magic words to get what she needed. The attendants weren't even at the door to the royal tower yet this morning, and her compulsion to make things right with Kyr was growing and growing until her skin felt too tight. "Apologies. My grandmother's ill and I haven't slept." She scrubbed a hand down her side and dropped her face toward the flagstones, each carved with a relief of lacy ferns. "My lord Mico, could you perhaps let our lord Kyrian know I've come and need to speak with him. Please."

"I am so sorry."

She lifted her gaze and narrowed her eyes. Even to her, who often felt off-balance talking to anyone besides Nonnina or Kyr, this seemed odd. She didn't understand why he was still apologizing to her. "I'll find him myself—"

Mico's thick brows rippled. "You cannot."

Kyr couldn't be so severely out of the court's good graces to be confined alone to his chambers still. Shame made her start to ramble. "I know. I know he's upset with me——"

"My lady, he's been tithed."

He was teasing her. People did that, and she often couldn't tell. It always made her angry.

Mico kept looking at her with that serious face so much like Kyr's, refusing to break into a grin and admit the jest.

"No," she said. "That's not possible." The towers tipped sideways.

Mico dropped his book and pencil to catch her by the elbows. "Here now——got you." He held her steady while she tried to comprehend.

"But he's——" *He's mine.* "He's our lord Kyrian. He's to be heir."

Mico pressed his lips together. "The kharis spoke."

She pulled away from his hands. "I have to go. The dock."

"They took him yesterday," he called after her. "The ship will be on its way back——"

She didn't listen to any more. She ran through streets filling with sunlight and people, through fields steaming with dew lifting in the day's heat. All the way to the stone dock where the Towers' ships were kept, to the farthest edge, where the stone carved in swirls like waves fell away to the actual lapping water. Where posts wrought like seaweed stood alone and unburdened by ropes.

The tithing ship was gone. Kyr was gone. *Gone.*

She would chase after——if only she still had her flier.

Alesta could not understand. Kyr hadn't done anything wrong himself. Even if the alberos and courtiers believed him responsible for her accident, the Lia guided by Hektorus' will should discern the truth of his spirit. Why would the kharis smoke have pointed to his name?

Unless the alberos were right about her. Unless she was so sinful, so utterly unworthy, unredeemable, the act of saving her was just as bad, or worse.

A sick certainty struck her gut, like the slap of waves against the dock. She had damned him.

Her knees sank to the stone. The sun burned into her back, then the part in her mussed hair. If she could, she'd climb its rays like the man in the story and ride it over the horizon, to where Kyr had been swallowed up.

"Grant me, O Hektorus, your divine concession." Her chapped lips murmured the invocation said at the start of every prayer, every opening of weekly chapel, as if she might conjure the god and beg him to undo this unthinkable mistake. She would offer anything—everything—in exchange for a sacred covenant to win Kyr back. "Grant me, O Hektorus—" Over and over. Until her throat went too dry to pray.

Someone else was saying something. Mico crouched beside her and pressed a stoppered bottle into her hands.

Lia medicine. The kind she could never afford for Nonnina. She clutched the glass to her chest. Oh gods, Nonnina would be awake and needing her and Alesta would have to *tell her*—

But she couldn't stop the howling grief that anchored her here, as close as she could get to Kyr, staring where she could not follow. She hadn't cried. She didn't want his cousin to think she didn't care. She croaked out, instead, "It isn't right."

He nodded in her periphery. "Tithings never are." His voice was low and gentle. "That was your flier, wasn't it?"

Her heart clenched. This was her fault.

"Don't worry, I won't tell. Too much lost already."

Tears stung Alesta's eyes then. "He doesn't deserve this."

"No one does."

"No," Alesta said, not sure if she was agreeing or saying she was beginning to think she did deserve such an end.

"I may have a way to help."

She turned from the blurring horizon to look at him. "Kyr?"

Mico shook his head sadly, but a glint sharpened in his eyes. "Everyone else."

They chained him to the rock. Couldn't trust fear wouldn't drive the sacrifice to run. To leap into the sea.

He wouldn't. Even now, after their passage through the poison waters, the night anchored far from either shore to avoid the flying devils that hunted Orroccio's night sky, Kyrian fought every instinct. He was still trying to do this properly. To meet their expectations for death.

Within, his emotions were in turmoil, like the churning sea around him.

They'd have to drag her from the ship, she'd said. A hundred times. She'd sworn. Until the monsters chased her back.

Saltwater stung his cheeks, whether from the sea spray erupting along the jagged dark coast or tears shed, only the gods could say. The air was all salt and spindrift. As if the world wept for the loss of him.

But it would not save him.

It would not unlock his chains that would break only under the teeth of the three beasts. It would not bar them from delivering him down to Teras and his destruction.

Worse than what waited for him, more inescapable than his fetters, was the thought that Alesta had used him too. He knew she didn't care for him the way he did her, but he'd thought she'd cared enough to brave a farewell, upsetting as it might be. Unless she feared he'd accuse her, reveal to the alberos the truth of her flier's accident. Unless she valued more than their friendship his position's benefit to her in this crisis. Or, gods, perhaps she always had. Like everyone else, wanting some version of him that wasn't who he actually was. Just another tool on her belt.

Now he'd be plenty of use to them all—holding off a monster's wrath he never expected to turn on him.

A keening rose in his throat. He swallowed it down, hard. The scent of kharis oil overwhelmed him. No amount of consecration could make Kyrian into what he'd fought his whole life to be, someone worthy of the future he'd certainly only have failed, of the girl whose friendship he'd perhaps mostly dreamed up. Drench him in the stuff, it couldn't touch beneath, where his weaknesses writhed horribly as the sea monsters they'd sailed past, while Soladisa sank beyond the horizon, like his faith drowning in his rising fear.

The alberos were gone now, already turned back for home. Everything he'd kept chained down within himself, for years, erupted. His hands beat against the iron. His head knocked into the stone.

Alesta was lost to him forever. He had no hope his ruined spirit would fly to the heavenly fields. It was as wretched as that damned flier's tattered wings. He sensed, instead, another fate.

Something huge and dark, howling toward him.

Part Two

PURGATORIO

Chapter Seven

BEAUTY IS TRUTH

One month after Kyr's tithing, Alesta returned to the Towers. She was late and had only wrenched a comb through her hair and put on a clean overskirt because Mico insisted she come. He'd brought more medicine for Nonnina, to help with her pain; this latest bout of her illness left her speech slurred and worse stiffness in her joints. Most days Alesta had stayed in bed, curled beside her grandmother, only dragging herself up to tend to the animals.

Even taking the back stairs as Mico instructed, Alesta wished she was home with her sheep. Each quick glance from another Soladisan burned like a brand more than ever before. When she slipped into the training room Mico's branch of the royal family kept for fencing practice, a dozen pairs of eyes turned on her. Mico had carefully gathered others to his cause, mostly people at risk for tithing, or who had siblings who were——several students from the university, as well as vintners' sons and laundresses. Shopkeepers' daughters. Lor, the seamstress.

And Rina.

Brocade skirts spread over a bench near the front of the gathering, arm in a sling of the same material, the courtier widened her dark eyes at Alesta before leaning near Lor and whispering something.

Alesta's shoulders tightened with embarrassment, even as remorse flooded through her. She hadn't had to explain to Mico the truth of Kyr's tithing. He'd worked it out for himself. Perhaps Rina had as well. She would only be justified in hating Alesta now.

No matter. She was here for one reason: the plan Mico had murmured to her on the dock that impossibly awful day.

She slumped against the wall as Mico stood before the group in a silk jacket the color of a sunrise. Notebook in hand, he thanked everyone for coming. "We're all here because we see a better way for Soladisa. I love my uncle the king, but our leaders are too comfortable with this deal with the monster. To be honest, the threat keeps everyone in line. It makes the government's and Arbor's lives easier." He cast his gaze from person to person, earnest and open. "My cousin——" He frowned, jaw tensing, as the memory of Kyr filled the room—people nodded, and Rina's brow creased and she gripped Lor's hand. Alesta's fingernails dug into the carved rosettes on the wall behind her. "I know you all loved him. I know his death is the reason many of you joined us today." Mico dropped his gaze to the floor for a moment before raising his head and saying, "We deserve to live unencumbered by Teras' demands. Hektorus' light shines on all of us; it's wrong for any of his children to be cast away. We are so blessed here—imagine what we could be when our future holds only hope. I truly believe Hektorus wants this for us." A fire caught in his eyes. "We must eliminate the beast."

The mournful air in the room now grew charged with intention. Anticipation.

Mico went on, "We'll all prepare for the possibility of being tithed, and to use it as an opportunity. But as we gather the proper resources for our mission, we can become more . . . proactive."

A girl leaned forward on a bench. "What does that mean?"

"Incur the Lia's judgment." Mico exhaled. "Send someone intentionally."

"Me." Alesta's rough voice rang against the polished floor and mural-covered walls. Everyone twisted to look at her again. But her words came easily for once, carried on an updraft of fervor, and there was a kind of beauty, even, in their stark truth. "I'm going. I'm killing the monster that killed Kyr." She couldn't bring him back, but she could do this.

Mico nodded but said, "We'll see, once we've prepared. We can't launch a full attack against Orroccio—all ships capable of sailing that far are under royal command, and safe passage through the sea only opens for the tithing. The sacrifice will be on their own. But we can all help them be ready. Our scholars can take out books on Orroccio for us all to study without drawing attention to our cause; the plan must remain secret. I can provide weapons, get my hands on some kharis, though that'll take some time. And I'm hoping we can help each other train to fight—with swords, and those of us with real experience killing monsters can teach the rest." He made Alesta a small unanswered smile across his little audience. "We'll need to be smart, and learn all we can about what we'll be facing. Practical knowledge of Teras is limited—"

"Can our lady the davina's daughter help?" A boy in shirtsleeves pointed at Rina. "Use your visions to See more about Teras?"

Rina twisted a hand in her skirts. "I don't have the Sight. Yet."

"That why a noblewoman like you is here?" The boy's chin

lifted. "Afraid of being tithed?"

The girl next to him wrinkled her nose. "What happens if you start with the visions? You abandon the cause?"

"Of course not." Rina splayed a hand over her chest. "I believe in our lord Mico's plan. The tithings are abominable. If I gain the Sight, I will use it to help." She drew a deep breath, then dropped her shoulders. "I'm studying, but Mother says I'm not opening myself fully, *rejecting the invitation to commune*." She sounded like she was repeating a regular bit of chiding. "And that's why the Sight-summonings haven't worked for me."

Lor angled herself to give Rina an appraising look, one brow cocked. "I can help you practice. Start small. Tell me what I'm thinking right now."

The boy who'd spoken up muttered to his neighbor, "Probably how terrifying Davina Bianca is." Alesta could only agree. She wouldn't want Rina's intimidating mother digging around in her head, either. Not that field laborers were invited to the summonings; it was mostly children of davinas who had an affinity for the Sight, and even they were said to be plagued by headaches and weakness after their visions.

"Here's what we do know," Mico said, "from other davinas' visions and the Arbor." Everyone quieted at once, as he opened his notebook. "Soladisa makes the tithing immediately after the ceremony, just to be safe, which means whoever goes will have at least two weeks before Teras' payment is late. The alberos chain the tithing near the coast, and Teras' three beasts fetch them down." His fingers flipped over a page, and he read. "'*The shimmering dark leopard, the burning red lion, the coarse-coated wolf*—they break the chains with their monstrous jaws and deliver the offering straight through the greatest volcanic vent to their master." Alesta tried not to picture Kyr being dragged underground by monsters as Mico paced before the benches. "Somehow, we have to gain an advantage before that happens. The element of surprise. There are other smaller vents that travel through the rock's seven strata—"

"Splitting into a maze of horrors," someone said.

"Full of demons," another added.

"Now," Mico said, "the topmost levels aren't inhabited by any of the great monsters that live deep in hell—"

Like Teras. Most terrible of them all. A familiar heat kindled inside Alesta as Mico spoke on, burning through the haze of grief that hung around her. The only times she felt alive anymore, it seemed, were when she imagined destroying that devil. Mico was righteous in wanting to end the tithings, to better honor Hektorus. And Alesta would help him to that end.

But she was here for revenge.

She was eager as anyone when they drew swords from the racks along the wall—designed to look as if each weapon were a flower plucked from a garden—and followed along as Mico demonstrated. Rina alone sat, pouting in her sling.

Lor, putting her lanky body through the positions Mico showed them, tutted. "Wish that arm was healed up already. Then you could show me some *pointers*." She jabbed the blade out at Rina.

The other girl gave a dainty snort and shrugged. "You've stuck me with pins enough times. I'm sure you'll be a natural."

The seamstress swept her sword out in mock outrage, making Alesta take a swift step back. "Never would I ever carelessly prick my lady's tender flesh."

Rina seemed to flush with anger, though she only rolled her eyes, and after everyone was sweating and sore and excitedly chattering about taking on every variety of monster in hell, she stood and followed Alesta as she put away her sword. "Lessie. I wanted to say—"

Alesta stared down at the delicate blue flowers picked out in the brocade of Rina's sling. Any time the weight of damning Kyr had shifted slightly these last weeks, knowing she'd hurt Rina kept Alesta pinned under her guilt.

And yet it was Rina who said, "I'm so very sorry." Alesta's gaze jumped up to meet the courtier's. "About Kyrian. I know you were such good friends."

Rina's kind words stung like acid. Alesta nodded, blinking back tears, before shoving away and racing out the door.

Two months after Kyr's tithing, Alesta stood at the forge, under a veranda in the Towers, shaping a spring for a new style of arrow she was devising. A frizzy curl fell over her eye. Concentrating on her work, she huffed a harsh breath to blow the hair back, but it stuck to the sweat on her face.

Mico leaned carefully nearer and tucked it behind her ear. "That's looking promising."

"Needs to be smaller." It was only a prototype. If the design worked, she'd see how far she could scale it down, to fit a bow compact enough to sneak onto Orroccio. The trick would be maintaining the force needed to drive the shaft through monster scales, the tension needed to kick the expandable spikes into monster flesh.

"You'll figure it out." Beads of sweat upon his brow and upper lip, his own hair curling in the steam, Mico calmly shifted the blade he was tempering from over the flames.

"Another tithing next month."

"And none of us are ready yet."

She huffed a harsher breath and laid the finished spring on the cooling table. Another youth chosen. Another family wailing and pressing whatever treasures they might have to them, praying they'd purchase passage to the heavenly fields, or at least gentler treatment from monsters.

Mico rested his own work across the anvil and moved away from the heat of the fire. "Here's something that will cheer you up."

Not likely. Cheer felt like something she'd left in another life. She plunged the red-hot tongs into the cooling basin.

"The artificers want you to demonstrate for them."

Alesta froze. "But they—" She swallowed. "They only make invitations at the Festival of Virtues."

"True." Mico leaned a hip against the work table, covered with papers, and flashed a smile. "But I work closely with a few of them, and I may have left the schematics for your mechanical bow in their path last week. They were intrigued."

She'd created that crossbow to help farmers more safely protect the coastline, take out branzonos from a distance, even without great strength, and without needing to be expert shots. Now she was attempting to improve on that design, though it would likely require skilled aim. She would practice before using it on Teras.

"Lessie?" Mico sounded like it wasn't the first time he'd said the nickname that had followed her around since childhood. "You're displeased."

"No." Only surprised. A little confused by the feelings battling within her. "I don't——" Everything she'd wanted. She didn't deserve it. "Do I need to attend university? I'm going to Orroccio." Killing Teras was the only future she could picture for herself now.

"Like I told you," Mico said, shrugging out of his quilted jacket and tugging off his protective gloves threaded with Lia fiber. "We need to play the long game. Gather resources and knowledge." He swiped the back of his hand over his brow. "Your inventiveness is proving just as helpful as I expected. More." His hands rested on the table, still and sure. "This new arrow you've envisioned. It's just what we require to take down these monsters. As a scholar, you'll have access to books and experts and materials, everything you need to contribute. And you'll be safer. We can't wait until next year's festival to get you into the university." Another smile. He was so free with them. "I need to protect you."

And she needed to trust Mico. Everyone would be safer that way. She couldn't let her passion to hunt down Teras lead her into some new disaster like how her desperate fight to not be tithed had doomed Kyr.

"Teras has ruled that rock as long as Soladisa has existed," Mico said. "It will still be there once we're ready."

And Nonnina needed her more than ever. "I do wish to be useful."

"As do I." Green shadows cast from the low sun through vines clinging along the veranda shifted over his face as he gave a softer smile. "Someday the kingdom will see how we've helped it, as I know Hektorus sees us already."

His reassurance was a comfort, especially when she stood in a university courtyard the next week, before a gathering of watchful artificers. Crimson and yellow leaves stirred in an eddy of wind between her and the straw-stuffed sacks set as targets along one end of the yard. The bow slipped in her clammy hands, but Mico was at ease with the teachers, complimenting and asking questions about their work. The king, doubly stricken by grief, had not yet officially made Mico heir, but he carried the expectation as Kyr had—better than Kyr had, already using his position to slowly accrue the information and supplies his mission would require. After he explained the details of the mechanism Alesta had devised for the new weapon, the artificers asked to see it in action. Mico shot Alesta a confident look and nodded.

He was like her—he saw something he wanted from the world, something he wanted to change, and went after it.

She lifted her bow and hit every target.

Nine months after Kyr's tithing, Alesta sat against the wall in the training room after a morning of lessons in the university tower, a book she'd borrowed herself from its library spread open before her. She barely took in the others who were lying on their stomachs, reading more volumes she'd carried here, or running through training exercises that were becoming as familiar as breathing, as familiar as the grief echoing through Alesta still. It stirred up anew each time the tithing ceremonies took another orphaned farmhand or merchant's daughter, while Mico insisted their group still needed time to prepare.

So she was preparing. Alesta wanted to know absolutely everything about Teras and had already worked her way through the most popular writings about the devil. She'd found this dusty account of the war between the gods tucked away deep in the library, and soon saw why it had lain unread for so long. Its cantos of faded lettering said Teras stole Hektorus' daughter when the god was already visiting Soladisa and had promised her to the first king as a bride—that she'd come to tend to her father, wounded from his victorious battle against the monsters' god, and Teras stole her in retribution. It called her the first tithing.

But the Arbor taught that the demigoddess' abduction was the cause of the war between the gods. The alberos and davinas were normally more careful not to let the trade ships bring in apocryphal texts. Alesta set the book aside. Its poetry was beautiful, but the information in it might not be reliable. She picked up a familiar volume of recorded visions instead.

Some are called to the Sight by other davinas; some carry it in their blood, until it stirs awake; some find it blossoming within themselves by pure grace, touched but by Hektorus' holy hand. My aunt was a great Seer, and therefore when I was sixteen, I joined the Sightsummonings, where our order used kharis smoke to invite Hektorus' divine visions.

When I was in my fortieth year, my great vision came to me, full of wonders and terrors. I Saw a beautiful girl who led me into the devil's rock, down through all its horrors, toward the beast that crouches at the farthest depths of hell.

Alesta had Davina Graziela's ancient writings practically memorized now—her accounts of the willowy, wheat-haired maiden shrouded in holy light leading her through the seven strata of Orroccio and the many different kinds of immortal monsters that dwelt in the different caverns and tunnels in each: hoofed devils and three-headed wolves and eight-headed hydras. A dim flicker of curiosity made Alesta wonder what possible structures and tissues might allow creatures with multiple minds to coordinate their animation, if a study might be made with the university's anatomists. She killed the thought; neither she nor any specimens would likely be returning from the rock's depths. Nothing ever did. She only needed to focus on surviving long enough to make it through hell and reach Teras. Alesta turned the page, checking her memory against the text. Each detail might be lifesaving when she was there.

Lor was flipping through a fat volume nearby, quizzing Rina, who perched behind her braiding ribbons into her long straight hair. "The seven strata of hell?"

Rina bobbed her head, reciting each. "The surface, the twilight levels, the mirror-maze, the dark levels, the inferno, the city of devils, and the source of all monstrousness, Teras' pit."

"Good. What lies across from the tithing cliff?"

Rina twisted her lips as she worked. "The largest pyroduct on Orroccio?"

"Which is called?"

"Who cares what it's called? If I'm tithed, I only want to know how to avoid it." She tilted her head over Lor's shoulder.

Lor clutched the book to her chest. "No peeking! If you're going to cheat, at least try Seeing the answer."

"There hasn't been a davina who could have visions without kharis in *generations*, you know."

"Are you planning on pouting your way past the all the monsters to reach Teras?"

Rina blew out a breath, fingers threading quickly over Lor's scalp. "The Umbilicus Whatever."

Alesta murmured, "The Devil's Umbilicus."

"The Devil's Umbilicus!" Rina declared with a triumphant tug at Lor's hair. "Thank you, Lessie. Do you want me to do yours next?"

"I'm not going to the festival." She had to study. And rise early tomorrow to attend chapel. She went at least twice a week now, at the Towers before lessons or down at the villa. The alberos hadn't seemed to warm to her for all that, but their admonishing looks and lectures were like a scouring brush over her spirit, reminders to temper her ambition to only serving Hektorus' will.

Rina's crown of braids was already woven through with yellow and pink ribbons. She'd be the perfect spring maiden at the Festival of Promises, celebrating the betrothals of those who had escaped tithing through their twentieth birthdays and honoring the sacred covenant Hektorus made his demigoddess daughter, allowing her to marry whoever she gifted her kiss to. The alberos loved reminding Soladisan youths that a kiss was a holy pledge, not to be made until they knew they wouldn't be promised instead to Teras. The priests never liked it when Alesta asked if that was the same daughter stolen by the monsters Hektorus went to war with.

Lor was again urging Rina to try to See something. "You'll be safer if you're a proper davina."

"We all might be, if I could have a vision of the lower strata before the lava pit." Rina tucked the last wisps of hair into Lor's braid. "All these books, and none of them tell what we'll encounter there."

"Start small. What am I picturing?"

Rina hummed uncertainly and lowered her face nearer Lor's ear. "The rosemary cake you're going to eat at the festival."

Lor's lids dropped closed as she gently shook her head. "Not even close." Setting down her book, Lor pulled back from Rina's hands and turned about, saying, "Maybe it'll help if you look into my eyes. Try again." She rested her palms on her thighs, staring intently at a blinking Rina. "Try very hard."

Rina bit down on a scowl, gaze sharpening. "Visions or not, you're the one more in danger. One misstep could send you to the rock." She grabbed the book and flipped its pages, too quickly to be taking in any knowledge.

No one besides Alesta seemed able to concentrate that day, and soon they all made their way out to the festival. Alesta read on under the generous kharis lamplight until she needed to get back to the farm and Nonnina. She'd refused apartments at the university—she had no interest in bonding with other scholars over late-night discussions or study sessions—and hired Vittore's eldest to tend to things and check on her grandmother on days Alesta had to be up at the Towers.

Garlands of flowers were strung between the colonnades, and girls with ribbons flowing through their hair and boys with wreaths of flowers crowning their heads were playing games and sharing baskets of food and shouting jubilantly for the announced betrothals. Alesta caught sight of Rina pulling Lor along and calling to Mico, circlet of leaves and colza blooms askew on his dark hair. They joined those holding boughs in a long archway and cheered as couples ran hand in hand through the tunnel of blossoms and gave a first, civil kiss to one another at its end.

Stalking down past the merriment, Alesta felt their hope like sharp shoots digging up through the earth—after a dark, gray winter, that promise of spring.

Time had passed in a blur since Mico had found her on the

dock and set her on this new trajectory. The harvest. Caring for Nonnina. A winter spent sweating in the forge, working on her crossbow, melting down failure after failure. Dark mornings rushing through chores. Shearing. Festivals she ignored, chapel she never missed. The sun and springtime coming back again, the seasons like a swirl of skirts, like the pieces of the old automaton she'd made orbiting around and around. And Alesta, untouched by it all, an arrow on a straight path, merely waiting for its chance to strike its target. For her revenge.

Its fulfillment would create a new chance, not for herself, but for these other youths, raising branches dotted with buds, that they might be free to make their own vows someday if they wished. Rina and Lor and everyone else on the island deserved to live a safe life. Mico was so kind, so driven, Alesta had no doubt when he was king someday, he would make all the ease and wonders enjoyed at the Towers available to every Soladisan. She'd been so eager to claim them for herself—to prove she deserved them. Now she only wanted to protect them for the kingdom. The promise of all those lives, all those futures, lifted her spirits as she left the Towers.

Eleven months after Kyr's tithing, Nonnina died.

Chapter Eight
UNTAMED TIDES

If Alesta were driftwood or sea-glass, she'd be worn down smooth by now. But she wasn't. She was a waiting blade. And this final loss gave her two things, like Hektorus' matched scales: deepened grief and sharpened purpose.

A few weeks after Nonnina's passing and before the next tithing, Alesta hurried out from a lecture into the halls of the university, through cloisters and across the courtyard, where she caught sight of Mico heading for the entrance to the far tower. She ran to catch up, past pavilions readied again for this year's Festival of Virtues, and fell into step beside him. "It's time."

"Lessie." He flashed his wide, dimple-free smile in greeting. "Good afternoon."

"Good afternoon," she returned quickly. "It's time."

He held the door for her and followed inside. "We've talked about this."

"We have." She stalked down the hall toward the training room. "I told you from the first day I wanted to be the one to go."

Inside the training room, sunlight from high windows bathed

the polished parquet floor, where some of the others were prac-
ticing. Rina, skirts tucked up into her braided belt, slashed her
beautiful, blunt weapon at Lor.

"Your form is weak," Lor told her, her own broad shoulders
perfectly balanced as she beat back Rina's attack. "Elbow up."

Rina huffed a breath, setting a few curls dancing where they'd
escaped the silk band holding back her hair. "It *was* up."

"Come on, keep up. You must be ready when those claws come
for you." Lor's sword clanged against Rina's, again and again.
Then its long edge whipped against Rina's side.

Rina swept back and gaped at her bodice. "*Lorenza.* You cut
my dress!"

Lor danced into position, smirking. "And I'll fix it up for you
later, with a fancy stitch. *My lady Corina.*" She made a little bow
to her, flourishing her blade to one side. "Slashed bodices will be
all the rage by week's end."

Rina kept her eyes on Lor's weapon as she engaged her again.
"Did I tell you I had a vision?"

Lor's mouth fell open. "You did?" She barely met Rina's next
strike.

Alesta, slinging off her bag, raised her brows. Everyone knew
how Rina's lack of the Sight weighed on her. Nearly as much as it
did her mother.

Rina gave a fierce little grin. "I had a vision of me kicking your
ass." She launched herself into the opening Lor had left and drove
the taller girl back.

Alesta and Mico grabbed weapons from the flower-garden racks
and soon joined the others for sparring, in the style they'd developed
together, more practical than fencing, a blend of grace and brutality.

Alesta faced off with Mico and saluted with her sword. He mirrored her before lunging at her right. Always fast with an attack, always first to strike.

She met his thrusts with the defense he'd taught her and said the words she'd rehearsed. "I can't wait and watch another field hand go when it should be me." Last spring, the girl had been a mere thirteen.

Mico danced back and sucked his teeth. "You're valuable to the cause." He came at her slower this time. "We may yet need other devices, weapons—"

She met each of his strikes. "I appreciate everything you've done for me." Procuring medicine for Nonnina. Getting the bow she'd made for more safely protecting the coastline into farmers' hands. Making her feel useful enough to keep going when facing each day felt as impossible as flying. She grimaced as Mico forced her back. "But Nonnina is gone now." The new grief was gradually receding, with occasional fresh waves that knocked her over, like an unruly tide. Her fingers tightened on her hilt. She was used to that. "There's nothing to keep me here."

"Keep your grip nimble," Mico reminded her.

Alesta adjusted and was soon rewarded with a strike to Mico's shoulder. "You've secreted away enough kharis for the mission. Collected the branzono poison. I've finished the new crossbow." She'd finally solved how to make it both compact and powerful enough for Orroccio, with a folding design. "Our Lia arrows are perfected." She whipped her blade around Mico's and drove it down, meeting him nearly chest to chest.

Mico smiled crookedly. "Is it so bad I don't want to let you go?"

"It was bad enough to damn Kyr." Her sword gave a metallic

wail against his as she drew away. "So, yes."

She'd once been desperate for this place to value her. Wanted it to love her. She could only show her value now in leaving it. Freeing it.

Rina walked over, patting the damp curls at the nape of her neck and breathing hard. "My lord Mico, I don't want to see her go, but everyone deserves their chance to be useful." She blew out a heavy breath as Lor joined them. "If I never have a vision, I don't know what I'll do."

Lor elbowed her. "You're helping the cause."

Rina rolled her eyes. "I haven't done anything. Just trained." She dropped her chin and pouted. "And my form is weak."

"It's not. Your form"—Lor scratched behind her ear—"is very nice."

Rina hugged herself with one arm, and Lor leaned in and cupped her elbow. "Is it aching again?"

Alesta swallowed down the old guilt, but Rina only blinked up at Lor and said, "It's fine."

Mico shifted in the corner of Alesta's vision, and for a moment, she could almost imagine he was Kyr.

The boy she had destroyed still haunted her, and not only when his cousin was around. The truth was, she was already on that island, surrounded by a full sea of roiling grief, untamed by any tide. Her world had turned to dust last summer when Kyr died and Nonnina's illness worsened. Anything she'd once wanted washed away. Any admiration or accolades. Welcoming skies or warm arms. All that remained for her was retribution, hard and jagged. She clung to it in the storm.

She didn't deserve to entertain even the momentary delusion

of Kyr by her side. She looked Mico dead on, at his rounder cheeks and his hair he kept clipped shorter, out of his eyes that were the same rich brown Kyr's had been. She pitched her voice low as the others drifted away to return their swords to the rack. "I owe it to him."

Mico was the only one to ever realize Alesta's true role in Kyr's tithing. Now he ran a hand over his damp hair and nodded. "Very well."

Alesta inhaled. She could already taste the sharp tang of her revenge against the monster, like the smell of the steel in her warm palm.

"You have a plan for how to ensure you're selected?"

Alesta shrugged. She'd fought so hard to avoid the kharis smoke's attention; getting herself tithed was never going to be a problem. "I'll think of something."

Rina zipped back over eagerly. "I'll help."

Alesta had avoided Rina's overtures of friendship for nearly a year. She'd shrugged away invitations to join her on walks down to the tailor's shop for special fittings and to wave her admiral father off when he made for Molissa with the cargo fleet. There was no point in letting anyone get close when Alesta was destined for Orroccio as soon as possible.

And besides, look what had happened to her last real friend.

But there was no putting Rina off now, as Alesta prepared to invoke the wrath of Hektorus and his kharis. Rina was determined to help her tick off each and every sin to guarantee her selection.

"I don't really think it's going to take that much effort," Alesta told her, as Rina followed her into the library. Alesta returned the books she'd borrowed, and they headed for the nearest reading table. She figured her reprieve from tithing this long was mostly because she was helping Mico to make Soladisa safer, along with her strident devotion to the Arbor and her university work, which she was due to get back to in an hour, assisting an artificer in his workroom, and a lecture after that—though she might as well skip her lessons, she realized. The point of going had only been to stay alive until she was equipped to deliver revenge to the monster who killed Kyr.

"You can't leave important things to half-measures," Rina replied, sinking into a chair and considering the list of virtues and sins covering the one wall of this chamber not lined with books, next to the arched entryway. She tapped a finger to her lips.

Alesta carefully wedged her hips between the carved armrests of the chair beside Rina, then looked around as well. Librarians rolled carts full of books to be returned and rode extending ladders that shot up like silver filigree branches, to pull others from the higher shelves. "What if I desecrate a holy book?"

Rina nodded. "That's destruction. Plus you'll be in discord with the librarians, who won't appreciate that at all, or your stealing from them."

Alesta watched a librarian hug a book to her chest and engage a lever, the wide pants of her uniform fluttering as she descended. No more hours here reading. No more classes or experiments. Alesta leaned back in her chair. "And once I've done that," she told Rina, "I'll lie about and do nothing else until tithing day. Except eat everything left in the cottage." Finally she'd fulfill what the alberos all seemed to imagine her doing. Better than letting it rot once she was gone. And she'd need her strength where she was headed.

"Sloth and gluttony." Rina's curls bounced as she nodded at each sin. "But what about violence?" She frowned. "Perhaps you had better punch me in the nose or something."

Alesta squirmed in her seat. Its narrow armrests pinned her uncomfortably in place. "Listen. I should have told you. But before I leave." She cleared her throat. "The flier—that was me."

Rina lifted her eyes to the plaster lilies swooping over the vaulted ceiling. "I know you helped Kyr—"

"No." Alesta gripped the arm of her chair closest to Rina. "It was my design. I failed to test it properly and account for the reaction that occurred—" She'd put it together afterward, how it was the kharis smoke that had caused the monster hide to eventually degrade. Just as the alberos said, the monstrous was weak in the face of holiness.

Then she and Mico had figured out how to use that power to destroy Teras, infusing it into the arrows she'd designed. The sacred books all said no human weapon could harm the devil, but now they had one made from a piece of a god. From her mistake that had sent Kyr to Orroccio, they'd made this chance to stop the tithings forever.

Alesta used to value how failure led to discovery. But hurting Rina and damning Kyr would be her last major mistake. Now she was so, so careful. Her teachers called her brilliant, like a gem—dazzling, but hard. She'd reined herself in. Tamed herself. Trusted the Arbor and Mico to guide her. She no longer reached too high.

She was aiming for only one thing now.

Rina fiddled with the tassel of her fan where it hung about her wrist. "Lessie, it was ages ago."

"Still. I am sorry. And I'm not punching you in the face."

"Well." Rina lifted her fan to tap it against Alesta's hand. "Just make sure you desecrate the book in a particularly violent way."

Alesta nodded, but butchering one of her last meals with an unblessed knife would be enough. She had one Mico had recently forged for her and not taken to the alberos for a dispensation yet.

Rina pursed her lips. "What about lust?" Her eyes slid slyly back at Alesta. "Maybe Mico could help you with that one."

Alesta flushed. Not because she felt anything like that for Mico. Those feelings had died along with Kyr. She felt safe with Mico. But a position at the university hadn't changed how her face and body and lack of family meant she was utterly ignored in the shuffle for matches as she neared her jubilee birthday, when the Arbor removed youths' branches from the tithing ceremonies, warnings against impurity turning quickly to exhortations to hurry up and pair off by the next Festival of Promises.

It was all just as ridiculous as ever, that these accidents of birth could prevent someone from wanting or loving her, when they didn't feel at all like the *her* she felt herself to be inside. They had nothing at all to do with anything she truly was or wanted. And she knew it had made it a steeper climb for her to gain a chance to study here, would have made her options finding a position as an artificer or scribe more limited than for less talented students. She hated how foolish it all left her feeling. Even now she wondered a little if Rina was making fun of her, contriving to make Alesta betray she actually wanted something like that with Mico. Which would be laughable to the court.

The question had become irrelevant. She had a prior engagement with a monster. She asked Rina, "Isn't your mother angling for your betrothal?"

Rina lifted her gaze to the ceiling again, letting out a long sigh and waving a hand. "Yes, because he shall be king, once Enzo finally names him heir, and my social position and future children are at risk if I never have a vision, and so on and so forth." She dropped her gaze to Alesta and gave her shoulders a little shake. "I won't have to worry about any of that once you slay Teras."

Alesta couldn't help smiling back. Rina's confidence in her made something clenched tight inside her soften.

Rina's mouth twitched to one side, and her bright eyes took on a more earnest sheen. "You're very brave to go. And we are counting on you. When I imagine being free of the threat—" Rina blinked back tears. "I can handle my mother or the alberos' judgment, as long as that's where it ends, and it doesn't come along with a swift trip to Orroccio."

Alesta dragged her thumb over her chair's sheen of beeswax polish. She knew descendants of Molissans were at greater risk of tithing if they lacked courtly status. But Rina would make a good match, with Mico or someone else, and would be all right even if she didn't become a davina like her mother, as overbearing as the woman was.

Alesta hadn't become the kind of friend who would understand why Rina seemed so upset, or know how to ask. She'd assumed at first—after Kyr—that Rina was only trying to be kind because of her loss. But she had never stopped welcoming Alesta in the same amiable manner she'd always used with Kyr. And Alesta had grown intrigued by how she designed most of her own clothes,

Lor helping to bring them to life, with a keen eye, like Alesta brought to her machines.

Now she was leaving, Alesta felt a new splinter of grief, that she hadn't been able to accept Rina's friendship.

Rina made a tiny sound of exasperation at herself and carefully wiped away the one tear that had escaped. "Now," she said, leaning in, "which book will you destroy?" She whispered as if the volumes all around them might overhear.

Right. Alesta's job wasn't to be friends. She didn't deserve friends. She was bound for hell.

She tugged her lip between her teeth. "*The Codex Anima*. It was Kyr's favorite."

Rina's eyes widened. "Oh! But why would you want to destroy his favorite?"

"That's the *point*. To do something awful." Besides, it wasn't as if it would even approach what Alesta had done to Kyr himself. She had never been delicate, and she was long past being precious about anything, even what Kyr had loved. Killing Teras was all that mattered. "And it's the holiest book I'm allowed to call up without a lecturer watching over me." She frowned. "Though I'm only permitted to study it in the reading room." Alesta certainly wasn't going to destroy it there and get herself detained by the librarians and alberos until they took her on their ship. She needed the chance to sneak her inventions and weapons along with her.

Rina lit up. "That's no problem. I'm very good at distracting attention."

Chapter Nine

LOST STARS

R ina's claim proved true the next day, as Alesta returned the *Codex* to the librarian in charge of the bibliosanctum. The collection of sacred texts kept by the university was smaller than that of the Arbor, but there was still a large chamber full of such books, nestled safe in the heart of the tower, away from the moisture and light of any windows.

Alesta had spent an hour in the reading room with the *Codex*, sitting under the statues of beautiful women bearing kharis globes in their upraised arms, pretending to read but mostly staring at the illuminated artwork of vines and roses, seas and stars, Hektorus shining and central among a pantheon of distant gods.

She couldn't stop thinking of Kyr sitting in this room, looking at these same pages.

Creamy-smooth, they were made of the Lia tree itself. She brushed her fingers along their margins and turned them until she reached an image of shades caught in hellfire, a chiaroscuro of black ink and gilt flames.

She shut the book.

When she laid it on the massive wood table before the entrance to the sacred texts, Fidelio marked its return in his ledger and placed it in the return cart behind him.

That's when Rina made her entrance.

She wore a gown with a bodice covered in a beaded netting that also extended up from her shoulders like a carapace. Her skirts were dyed in deepening shades of blue, leaving her looking like a treasure unexpectedly caught from the sea.

She resolutely avoided looking at Alesta, in her simple skirts and blouse, as she swept up to the desk and waved a long piece of parchment at Fidelio. "Good afternoon, Fidelio!" she sang out. "I need all these books, if you please."

"My lady Rina," Fidelio replied in a pointedly low voice, reaching out and capturing the list. His lips tugged into a shallow smile. "This is quite an extensive catalog."

"My mother sent me to study them all in hopes of kindling the Sight in me." Rina shrugged. Her beading clattered.

Alesta fought back a smile, trying not to draw attention to the fact she was still standing there. It wasn't hard to be invisible next to Rina, though.

"Of course." Fidelio drew up straighter. "The davina is very wise."

Rina tapped her painted and gem-studded fingers on the table's polished wood.

Fidelio turned to the assistant librarian just reaching for the cart beside him. "Pietro! Leave those for now. Help me gather these for our lady." Pietro pushed back his hair and made Rina a gallant little nod with his sharp chin, and the two of them went through the archway toward the requested books.

Rina began to follow them, tracing her fingers over the books waiting in the cart and raising her voice as the librarians withdrew. "*Can* volumes bound in Lia paper spark visions, do you know?"

"I will see what information about that I can find," Fidelio said, holding up a palm, but smiling again. "If you would be so good as to wait right here, please." He hurried to his task.

Alesta ducked around the table and, hidden behind Rina's skirts, snagged the *Codex*, slipping it under her loosened bodice. The beautiful thing about being fat and invisible was no one noticed if you were slightly bulkier than normal.

As Alesta rounded the table and readied to slip out of the library, Rina turned and threw her a wink over her shoulder.

Alesta headed straight for home, cutting through the Towers' vaulted halls and balmy courtyards. It was almost summer, and as she hurried through the atrium beside the Arbor, the *Codex* tucked under one arm, the sun glinted off the highest panes of glass like one of Mico's fortified weapons. But the Lia-powered waterworks spread mist over the atrium's foliage, just as they ran under the tiles through the Towers, keeping rooms cool this time of year, and warm in winter.

It might have been easier than robbing the library, Alesta thought, to smash through the glass secured in winding iron branches and flowers, punch the nose of any albero who got in her way, and snap off a living bough of the Lia tree. Take a great giant running leap to Teras. A small part of her, a sharp sliver where her months of devotion met up against her old resentment, would love to see the looks on the faces of the alberos out there keeping the

Perpetual Adoration, or trimming carefully selected pieces of Lia with their special tools oiled with the tree's own fruit.

The image cracked a laugh from somewhere buried inside her—right as she rounded a large potted lemon tree and ran into Albero Paolo's disapproving eyebrows.

He drew up tall and clutched his hands together. "This is a place of solemnity, not wanton frolicking—" He always found something to harp at her about, no matter how committed to the Arbor she'd been since Kyr's death, which she suspected he blamed her for, despite not knowing how right he was. "Not a care for how you corrupt the sanctity of this place, or those who strive to keep it."

She ducked her head and apologized before he was even finished, but he and his admonishments followed her as she hugged the *Codex* to her chest and exited the atrium, beside the glass shed of anointed shears and scrapers and axes. She could show him her own piece of Lia, rip a page out of the book right before his eyes. But she had no intention of spending her final days on Soladisa listening to his harangues. She had more sins to commit, and no one beyond Mico and the others he'd recruited needed to be aware she was doing something wicked. All that mattered was the Lia's judgment.

Which she would never bring down upon herself if she stood here enduring the albero's instead. Worse, she'd never escape Teras' three beasts if he caught sight of what book she held and hauled her off to the sanctuary rather than letting her prepare before her tithing.

Fortunately, she saw Mico making his way down the steps from the davinas' hall. She threw him a desperate look, and he approached. "Excuse me, Albero." He gave a quick bow. "I was just with Davina Bianca, and she mentioned needing to consult with you about the upcoming tithing?"

Albero Paolo frowned. "Everything should be arranged. The davina is always insisting she needs more kharis—" He nodded goodbye to Mico and rushed for the steps.

"He'd better be careful," Mico said, accompanying Alesta across the yard, "or one day those eyebrows of his will crawl right off his face and begin munching his precious foliage."

Alesta snorted. "Thanks for saving me."

He stopped, his earnest expression trained on her. "Thank you for what you're doing. You're ready?"

Alesta flashed the cover of the *Codex* at him.

"Sacrifice is never easy." Mico dropped his gaze, and when he lifted it, he couldn't seem to meet hers again, looking instead toward the mural beside them. "But the hard thing is often worth it." He stared at the image of the first king of Soladisa, and his queen.

"Kyr used to worry, too," Alesta said, "about living up to all the kings before him."

Something in Mico's eyes flashed, like the gleaming mural tiles. "That's not good enough. I need to be better." He pointed with his chin above the king and queen and tree, where the god shimmered in gold. "Hektorus never wanted us paying tribute to the monsters that crawled out of the ashes of his war. If we want to live in his image as the Arbor teaches, our devotion belongs fully to him."

A fierce conviction threaded through his voice. The only time Alesta had seen Mico angry was during chapel readings about Teras. After Kyr died, Alesta had gone through the motions with the Arbor, just as dedicated as she was to her training with Mico, looking for comfort, trying to feel the same fervent devotion Mico clearly did. It came easiest when she focused on hating monsters, but she was always left feeling like she was seeking something more she never found in her careful prayers to Hektorus. She assumed she could only find it on Orroccio, in making atonement for her transgression. Soon it would be within her reach.

Her faith might be an awkward, uncertain thing, much like her, but she could serve as a weapon in Mico's sure hand.

She told him now, "Even Hektorus lost his own daughter to them." An altar to her filled one corner of the courtyard, eternal-burning kharis set under a lithe statue with a mournful expression and a swirl of golden hair.

Mico nodded, as if trying to convince himself of something. "And you follow in his footsteps, delivering holy retribution." He reached out and squeezed Alesta's arm. "He will be with you, even there." No smiles today. "I'll make them send one last tithing ship. Somehow. If you can escape once it's done—"

"We all agreed." Everyone in their movement had: kill Teras, throw themselves to the devil as its tithing if they failed, and don't count on anyone making it across the poison sea to bring them home if they succeeded. He didn't need to worry about her. "This is what I want, Mico."

"Good—good luck." His hand lingered still, before letting her continue out the courtyard and on her way.

The heat baked into Alesta's skin and clothes as she hiked down the island, passing orchards with trees in bloom or plumping with early fruit, vines climbing upon their lattices, bees and golden beetles dipping their pollen-dusted bodies into their trumpets or droning to the highest magnolia blossoms.

In a few days the moon would wax and the path to Orroccio would open. Yesterday she'd put things in order at the farm, for Vittore or whoever Kyr's mother allowed to take over. She only needed to desecrate this book, then ready herself for tithing.

And say goodbye. As she passed the villa, the cypresses standing like guardians behind it beckoned her. She detoured to the little cemetery they edged and dropped to her knees before the small carved rock she'd laid in memory to Nonnina. It was nothing compared to the monuments to Kyr's ancestors, statues of Hektorus bearing their spirits to the heavenly fields or thick kharis smoke rising and erupting into birds that almost seemed to break from stone to sky.

Alesta let the *Codex* thunk beside her and lay on the ground beside Nonnina's grave, next to those of her parents. Sunlight filtered through the branches to fall upon the matted grass like lost stars.

The earth had devoured everything she loved. Her family, all delivered here by the devil's breath. Kyr, lost far below ground, cut off from the real stars, from all the light he loved. He would never ascend to the heavenly fields because nothing from Orroccio ever left. The spirits of the sacrificed burned forever and ever deep where Teras swallowed them down.

Maybe she would burn forever too.

After she took Teras down first.

No monument stood here for Kyr. So, book tucked against her hip, Alesta visited the old barn one last time.

She shoved the great doors open, revealing a craft larger than the one that had damned Kyr and set her on this course she was finally about to fulfill.

Her secret project.

The wood frame bowed wide enough for three riders, necessary for powering its flight without any use of kharis. Its wings of silk, painstakingly gathered from the scraps of the artificers' works, arced overhead. She'd never tested it. She didn't have anyone to operate the machinery with her. Outside of classes and training, she stuck to her sheep's company these days. Still, she'd worked obsessively on this new design, something in her feeling almost as if she could fix what she had broken that day at the festival, if she could only get it right this time. As if she'd won a sacred covenant from Hektorus, where fulfilling a nearly impossible challenge could secure a boon beyond hope.

Kyr's things, she'd been unable to clear away. His pots of paints sat congealed and hardened where he'd left them, brushes laid out like dried bones picked clean. His art still decorated the space. Even whatever he'd been toying with while she worked feverishly on the first, doomed flier. A painting of sheep speckling a hillside that lifted to a sky full of clouds, as rotund and fluffy as the flock, rested yet on his easel. She'd stared at it so many hours from across the barn while she worked alone, just like those last weeks when she'd beg off going for a swim with Kyr, after a round of teaching him fighting, saying she had more work to do. Normally he'd cajole her, peeling his paint shirt off, racing her down the hill toward the shore. But leading up to the festival, she'd stayed, watching his broad back as he disappeared through the fields. So sure her work was the key to never losing him.

Alesta trespassed into Kyr's workspace, kicking up dust gathered beside his old chair. She skimmed her finger over his brushes. An eye gazed at her from behind the landscape. She'd been so distracted earlier that season, trying to come up with an idea for the festival, she hadn't taken note of how Kyr filled his afternoons or makeshift canvases. She tugged the painting to one side to see what Kyr had seen before he died.

It was her.

The bark's edge bit into Alesta's fingers. She'd always told Kyr off if he'd tried to sketch her, on lazy days spent together out in the pasture. The painting was worked in his most experimental style. In it, an Alesta made of rainbow daubs of paint frowned down at her work, yet the curve of a burning horizon reflected in her eyes, and an impossible sky overfull with stars reared up behind her. And he'd made her too pretty. Sometimes beauty was not truth but a lie. Kyr always was too kind to her.

And it had been his undoing.

Well. She shifted the *Codex* in her grip. Now everyone would see the truth of her. The truth she'd surrendered to, along with all the teachings of the Arbor, once Kyr's death had proved it. She would show them she was as sinful as they'd all expected. They could congratulate themselves just as long as it took until she rid them of Teras' hold over the kingdom.

When she entered the cottage, Alesta kissed her fingers and pressed them to Nonnina's shell resting on the little altar, next to the ones for her mother and father, worn smooth along their ridged curves from years of blessings.

She would not allow her fresher grief to wear level. She needed its ragged edges to prod her, even if it felt most days like she'd swallowed a knife.

She sat on her low stool, spread the book across her lap, and began tearing out every page.

The thick Lia pages ripped smoothly, giving up the little screams of things rent that could not be restored. Alesta shoved a handful into the fire.

The smoke turned yellow and blossomed into the room. Alesta

coughed, and a feeling like fire filled her lungs.

And blood.

And mind.

The room's walls fell away into a vast blackness, and Alesta barely had time to realize this must be a vision like the davinas Saw before a monstrous form thrust through the smoke. Its skin burned red, bright enough to sear Alesta's eyes as they took in the beast. Nostrils venting black smoke like a volcano. A snout filled with uncountable teeth, each as tall as herself.

Teras.

That mouth opened wide and roared.

The noise nearly tore Alesta apart. The despair and anguish it carried wormed into her thoughts, her heart. Alesta fought to keep her feet under her. She was burning, inside and out, skin charring and flaking away. And still the abomination roared. Teras' monstrousness pounded against her like waves.

But she was an island of enduring grief, and met them with a force just as fierce.

Alesta roared back. She broke off pieces of herself, charred dark and half-shattered, and dug them into the monster's face. Dragged them down with all her might.

The apparition split and splintered away.

Alesta bolted for the cottage door. Drank in fresh air, suddenly cool in comparison to that taste of hell she'd gotten. She dropped her palms to her thighs as her chest heaved.

By the boughs, books made of Lia paper really could spark visions.

But it never should have worked like that on *her*. Alesta's heart panicked all over again for a moment—visions were only for davinas and their daughters and other nobles invited to the

Sight-summonings. The idea of stepping out of her place again set her pulse skittering through her like spiders. She scrubbed her sweaty hands over her skirts and reminded herself it didn't matter now. She wanted to bring down the threat that had been hanging over her head her whole life. And maybe the vision was due to her faithfulness to the Arbor. Maybe it was a blessing from Hektorus, approving of her quest.

Maybe it was a warning.

A fierce headache had taken up behind Alesta's eyes. If the holy Lia was trying to caution her away from damnation, it had the opposite effect. She'd already known Teras must be a horror. Seeing that fire that had consumed Kyr, those teeth that had destroyed him, the monstrousness that had stolen and obliterated him, only set her raging to go in pursuit of that devil in earnest.

She left the door of the cottage open to allow the yellow smoke to dissipate, and destroyed the rest of the pages outside, mashing strips into the slop and waste of the animals.

She preserved one. An illustration of constellations above a peaceful sea. One piece of something Kyr had loved, to keep her anger awake. Like her own monster chained within herself, starved and stoked and ready to snap. This was the only claim she could make to Kyr's memory, or tokens that would invoke it. She folded the page and tucked it into her breastband, over her heart.

She would follow Kyr over the horizon and down into the dark and flame. But she was bringing a surprise for his killer.

All her stratagems and machinations planned with Mico—and her grief. She would carry it with her. Let it sharpen to a blade she would plunge straight into the monstrous heart of Teras.

Part Three

INFERNO

Chapter Ten

DOWN INTO THE DARK AND FLAME

They chained her to the rock.

The alberos came for Alesta quickly the day of the tithing ceremony. She was ready, dressed in her skirts and blouse and bodice, with all her jewelry on, leather wristbands and clay bracelets and a wooden pendant around her neck, as if she'd still had a family to adorn her for tithing.

Even the safe passageway through the poison sea had pitched their ship like a child lobbing a ball from hand to hand. Waves to either side teemed with monsters, kinds Alesta had never seen—ropey red tentacles clutching at foolhardy seabirds, violet-green shimmering beasts leaking milky clouds of poison, armored limbs with snapping claws, and hulking shadows deep below. Now the water writhed all around like one of those leviathans she'd spied in the distance and dragged the massive scaly hands of its tide over the rough shore of the stony island.

Orroccio. Not in descriptions or paintings or visions, but at last before her own eyes. Under her own leather boots. Massive and black, already biting at her with its sulfur scent.

The alberos led her, pinned between two of them, to a cliffside where chains hung several feet apart from metal spikes driven into the rock at head height. Their mangled ends traced arcs in the fetid, salty breeze.

The alberos removed the twisted, broken metal and locked a new pair of manacles to the chains. One albero gave Alesta a shove between her shoulder blades. They pressed her to the wall and closed the irons around her wrists.

They left her as an offering to the monster. She didn't waste time trying to look scared, or contrite, or sorrowful. She was too busy scanning behind the alberos' heads, checking the landscape against the descriptions from Davina Graziela and other accounts. The island stretched upward to a peak at its far end. Much nearer, she could see the entrance to the Devil's Umbilicus, the great pyroduct that descended straight to Teras' pit.

Her heart raced only from the thought that she might be too slow, and fail Kyr's memory, and all the others. Her palms were clammy only from the sea mist.

The alberos said a lot of prayers over her, but nothing addressed to her. She was already monster food to them. They climbed back in their ship. She watched as it became a mere smudge far out on the waves.

Now it was just Alesta and the rock, and her heartbeat thrashing in her ears like the incessant waves.

She twisted her arms and beat them against the obsidian wall. The clay of her bracelets shattered. The substance she and Mico had concocted—using some of the branzono poison he'd collected from one slain on the beach—leaked out and began eating away at the irons. It left her wrist guards, their leather tanned in kharis oil, smoking a little but intact. Impatient, she pulled as the metal frothed and melted, and freed herself.

She unlaced her skirts and shimmied them off, over the belt slung low on her hips and leather breeches underneath. The skirts fell heavily, weighed down by the supplies sewn into hidden pockets inside. Alesta pulled the ribbons Lor had supplied her with and drew the fabric into a sack. She threw it over her shoulders and stood. It felt strange, wearing only clothing that fit so tightly all over, showing off the full shape of her belly and bottom—if there had been anyone to see and judge. Instead of feeling exposed, she felt a satisfying self-possession. All the times people at home had told her to feel ashamed seemed very small and meaningless in the face of her purpose here. All the times they'd told her this place held her doom, that she'd be trapped and consumed here someday—but she was prepared. She was already free.

No accounts reported how long she was likely to have before Teras' three beasts came for her. She hustled away from the rocky beach, skirting the gaping hole of the Umbilicus. The ground was uneven as she headed for the obsidian peaks, where Graziela said a smaller pyroduct led down into the maze of lava tunnels. This bit of cover between Alesta and where the beasts would emerge soothed the worry pinching at her shoulders like the talons of some great seabird. Nothing grew on Orroccio, beyond a little blue algae: no trees, no vines, or even patches of grass. Glassy, dark rock jutted up from the rougher land she half-crawled over. Alesta willed her boots to crunch more lightly over the gravel—winged devils roosted up in the heights of the dormant volcano. They were nocturnal, but she wasn't betting her life on the sound sleep of monsters.

The remains of those defeated in some sky battle between the beasts rotted on the rocks, adding to the acrid smell of the place. Claws or teeth had slashed their-hides open and ravaged their insides. Smaller carcasses of half-eaten seabeasts were littered among them. Alesta picked her way around, searching for any sign of the other tunnel. The records made it sound like it should be a clear break in the rock.

But she saw nothing. Piles of ashy rock vented steam here and there. The folds and pockets of the island seemed to shift as she worked her way toward its peak, each tantalizing with the possibility of the entrance. Any moment now, the leopard and lion and wolf might come hunting. She needed to take on Teras on her own terms, sneaking up on it through its devil's nest, not dragged before it like every other tithing. She needed to disappear.

So where was that cursed entryway? She stuck her head into a few crevices, hoping they would go on, bracing to find a burrow of monsters. She had blades ready on her belt, though she left her crossbow folded in her bag. That was for Teras.

An abundance of the charred-looking rocks tucked themselves up against an eruption of obsidian. Alesta climbed closer, hoping their steam might obscure the pyroduct. As she passed one crumbly pile, she realized it spread over the darker ground almost like a torso and limbs. She fought a shudder and marched on. At last one shadow grew sharper as she neared—a shaft half-caved in, not wide enough for her to stretch her arm across, sloping down precipitously. Deep claw marks, each spread nearly a handbreadth apart, striped over the fallen rock. Like some creature—one far too large for this first stratum of hell—had almost pulled the opening in on itself. A chill bristled across her skin. But she couldn't worry about that now. With a final glance at the ashen-gray sky, Alesta descended.

Orroccio swallowed her whole.

Graziela said the monsters in its first levels were not as cunning as some below.

Alesta clutched that knowledge like a shield as she started through hell. Tracing one hand along the wall of the tunnel as it widened and split, she followed where the wheat-haired maiden had led the davina in her vision, always to the left. Alesta could still see where she went here in the uppermost underground stratum. Light seeped down through cracks, water trickled along walls, algae clung to the sharp curves of stone.

A skitter—a shadow. Something that was all jagged, black angles moved on impossible joints across the tunnel. Alesta's heart stuttered. Nothing so large should be encountered here, not yet. She raised her forearm and the kharis-soaked leather she wore between them, and the devil bent away horribly. At least one thing the alberos had hammered into her was true, and useful. Monsters were driven off by the Lia's goodness and divinity. Or they simply sensed its power to hurt them.

That was almost too bad, she told herself. Alesta's other hand skimmed over the handles of the knives Mico had made her, snug in her belt. She would not mind killing any beasts that refused to back down, big or small. She was beyond ready to destroy some monsters.

She kept telling herself this as she caught glimpses of others— more of those made of quick black spikes, and more lumbering beasts with bones protruding, and creatures with limbs made of serpents that set the shadows writhing. Each almost as tall as her. But her wrist guards and the wooden Lia pendant Mico had managed to procure sent them all shuffling away in the network of tunnels and chambers she progressed through.

Darkness banished the last of the light, and Alesta paused to crouch and pull her firestarter from her bag. She dug out the precious fragment of eternal-burning kharis Mico had sneaked away, touched spark to Lia, and let it kindle a small but holy flame in this hellish place.

The darkness did not surrender, though. As she recommenced her journey through the maze of stone, ever downward, shadows feuded with her light, rolling over craggy walls and fleeing in long black streaks only to rush back to where she walked past stalactites and collapsed walls. She bore the light before her, keeping her other hand to the flickering stone at her side, for what felt like hours.

Something growled, sending echoes running up and down the corridor. She braced her forearm against the sound and turned again. The gloom here did not scatter at all but reared higher, a monstrous silhouette. Light glinted off a multitude of eyes.

She was face to face with a demon taller than her.

Its mouth split open. A hundred sharp teeth caught the kharis light. They snapped together. The beast hissed. It loped away on muscular limbs that jutted from its swollen body to the back of the small den she'd stumbled upon. Alesta was already retreating, to her last false turning. She hurried on, listening for bounding steps behind her. The back of her neck prickled painfully, until she was several more turns and tunnels away.

She swallowed down her alarm, and the sound of her

throat-clearing echoed loudly along the rock. She froze, a rabbit waiting out a hawk.

For a split moment, Alesta felt a tug of dread. Regret threatened to close on her like some devil's powerful jaw taking hold. Like that caved-in entrance. With the wide claw marks. Everything she'd studied, all the writings of the davinas, had said she would not have to face such devils here in the twilight levels. What else in those accounts was wrong? How else was Alesta unprepared for what she'd walked into? She was already deep beneath the surface, but even if she ran all the way back, only Teras' beasts waited for her up there. Orroccio's small coastline bounded her world now.

Her kharis danced, as if its bright yellow flame tried to escape the splinter of Lia. Alesta drew a deep breath, exhaled, and walked on.

This was where she belonged. *A place of sin and howling sorrows*, Graziela had written. But Alesta had been in a dark and horrible place since that day a year ago. Now at least there was something she could do. Make things better. Atone.

Purge some of the sin that stuck to her inside and out.

Nevertheless, she started watching for any other smaller caverns breaking off the tunnel, and after what might have been minutes or an hour, found a tiny nook—hiding no monsters—to shelter in while she slept. Alesta ducked and dragged herself inside.

She checked over her things in her pack, readying those she'd had to disassemble to sneak past the alberos, fitting more supplies to her belt. Thin and strong Lia rope. Mico's arrows. Her crossbow. She popped one Lia seed into her mouth and chewed. For the food of a god's tree, it was awfully bland. But she would have no need to drink or eat anything else for days now. Graziela traveled here only in a vision, one that broke off before she'd been shown all the way to Teras' lair—the growing feeling of madness as she Saw deeper and deeper overwhelming her. There were still more levels through Orroccio she foretold, of dark mirror-stone, half-flooded caverns, blue fire, and pools of lava. And beyond that, places never seen at all by any human or described in any text, a thought that might once have fed Alesta's curiosity and ambition. Now she recited the seven strata recorded in the Arbor's holy books to herself like a perverse prayer: surface, twilight levels, mirror-maze. Dark levels, inferno, city of devils.

And the source of all monstrousness, Teras' pit.

No way to know precisely how long traversing them would take. But Alesta and Mico had calculated it wouldn't exceed the two full weeks before the tithing was forfeit, when Teras would punish Soladisa with tsunamis and eruptions of its isle. She had enough Lia to keep her alive that long.

She would make her way free and unchained, not dragged by beasts straight to the tyrant's maw. Spring her surprise attack with the weapon she'd designed especially for Kyr's killer. The comfort of how near her revenge drew allowed her to recline her head on her lumpy bag, curl up, and try to rest. She left the kharis burning between her and the entrance to her little cave and fell into the softer darkness of sleep.

Nothing but shadow and flame surrounded her when she woke, an unknowable time later. For a moment she forgot she wasn't in bed at the cottage and sat up only to knock her head against the low curve of the stone. Suddenly, the reality of all the weight of all that rock above her seemed to press down on her. On her lungs. The urge to smash again against the stone overwhelmed her. She clawed her way out of the crevice on her hands and knees and breathed hard.

Her forehead rested against the ground. Kyr, she reminded herself. Rina. Lor. The better Soladisa that Mico could make after they were all free of the tithings. Slowly, her insides unclenched. And she added one more name to her count: *Teras*. It didn't matter how much stone lay above, only that which was left between the devil and Alesta. She would fight her way through it. She might have been a weak, sinful thing, but that should only ease her way to hell's depths, drawing her to Teras like iron to a lodestone. She slung on her pack and belt, lifted her kharis, and set off again.

She reached a tunnel so steep, she almost resorted to the rope. She shuffled down it on her backside, kharis balanced precariously between her teeth, limbs shoved against the walls, like some sort of bizarre crab. Below, the tunnel opened into larger chambers of glassy stone. Her light revealed shapes beyond the translucent walls, and she stepped carefully around shattered piles. She did her best to follow Graziela's directions, but her path was spreading into the vast mirror-maze of the third stratum.

Here Alesta had expected the larger monsters that again menaced at the edge of her firelight, hulking on two legs, almost humanlike, but unclothed and throwing shadows spiked with horns and claws. Voices echoed around her, rough and strange, speaking in what seemed like conversation, not mere growls or squawks like in the levels above.

Until hell went silent, and its devils disappeared.

For a long stretch, there was only the pad of Alesta's footsteps, the soft echo of water dripping somewhere. Strange shadows cast by some other source of light, green and glowing, mingled with the kharis'. She was sure one towering shadow kept darting from her view, only to loom again just at the edge of her sight. Alesta imagined she heard the hiss and whisper of her name and wondered if this place, the evil of it, could be bleeding into her mind like the shadows did her vision.

Too many blurred forms passing behind transparent rock. Too many times whirling on something only to find her own reflection in the black glass. Too many shadows eating in at her periphery.

Alesta gripped the burning Lia until splinters pricked into her fingers, as the labyrinth of half-mirrors seemed to shift around her. Impossible streaks of obsidian veiled the clearer glass. This didn't feel like when she'd Seen with the kharis smoke before. Could Orroccio be driving her mad? After only a day—or what Alesta at least thought had been a day?

If a mere vision of this place could make Graziela collapse into a three-days' sleep after her great Seeing, what might setting foot here do to a person? To someone as corruptible as the alberos were always naming her?

Yet Alesta set another foot down, and another. She walked on through hell, trying to think only of her purpose waiting at its bottom. The kharis flame clung to her vision like a golden ghost amid the darkness. Like Kyr.

She rushed, though, as if she could leave the shadows behind. As if a thousand more weren't waiting for her in the next chamber of stone, or the next, as she passed to a lower area broken into smaller caverns and deep chasms. It was danker here, moisture and darkness sticking everywhere like tar, puddles capturing her kharis in an upside-down, distorted world.

Perhaps her hurry was why she missed any warning signs as she turned directly into a nest of monsters.

Chapter Eleven

MONSTROUS FACES

For one heartbeat, Alesta caught sight of their gray, chalky skin straining over stout, upright frames. Their milky scales, scattered about their shoulders and running down their forearms and hands to become long pointed claws. Their wide-set eyes, wincing in the sudden light.

Then her pulse set off sprinting. Although these beasts weren't much bigger than branzonos, there were so many of them. Alesta whirled away, but her hand struck against the stone wall and her kharis was knocked from her grip.

It fell down into a deep crevasse, its light smothered by dark and distance.

She stared, agape, back into the monsters' flat-snouted faces lit only by the eerie green light. When she took one slow step back, they began to speak. Their voices were throaty and sharp at once, like the snap of branches.

"*Human.*"

"Who gets to eat her?"

"Whoever catches her."

Alesta drew a slow breath in and slid back another step. So many large, oily eyes locked on her.

"We catch her together, we share."

One monster's lip curled, revealing thick white teeth. "I'll take a leg, and her heart."

Alesta's fingers pinched the pendant sitting at her collarbone. Her other hand drifted nearer one of the hilts at her belt. Could she lose them in the maze of caverns? Her limbs tensed, ready to run.

"That's too much for one."

"A leader deserves an extra share."

"Yes. Which is why I will take her heart—"

"You think you're the leader?"

The two largest monsters arguing jutted their chests out at one another—then, as she made to run, they lunged for Alesta.

She jerked back, brandishing a knife. Too fast, one struck it from her hand, and they had her by the shoulders. Alesta's heart pounded. This was different from sparring with Mico, from tackling one lone branzono on Soladisa's wide, bright shore.

But monsters weren't the only things with claws here in the dark.

With a twist of her fingers, she engaged the wrist guards she'd designed. Blades snapped out.

She jabbed the Lia pendant, soaked in kharis oil, at the monster on her left. It recoiled and growled and loosed its grip enough for her to turn on the other. She drew back her arm to drive her surprise-blade into its chest.

A massive shadow detached itself from the surrounding darkness. It swept around her, grabbing hold of her arm.

A swipe of claws. A flash of spikes. This new beast sent the first monster sprawling back. It plummeted down the crevasse with a shriek.

The other monsters laughed, a sound like the pop and rip of wood devoured by flame. Until the large interloper clawed at the second monster, still holding Alesta.

This one fought back. It stabbed its long white nails out. Alesta flinched away as they sparked over the bigger monster's skin— dark blue with pale veins disappearing under serrated scales. The two monsters battled, trading jabs.

Alesta, caught between them, could feel the strength of the towering beast, hard muscles taut against her back. She felt them coil as the monster one-handedly threw the other over the crevasse's edge.

No laughter now, only howling and yelps as the other monsters all fled farther into the maze.

Alesta slashed her free arm back at the final monster. No one was eating her. No matter how tall. Or spiked. Or terrifying to other monsters.

It didn't react to her blade slicing over its bicep. Its grip on her remained a vise. It hauled her up over its other arm and carried her off through the darkness.

She shoved at the beast, kicked, but it held her clamped tight against its chest. She could see only an armored shoulder and that the monster was bearing her back the way she'd come, to the level of black glass. She jammed her wrist-blade again at its arm. The blade's edge skittered over the monster's triangular scales—until it lodged into the beast's flesh at the juncture of arm and torso.

The devil struck back fast. Alesta never saw it react, just felt it cut across her belly and ribs. She gasped at the pain. Before she could gather herself and strike again, the monster climbed a jagged riser of the stone and dropped her.

She cried out. Her hand streaked down a wall of obsidian. The ground crashed against her knees and shoulder.

Instinct drove her to curl into a ball, sheltering her head and tender belly. Was it leaping after her? Were there worse things waiting in whatever pit she'd landed in?

When nothing happened, she forced herself to move. Clutching her stomach, she scraped herself up to sitting, elbow dragging over the grit and cold of the ground. Weak luminescence bled from somewhere near. From the other side of the translucent obsidian wall that reached a dozen feet above her.

The monster watched her.

Not much more than a silhouette behind the cloudy glass, standing several paces away, it appeared perhaps more human-shaped than any of the other beasts she'd encountered. That was hardly reassuring when it was also so much larger than them; Alesta still had to crane her neck to take in its full height, from what might have been some ragged clothing up to spikes and possibly horns lancing up into the murk. A wine-colored glow seeped as if from cracks near its shoulders. Maybe it was hurt.

She hoped so.

Alesta certainly was. She'd lost her eternal-burning kharis. She was pretty sure she was trapped.

Well, that was unfortunate—what was she going to do about it?

She still had her pack. She could explore where this glass pen subsumed into shadow. See if there was a way out. This monster, while giant, hadn't spoken. Maybe it wasn't as clever as those geniuses back in the lower level.

She retracted her wrist-blades, then shrugged her bag off her shoulders, wincing as the movement stretched her cuts.

Her eyes were adjusting to the lack of kharis light. She darted her gaze from her pack to the monster, to check that it hadn't moved, that it wasn't attacking again. Its veiled form only loomed there still.

Such a creep.

Rising to her knees, she tugged the laces of her bodice loose. Her blouse was damp underneath—sweat and blood.

She glanced again to the monster. It had disappeared.

Probably just back into the shadows of the greater cavern. She dug into her pack and pulled out a small metal pot. A balm of lanolin and kharis. She pried the lid off, lifted her blouse, and daubed it over her wounds.

A hiss escaped through her clenched teeth. There were dozens of small cuts, like little bites almost. As if the monster had seized her in its jaws and not its arms.

Her front and side stung, and all she wanted was to curl up again on the ground. Instead, she stood and shuffled around the pen, hands out, feeling if the walls closed her in completely.

The space was barely wider than the spread of her arms, and grew narrower as she pushed on, around a gentle curve. The dim lessened farther into the cave. Green luminescence trailed down the wall from ledges high above her head. And it spread over the opposite wall, fainter. Smudged with glistening dust. Worked into images.

Hills. A starscape. There was no art in Orroccio, the alberos said. Alesta stared, unaware she had drawn nearer until her boot stepped on something softer than rock.

Cringing, she crouched and retrieved it. Lifted the small bundle to what light the wall afforded.

A ragged jacket. Artful embroidery long frayed. Fancy buttons gleaming weakly under scratches and dust.

Kyr.

Her hands squeezed the fabric so hard, they trembled. It made no sense that he could have been here. Unless he escaped his chains as well, found the other tunnel, hid here. Until this monster trapped him too.

How was that possible, if Teras had never punished Soladisa for the missing sacrifice?

His jacket might have been stolen by one of the smaller beasts once Teras devoured him. Alesta turned again to the illuminated wall. But this was his work. His hand. Him.

Her fingers reached for the smears of luminescence. Rested where Kyr's had touched.

She followed his final creations, greedily looking over every picture. Faces and towers and trees. They gave way to etchings. Then frantic scratching—monstrous faces supplanting all others.

Her hand pressed against the uneven gouges. It didn't matter how Kyr had come to this place. He'd still been so buried, so lost. And the monster that had trapped her must have eaten him, like those other monsters had been ready to do to her. Like it would do to her soon, too.

Her hand clenched, nails catching on the gashes in the stone. As if she could pull Kyr back from what had happened to him. She had worked all this time and come all this way to deliver revenge to the monster who'd killed her best friend.

Alesta's spirit could never rest until both she and Teras paid for what they'd cost everyone. She still needed to slay the devil at the root of hell.

First, she would end this one.

Alesta worked out a plan over what she hoped wasn't more than a day or so. Not being able to tell night from day only fed her worry that time was slipping through her fingers like one of Lor's satin ribbons. The kharis balm had her wounds healing, but wasting time sitting here trapped was cutting into her two weeks. She finally ate another Lia seed, anxious she'd run out as she fell behind schedule.

She wondered what Kyr ate while trapped here. Why would the monster let its meals waste away—long enough for Kyr to create all those pictures, sharpening whatever rock he'd used to make the etchings—instead of enjoying them immediately? Why keep her trapped here like a sheep in a pen?

Sometimes she caught the monster seeming to stare at her from the farther shadows, spiked shoulders angled in her direction. Or lurking nearer, head turned away, looking out into the glittering black.

It was a devil. It loved to torment. Maybe it could taste the built-up fear and pain when it finally consumed its captives.

She studied the chamber's ceiling, looking for what she needed to implement her plan. Rock jumbled about up there like brawling monsters. Stalactites speared through the mass occasionally, dripping with luminescence, and giant blocks of shiny obsidian slid across the ceiling—

The immensity of all that massive weight of stone struck her again. The crossbow she was preparing clattered from her hands.

She pressed them to the ground. Willed herself to steady. Fought to breathe. She and Mico hadn't known to prepare for this. How much worse must this have been for Kyr, who'd never chosen to come here, who she'd last seen splintering under the weight of the court's judgment for the first time in his life? The thought made her chest clench tighter.

The monster trod closer to the wall between them.

She leaped to her feet. Hand to hilt, lungs flooding with air, she stared at its horrific outline, where the unholy glow of rock and skin painted over claws and scales and, rising atop its head, over a face masked in gloom, a pair of curving, serrated horns.

"Monster!" She slammed her palms against the stone, at the beast obscured in shadows and her own reflection in the dark glass. Everything the Arbor had taught her to hate. "Abomination!" *Slam.* Her hands blocked out her mirror-face twisted up in misery. "I hate you all!" *Slam.* "*I hate you!*" *Slam. Slam. Slam.*

She didn't even care in that moment if she provoked it into attacking. Let it haul her up and try to end her. Let her vent her rage and get free of here.

It backed away. She sank to her knees, fists and forehead against the obsidian.

She had killed Kyr just as surely as this monster had. She was more culpable, even. And she couldn't stand it. Couldn't ever forgive herself. Atonement for casting him into this place, for whatever he'd been through here, was impossible. All she might do was wreak vengeance on his behalf, and hope she destroyed herself in the delivery of it. Mico's kind words about trying to send a ship for her were a pretty fantasy she didn't deserve.

She readied for her escape. She had her crossbow. The arrows, and the mechanism she'd designed to retrieve them, tied onto the slender Lia rope.

And the poison Mico had collected from a branzono corpse for her. It was strong enough to protect those sea monsters from the greater seabeasts. Coating the arrowhead, it would make sure this devil went down in one blow. She only needed to strike it at the vulnerable spot under its arm where her blade had pierced, deep enough to trigger her arrow's splintering design. The poisoned Lia spikes would break off and burn this thing up from the inside.

She couldn't hit it directly. The wall stood in her way. She calculated.

This rock was likely only to shatter under a direct hit from these arrows. But aim at the looping formation of rock above the wall just there—let the arrow carry the rope through it, and deflect off the cavern ceiling. Kill the monster, then let it act as a counterweight, more reliable than that curve of rock, for her to climb out of here.

One shot. Taking it felt as risky as invoking the trickster god in the old stories, who would be bound to stand before you but tempt you into a terrible bargain. If she did this wrong, the beast would understand her threat and probably attack. At least take her supplies. She dragged her teeth over her lip. Or she could kill it but still end up trapped in this pen, with nothing to bear her weight, only a few Lia seeds left, eventually just as dead as the monster.

She waited to prepare her weapon until the monster stood facing the greater darkness. In position, she watched for it to turn her way again. A bit more. Her finger brushed the trigger.

It leaned its weight upon one leg, shifting. Exposed its shoulder. Her finger squeezed.

The monster crossed its arm over its chest, plucking at the spikes extending from its elbow.

A gesture so familiar, it set a shudder through Alesta even as the heart of the crossbow engaged, and the arrow flew.

It tore a name from her tensed lips.

"Kyr?!"

Chapter Twelve

€LAWS AND †EETH

The name struck him first.

Then the arrow.

Fuck. She'd shot him. It *hurt*.

She'd recognized him.

Fuck.

The arrowhead hadn't pierced deep. But a feeling like fire spread from the wound. He hurt all the time, but this was different. He stifled a roar.

She was banging her fists on the glass. Shouting that name. That wasn't him. That wasn't him anymore. His scales had bristled at the arrow's strike, and they wouldn't calm. Not with the pain and the noise.

The shaft tore from his side. It zipped away on the rope she pulled until it caught across the snarl of rocks high above. She'd tracked him down in hell itself just to rip him apart again.

He doubled over.

Her boots thudded to the ground. She'd climbed the rope, out of the shelter. He stumbled back. Lifted his gaze to her face.

She was more striking than he remembered. But then, she was older.

They both had changed.

Her brows lifted. Eyes widened. The black of her pupils drowning their brown. Her jaw trembled, her lips still closed, as if holding back a scream—the horror about to break through the shock.

Anger burned under his monstrous skin as hot as whatever she'd hit him with. Anger that she was here.

And drawing closer. She was *here*, beside him—

"Kyrian?" His name clawed up her throat and skittered about the cavern, breaking into echoes.

"Don't touch me!" He retreated another few steps, until his back hit the wall behind him. He bent over farther, sliding down to the stone floor.

"No," she whispered. Her voice was hoarse from lack of use, and then shouting when she'd realized.

Kyr was *alive*.

And he hated her.

"I won't." She stepped back. His features were still clearer to her now this close, with no glass between them—the dark claws, hands like blue stones. Black plating crusting over his chest and shoulders like bark, stretching up his neck like a high stiff collar. His face, still so like the one she'd known, the one she'd seen only in dreams and nightmares for a year.

He was so pale now.

His skin had once been sun-drenched, but it was stark against his hair grown into long tangles, the scruff covering his jaw. His eyes were nearly as pale, faded to a faint charcoal.

"I'm sorry." This was so insufficient to what she owed him, like a Lia twig attempting to hold up the entirety of stone above them, she rushed on to clarify. "For shooting you."

"So you're not here to finish the job?" He clutched his side and grimaced. His teeth were just a bit sharper, stonier, than the smile she remembered. "Fooled me."

"I didn't know it was you! Why didn't you *say* anything—?"

Between those clenched teeth, he snapped, "I didn't want to talk to you." No, of course he wouldn't. What was there to say to the girl who'd damned you? What words could she, of all people, possibly speak in true apology? Kyr drew a ragged, shallow breath. "What did you tip the arrow with?"

Her turn to wince. "Branzono poison."

He'd moved again when she'd cried out, so the arrow hadn't lodged where she'd aimed, or deep. It hadn't even engaged the splinter mechanism. She'd pulled it free before the poison could be dangerous. Still, the soft light caught and went jagged on scales rent and twisted, like petals of some perverse, sharp flower. And something darker than the seeping glow of his shoulders dripped from the wound, through other raised scales, all the way down to the tattered breeches clinging to his hips. She dared a step forward. "Let me see."

He ducked his head, so his hair fell over his face like a dark curtain. "No."

She tugged her pack off one side. "I have kharis balm—"

"*No.*" He jerked his gaze up to her. Stared. "How are you here?"

"How does anyone get here?" She made a tense little shrug.

"The alberos." That was such a simpler question than how he was here. How he was this.

He shook his head. "You were supposed to stay. If I had to come, at least you would stay there." The fist he balanced on clenched, claws scraping into the ground. She thought of the etchings. The panicked—or angry—hand that had created them. He couldn't stand for her to be on the same island, let alone touch him. "And you're not chained and waiting for the beasts."

He'd probably be glad to see her dragged off to Teras. "Neither are you." How had he survived? And then how had Soladisa?

Kyr huffed. "Enzo anointed me with a year's worth of kharis, in hopes of my spirit passing to the heavenly fields." His laugh turned sour. "But Teras doesn't consume the tithings like we thought, only toys with its payment, then lets all the devils of its lowest pit give chase. The kharis merely allowed me to ward them off, to escape and linger here. Long enough to turn into this." His voice, more gravelly now, dragged like a heavy sword over stone.

"Kyr." Her own voice wavered dangerously. She'd managed to swallow down a sob of joy when she'd first seen him, but the idea of him trapped here alone for a year felt like a crowbar to her chest. "How did this happen to you?"

His lips, a wine-stained color now, twisted. "Orroccio changes you."

A frisson of fear scurried down her spine. How long did she have before she began changing, too?

Kyr tilted his head. "But you're not escaping."

"No." She had time enough to get her job done before she needed to worry. "I provoked my tithing to get here and came down the smaller pyroduct. I'm going to kill Teras."

She thought, as he drew a long breath, he was going to laugh again. It was worse. The furious, dismissive noise he made in his throat, so like the growls of the creatures she'd passed in the dark above, almost sent her running. Her hand strayed to her stomach.

She had shot him, but he had slashed her first. Thrown her in that pen. He had every right to be angry with her. Maybe that anger had grown, just like the rest of him.

"How could you be so selfish?" he demanded, beating his hand against the ground. "You escaped *before* the three beasts brought you to Teras? But that's the payment!" His lip curled in disbelief, as if she were something utterly foreign to him, something foul. "How could you leave all of Soladisa unprotected? Leave Nonnina to be buried in fire and ash——"

"Nonnina's dead!" Her voice broke at last. "She's dead, and you were dead, and there was nothing left for me. So I'm here to save everyone else." Somehow it sounded so unreasonable, almost pathetic, echoing against the endless stone of this stark place, in the face of Kyr's flashing eyes and furrowing brow.

"No." His expression softened a moment, going slack. Then he pressed his lips into a line and drew a sharp breath in through his nose, looking even angrier. "Ridiculous. You're going back."

"I can't. I have to finish what I came here for." The horror of this struck her, soured in her mouth, as she said the words. Kyr being alive didn't change that. She couldn't leave Soladisa to endure Teras' wrath or abandon the mission Mico and the others had charged her with, even if every atom of her wanted to run home with Kyr this instant.

Kyr lurched to his feet, scowling, hand to his side. "I can't drag you back there like this, but——"

Only winged beasts from above and Teras' minions from below would find them there. "There's no going back," she said.

"You think I don't know that?" He clenched a fistful of hair at his temple, then flung his clawed hand down, thrashing the air. "Damn it all, Alesta."

Even with his anger, even with the little hiss his teeth made, her name in his mouth was beautiful, washing over her like sunlight. No one had called her by her full name in ages. No one had been left to. It was the name of a girl who hadn't yet believed her own cursedness. A girl who had believed she might fly.

Now she was only someone who could save others' dreams. And not by returning to her chains. She shoved the loose strands of hair from her face. "I have nearly two weeks—"

"You have no idea." He drew up tall—which was really tall, eight feet at least, even before accounting for the horns curving over his head like a dark nimbus. "No idea what you're facing."

He had no idea how hard she'd prepared, how she'd worked to atone. "I've studied all of Graziela—"

"You can't study for what's waiting down there. It took me ages to claw my way out. It cost everything to get this far." His voice hitched and went hollow, but he filled it at once with hot anger.

"Why didn't you keep going?" All that time mourning him. "Come home?"

"Like this?" he hissed, spreading his arms wide, unfurling his claws.

She hated to see the anguish in his eyes. Hated that he was right; Soladisa would see only proof of damnation. "Kyr—"

"I can't go home. I have no home. I'm not Kyrian anymore." His hands swept down, again and again, punctuating each denial, as if he could shake off that place, that name. "Here, you're no one. You're nothing. You're meat, or you're teeth and claws."

His despair broke her heart, but it could not drive her away. She already felt like nothing more than a weapon waiting for the chance to kill. She knew she deserved nothing beyond the depths of hell he was warning her against. Kyr was alive, and as miraculous as that was, it would not stop the moon's waxing. It did not absolve her from how he'd been sent here. The pain he'd clearly endured. She couldn't undo that, or force him to go await Mico's unlikely rescue when Kyr had refused to ever meet the tithing ship even after making it up here. But she could still avenge his suffering by putting an end to Teras. "I can do this," she told him. "I'm prepared—"

His face shuttered. "You're not."

She knocked a fist against her chest. "I escaped the alberos' chains. Evaded Teras' beasts. Found my own way into hell."

"You're going to get everyone killed. Starting with yourself."

And *that* would probably make him happy. Her nails dug into her palms. "If you're so worried about everyone, and such an expert, then show me the way—"

His nostrils flared. "I don't want to take you down there." He was almost shaking with fury. She met his glower, hoping the effort of fighting back tears made her look fierce and unrelenting. Why did she only cry at the worst times? But she'd come all this way for him, and he loathed the very idea of being near her.

"Very well," she choked out. She felt her face screwing up more, with hurt and self-hatred. "I was doing just fine before you attacked me and threw me in that pen."

His mouth dropped open a little, and it was so *him*, even under all the changes, even after all this time, she clenched her hands to the straps of her pack to stop herself from throwing her arms around him. He wasn't her friend anymore. She didn't deserve him by her side. She needed to retrieve her rope and arrow and get moving.

"That band of monsters you ran into," he said, when she started to move. "They hold a grudge against me."

She wasn't sure what that had to do with his hauling her here, but was glad for the excuse to turn back. "Why?"

"Monsters are very territorial. I took this level from them." That must be why so many other larger beasts had greeted her in the twilight levels, too, she realized. He'd chased them up there. "And now I'm displaying a weakness—"

"Can't I do anything to stop the bleeding at least?"

"That's not—" He scratched his claws over his forearm. The scales that had stood up had settled back over his skin—what he must have actually cut her with, it dawned on her. "I heal fast. A few days and it will be fine."

"Well." The straps twisted under her grip. "Maybe you'd better clear out until then." She couldn't help the hope that kindled painfully in her chest. Couldn't help the steps she took in the wrong direction—nearer to him. Greater than any pull of gravity upon a flier, more than her duty to Soladisa, stronger than the lure of Teras to sinners, he would always be the primary force compelling her. Alive or dead, boy or monster.

He didn't shout her away this time. His shoulders, overgrown with a spiky carapace, dropped. He blew out a hiss of breath. "Fine. If you insist on doing this, you're going to need a guide to see you all the way there. So you don't get eaten in the first five minutes and damn all of Soladisa." Like she had him. "I was sacrificed for you; I can't let you throw your life away now."

Chapter Thirteen
No Such Thing as Safe

She no longer had the eternal-burning kharis to drive away monsters, but as Kyr led her down through the clammy caverns and another web of pyroducts—into what she took for the start of the fourth stratum, the dark levels—they didn't encounter any. Beasts lumbered or loped or scurried in the distance, but none crossed their path.

The monsters were fleeing before him, she realized, as another scuttled away at the far end of a chamber. Which was ridiculous. It was Kyr. She'd seen him help bumblebees who'd become trapped in his paint water to freedom, and pour them a safe puddle over the ground, on scorched summer days. He'd met every courtier, unfailingly, with a polite greeting. Listened patiently to each piece of gossip Rina shared.

Befriended his awkward, ugly neighbor when no one else would.

It was laughable for anyone to fear him.

Wasn't it?

His seething breath filled the darkness beside her, punctuated by the thump of his footfalls. She couldn't see well, except where dense patches of luminescence painted the walls. It was a struggle to keep up as Kyr moved with long strides easily around stalagmites and over the uneven ground, ever downward.

When they came to a passage completely slimed over with luminescence, she was relieved, until her boots nearly slid out from under her.

Kyr's hand shot out, but he retracted it just as quickly.

She recovered her balance, the knowledge that he was truly pained by her presence more bitter than the lemon pith Nonnina used to love to chew. Still, Alesta had spent possibly two days not traveling thanks to him and didn't have time to waste falling on her rump.

Kyr's claws dug through the glow into the stone of the wall and floor, keeping him steady. "Kyr," she asked reluctantly, "I could use a hand."

He didn't reply, only slowly raised his free arm, claws curling away from her. When she extended her hand, he spoke. "Not the scales. They react protectively and I might cut you." His gaze fell from her hand to his feet. "Again."

Did he mean he hadn't hurt her on purpose? Though he'd still caged her in the stone pen. She chewed her lip. At least he was warning her now. So she took hold of his arm just above his wrist. His skin was blue as agate there, with pale veins, and her fingers wrapped barely halfway around. But, she decided, despite the armor, despite his being nearly twice her size, he still felt like Kyr. It was still him.

This, and any other piece of monstrousness wrenching Kyr away from what he'd been, spoke only of her own corruption and failings that had sent him here.

Cheeks burning with shame, she turned her gaze toward the luminescence around them, wishing she knew what produced the glow—nothing of the sort grew back at home. She was just wondering if it might be harvested and cultivated on Soladisa, as a light source for those without access to kharis lamps—perhaps in specially designed lanterns to enhance the intensity—when she almost fell in a puddle of the stuff. Kyr twisted under her grip, his fingers securing around her forearm. He let go immediately, with a little shiver.

"Is your side hurting?"

"No. It's the kharis." He nodded to her wrist guard. "Where did you get so much?"

"Mico." The name reverberated off the tunnel walls, joining the plink of luminescence, as she realized this was why Kyr had refused the balm, when she'd unthinkingly offered it. She wondered if all forms of Lia were painful to him. "It was his idea to figure out how to kill Teras."

"But he sent you?" Kyr's tendons tightened under her hand.

"He gave me a reason to pick myself up when I wanted to lie down and die." Kyr shouldn't judge Mico for trusting her. Better she come here than anyone with a real chance at the better life he would make possible. No position at the Towers or betrothal kiss was ever meant for her. She was like Hektorus' daughter, disappearing from the Arbor's stories, gone to the monsters. That loss had led her divine father to come kill their god and subdue them. And Alesta's sacrifice would make their home safe again. "He wants to help all Soladisans."

"He's going about it a terrible way." Kyr's lips twisted. "Still. He's trying. He'll likely make a better king than I ever would have." He let out a sigh like a gust, claws striking against stone. "When did I ever really try to better protect the kingdom?"

Alesta raised one shoulder. "You saved me."

"It was a sin." He bit the words off, between his sharp teeth.

Even having lived with that knowledge for a year, that saving someone so sinful as herself had damned him, something within Alesta still railed against the unfairness of it. "But why——?" She squelched her protest. She'd learned better than to question Hektorus' will.

"Surely you know." Kyr angled his head, eyes boring into her, wretchedness nearly strangling his next words. "Don't make me say it."

"No," she gasped quickly. Of course she knew it was her fault, and the evidence of her abomination was all around them, written upon his very body. She couldn't bear to hear him condemn her. To say aloud that it was her wickedness he was paying for. "Don't."

At this he looked even more pained, mouth closed, brows high, eyes ringed with hurt. His gaze traveled over her face, as if searching for something.

"I should never have asked it of you," she blurted out. "To take the blame. It was unfair." If only she'd surrendered to her fate before tangling him up in it. She needed to remember that now, even— especially—knowing Kyr was alive. Remember her duty here.

His jaw trembled above where his neck was overgrown with skin like basalt. He swallowed, throat bobbing hard, then squared his shoulders and nodded.

She should be glad for the chance to apologize at long last, but seeing the heartbreak she'd subjected Kyr to, the way he clearly wished her a thousand miles from his side, felt far worse than any other torment hell might have in store for her. They left the tunnel for another dark cavern, and as the glow faded, she removed her hand from his arm.

He wanted to hate her.

He was more angry she was here. Angry for reasons as numerous as the heads on a hydra monster he'd once encountered deep below. Where he was taking her. Because he was still a fool when it came to her, apparently.

Like thinking she could stand to hear the words he'd never been bold enough to say before from his monstrous lips *now*. Gods, the way she was reluctant even to touch him.

She pulled away the first chance, as they passed to drier, darker caves. It stung sharper than the poison's bite.

And wasn't she wise to be afraid? When he'd tried to protect her, after catching her startling scent and following her down from the mirror-maze—when he'd taken her from that fight to where he'd once sheltered from the other monsters—he'd hurt her. There was no such thing as safe in Orroccio. Though—even with the complication of defending a human—nothing in these levels would pose any real threat to him.

Damn it, he was sick to death of reminders of what he'd become. Her kharis that burned like a brand. The pained look in her eyes, confirming he was every bit as monstrous as obsidian mirrors had shown.

He endured her furtive glances as they traveled through places he'd never imagined trespassing into again, suddenly too aware of how bad his fidgeting had grown in hell, spared only when she needed to rest. He told her he didn't need much sleep and kept watch. He stood a few paces off, feeling the pull of the moon and tide somewhere out in a world he didn't belong to any longer.

Trying not to look at the girl he'd traded it away for.

For a long time, he'd tried to hate her. Tried to believe she had only been using him. Tried to make it harder to miss her.

He flicked his claws over his scales. Even when doubt had reared up in him in earnest, he couldn't wish their places reversed. Mico's plan, putting Alesta in this danger, splintered his anger in another direction. Though, Alesta was the smartest person Kyrian knew. Perhaps it was merely another failing within him, that he couldn't understand why she would insist on taking on Teras. He'd always felt unsure, being told by his mother and the alberos that so many of his instincts were wrong. Burying any ideas he had for the kingdom along with the parts of himself they found unacceptable. Listening when they told him Soladisa didn't need fixing, only for him to fix himself, to be worthy of leading it.

Like raising the issue of university invitations, that day Alesta killed a branzono, and letting Albero Paolo shut him down. Or the time he'd tried to cover a tenant's rent with his own allowance, saved up for whatever books came back on the trade ships that year. The farmers had just lost their son to tithing. When his mother discovered how he'd tried to help, she'd pointed out the unfairness to their other tenants, good people who had served Hektorus faithfully and not lost a son to sin. So Kyrian had suggested lowering the rents for them all. His mother told him people were taking advantage of him, and the albero she had to dinner after chapel said Kyrian needed to stick to the right way of doing things. Give to the Arbor, and allow them to help those who truly needed it. Breaking custom could undermine the king's rule, invite sloth into his people, threaten everything. Kyrian's misguided attempt to help would only end in disaster. Just as saving Alesta had. The Arbor's clear edicts had been the only beacons through his uncertainty.

Kyrian leaned back against the cavern wall in the corner where Alesta had curled up. He coiled a hank of his hair around one finger until it cut off the flow of blood. It was surely better for his kingdom he'd been banished here. He'd never been as suited for serving as heir as Mico would be. How could Kyrian ever lead when all he did was echo others? When he and Mico studied the same books together, the same tales of heroes, Mico would declare he wanted to have new poems written about his deeds someday. So sure of himself. And Kyrian had mimicked Mico, had tried so much to be like him, like Ciro. Until he worried he didn't even know who he was, himself, anymore.

So long he'd felt lost in the dark. And that darkness was inside him.

He'd felt its eruption approaching the day he'd been brought here—the truth of himself made evident at last.

His wayward gaze pulled to Alesta, luminescence painting over the curve of her cheek, pooling in the dimple of her chin. She slept peacefully even in hell.

He'd spent so much of the life he'd lived on Soladisa pretending. Hiding. He hadn't had to do that with Alesta. Most of the time, at least.

There was no hiding now.

When she woke, her sidelong looks resumed, itching over him worse than his monstrous skin.

Until they arrived at the first flooded cavern.

Then Alesta stared only at the dark waters. Glints from the faint luminescence here writhed on the crest of subtle waves, stirred by what swam beneath.

"I could carry you?" he offered. "Maybe?" If his touch were less repellent than the unknown submerged threats.

She looked at him then, horror drawing her brows together. "No!" An affronted flush covered her cheeks. "I mean—" Alesta tugged at the bottom of her bodice. "You're injured."

He nodded, accepting the offer of saved face. Trying not to recall the miracle of her softness against him when he'd stolen her away from those other monsters.

He waded in.

The inky pool spread wide, its reaches lost under the jaggedly arching ceiling. The passage would narrow and climb again, out of the water, to wind through this vast rock, back down through other cavities and grottoes and fiery pits. He fought off a tremble, as he had before when she'd asked him to guide her, at the thought of returning through them. At what they held, and what he'd done there. His body may have broken faith with him, in becoming the diabolic thing it now was, but he would not allow it to betray his fear, or stoke Alesta's. Any more than its mere existence did.

She followed. The water that came to his shins reached her thighs.

Something swished past. Long and dark and low.

Alesta froze. "Will they run away from you, too?"

She'd noticed how other monsters feared him. He picked at the stray scale resting against his knuckle. "Probably?" He hadn't bothered to notice when he'd come through here before. Hadn't cared.

By then he was dragging himself pointlessly upward. Knowing he was already utterly damned. Almost wishing some fiercer demon would end him.

Her steps drifted nearer to where he waded. Her eyes searched the ripples they ventured through, almost as wary when they flicked up to him every few moments, every few steps she took closer to his side. He could feel the warmth of her, amid the cold water and dank air. The scent of her. Like the sky.

She drew a blade from her belt, the one she'd always worn while tinkering on her inventions—over breeches he had never seen her wear back home, stuck slick to her curves as the water sloshed against them. Her thumb engaged some mechanism on the hilt and the blade snapped out to a sword's length. "Had to sneak everything past the alberos," she said, as she scanned the water with weapon ready.

The wry quirk of her mouth was precisely the same look she'd give him back in the villa's chapel, when the visiting albero would drone on too long about cultivating harmony or maintaining chastity, and Kyrian would twist toward the back pews to catch her eye.

Memory was more treacherous and deep than these waters. It threatened to drag him under, drown him in a false hope that he could ever earn more than a few flashes of expressions other than fright or loathing. That their friendship had indeed once been as true as he'd believed.

Another something sluiced through the water, sending rills up from either side of its eel-like form. Alesta looked ready to swipe at it, so he sloshed between them, put an open palm to her back, and hurried them from the final lapping stretch of the dark pool.

"Save your fight for Teras," he told her once they reached the rimstone crawling up the cavern floor.

"I brought plenty of fight." Her cutting smile only grew, even this close to him.

His hand fell from her back. "Better to avoid them."

She did not pull away. She balanced the blade over her hand as she looked him dead on. There was that same intensity, written in the unforgiving, eager lines of her face. "We're already in hell. We may as well sin."

She always believed she could reach out and change the world. Even this cursed corner of it. She knew nothing of how this place would reach right back inside and hollow out a heart. Like molten rock had carved these tunnels they climbed now. The futility of trying to protect her set his tattered spirit blazing with anger again. It had gotten him damned before. And now she was here.

She was *here* and he was *this*.

That he could not hate her, could not resign her to the deeper damnation waiting, could not help endeavoring to keep her safe in any small way, would likely be what caved in his heart completely.

He had to warn her off somehow. Even if it made him a thousand times more damned in her eyes.

Alesta had drawn ahead. "No," he said, catching up as the passageway descended and opened into a dark maze. "That's not—"

Something launched itself from above. Huge and fast and silent. Kyrian dove in front of Alesta. Too many legs rammed into his chest.

Fangs in his face. Fire burning through his skin and blood. Screams shredding through his head, from Alesta and monster and maybe himself—cut off with a sharp crack of pain and darkness.

Chapter Fourteen

DROWNED IN MONSTROUSNESS

Lightning broke across the air from the monster's fangs to Kyr's face. For one moment, Alesta saw the entire spidery beast lit from within. Its bulbous form menacing from above. Sinew and joints. A great throbbing heart.

The electro-luminescence revealed more of the demons, scurrying along a ledge over the passageway. It sizzled across Alesta's vision even as the cave again went dark. Kyr fell back, cracking his head against the curving stone—borne down under the many legs of the monster that had tried to attack her.

Alesta threw herself upon it, driving her blade forward. Remnants of the monster's crackling blue fire streaked still before her eyes, but all the grief she had distilled into fury and purpose for a year guided her hand. She would not lose Kyr again to any monster.

The tip of her blade clattered against a metal-like hide. The spider-devil reared and turned on her. Skittering sounded behind her. Cloying pungency choked the air. She struck again. The bulging form loomed. Legs thrashed against her. Her sopping boots skidded over the ground. Alesta fought to focus. She had seen inside the demon. She had seen its monstrous heart.

Again her blade found no purchase, sliding over an impenetrable casing. She did not relent. Her pliant wrist guided the steel to hunt for weakness. At last it dug into yielding flesh.

The thing screamed, and only then did Alesta become aware that she had been screaming all along as well. She roared louder as she wrenched her weapon through muscle and blood. The monster tumbled to the ground. "Nimble grip," she spat.

She wheeled, expecting a dozen more of the same devils to come pouring down on her from the ledge and dark reaches above, but the others scattered. Scraping and chirps faded into the black.

She crouched, balancing with her blade and groping for Kyr. Her hand stilled against rough skin, fumbled up over his collarbone, to the slack flesh of his face. "Kyr?" She swiped her fingers down, searching out his pulse. His skin there held the coarseness of a cork tree, or the volcanic rock along the coast. Alesta could barely discern if she felt a thrum of life or merely her own trembling. She set down her weapon and cradled Kyr's head in both hands, seeking any sign of bleeding.

His hair was wet. Copper assaulted her nostrils.

They couldn't stay, trapped against the narrow passageway and under the ledge. Those spider monsters could return. Or something worse could pin them down here.

She retracted her blade and fit it to her belt. The scales that had bitten up from Kyr's arms and torso were settling already, but she could not simply drag him by the shoulders, with those horns—like a stag beetle's, and serrated along their edges. She couldn't let his injured head scrape over the stone. He was too big and heavy to lift all the way against herself.

She recalled his clear doubt that he could carry her again, back at the water. Mortifying. But nothing like getting him killed within two days after he'd somehow survived here for a year. Hoping the Lia rope wouldn't hurt him like the kharis oil of her wrist guards, she pulled it from her belt and looped it about him, crossed it beneath his head, and drew it over her own shoulders.

She hauled him away, to the first corner of this maze she found with a patch of luminescence reassuring her nothing lay in wait too near. Helictites twisted through the space like searching fingers. She slipped her bag off and checked Kyr over again, easing his head to one side and the other. Dark blood trailed from his ears.

His lips let out a sigh and he nestled his cheek into her palm.

Alesta was so relieved he was alive, she didn't startle away—it would not do for Kyr to find her pawing at him in the dark. He didn't stir again, though Alesta felt a regular warm huff of breath against the heel of her hand.

The cave's green glow limned his face, and she could finally get a good look at him, now he couldn't glare her away or turn to the shadows. He didn't appear so very different, just here, even if the rest of him seemed drowned in monstrousness. His features were extreme versions of the boy she knew. Cheekbones sharpened. Lips darkened. Brows thickened. A silvery scar traced down one cheek, and four in parallel cut through the scruff shadowing his jaw. His curls had gone black and straight with a year's growth.

And somehow this place had worked itself upon him, until he bore the spikes and claws and scales of monsters. A ruff of delicate skin curling about behind each ear. That bloody glow seeping from where pale skin, webbed over with strange patterns of veins like stone in Soladisa's quarry, joined to the coarse plating over chest and shoulders and shins. He didn't look like just one monster or another she'd seen, but then she hadn't yet witnessed what dwelt in Orroccio's deepest reaches.

He'd endured here so long. It was nothing to wait in the dark for him to wake.

When he did, it was with a moan—then he jolted upright. Alesta scrambled back as he clawed the air between them.

"Kyr! It's only me!" *Only the one who sent you to this nightmare.* She cleared her throat as she stood. "It's me."

"What—" He was wild-eyed.

"Are you hurt? I think you were bleeding—" She reached to feel again, to see if there was swelling.

His hand snapped up. Claws captured her wrist, then flung her back. "What happened—?"

"It's all right," she told him. "A monster attacked us, but—"

"No." He froze halfway to his feet. The rope dropped to the ground around him. "No, no, no—"

Why was he so upset when she had dealt with it? She'd told him she could manage this mission. "I took care of the monster. And you."

"Alesta," he rasped, "what did you do?"

"I killed it." His eyes widened even more. "I told you I could handle myself. I've been preparing ever since I damned you to this."

Hektorus' breath, his expression. His brows drawn, his mouth half-open in horror. Like she was plunging another poisoned arrow straight into his heart. Or as if he was watching someone he cared for sail away on the tithing ship.

It didn't change when he asked, lips barely moving, "How long was I out?"

"It felt like hours." Her boots were still damp. "It probably wasn't, quite—"

He fell back to his knees and dug into her bag. "What kharis do you have? Something you can absolve yourself with?"

"There are no alberos to fuss over us here!" Like she'd said, what was the point when they were already damned as they could get?

Kyr pulled the wax lid from the tin of balm. He scraped some out and reached for her. Smoke hissed from his hand at once.

"Kyr, what are you doing?" She hurried to rip a pocket from inside the bag, to wipe his hand.

He knelt before her, unconcerned with his burning flesh, face still caught in a look of terrible longing and dread. "Within the hour—"

"I cannot believe you're still twitchy about the old rules." She was getting annoyed. "And I might need this balm, if I have to fight my way through other monsters to reach Teras." She cleaned what was left from his fingers, though most had burned away. She'd never seen Lia react like this.

His voice was thin as thread. "I tried to tell you. This place—"

She could barely attend to what he was saying. Something was distracting her. Her irritation raked deeper. An itch at her collarbone. And wrists.

It burned.

She dropped the cloth to tear the pendant from her neck. "Why—?" It smoked. Like her skin where it had lain. "Why is it doing that?" She twisted her wrists to see the skin of her forearms shimmer with blue luminescence. She felt it crackling underneath. "Kyr—!"

Her hand tingled where it still grazed his. Strands of his lank hair lifted as if stirred by an unseen storm. Panic flooded her limbs and gut, just ahead of a surge of lightning burning through her. Sparks shot from her fingers—almost like claws.

Alesta illuminated.

Light streamed from her hands, carving through the darkness all around. A wail escaped her lips. Her eyes flared with panic.

"Here—here—" On his knees still, Kyrian grasped her by the elbows. "Just like my scales. You breathe. It will stop when you calm."

"It burns!" She writhed in his grip, tearing off her wrist bands. Light ripped through her arms again. She cried out. The hair fallen loose about her anguished face lifted as if she were underwater.

"I'm sorry." He shivered at her lightning's bite. "I am so sorry. Try to breathe." More sparks. More gasps. He asked, desperately, "Remember when we were ten and I got that terrible splinter on some bark?" Alesta's rounded eyes didn't reveal that she even registered what he was saying. He carried on anyway. Inanely. "I wouldn't let anyone at the villa touch it and my mother despaired, saying my hand would inflame and fall off. I was so upset I ran to the cottage." She was biting her lip now. The lightning sputtered. "You told me to keep the tea you were making for Nonnina hot while you made a poultice, and I was arguing with you that I wouldn't let you put anything on it, when the steam from the cup drew the splinter straight out."

Alesta drew in a long shuddering breath. "That wasn't it. The difference in temperature created suction."

"That's right." He rubbed his hands toward her shoulders and back down. "You explained it to me while I drank the tea. Then Nonnina came in from the fields and said she'd give me a splinter cracking her herding staff over my head if I drank her tea again."

Alesta's mouth pulled into a frown. "What is the point of this story right now?"

He dropped his hands from her. "To distract you."

"Oh." Her pulse flicked fast at her throat. "It worked."

Alesta could be quiet at times, but she was always sure to draw breath to argue natural philosophy. He sighed, with relief and exhaustion. "I've told myself a lot of stories down here."

"Kyr. Why did this happen?" She stared where a tracery of blue incandescence covered the bottom of her arms. "What is happening to me?"

He squeezed his eyes shut a moment, as if he could find escape in the deeper darkness within. He should have warned her sooner. He should have told her so much before everything changed between them even more. Every time he'd thought he'd already lost her completely, fate cracked the chasm between them wider.

He reached for her again, like a supplicant, to the broad altar of her hips. Praying he might hold onto this last moment before she knew all he was. Praying for absolution that after this confession could never come. "It's the killing."

Her nose wrinkled—with confusion, if not disgust. The light from her skin dimmed away as he explained. "The absolving with kharis must counteract it. Otherwise, killing a monster stains you with its monstrousness."

"Monstrousness." Alesta's breath became ragged again. "I'm going to become that? That thing?"

"No." His fingers pressed into her sides to steady her as she swayed. "Only a little. Just a little, for each life."

Her brows drew together. Her lips pursed. "That means, if you're—" The smartest person he knew. "You must have—" Her shrewd gaze fell on him like a spear.

A sigh cracked from his chest. "Alesta, you didn't damn me to what I am now. I did this to myself."

Chapter Fifteen

A THOUSAND DEVILS

arely a sign of the monstrous lightning remained upon her skin now. For Kyr to be what he was—the mark of so many different monsters left on him—he must have killed hundreds. A thousand devils.

A wisp of smoke from her wristbands trailed up through the shadows, the smell of kharis sweet and thick, and an unbidden vision pressed into her mind. Alesta fought off the Sight she knew didn't belong to her by right, but for a moment, she Saw Kyr slashing new claws at a scaled throat, hunched over a fallen monster, ripping another apart—more and more monsters slaughtered and bleeding, and Kyr covered more and more in the blood and the scales and the spikes.

No wonder so many of the others feared him.

His neck bowed, his forehead coming to rest against her stomach. Horns pointing as if in accusation. Her hand fell to the back of his head. "Not only you." He was put into this position because of her. Guilt gnawed at her gut, ate into her bones, deeper than ever before. "It wasn't only you."

"There have been others." He didn't understand her. "When Teras throws away the tithing for the horde of devils to chase down. The kharis oil I was anointed with meant the three beasts and all the rest could barely stand to touch me once they claimed me as the payment, so I could escape, and stay myself longer, but others have made it out too, occasionally."

The oil hadn't protected Kyr from changing, though. Not forever. So the amount of kharis was key. They knew timing was important.

Kyr dropped to his knuckles as she shifted away. "I should never have led you down here," he muttered. "I should have made you go."

She found the fallen pot of balm. "Go? Where exactly was I meant to retreat to?" Kharis in wood or leather against her skin hadn't staved off the monstrousness like the alberos' oil. Absorption must be crucial. Perhaps it wasn't too late.

"I wanted to prevent just this. I'll take you back now. Before something worse befalls you."

"Kyr. I'm not turning back." He looked up at her, where she crouched, in time to see her slather the balm over her arms, where the luminescence had shone.

This had seemed like a sensible test, but her nerves were still frayed from the lightning, and a headache from the vision had set in. Her teeth clacked as she grimaced and braced her hands to the ground.

"Why would you do that!" Kyr grabbed her shoulder.

She kept her eyes trained on her skin. The balm burned away, like oil in a pan. Traces of lightning arced around her fists. The jagged webbing persisted on her forearms.

The monstrousness had taken hold in her.

She chewed her lip. "Even a bath in kharis oil probably wouldn't restore you now."

"Of course not. But you aren't—"

"Doesn't it hurt you?" she interrupted, angling her head at him. "The lightning?"

He let go of her arm and pressed his lips together. "I've taken on monstrousness from deep in hell." His hand traced along the rough, dark skin over his collarbone. "It protects me from worse fire than that. You only bear a fragment of that monster's power. And none of whatever shields it from its own force, it seems, which is why it hurt you and not me."

That seemed unfair. "Maybe I should go kill a few more and see if that helps."

"No!" He leaped to his feet, as if to block her from making a run for it right then. "You can't kill again." He saw she remained where she was, on the ground by the pack, and wrapped one arm about himself. "Please." His feet shuffled back, to the wall of stone behind him. "The others who escaped. They lost themselves. Killed until they weren't human anymore. To wander forever in here. Or some of them kill sea monsters, trying to return to Soladisa, but by then—"

"The branzonos who come ashore." The beads of sweat that had broken out on Alesta's brow and neck from the pain went cold. "They were—they were *us*. They could be former sacrifices."

"At least some of them. Driven there by some instinct they maybe don't even remember."

The image of the one she'd dissected rose in her vision. "They have no organs to vocalize with. The gills wouldn't allow for speech."

They wouldn't let them say they were only trying to come home.

The rough stone floor cut into the pads of her fingers. Gods. What had she done?

It was as Kyr said. *This place.* She'd known it was evil, the root of all sin, as the alberos taught every week at chapel. She felt it now, could see the depth of its wickedness. To bring itself to their shores, to creep into their very bodies. To make her hurt her fellow Soladisans.

To hurt her friend. She craned her neck up at Kyr. It was as she'd told him, as well. He was not alone responsible for what had happened to him. She bore that blame.

"You're not corrupted yet." Kyr paced in the little room the stone walls afforded. "No one will see that small bit. Easy to keep hidden. You can still go home."

She did not deserve to ever leave this place or return to Soladisa, like the youths whose chance for the same she had denied. A little lightning wouldn't send her running. "Not until I've seen to what I came here for." It was more vital than ever, she knew now. She gathered up the rope. At least she, and Kyr, could still touch Lia fiber not soaked in oil.

"We're heading into the heart of monstrousness," Kyr said. "The lower reaches aren't like those above. I can't protect you."

She tucked the balm and pendant away. "I'm not asking for your protection." She cinched the bag shut. "Not again."

He flung up his hands. His claws raked the darkness back and forth. "Why can't you see, at least now, the danger you're diving into? To provoke Teras?"

"It doesn't matter if it's dangerous." Why couldn't he understand this was all that was left for her? All she was good for?

"What happened to doing whatever it took to survive?"

You happened. You died. "The kingdom will survive. This is my sacred duty." To Soladisa. To Kyr as well.

"There's nothing sacred here." He scoffed, pacing again. "This place burns it all away. You either fall to the monsters or become one."

"Maybe it takes someone as damned as I am to set it right."

Despair grated his voice. "Nothing here can ever be made right." He paced back her way, eyes flashing like molten silver. "There's no escape from here! If you keep going, you'll burn!"

"Then I'll burn!" She shot to her feet and blocked his steps. She'd burn and burn to light up this dark place for him. The pain of what she had to say fissured through her, worse than the lightning. "You were my best friend. I know I failed you; I dragged you down into all this surer than any of the three beasts, and you don't have to be my friend anymore if you don't want." Kyr showed no reaction, staring down into her face with that old look of blank focus. So familiar, no matter what changes had been wrought by time or sin. "But I came here for you."

His gray eyes flared and his mouth opened. "You—"

She rushed on before he could argue more. "Whatever you had to do, Teras was the one that compelled you here. I swear I will reach its pit and destroy it. No one else will ever have to endure what you did. No one else will ever have to pay the price again."

She threw the bag over her shoulder and stalked into the maze.

"Alesta—"

She knew now he wouldn't leave her side. "You just admitted you were only worried for my sake. You're not afraid. You're big and scary and only got knocked out because that monster saw me coming first. I guess you'd better keep up, then."

She fought away a grin at the sound of him stomping after her. When he fell into step beside her, she asked, "Is your head all right?"

"I've killed some monsters who heal fast." He shoved the wrist guards he must have picked up at her. They looked worn and frayed. "Kharis oil burned away. And you might need them for when you go home. Eventually."

Her steps didn't slow as she put them on. Not until another thought occurred to her. "Wait." Her boots scuffed to a stop. They were still days from the bottom of Orroccio. Consuming any Lia seeds now seemed inadvisable. Possibly fatal. Certainly they couldn't sustain her if contact burned them—and her insides— up. "What am I going to eat?" She turned to Kyr, who had tensed, looking around for a threat. "What do *you* eat?"

His shoulders dropped. "Monsters are immortal, or near enough. Don't need to eat that often. However much they seem to enjoy slaughtering each other." He began leading the way through the tight passageways of stone again, not looking at her. "I've been trying to stretch out how often I have to kill anything. Scavenge when I can. I'm pretty sure killing larger monsters has a stronger effect, so the tiny ones—that make the luminescence—" He drew a claw through some that trailed down the wall beside him. "I've eaten plenty of them before." As the glow seeping from between his other monstrousnesses showed, she realized. "It won't harm me to kill some for you when you need. Should be enough to get to Teras."

Teras. Whom Alesta would slay, promptly inviting what she had to imagine would be a pretty strong effect of monstrousness upon herself. She fought a shudder, like a door had slammed loudly behind her. No matter. Her purpose was here, and Mico's thought of sending a ship through the poison sea when Teras was no longer around to part it had always been an idle hope.

But as she struggled to keep walking on suddenly shaky legs, she looked back over at Kyr, and her stomach knotted. He'd already killed so much because of her, and if she was going to become fully monstrous anyway—"You don't have to—"

"No. If we do this—" He stopped and waved his hands vaguely. "This is how we do this."

She supposed she owed him at least this much, if it was what he wanted. Still a stickler. She nodded, and they continued through the maze as it dropped steeply through the mountain.

Kyrian waited as Alesta ducked under a low archway of stone he'd folded himself in half to pass through.

She muttered, "Are you sure you're not just trying to keep all the good monster powers to yourself? You heal quickly, barely need to eat, don't sleep—"

He huffed. "Honestly, I think being knocked out was the best rest I've had in ages."

She drew up straight. "No wonder you were so grumpy when I first found you."

He slapped the arch where he'd shielded her from anything that might have been hiding above in this new chamber. "You'd just shot me."

She shook her head, walking on. "You abducted me before I shot you."

His voice dropped low. "You were about to kill them." He'd tried, at least, to prevent any monstrosities from rebounding on her.

Her mouth opened, then pressed into a line. "Right. Well. Good thing you heal fast." She pushed her hair that refused to stay braided behind her ear. Stubborn as the rest of her. "And I'm keeping watch tonight. Or whenever we stop. You know what I mean. While you get some actual sleep."

Easier said than done. For now, they continued through the last of the darkest levels. He felt her eyes on him, darting between his monstrousness and the creatures they caught sight of down tunnels and in shadows. Identifying similarities, doubtlessly. Cataloging all his sins.

Everything lurking kept well away from him as always, but there were other frights as they pushed lower. When they crossed the chambers where air from the surface squeezed through vents in a howling, mournful wind, Alesta's hand strayed again to a hilt at her belt. That would do no good at all here. The haunting breezes sang like an infernal choir, their wails echoing through the gloom, chasing them around corners of the maze of black rock, stirring unaccountable, swelling dread through Kyrian's insides. It was unnatural, excessive, even as he almost tripped over the dried-out remains of some monster that had succumbed to this place. Even knowing this was far from the worst thing waiting for them here below.

In the murk, Alesta's eyes glistened with unshed tears. "The Caverns of Lamentation?" she asked, her voice hollow, and he nodded. If they didn't hurry, they'd forget where they were headed at all, lie down, and never get back up. He rubbed one palm against an ear, put his head down, and barreled through the place as fast as possible, just able to hear Alesta's footfalls assuring him she was right behind.

They couldn't rush through the passageway to the next level, though. Timing was everything there.

The poison grotto filled and emptied with the tide, sulfurous water pouring in from the high reaches of the long cavern, dashing over the rocks, and spattering over the opening to the last tunnels that ran down to the levels of lava and fire. A stone bridge traversed the sloshing water trapped in the bottom of the cave.

"That's a bit of good fortune," Alesta said. "Graziela said it's completely covered half the time." Only Alesta would call anything about this place, with poison somehow more concentrated and caustic than even the worst parts of the sea, fortunate.

The tide was coming in, an occasional splash clawing over the side of the narrow bridge. "We should cross now," he told Alesta. "Or it'll be hours before the bridge is fully clear. Watch your step."

They made halting progress, in single file, pausing when a wave drove itself too high, then darting forward. Careful of their footing on the poison-slick rock.

"Where is the light coming from?" Alesta's voice was hushed as they ran a few steps. "Does moonlight cut down through here as well as wind and water?"

He only shook his head.

"There's no luminescence, only—" They stopped for another wave, and he half-turned to see her head tilt upward, her mouth drop open. "Only—" Her breath shuddered and caught.

"They shouldn't bother us." The creatures roosting on the cavern's soaring ceiling watched with wide glowing eyes, bright like perverse stars crowding a hungry sky. But the bat-like things hadn't stirred when he'd last crossed. They'd chosen other prey— smaller monsters captured and impaled on the stalactites among their nesting ground, their corpses half-gnawed away to blackening blood and white bone. "Come on." The only option here, as in all of Orroccio, was to keep going.

She'd taught him that. To do whatever it took to survive. Like when she'd asked him to cover for her at the festival. He'd thought of that plenty here. Her example had been even more useful than the brutal fighting she'd shown him that last dying spring.

He took a wide step over a retreating splash. They were nearing the waterfall. Its curtains of water split and diverted haphazardly—they'd time it perfectly so Alesta could leap through safely.

"Kyr!"

He turned to see her pointing upward. The jumbled constellations across the ceiling broke as the creatures launched downward.

"But they—" His stomach dropped. He'd already been mostly monster when he'd reached this grotto before. Now he had Alesta with him—and they must have been able to sense or smell the human in their territory. *"Run!"*

Nothing to do but keep going, to try to outrace the things, whose shrieks carried over the rush of water louder than the crying winds in the last chamber. He almost slipped whirling around Alesta, letting her be first, putting himself between her and the pursuing monsters—who spat globs of fire with every shriek, he saw over his shoulder, just before one struck him there. He hissed and hurried after Alesta. The fiery illumination revealed the monsters better, as they gained on them—their leathery wings swept back to dive fast and long bushy tails like wolves' streaming behind them.

Poison slapped against the bridge, and he yanked Alesta back from its spray, then shoved her forward through a gap in the tumult of acidic water just before a screaming bat flew low, fangs and claws ready to attack, and ignited the waterfall into a cascade of fire.

Kyrian shot through, eyes clenched tight. More screaming from the wolf-bats, but now it was anguished yowls as they sped into the flaming waterfall and dropped into the churning waters, or echoes as they reeled away. As he kicked a fallen, screeching ball of fire back through the falls and watched to be sure they wouldn't be chased further, skin stinging, Kyrian asked Alesta, "Are you hurt? Did I hurt you?"

"No. At least I landed on something soft."

His arms dropped from where he'd been rubbing away the burn of poison and flame. Nothing was soft in Orroccio. Except—

He turned to see Alesta fallen forward across a bloated lump bigger than himself, purple and speckled white in the tunnel's luminescence. More dotted the passageway like barnacles on a ship, or boils or blisters, each fringed by dark green fronds— though these were no plants. Kyrian leaped forward to pull her away, but a burst of blue spores erupted into her face.

He coughed away a few stray spores. She rolled over, wheezing hard. Her curls snaked about wildly, obscuring her face.

Kyrian croaked out, "Are you all right?"

Alesta looked up to him, a sharp-toothed smile cutting across her face covered in winking sapphire scales. "I'm perfect."

Chapter Sixteen

THE GIRL WHO STOLE THE SKY

yrian squeezed his eyes shut again. It had to be another nightmare. He'd had a thousand of them here, seen as many horrors in his head as in hell itself, until he sometimes didn't know what was real. Maybe it was all a nightmare, maybe Alesta was still back at home and safe—he scraped at his face with the hooked joints of his fingers, wiping away the blue spores, before looking again.

Alesta stood before him, every exposed inch of her skin hardened into fierce scales. Her fangs bit into her lip as her smile turned coy under his stare.

"Alesta—" He choked on the misery rising through him like bile. "I'm so sorry—"

She shook her head. "Why?" The firelight glimmered over her, blue and sparkling like the sky. "This is what you want me to be, isn't it? So I won't turn away from your frightfulness? So we can be together?"

"No!" he rasped, even as she stalked closer and raised a clawed hand to his cheek. "I never wanted this for you." He'd failed again.

"Didn't you?" Her frozen smile gleamed coldly. "Didn't some part of you wish to see me punished?" Her fingers clenched, digging into his skin. "Like you?"

He couldn't raise his hands against her, not even as she drew blood. Instead he clawed at his own face, too, unable to bear the condemnation in her stony eyes.

A nightmare. Real or not, the worst nightmare yet.

When his hands fell away—along with a sprinkling of spores— Alesta wasn't standing at all, but lay limp across the tongue-like blob, unconscious. Its purple flesh was roiling, the fronds around it already reaching up to wrap about Alesta's wrists and ankles.

Kyrian slashed the fronds and pulled her free, stumbling backward and collapsing onto his knees. He'd witnessed one of these things devour a monster nearly his size, rendered helpless by the spores while the thing held it tight and absorbed it.

Alesta's face still appeared monstrous to him. That hadn't happened to the beasts he'd seen eaten, but then again, they'd always borne fangs and scales. The guilt he already carried expanded to press painfully at his ribs, to burn in his throat. He held Alesta across his thighs, an arm under her shoulders. She was still asleep—or worse, oh gods—and he was babbling apologies. He dropped his forehead to hers.

Her skin felt smooth. Soft.

He pulled back and she was herself again, thank Hektorus. Only a nightmare. A hallucination. Already wearing off. "Alesta?" Blue powder caked over her face still. He rubbed it away from her cheeks and brow with his fingers, his thumb gently sweeping it from the folds of her eyes. "Please wake up." What if so many spores were deadly on their own? "Alesta! Please, please wake up—"

Alesta turned from where she'd fallen—she didn't remember onto what, now—and gasped when she saw Kyr standing before the burning falls, their firelight licking over his smooth skin and cropped curls. Just as he'd looked at home. "What—?" She rushed forward, throwing her arms around him.

"Ow—" He tensed under her touch.

But her hands wouldn't stop. She dragged them over his shoulders, down his chest, and her human nails somehow clawed open his soft skin. Something emerged from between its folds—long, thin jointed legs first, and a furred body—then more after it. Spiders spilled from inside Kyr, who gaped at her and made a strangled noise in his throat. Alesta desperately reached out for him again, as if her hands could put right the horror they'd worked on him. Instead, one plunged into the stream of skittering monsters and drew back clenching Kyr's heart, red and bulging between her fingers.

Kyr collapsed at her feet, and then she was fainting—she was on the ground—no, the purple thing—no, someone's lap.

She knew she was still dreaming, because Kyr was holding her, his distraught voice saying, "Cara, please. Wake up, Alesta. Please—"

When Alesta finally opened her eyes, Kyrian didn't even think about his scales and claws as he cradled her face. She was herself. She was all right. Relief rushed through him, setting his chest heaving, almost moving him to do something foolish.

She was so near. Her freckles and fever spots dappling her cheeks. Her full lips, drawing in a slow breath.

Dazed and blinking, she lifted a hand to cup the back of his. The second her fingers touched his skin, though, her eyes widened, and she jerked away from him, right onto the floor. "What was that?"

"I—" Something else was flooding through him now, more like the poison in the grotto. Twisting up his insides.

"Some kind of—fungus?" She swiped at her face, and stared down at her hands like they were covered in the awful stuff, though he'd already cleaned it away. "I thought—I saw—" She lifted her gaze to him. "Something horrible."

He rocked back on his heels. He couldn't imagine what might be more terrible than this place and her guide through it. Who clearly scared her just as much as all the other monsters attacking her. He stood. "You—got a much worse dose than I did." He swiped at his eyes. "I hallucinated too, only a moment, then I got you away from it. Otherwise it would have—"

"Killed me. Like everything wants to here." She blew her curls out of her face. "Graziela did write there would be torments in hell, punishments for the damned, all that. I knew what this duty meant." She scrubbed her palms down her thighs and stood. "That does *not* count as sleeping, by the way. You're still taking a turn when we stop again."

He resisted when they found a recess off the last cavern they traversed before Alesta tired. He only agreed after she had slept. He'd gathered some of the tiny monsters that propagated like algae high on the cavern wall and crushed them dead in his palm before scraping them into Alesta's, for her to safely eat. Then he lay across the entry to the alcove to avoid seeing her reaction to what his world had become.

What could she possibly think, when she'd experienced more than enough horrors here already and was still insistent about marching straight to the greatest monster in this place? She'd always been bolder. While he contorted himself to fit everyone's expectations, she'd devised her own ways to fight back.

Except now, she was talking of sacred duty and damnation, like she believed everything the alberos had always said to her. Like she believed she belonged here. Like all her dreams meant nothing.

He couldn't stop fidgeting. Scratching at scales. Resettling on the stone floor. He never really slept anymore. Between the discomfort of his monstrous parts and having to stay on guard—not to mention the nightmares—sleep was as annoying a necessity as eating.

"Here." He turned his head to see Alesta beckoning where she leaned against the wall, below streaks of luminescence. She laid her hand to her thigh. "I promise to shove you away if anything attacks, before you can go all spiky on me."

He hesitated. She'd come for his sake, she'd said, and his heart had kicked in his chest like it was trying to leap into her hands. But if what she said was true, then surely she'd have been at the dock that day. She hadn't come, breaking a vow that had felt as strong as a sacred covenant to him. And he'd seen inside monsters he'd killed, seen how their viscera were as horrific as their outsides. Wondered if his heart was made strange, if it still held the capacity to feel what it should.

She angled her head as if she were the one who'd trained for royal authority. "*Come here.* What's the point of being fat if you can't be a pillow for your best friend who hasn't had decent sleep in ages?"

There were many reasons, in his opinion, starting with the lush wonder swelling above her bodice—also a reason he should keep his monstrous self far away from her.

Definitely not the reason he gave in.

He wanted to believe they were at least still friends. Wanted to forget how she'd startled away when he'd held her too near. Careful of his horns, he laid his head across her thigh. They'd sat like this often in the fields at home, Alesta shielding his eyes from the sun so he could read aloud while she watched the sheep. "How long has it been?"

"Since you've slept properly?"

"Well, yes. How long since I left?" He dug a claw into the floor where he'd folded his arms. "I can feel the tide and moon, now. So I know months pass. But I've lost track."

Nothing but the sound of her breath for moments. "One year." Her fingers brushed a tangle of hair from where it tickled over his brow. "I was a summer tithing like you."

He closed his eyes under her touch, wanting to imagine them back home. Back before everything. The air was too dank. No sun burned through his eyelids. "I sometimes thought maybe Soladisa was a dream. That you were."

Her voice was quiet, seeming almost to come from inside his own head. Like so many times he'd imagined her speaking to him here. "Did you really never consider trying to come home?"

"By the time I figured out what I was doing to myself—" His claw dug deeper. "I couldn't. I'd heard what happened to some of the others, by then, how they left." He'd opted, once again, to do nothing so bold. Only to ruin himself slowly. Trading away who he was gradually to eat or fend off other monsters.

He couldn't tell her how he had lingered for weeks after making it all the way through Orroccio. How he'd crouched inside the last tunnel. How he'd listened to that season's sacrifice screaming before Teras' beasts bore him away, then clawed and caved the tunnel in on itself and vowed never to return. What could he have done? Scared the youth with his own monstrous form? Stolen him away and damned the rest of Soladisa?

He'd failed his people already, with his sin of omission, never attempting to fix their curse while he still stood a chance. Like Mico was actually doing. Kyrian possessed no such principled determination. His sin was ever an omission, like himself. A blank. A void. An echo at best. Look at what he'd resorted to without the Arbor's clear guidance. The sickening violence. Even now, Kyrian had encouraged Alesta to return home, leaving the island at risk with no payment to Teras. He was as grotesque inside as he feared.

And still he grasped for her mercy, to explain why he couldn't have saved the other tithings. "I did go to the surface once. But my eyes—"

Understanding dragged Alesta's voice lower with each word. "They've adjusted to the dark."

He swallowed. "Killed too many monsters that live in it. Can't see up there. Only at night, and even then. It hurt to look at the stars."

"Oh!" His head bobbed as she moved. Something rustled.

He opened his eyes. "You make a terrible pillow."

Then the night sky dropped before him. A starscape of gilt and ink. Constellations staking out wide reaches of the heavens.

"I stole it." Before, she'd sounded almost giddy about being able to sin without the harping of the alberos. Now as she clutched the page, her voice tightened with worry. "I'm so sorry."

"Why would you be sorry?" he breathed. She'd given him back the sky. Hektorus' Throne. The Seven Tears his daughter had shed. The Gorgon, the Hydra's eight stars, the Silver Bough, the Golden Scales. Each painted star pricked through the shroud he'd been sure had muffled his spirit for anything such as books or art. Each gentle wave below them washed clean some part of himself long buried.

"I destroyed your favorite book." Alesta's words came quickly and laden with guilt. "All the rest of the *Codex Anima*. To make sure I'd be tithed."

His eyes scanned the creased page still. Drinking in the contrast of light and dark, sharp form and deep color. He could barely murmur, "This wasn't my favorite."

The parchment crumpled at the edges. Alesta dipped her head over his, nose wrinkling. "It wasn't?"

"I gave you my favorite."

"You did?" She sat back. "That tattered volume?"

"I must have read it a dozen times." The last few while working up the courage to make a gift of it to her, hoping she'd simply accept it. That she'd like it. He reached a finger out. Not quite tracing the stars reflected in the waves.

"I wouldn't," Alesta warned, though she didn't move the sheet away from him. "This paper's especially potent Lia. I think it was giving me a rash. It might ignite. And that wouldn't be good, trust me." She tapped a finger on the cut edge. "It's fascinating. The Lia and monstrousness react destructively when in contact. It's not just monsters repelled by its goodness or degrading on exposure, like the flier's wings, though it does make sense the Lia can prevent someone turning monster, if you absorb enough kharis soon enough. But it goes both ways. My skin was burning, and the oil burned away too. I wonder—"

It was like the old days, drowsing in the sun after a swim or helping pen the animals or working in the barn side by side, listening to her theorizing. She talked out questions of whether the alberos ever knew as part of the Arbor's sacred knowledge, if the rules for absolving had been taught by Hektorus long ago or developed over time and the reason forgotten. Kyrian fell asleep stargazing.

Chapter Seventeen

BLOOD AND FIRE

Orroccio began fighting back in earnest. For a place the alberos had always told Alesta she belonged, the rock didn't want to allow her farther into its depths, into the fifth stratum of the inferno. Scarlet light cut through the darkness, glowing from cracks in the basalt. Steam vented even where chambers fell back into black. The ground grew hotter. The soles of Alesta's feet stung an hour after she and Kyr set off again, once he'd slept. She'd slipped the *Codex* page back between her breastband and blouse, carefully, to keep it off her skin.

Red-rimmed silhouettes were the only signs so far of the fiercer monsters both Graziela and Kyr warned her waited in hell's lower levels. Kyr guided her away from their nests and pulled her into gaps in the stone to let them pass by. Alesta almost wished she could get closer looks at them, wished she had someplace to record all her observations through hell. This was beyond even the sort of groundbreaking research she'd dreamed of performing some-day at university, but she could only dream again of making her own codex of her discoveries here. Like the minuscule monsters Kyr had given her to eat. Even crushed, their varied structures—rings of teeth, long spiny bodies—were transfixing. And they also made her wonder how Kyr had ever survived here. He'd eaten the same three things most days back on Soladisa. None of them with antennae or more than four legs.

His own monstrous parts seemed to protect him from the increasing dangers as the maze opened up into a wider net of caverns. Smaller monsters scurried—always away from Kyr—on four legs, atop broken columns of stone and along narrow ledges. A leathery, hoofed demon with spiny teeth chased a little loping creature straight over where a crevice erupted suddenly with steam. The prey glowed golden-hot and dropped into a simmering pile the other beast fell upon. Kyr didn't flinch as the gust of heat burned through the air and slapped across their faces.

Alesta's hair stuck to her cheeks. And her feet were shouting now, even with her boots' thick soles. She hurried down the next slope of stone. Kyr easily kept up—he'd been adjusting his stride to match hers. "I can't use the kharis balm I'd planned," she explained. "To protect my feet." The heat intensified. She could barely speak—couldn't think. It felt like the time when they were little and she got caught halfway across Soladisa's beach, between the water and the shade, bare feet aflame, unable to choose which way to run.

Kyr spread his arms as he sidled next to her. "Come here." His fingers tensed back. "If it's all right?"

Alesta was too desperate to worry about embarrassment. He'd managed to get her from the fight with the band of monsters to the obsidian pen, and she'd stabbed him halfway there. She threw her arms around his neck. He bent forward, slid an arm under her knees, and lifted her.

He didn't seem to have any trouble as he bore her down the slope and across another cavern. As the pain in her feet receded, another warmth flushed up her chest. Kyr no longer smelled of Soladisa's foliage but of something earthier, like petrichor and dark wine. She said, for her own sake as much as his, "You can't carry me all the way to the bottom of hell."

This close she could see how his pupils were almost slits and the whites of his eyes like onyx shot through with pink veins. His jaw pulsed. "I should carry you back to the surface of this rock."

"Where I can have an excellent view of when Teras burns Soladisa to a crisp?" At least she knew now he didn't merely want to deliver her to the three beasts.

She felt his growl under her arm draped across his chest. "Plenty of monsters down here are better resistant to the heat. You just need to borrow some of that resistance."

"I thought you said no more killing."

"Scavenging." His grip tightened, long fingers digging into her side and thigh, though he must have been careful to keep his claws pointed away. "I'll find something for you to use."

Instead, something found them.

A beast nearly as tall as Kyr lumbered out of a side tunnel. There was nowhere for Kyr to duck out of sight, and it did not retreat like so many of the other monsters had. It stalked forward, at an angle toward them.

Kyr's steps sped. The creature broke into a run, making to intercept them.

Alesta's fingers hooked against the rough skin around Kyr's back. "Shouldn't you put me down?"

"No." Kyr's face was a mask of concentration. His nostrils flared.

The monster gained on them. Scales like Kyr's completely covered its massive form, shimmering over broad hunched shoulders and barrel chest in the ruby light. Rows of teeth in a too-wide mouth glinted as it panted.

Alesta could make out each razor edge as it drew nearer. And nearer. *"Kyr."* She needed to draw her blade or bow. If this monster slaughtered her, it would be killing every person on Soladisa. Why had she ever thought she could do this? She should have fed herself to Teras and its horde and saved them all for a few months at least.

The monster lunged for them. Kyr darted to one side, leaping over the dark crack splitting the floor he'd been running beside. The beast didn't slow at all, but followed them—

Steam burst from the fissure, shooting up over scales and teeth in a flash. The monster dropped with a wet thump behind them.

Kyr slowed as they approached a tunnel at the far side of the chamber. Alesta was clinging to his neck, almost cheek to cheek with him. She breathed, "You planned that."

"I can feel where the steam is coming." Kyr made a little shrug under Alesta's arms. "Good trick for when you don't want to actively kill, but you're hungry. Or someone else is."

"You learned lots of good tricks like that?"

"Oh, sure. You know. Playing dead. Hiding. Did a lot of hiding."

The lump that had been the monster slackened, scales flaring loose like a horrific succulent. Alesta eased her hold, mindful of the spikes upon Kyr's shoulders, and angled her face at his. "I suppose he'd be no good against the heat."

He arched one dark eyebrow as they entered the passageway. "I'll scavenge you better."

When they had crossed another roasting hot cavern, Kyr turned under an archway of twisting stone into a smaller chamber, insulated from the worst of the heat. He found a ledge to set her upon. His face looked down into hers for one breath, then he moved back the way they'd come. "It should only take a few minutes. Don't move."

Like she was going anywhere on her own. "Thank you."

His gaze didn't return all the way from the archway to her. He waggled his head the slightest bit. "What's the point of being a giant, hulking monster if you can't carry your best friend over the fires of hell?" He slipped from the alcove.

Alesta hugged her arms tight around her knees. Nothing sacred, he'd said. Nothing set right. But if Kyr could forgive her—if they could be friends again— A lightness spread over her sweltering skin. Who cared if they were dancing around the real issue, that it didn't matter if she corrupted herself with a dozen monstrosities? If she destroyed Teras, she'd bring all its damnation down upon herself anyway, and there would be a mountain of monsters looking for revenge atop her. If she failed, she could only hope her death still counted as Soladisa's tithing for the season. She wasn't getting out of here unscathed. Probably at all. But she'd never thought she'd have a chance for real absolution from Kyr himself first.

He was back as soon as he'd said, with a bundle of bloody hide in one clawed hand. She untied her boots as he sliced pieces to fit inside their soles.

"The blood will help, too." His lip curled at the gore and stickiness. "Unfortunately."

How *had* he ever survived? But then she remembered his intent look as he'd drawn that monster to its death. Every scale dotting his own arms and torso showed how adept he'd become at killing. He hadn't hidden and played dead always. She shoved the monster skin flat into her boots. "Again. You're hoarding all the useful aspects of monstrousness."

Kyr's eyes narrowed. "It's a trade-off," he said flatly. "My skin started to burn after a while when I tried the surface, just to feel the sun. Literally burn. I ran back to the tunnel when I started smoking."

She remembered the blackened forms she'd passed before finding the tunnel down into the island. "The branzonos—" She bit her lip, squinting to visualize. "The way their skin steamed and charred. Maybe it was from monstrousness they'd acquired deeper in Orroccio, that wasn't suited to the sunshine." If they really were previous sacrifices who'd endured, possibly for centuries, taking on different monstrous forms—only to be greeted by a shepherdess with a vendetta against monsters. Her toes squelched back into her shoes. As long as they didn't burn. Not until Teras. "It must have been a very fresh kill you found."

He eyed the leathery pelt in his hand as she relaced her boots. "Monsters fight among themselves so much. More than they need to eat. Makes it easy to find what you need. Many of them only eat live prey they kill themselves." He held out his clean hand to help her down. "We'll see if that's enough."

It was better; as they pressed on through smaller chambers where narrow streams of lava coursed down the stone walls, the heat of Orroccio licked over her soles, but it did not bite.

Which meant she failed to feel when she neared one of the cracks that would suddenly release scalding steam. Not until the vapor nearly seared her eyebrows off and Kyr hooked an arm around her, spinning her away.

"Sorry." He pulled his hand back. "No time to ask."

She released a short, sharp breath, staring at where she'd just been standing, still flooding with steam. "Please don't be sorry for saving my life."

She jerked her gaze up to Kyr's, aghast. Her eyes widened. Of course he was sorry he had—he must have stewed in a year's worth of regret for trading his life away for hers. "I mean." She swallowed. Shrugged. "You always have my permission." Oh, gods, that was *worse*. How had she managed to say something worse? Her awkwardness burned more than the blazing stone had. She'd never meant to discount what she'd cost him. To ever be flippant again asking his help. Maybe if she was very lucky, Teras might decide to meet her halfway and swallow her up right where she stood. All this steam made it hard to breathe. She plucked at where her blouse stuck to her skin.

Kyr was scratching a thumb over the scrap of hide he still held in one hand. His gaze dropped to her fidgeting, then reared back up, all the way to the cavern's misty heights. "I'll remember that." His voice sounded strained as he said, "Things are only going to get deadlier from here on out."

"I know." Following Kyr across the chamber, gauzed in vermilion steam, she gladly jumped on this new topic. "Graziela's writings imply the devils grow more and more diabolical closer to Teras."

Lava-light licked down Kyr's profile. "Graziela didn't See all the way there."

"I've Seen Teras."

He looked at her sharply. "You had a vision?"

She cringed, feeling too much like she'd again taken what wasn't meant for her, like the kharis fire she'd once begged him for. "A little one," she admitted.

His eyes darkened. "There's nothing little about Teras."

The image of the devil's boundless horror overwhelmed her memory. "No." And if Kyr was right, and larger monsters had a more profound impact on the human who killed them—then surely ending one as incomparably colossal as Teras would utterly doom herself as well.

At the moment, she wasn't sure how the deepest pit of hell could compare with the way her thighs were chafing. She couldn't even use balm as she did at home because she'd mixed holier-than-slightly-monstrous-thou kharis into it. Another of her plans gone awry. "Clearly we didn't discover every detail about Orroccio," she conceded, as Kyr ushered her around another steam vent near the edge of the chamber. "But Mico and I did prepare for what's waiting. Together, we—"

Kyr swept her to one side, and she expected another jet of steam, but there were only the others they'd passed, scarlet vapor blossoming through the space, and Kyr pressing her to the wall. Pinning her hand to the stone. Rasping, "Hold still." Before clamping his mouth to her throat.

Kyr's mouth was on her, and suddenly any discomfort evaporated as her body sparked with another sort of awareness. The longer his lips pressed to her skin—and light prickles of his teeth, and, *gods*, the barest trace of his tongue—all the heat of this place burned inside her, flowing down through her like lava, pooling to an entirely different warmth building between her thighs.

His hand clutching the shred of bloody hide pushed against her neck, following as his mouth worked lower. His leg pressed into her hip, and she wanted to pull him flush to her. Her free hand fumbled across his back.

He broke the seal of his mouth against her collarbone. His breath whispered over the sheen of sweat on her skin. "Play dead. It only eats what it kills."

Chapter Eighteen
NO OFFERING BUT BLOOD

*S*he tasted of salt and heat.

Alesta's eyelids fluttered. He thought he saw the moment she caught sight of the shambling dark monster behind him. She let her head fall away, leaving her neck exposed, mottled with the blood of the beast he'd killed for her. Her hands went slack and gently curling, against the cavern wall.

He hadn't thought this through. He'd seen the monster and acted to shield Alesta. But what would guard her from the impulse building within him now, as he playacted mauling her, to fit himself fully against her curves, to lose himself in the wanting he'd fought off, to drag his mouth up to hers?

Or lower.

It took everything to wrench himself away. He dared a look back for the monster. Saw it was gone. Withdrew his hands.

Alesta shuddered.

It hit Kyrian with more force than ever before, more than any strike another devil ever landed against him, more than the great

bells of the Towers used to drive waves of nausea through him—
he was a monster.

"Sorry——" His voice was thick. He swallowed down the pain.
"You said—to save your life——" She'd just begun to grow at ease
around him, and now he'd reminded her how horrific he was.

Her mouth tensed. "It's all right." But she stayed slumped
against the wall. Held her palm to her throat. As if she expected
him to attack her in earnest.

And hadn't he been burning to do just that?

He ignored the sourness churning in his belly. "It's gone now,"
he reassured her. "Figured that one wouldn't bother me. As long as
you weren't a temptation." The words nearly stoppered his throat
again. He gestured with the hide at her fingers slipping over where
he'd bloodied her neck. "If it looked like——"

"Of course." She gave her shoulders a brusque shake, and
stood, adjusting her pack. "Practical. Better than killing." But her
voice was husky with fear.

He wished he had anything to give her to help her clean her
neck and hand. He had nothing to offer but blood. And more horrors. He had to prepare her for where they were going. "It's not
just that monsters are combative amongst themselves. Or looking
for any meal. Humans are treasured food."

Alesta nodded, as he began to lead her on through the next passageway, where pale gypsum flowers curled from the ceiling like
tentacles. "Like with that band of them. That fought over me."

"Though closest to Teras, monsters are almost more like a
court. We'll have to disguise you before we venture much farther."
He checked ahead of Alesta, as the curve of the wall sharpened,
heart singing praises to Hektorus for the chance to talk about

anything besides what he'd just done.

What he'd just done. His mouth still savored the taste of her, even as he kept relating more of Teras' last strata of hell and all their monsters, some almost more human-like, though shimmering golden or veined green or aglow, some newly spawned crawling in dark fissures or where lava flowed, some flying like motes in sunlight—or more like pricks of light in the darkness.

He wasn't afraid anymore of returning. What greater hell than the anger and despair roiling through him—not aimed at Alesta but at fate's mockery of him. As if the nameless trickster god mentioned in his books had caught him in a terrible bargain, that he could only now do what he'd wanted so many times. If she'd ever given any sign back in those days that it would have been welcome. To know now it could only inspire revulsion.

Even while every little familiar gesture Alesta made as they walked together, like they once had through golden fields—tucking her hair behind her ear or biting her lip—drove him closer and closer to diving over a cliff's edge to the utter ruin of his heart.

So much had changed, and nothing had changed. He never stood a chance. As it had been back in another life, on another island. Alesta had never had feelings for him beyond friendship.

He'd had to understand. It was just like how his cousins would talk about pretty girls—would gaze at them when they all went swimming in the cove. And Kyrian would gaze, too, considering how the light fell across their backs, so smoothly, planning a painting of yellows spread over swimmers' forms and scattering over the choppy water. But he didn't feel anything that his cousins seemed to feel.

Not for anyone but Alesta.

Those feelings were rooted deep inside the friendship they'd shared almost as long as he could remember. And in the last years before Orroccio when they'd unfurled strange new leaves, sent shoots of wanting—wanting to take her up in his arms like he finally had when the band of monsters attacked her, wanting to explore with her in ways the alberos would douse him in kharis for even considering—he was met only with her insistent indifference.

She was too clever not to suspect how he felt. He had sensed the discomfort growing between them. He was a monster even then for wanting what he did, when such a transgression might have tipped Hektorus' scales against her at the tithing ceremonies. She'd tried to be kind, to remind him of what a best friend should be. Of how she did not feel any of that for him.

She'd have been perfectly content to see him married to someone he'd have to keep on pretending with or hiding from, for the sake of the royal line, and go off and do all the wonderful things she was meant to do.

Dying for her had seemed like such a better end.

He hadn't even managed that properly, but mangled himself into something no one could ever feel for.

Now they were going to Teras, he'd get another chance.

"Tell me about your plan," he asked her. "For Teras."

Alesta was nearly hugging herself, plucking at the straps of her bag. "Right. Mico and I"—she swallowed, eyes going a little unfocused as one finger traced from the strap up her neck—"together. Um. We created a weapon that no monster can withstand." She gave a little jerk of her chin.

He tamped down his annoyance with Mico, again. He was only irritated his cousin reminded him of his own failings. And had put

Alesta into this situation. "Teras isn't just any monster."

Her gaze sharpened down to a glint of satisfaction. "That's why Mico infused the arrowheads with Lia amber. Special arrowheads I designed to spring open into many spikes once they're lodged deep. They break off if you try to remove the shaft, so the arrow's holy power will burn on inside Teras until it's dead. And Mico extracted the branzono poison to give it a quick kick." She grimaced. "Which you got a taste of. Sorry again."

Kyrian couldn't shake the feeling Mico couldn't possibly have fully prepared for Teras. "I know his Lia-forged weapons stay sharp and all, but will Lia in steel still have a real effect? Your wristbands were less repellent than your flame."

Alesta shrugged. "I'm mechanics, Mico's magic."

"Right." It was strange to think of Alesta spending so much time with Mico, as he once had. That they'd shared months and months together. Without him.

Alesta tilted her head, considering. "It's some terribly long, complicated process to create the rosin, and magically forge the steel with it, using even more Lia. He's been developing it for ages. These are all he could make in time. But the Lia is still reactive once it pierces skin and reaches blood. And, thank Hektorus, it will endure in the steel, unlike, say, the balm I made, even in contact with Teras' monstrous flesh. We tested it." Guilt shadowed her face. "On branzonos."

Kyrian stared down the long pyroduct winding into shadow and flame. "So you just need a way to get close enough to take the shot."

Alesta blew out a breath. "Without being eaten by all those monsters in its court."

"They'll be riled up," he said, guiding her to the left in a division of the tunnel. "We can all sense the tides and moon. They'll be expecting the new tithing."

"And I'm overdue," Alesta said grimly.

"There are revelries leading up to when Teras gives the sacrifice to the rest to fight over. Dancing, and—" He waved a claw. He'd blocked out most of these memories, of that first metallic terror. The tumult of monsters whirling, striking their strange instruments of bone and sinew, snatching up smaller creatures to eat, or worse. The moment when Teras' beasts, unable to hold his anointed flesh, cast him to the horde. Coming back to himself hours or days later, baptized fearfully anew in monstrous blood. But he could use it all now, to help Alesta, and the kingdom. "If they're growing more wild with the tithing later than usual, it may actually help to provide some cover to gain access to Teras."

The space opened up around them, the walls carved wide by trenches of flowing lava. Alesta's face was screwed up with concern, its lines and planes painted in black and red.

He may never have worked to free Soladisa like Mico, but he at least could make her confident in her guide now. "I'd read about the source of all monstrousness. Before. The boiling lava, the abomination unto Hektorus, the wellspring of all devils. But Teras doesn't simply crouch in its flow. It's tied to it. Rooted in it." He cast his gaze up to one side, barely seeing the luminescence trailing from a high ledge as he pictured Teras' lair. "I remember a giant archway—monsters can enter there to make petitions during the balls before the tithing." He'd heard more about this as he sneaked away through higher levels. "For power, or status, or against others in the court. We should be able to make our way there. Get close."

He slowed to check around another tightening bend of tunnel.

Before he could move on, Alesta reached out for him, all that concern on her face still, almost devastating in its tenderness. She laid a hand lightly on his wrist. Where he'd told her it was safe. "I'm sorry to make you go back."

How she could still touch him at all after the way he'd scared her only made him more determined to help as much as he could. He shrugged one spiked shoulder. "I'm glad you found me," he said, before leading on around the turn.

Maybe he was always destined to die at the bottommost pit of hell. Maybe fate hadn't played its cruelest trick on him yet. Kyrian didn't know. What he did know was that his fate and Alesta's were tangled together, and he would do anything to see hers corrected, to make *her* go back, all the way to the safer shore of Soladisa.

Even kill Teras himself.

Chapter Nineteen

STARS MADE OF MONSTERS

Alesta awoke to stone trapping her. Orroccio had finally fallen in on her—it would crush her, and flatten her lungs—

She couldn't breathe. She beat her fists against the stone pressing near, and they sparked like flint. Lightning flared up her arms. She couldn't draw breath to scream.

Something jerked hard on her shoulder. Somehow rolled her away from the stone. She wasn't trapped, wasn't buried under a mountain of rock. Before her was only Kyr, in a field of stars.

He sat back as she wheezed for air. "All right?"

She'd gone to sleep at the edge of a small cavern as far from the fire and heat that they could find and must have rolled over in the night toward the wall. Now she could see the actual ceiling angling down—painted over with luminescence in whorls and bands and constellations.

"Nightmare?" Kyr clasped his hands together, arms around his knees. She could only shake her head. He waited as her lungs slowly filled.

She sat up and scraped sweaty hair from her face and shoved

it behind her ears. Her voice was nothing but a shaky whisper. "Sorry if I scared you."

He nodded seriously. "You're definitely the scariest thing down here." Then his dimple winked in the glow of the sky he'd painted while she slept.

Kyr smiling had her lungs ready to give up on her again. She'd never thought to have been granted such a blessing in hell.

Though thinking about his mouth was dangerous. How it had felt moving over her skin. How those bruised-looking lips might taste against her own.

He'd only been protecting her. Because the fate of Soladisa depended on her reaching Teras. He'd never seen her that way, never could, even before she'd cost him everything.

She let her head thump against the stone where she leaned back. "We should get moving. Though I hate to leave this so soon." Every step toward Teras was one step closer to losing herself, and losing Kyr again, for good. It was how she had to serve her kingdom. That didn't mean she was eager for this reprieve with Kyr to end, this little sanctuary of time, in a cave carved by fire, under stars made of monsters. "Your work is beautiful."

"I hadn't done any since right after making it through Orroccio. It's nice to see that maybe"—he scratched at a scale on one knee—"maybe I'm still capable of more than merely destroying myself bit by bit."

"Kyr." Her gaze dropped from his unfinished sky to where its green starlight stroked down along his horns and through the long coils of his hair. "You haven't destroyed yourself. You survived. And you found what light you could even down here in the dark."

His hand fidgeted faster, fingertips glowing with smears of

luminescence he must have taken from where it traced over the walls. His other hand bore a blot on the back of it, a makeshift palette. He'd been in the middle of painting when she'd awoken in a panic.

"I'm serious," she told him. "The pressure of this place was getting to me within hours. The weight of it all above——" She drew in a long, shallow breath, drinking in the firmament he'd crafted as well, letting it soothe the lingering edge of her fear. She exhaled slowly. "Sorry to be so ridiculous."

"It's not ridiculous."

She scowled at herself. "I prepared! To endure whatever it took to——"

Kyr leaned over and dabbed some of the luminescence right onto her nose. "Now you're ridiculous."

She stared at Kyr, half-obscured in the glimmers of luminescence. He grinned, tongue poking at his teeth, but the longer she sat agog, the more worried he looked, smile going slack. He ducked his head and hunched his shoulders a moment before she pushed him, just below his collarbone where no spikes or scales protected him.

Still, it was like hitting the wall of stone behind her again. Immovable, he swiped the entire blob at her cheek, but she caught his hand and forced it back into his face.

Kyr made a disgusted noise, though she was pretty sure he could have fought her off harder. The gleam in his eye was visible even as he scraped at where a glob had lodged between it and his nose. "You perfect calamity." He flicked his fingers at her.

She wiped at her nose with the back of her hand. "You started it!"

He drew his head high and said in his most courtly tone, with a broad smile, "I am simply helping you with your disguise."

Their gazes fell at the same time to their hands resting against the floor, palm to palm.

How many times had one of them grabbed the other, pulling them along to some game, or a swim, or to hide from all the others who would never understand them the way they did one another? How many times in those last years had she forced herself to let go, to hide how much it meant? And now it was time to face Teras. Alesta swallowed. "I wish we could go back, to when we were both safe on Soladisa."

Kyr shook his head. "The horizon was always in your eyes." His smile waned a little as he played with her hand, gently twisting it this way and that. "I thought you would fly away. You'd say over and over how desperately you wanted to stay, but I could see it. Once you built your freedom, you could escape." His smile extinguished. He let his hand drop back to the stone. "And I'd still be stuck on a rock."

She wanted to cling to his hand before he could draw it away. To explain her struggle to save herself had never been meant to hurt him. That she'd been trying to escape not only tithing but the pain of wanting something she could never have.

But that wasn't why she was here. Kill Teras. Save the kingdom. Atone.

None of that would actually make a difference to Kyr. He thought all he was now was a monster, his potential nothing more than losing himself piece by piece, still wearing away under the calamity she'd unleashed on his life. If she simply left him here like this, without making true amends to him—

Alesta bit her lip. Considered possibilities. Impossibilities.

Resources. Counterbalances and points of inflection.

She would be ridiculous. She would try, however she might, to find a way to send Kyr home.

He slipped his hand from hers. "We should begin scavenging for what we'll need."

Over the next few hours, they found several things Kyr said would be useful for camouflaging her: a thankfully dried-out pelt of some furred devil and some rocks that didn't look that different from the thousands of others they must have walked past, in the persistent red tinge of these levels. Kyr draped the monster fur over her head like a scarf and slipped the rest into the pack.

Then they came to the top of a vast open space, several times over as large as the greatest royal hall at the Towers. Trails of lava glistening across its floor far below made its depths appear like the scaled skin of some monster more massive than all of Orroccio. Kyr, face uplit with scarlet, horned shadow stretching tall over the curving stone, gripped her hard by the shoulder as they descended the long winding ledge to a dark archway just above the roiling crust.

It led to a tunnel formed to a high point along its ceiling, interrupted by stalactites, like a spiked spine. This opened into more passageways and chambers bearing signs of territories staked out—rough stone carved into twisting columns and arches, like lava frozen mid-flow, and shaped into halls breaking off into dozens more shadowy walkways and colonnades—all bathed in the creeping light of fire or luminescence.

Echoes brushed up the passages as well, of laughing or screaming, drawing Alesta's eye to search for any approaching monsters. This was the sixth stratum. The city of devils.

"Most will be at the revels," Kyr said, hurrying her around a corner and away from whatever he'd been able to see coming. "And their attendants will be keeping a close watch on their territory while they are. If we're careful, we can pass by and find a place to hole up away from anyone hanging around. Get you costumed." He glanced down one stone alleyway, shook his head a little, and led her on. "Fortunately, I've been working on mine for a year. At least turning myself into an abomination will have been good for something."

She was tired of him saying such things about himself. "Stop being so dramatic."

"I'm eight feet tall with *horns*. I'm inherently dramatic." He stalked ahead.

"Artists," Alesta muttered. She caught up and waved her hands up at him. "You honestly think you look more ridiculous now than you ever did at home, with your face all painted gold?"

A crease formed between his brows. "You never saw me with my face painted gold."

She ran her fingers under the hair sticking to the nape of her neck. "I sneaked up to the Towers the night of the first ball you attended." Kyr's mouth fell open a little, and she shrugged. "I just wanted to see everything. I climbed a tree in the next courtyard and watched the dancing."

"And me." His lip curled up. There he was. A remnant, at least, of that beloved and confident future king. "You never said."

She snorted. Never mind. "I was avoiding telling you how desperately you needed more dancing lessons."

He drew a breath as if he was about to say something else, but around the corner emerged several large monsters.

They were human-like, and tall, with skin like white onyx or sulfur stone, draped in shimmering or furred hides across their chests or around their waists. Some had long iridescent manes. One with flames running along his broad shoulders lunged forward, jutting his chin at Kyr. "What are you doing here?" His voice was throaty with the scrape of a hiss on top. "This isn't your territory."

Kyr shoved Alesta behind him. "Passing through—"

The monster slammed his palms into Kyr's chest. "Is that all?" Kyr knocked him back at once, into the arms of the other monsters crowding nearer. Alesta braced herself for an eruption of more violence, but everyone froze as if arrested by the tension suddenly choking the air—coiling in taut muscles—hardening the grip of the monsters around the forearms of their leader, it seemed, with the flames framing his craggy face. He never took his pale eyes off Kyr, and as Alesta pulled the hide down tight around her and peered past Kyr's elbow, she could swear a spark of fear mingled with the animosity in his voice. "You've already stolen an entire upper level; you won't take my master's territory."

Kyr snarled, "Then he should find himself some guards who won't abandon their posts while he's off dancing."

A monster to one side of the group, holding a leather drawstring pouch, scoffed, "None of your business if we have a bit of fun ourselves, with the tithing still not come. Some dice, some food."

The first monster barked a laugh. "More food now."

Several mouths pulled into fanged grins. The other monster tossed and caught the bag idly, though the stones clattering and crunching made Alesta wonder how much damage it could do if swung as a weapon. Again and again the dice rattled. The tension strained—ready to break on one wrong word or move.

Kyr muttered through a clenched jaw, "I have no interest in this territory. There's no need for violence—"

"No," the leader answered, teeth yellow in his firelight, "but it sounds like fun."

Kyr's shoulders sank just a fraction, as if weary, before he turned to one of the other monsters who hadn't spoken, still holding his leader back from a full-out fight—or shielding himself. Kyr pitched his voice low. Almost gentle. "Do you think," he asked the monster, "that's what the hundreds of others thought, before I killed them?" Alesta's stomach dropped. These had to be the wrong words, as the other monsters shuffled their clawed feet in readiness, as their leader's eyes thinned, but Kyr didn't stop. "Do you think they were enjoying themselves right up to the moment I sliced their stomachs open? Ate their hearts? Ripped their bones apart?"

The bag of dice clacked again. Kyr's shoulders twitched, once, before his claws lashed out and grabbed the pouch from midair. His fist clenched hard. Stone gnashed against stone. "Do you think it sounded something like that?"

The monster caught under Kyr's stare pressed himself back, pushing his leader forward now rather than restraining him.

Kyr dropped the bag, and dust plumed from its opening. His voice ground down to an unconcerned growl as he swung his gaze back to the fiery monster. "Do you think I can't crush you like a fresh-spawned grub and be dancing before the smear you leave behind is dry?"

His spikes were a sharp silhouette before the wavering flames. Alesta wasn't sure she'd drawn a breath in minutes.

She nearly jumped when the monster huffed and shook his fellows' hands off him. "This thing's not even human enough anymore to bother over." He jerked his head toward the corridor they'd come from. "We have our posts to get back to."

Kyr waited until they'd returned far down the passageway before pulling Alesta along in the other direction, tucked under his shoulder and hidden from them.

His gaze wrenched from the creatures to her, full of concern. "You're shaking—it's all right, I could have handled them if I'd had to—"

Alesta couldn't hold it back any longer. Her laugh spilled out of her. Kyr's face went slack. She drew a long breath in through her nose. "I'm sorry—I'm just picturing them seeing you take stray caterpillars from the kitchen garden out to the fields, before your cooks could squish them."

Kyr's mouth turned wry. "I appreciate you not bringing that up while they were still considering eating us." The press of his lips lingered, and he let his arm slip from her shoulders. "We need to find that place to hide." He turned his gaze down another narrow hall leading off at an angle. "This looks promising."

They found a small unclaimed space—likely left empty because of the copious luminescence that dripped from stalactites to leave slippery pools over the uneven floor. Alesta pulled the pelt from her head and ruffled at her hair.

Kyr slung off the pack from the crook of his arm, away from the worst of the glowing puddles. "You should probably take out your braid."

If this mangled plait could even be called that. She dragged her fingers through what little remained braided, knelt beside the pack, and began uncinching its ribbons. She piled the rocks Kyr had collected to one side, laid the folded crossbow and the quiver of splintering arrows beside them and the pelt, and stuffed everything else back into the hidden pockets.

"I can carry the crossbow," Kyr offered.

"And hide it where?" Her gaze traveled pointedly up from his bare feet to his threadbare breeches stretched over his thighs to his bare chest. She swallowed and stood, pulling the fabric up over her hips. "I can wear my skirts again." She paused, tying the ribbons at her waist. "If they'll fit in all right among the monsters?"

Kyr nodded, eyes on her hips. "We can add some strips of hide—everything they wear is made of other monsters. Skins. Bones and teeth for buttons." His hand flexed at his side. Always so fastidious. "You might want to wear just your bodice?"

Leather would fit in all right with monster skins. Alesta began tugging at the laces.

Kyr turned on his heel. "I'll find the rest of what we need," he said, making for the passageway again.

She pulled the bodice off—careful to balance the folded *Codex* page atop the crossbow—and her soiled blouse, crusted with sweat and blood and spatters of luminescence.

She ran her fingertips over the little bite marks trailing across her belly. The kharis balm had at least mostly healed them, leaving silvery traces like those she already bore there, and over the sides of her hips and breasts.

Like the webs of monstrousness peeking out from her wrist

guards. Kyr was right; it would be possible for her to hide them or explain them away on Soladisa. She wondered how many farmers and fishermen over the years might have hidden something like this, if they'd shirked getting absolved after killing a sea monster, not wanting others to see how Hektorus blighted them for their sin. Kyr didn't have that option. He couldn't return to the villa and its gardens and pretend nothing had changed.

What he could do was take the credit for killing Teras. She grabbed her bodice and pulled it back over her head. She was resolutely not thinking about what was going to happen to her when she killed the greatest monster in this place. A few zigzagging scars would be nothing in comparison, she was sure. So the glory could go to Kyr, as he had once taken the blame for her. It wasn't a perfect solution; Alesta knew too well how their home treated creatures it saw as ugly, knew from her own experience others might not see all the goodness in him. She pulled her laces tight again. But at the very least they'd have to accept him back into the safety of Soladisa.

She frowned at the parchment she tucked carefully back between bodice and breastband. She didn't know how to reconcile the Arbor's teachings that had been drummed into her all her life with what she knew of Kyr. She'd resented the alberos but only really ever questioned how to make them accept her, how to earn her safety. And Kyr's loss prompted her to take their tenets more to heart, drove them deep into her spirit like garden stakes into the earth.

The unfairness of what had happened to Kyr, though—being selected for tithing, being turned monstrous for surviving it—

Those jagged scars down her arms shivered with blue fire.

Her anger, churning up doubt, left her more scared than when those monsters had caught her and Kyr. Maybe it was better she wouldn't have to ponder such philosophical questions once she was a giant devil hidden away at the bottom of hell.

Her fingers trembled where they tied her laces into a knot.

She distracted herself, checking over the crossbow and splintering arrows, strapping them to one thigh, and looping the retractable rope to her belt. And planning for how to actually get Kyr off this island. They couldn't count on another ship necessarily. Anyway, she couldn't tell Kyr yet about what Mico had tried to promise, or he might haul her back up to the surface to throw her aboard, and she had to kill Teras first. This was truly ridiculous. She chewed her lip and dreamed bigger. Maybe she could build Kyr a way to fly home. Maybe her work mastering flight would save him in the end, as it had once damned him.

If only she had more than monster pelts and rocks.

She put on a brave face when Kyr returned with more supplies, although none of them would help much with crafting him a way home. Grudgingly, she focused on preparing to reach Teras, kneeling across from where Kyr laid out piles of sloughed-off scales, shards of rock, hides, and claws. He set about grinding up the latter with another rock, and began by painting her face with the crushed pale powder. She closed her eyes as he skimmed his fingers over the planes and curves of her face, never nicking her with his claws. The darker rocks he used to lay a shimmering gray-green over the tan skin of her arms. He held it out for her to draw over her neck and down to her bodice, then scooped up some of the nearest luminescence and worked it together with a silvery dark blood he scraped off one hide.

They stood so he could more easily press thumbprints of the mixture over her skin and dot a scale or chip of iridescent rock to each, up and down her arms, over her shoulders and back. She drew her hair out of the way, from one side to another, as he attentively worked across her shoulder blades, fingertips light, under the glow of stalactites like lanterns.

Alesta shivered as he reached the space just under one ear. Where before his mouth had swept over her skin. "Ticklish," she said with a little shrug.

"No, you're not." She wasn't. She'd never been. But he simply held out handfuls of the paste and spangles so she could apply them herself, across her collarbones.

They tried wrapping the remaining hides around her skirts, but they kept dragging one another down.

"Where's Rina when we need her?" Alesta grumbled the third time her costume hit the ground. "I should have let her teach me a thing or two when I had the chance. All those times she fussed over me or tried to fix my hair."

Kyr sliced one pelt into thinner strips. "She your new best friend?"

Alesta tugged a skin around her hips and fumbled at tying it snug. Remembering how she hadn't allowed herself to become friends with Rina at all. "Why, you haven't made a better one here, have you?"

He cocked a brow, eyes on his work. "Not a *lot* of candidates." He handed her the strips, and she settled for tucking them each into her waistband, hanging all around like ribbons, while he gathered up some more of the paste. "Though I did spend one cozy stretch hiding deeper in a cave where a hydra decided to camp out."

She looked up from her skirts. "*Eight* friends!"

He twisted back from a pool of luminescence to raise his palms as if in praise to Hektorus, his face an exaggerated mask of enthusiasm. "My mother would be ecstatic."

He hadn't asked about her. He didn't now, as he mixed together more shimmering paste. Alesta blurted, "She misses you." She owed that much to the woman she'd seen every week for a year only through the black veil she always wore.

"I'm sure she does." His hands stilled, though he kept his gaze cast down. "How is she?"

"In mourning. Never happy to see me at chapel. Feeling vindicated in her poor opinion of me, I'm sure." His mother had rightly blamed her for Kyr's death, even if she thought Alesta had only encouraged his work into dangerous directions, had been part of that side of Kyr that wasn't a perfect courtier and heir. "My getting tithed probably cheered her up."

Kyr rubbed his hands together swiftly. "I wonder how good old Octavio is doing. Maybe we can pop in on him on our way to the revels." He beckoned Alesta to lean nearer. "Almost done."

He daubed the mixture along her hairline, down her temples, and over her brows, and covered half her chalky face with the last of the scales. Then he pulled a golden thread from the remaining hem of one leg of his breeches and shredded it into shorter glinting strands. "Your eyes will be a giveaway," he said, meticulously pressing it to her lashes. "This will hide them some. Try not to look anyone dead on." His own eyes were stony, his slight pupils swelling black against silver.

Finally, he brushed her hair from where she'd swept it over one shoulder and painted streaks of luminescence through it. She let her new lashes fall closed as his arms went around her and his fingers skimmed up her scalp and down her curls, chased by tingles over her skin. When he was finished, she held her arms out, watching the light trickling from the ceiling break and scatter over the scales. "How do I look?"

He stepped back, scraping one hand over the other. His brow rippled and he sighed. "Like a nightmare."

"Good." She was ready at last to descend to the lowest level of hell and take the final steps to Teras.

Chapter Twenty

DANCE WITH THE DEVIL

Alesta was surrounded by monsters.

Strange music bled from the next chamber, cut into by the snappish conversation of the devils all around. Observing them only from her downcast gaze and in her peripheral vision, Alesta felt as if trapped in a nightmare, the kind where you sensed a devil creeping up on you but never springing, until the dread brewed thick enough to drown and you woke gasping.

She ordered her imagination out of her way but wasn't positive her impressions of the monsters weren't still distorted. Their movements seemed as unnatural as those of courtiers—with greater contrast of languid and sharp, all sinuous with startling jerks. Some devils still scurried on four legs in the shadows, ready meals to be grabbed and gobbled up by the larger ones—creatures made all of golden planes and folds, shimmering green limbs, veined stony faces, horns carving the dark, or scarlet skin fringed with a thousand wisps feeling out into the gloom. All dressed in oddly draping scarves or hides secured with polished bone.

Kyr had thrown a furred hide across one shoulder, and plenty of the monsters clutched each other possessively, so he and Alesta blended in well enough as he guided her through the masses, one arm wrapped around her painted shoulders. Alesta allowed herself to lean into it, to soak up the comfort of Kyr warm and solid beside her. She might have only an hour left to trespass upon his kindness. She had not known when she set out on this errand it would mean becoming what she'd hated all her life. She'd avoided for so long being used as a sacrifice, and grabbed the chance Mico offered as a way to control her circumscribed fate. At least she was choosing how she lost herself to Teras, this way. And putting an end to it all.

They'd wound about the base of Orroccio—the final stratum—through towering halls, then passed through several successively grander ballrooms where they skirted the monsters throwing themselves into the revelries, dancing or eating or other carousing leading them off into the shadows. The air was pungent with a rancid perfume, trailing from certain devils, blossoming through the space like rot as they moved to speak to each other, or lift goblets of hollow horn and sip whatever dark liquid stained their eager lips and keen teeth, or drape their bizarre forms across geodes broken open into glittering thrones. Tall slabs of rock like tables were strewn with shards of gemstones and laid out with confections that Alesta, as she and Kyr squeezed past, saw were, in fact, eyeballs. Their slitted pupils watched her as Kyr led her toward the other end of the room, past more couples twining and lurching, locked in their frenzied dance.

Upon the walls, elongated, horned skulls grinned from a mosaic of bones—sunbursts of femurs, undulating waves of ribs, fine details made of clawed finger bones. As Alesta stared, something trailed against her shoulder. Twisting, glistening viscera hung like streamers. She startled at its damp touch, eyes darting to a nearby monster as tall as Kyr, who wore—*by the boughs*—a human skull like a mask. Remembering Kyr's warning, she dragged her gaze from what could only have been a previous tithing's eye sockets, but now she saw others—all formidable, resplendent monsters, surrounded and fawned over, each proudly wearing fragments of someone's face over their own like a prize. Reminding Alesta that every single devil in this place would readily devour her.

They were left alone so far—even in this crowd, Kyr was among the more imposing. Others shifted out of their way as he pulled Alesta into an antechamber of sparkling, pale stone, where monsters lined up gossiping and adjusting their grisly finery. He tightened his hold on her, crushing her to his side with the vise of his arm, and bent near to trace his nose over her hairline. Alesta suppressed a shiver as he breathed, "Should be all right, my scent's covering you. Here we go." He swept them past the waiting monsters, through the tunnel of jagged diamond, as if they were falling through a shattered mirror.

Alesta snapped her gaze to Kyr as the monsters they passed flashed vexed looks at them. "Won't this cause trouble?"

He only marched them on, posture stretched tall, horns tilted back. "You have to act like you own the place. Like you belong. Learned *that* trick at the Towers."

And no one stepped forward to challenge them. They reached the front, where two guards with bone spears blocked the passageway, just as a monster crusted over in iridescent gems plucked one free from his forearm. He added it to a pile of monster parts upon another tall block of stone—wicked dark thorns, shimmering bronze fingernails, molted skins, and sharp triangular teeth as long and wide as one of Alesta's thumbs.

The monsters Kyr had cut directly in front of began muttering as the guards let the jeweled devil pass through. The bone-spears crossed again with a clatter. "Main ballroom's for those from the city only."

"I've come to request an audience with Teras." Kyr's voice was slathered with the expectation of compliance.

One of the monsters behind them, with shifting skin like liquid gold, gave a mocking laugh. "Waste of time. Teras does nothing but wallow in the lava."

The taller guard wrinkled his leathery green nose at Kyr. "And why would Teras see you, of all . . . *people?*" He waved a clawed hand, his too-long neck swiveling, already looking past to the next in line.

Kyr ignored the insult, like it wasn't even worth his notice. "I've earned the right."

The monster at their backs huffed. "The escaped tithing. Knew I smelled human somewhere. *Such* a waste. Teras squats upon all that power, only to let an offering slip away."

Another behind him apparently agreed, sneering, "Interlopers. Humans and their gods."

More discontented mutterings brewed down the line, as the first monster ranted, "They made us godless children, and still we are subjected to them. I can't wait to eat this tithing's heart."

Alesta huddled against Kyr, who pressed her closer. The chips of rock and scales along her arms bit into her skin like her anxiety. The underlings back in the emptied city were one thing, but surely pushing their way in here wouldn't get anyone to allow them near Teras.

"How much longer must we wait?" someone called to the guards. Clawed feet shuffled forward. The golden monster gave Kyr a shove.

Plainly hoping to clear the disturbance before it grew, the shorter guard told Kyr, "An offering is still required to enter, for a chance at the tithing."

"Something properly monstrous," the other added. "Nothing of yours with the touch of human at its root."

Jeers rose from the crowd. "Wait," the nearest monster snapped, amidst the din, "that human scent, it's not him, it's—"

Kyr turned away, and Alesta wondered for a moment if they were retreating—until he let go of her to snatch up the monster menacing behind them. He gripped its head between his claws and with one twist snapped the creature's neck.

"Will this do?" Kyr dropped the monster into the arms of the scrambling guards. One's tongue flicked out at the blood running from the slackening mouth over golden skin. The other snarled a smile up at Kyr.

"Enjoy the revels," he said with a nod, and then they were moving through the passageway as Alesta's pulse spiked wildly.

"I can't believe they let us pass," she breathed.

Kyr's shoulder sheltering over her made a stiff shrug—he was clinging to her more tightly than ever. "Strength is everything here," he said roughly. Sharp facets of crystal winked at them among all the milky stone. "It's why Teras rules, if you can call the anarchy here that, despite no one seeming to like it much. And our god defeated theirs in the old war, so they assert their strength by killing and eating humans."

"Terrified, chained children. Very fierce." It seemed that in every corner of the world, those who had been trod upon, who had lost those most important to them, were left cornered and lashing out, fighting for scraps of dignity. Wasn't that how Alesta had arrived here herself?

Where did it end?

She could only hope it would be with her driving her poisoned arrow into Teras' flesh.

The rock gave way to the vastest ballroom yet, so large that, for a moment, Alesta imagined they'd emerged outside under the night sky, and Kyr murmured in her ear, "There's the doorway."

Across the space as wide as several crops' worth of fields, a stone archway cut through the black stone. And through it, something seething, writhing, dark and bright.

Monsters wheeled around the room, its floor expansive enough that multiple groups of musicians spread among them played the same eerie waltz, layering over each other like moths' wings. The alberos had always said Orroccio had no forms of art, and yet here were ornamented caves and a hellsong brushing against Alesta's ears.

"We only have to dance our way across," Kyr went on, "then appeal for an audience with Teras."

"Across that." Alesta's voice came out level as she fought down the bubble of hysterical laughter rising up in her. She failed, and it burst from her, shrill as the peculiar music fluting through the sultry air.

Kyr rounded on her, shoulders hunched, as if he could hide her from the hundreds of devils at hand.

She clamped her lips together and drew a long breath in through her nose. "I don't know how to dance like this." For all her teasing, she was the one at a loss. Never in her planning with Mico had they imagined anything but fighting through Orroccio's hordes, never disguise and dancing. It was too much, as the threshold to her target, to her transformation, lay visible just beyond.

Monsters nearby began hissing about the great killer of the upper levels. Staring at Kyr. He was drawing all their attention—for now. They couldn't linger. They needed to move.

Kyr slid one hand behind Alesta's back, as the other found her trembling hand and clasped it hard. "We'll make do." He pulled her into a whirling step. "Together. Just hold on."

She shuffled her boots after the patterns of his steps, keeping her eyes turned away from the monsters spinning frenetically around them—like gears, and she was careful never to let her gaze slot into any of theirs. A couple reeled near—had that monster just *sniffed* her? Ragged lace upon another's sleeve brushed Alesta's cheek like cobwebs. She shuddered away before its claws could test her false scales. Devils and demons revolved too close, like the insidious coil of a snake. The obsidian walls, full black and mirrored, reflected their forms and faces, multiplying and blurring the monstrousness.

"You don't have to be afraid." Kyr stared down at her, unreadable emotion pulling along his cheekbones—concern or resolve or sorrow.

She lifted her brows, stiff with paint and scales. "Words I'd never expect to hear in Orroccio. Least of all from you, after all your growling about the dangers."

Laughter and music reverberated through the cavern's airy reaches, where tiny creatures flew aglow, and streams of lava draped down the walls, festooned themselves along narrow ledges, and sputtered over little cliffs to light the air like sparks.

Kyr twisted his lips together. "I ought to have warned you away sooner. Properly. But it's true, there was no safe place for you to wait it out." His hand tightened at her waist.

She let him draw her along in his orbit. "What do you mean?"

Kyr didn't answer, focused on guiding them around a clump of other couples. He was working them through the revelers, threading them across to her waiting fate. Finally he murmured, eyes still on the crowd, "I always wished I could bring you to a ball, at the Towers."

With the lava coursing over stone and lights of the monsters drifting through the air, Alesta couldn't tell if she was falling or floating. She anchored her gaze again to Kyr. Her best friend. That swooping feeling in her belly was from the lavafalls and luminescence confusing her balance. It was definitely not from how she was still wholly, hopelessly in love with the boy before her—further beyond her reach than ever before, beloved golden son of Soladisa and someday king. Because of how she'd failed him. Because of what she was. Because of what she now had to do.

"This is a sorry substitute," Kyr said, focused on their joined hands, voice wearing thin as whatever bone-reed trilled nearby. But Alesta was happy to pretend, if for only a moment, that they were safe in each other's arms, that they could go on dancing like this forever, among the shifting constellations of monsters and flowing rock. That here, they might be enough for each other, just as they were. Kyr looked, almost reluctantly, to Alesta. "I can't help being glad, though, before—"

Before broke the spell. Before she destroyed herself. Before she left him again to his unjust punishment. Once again failing.

Once again all her efforts not good enough. She tore her eyes from his. In the wheel and romp and dancing, they caught on a figure less monstrous than the others. "Kyr, look!" She pointed with her chin to a girl dressed in mismatched and ragged frills—Soladisan clothes—that only half-covered a patchwork of creamy and vermilion skin, scales like rubies spreading along her temples to milky pale eyes, gleamings from lava threading up and down her chestnut hair. "Another who's survived, like you—" Maybe Alesta would not be leaving Kyr all alone here. Maybe he and this girl could find a way home, once Teras was gone.

Kyr followed her gaze, then gripped her hard. "That's not a human." He steered them away just as the girl raised one sculpted brow. "That's a monster who has eaten a great many humans."

"What?"

He drew her closer, so she could see only where his jaw tensed. "Humans are prized food for a reason," he pushed out between his teeth. "If monsters kill and consume them, it makes them stronger, somehow, and they can claim their humanity, just as monstrousness spreads to humans who kill them."

So Kyr could remake himself as human if he wanted. The possibility cracked open like a dropped egg. He could have killed Alesta to win back some of what she'd lost him. "This means there is a way to return—"

"That's no path home." She could almost feel the dark rumble of his voice in her own chest.

It wasn't. How many lives would it take to restore him? As many as the monsters he'd killed? More questions poured through her mind. How could the alberos explain this? Was this why the monsters seemed more human down here, where Teras had gifted them humans for centuries? What did it mean that someone might kill and kill and be made less monstrous? And yet grow stronger and stronger? Alesta's head spun as much as the dancers. None of this fit with anything she'd been taught.

"There is no way home for me," Kyr said. He took a long breath, letting her spool away a little on their next turn, the whisper of his claws across her back. The great archway loomed nearer. He pitched his voice low. "Give me the crossbow."

The floor seemed to drop away. But even unmoored among the cascading fire and all the monsters, Alesta's resolve steadied. "No."

"This won't be like killing the others. It will corrupt whoever—"

She gritted her teeth. "I know."

"We can't risk what we may become."

She squinted up at him, sharply.

Maybe it was the lavalight, or maybe a flush actually warmed in his pale cheeks. "We know the others lost themselves when they became too monstrous," he said. "They've attacked Soladisans when they finally reached home. Like the one that killed Ciro. We can't know what horrors something that powerful might wreak upon the entire kingdom." He dropped his voice even more, to a resolute mutter. "So I'll kill Teras."

She hissed, "And then yourself?"

He pressed his lips together with a huff. Like he hated how she always pounced on what he wasn't saying. But he didn't argue. "Before I can change into anything worse."

She straightened against his palm at her back. "Well, I'm not giving you the bow."

"Alesta."

"I'm not letting you do this. You could make it home—" Her

face heated. This was a foolish place to have this argument, but she was just as foolish in the hope she tried to cobble together for him. "Mico's going to try to send a final ship."

"He's——?" Kyr's brow furrowed. "*Alesta.*"

She didn't relent. "And if they know you helped rid them of Teras, they'll have to welcome you."

He cast her a skeptical look. "Because they're so good at seeing past surfaces there."

The words bubbled up from deep within her, like the lava all around. "You think *I* don't know that?" Her gut twisted. "But at least you'd be *safe.*"

If anything his expression turned more bleak. "I'm not risking that. Just as you shouldn't risk shooting Teras."

"I've trained with the bow. I invented it. You're a painter."

"I know this place, these monsters," he countered. "I've survived. Which is exactly why I don't deserve the chance to go home."

"*You* don't? I'm the one that deserves to stay here. You were only trying to protect me."

"Exactly!" The word pierced her heart as if he'd speared a claw through her chest. Kyr callously reminding her again of her unworthiness made her want to fling herself before Teras simply to end the pain. "Please let me finally do something to protect the kingdom. Let me purge my sin instead of being trapped here forever facing it."

"And you want me to go on, knowing I'm the reason you had to? When you were trying to help me? Kyr, it's torture knowing this was all my fault, no matter how the alberos or kharis say what you did was somehow a sin——"

"It was!" he burst out. "It was lust." His hand holding hers clenched hard enough to quake. The other flexed against her back. "I protected you because I——" He drew a ragged breath. "It was selfish. I couldn't lose you."

Alesta couldn't feel her feet, though she knew they must still be moving, that the chamber still spun around them. She was aware only of Kyr's eyes, burnished in molten light, edged with anguish and want.

He swallowed. "I can't." He was looking at her as if she held his salvation on her lips. "Please, Alesta."

This must be like what great natural philosophers felt making a vital discovery—all she thought she knew metamorphosing, the world she thought she understood falling apart and remaking itself at once. The answer working itself into everything, revealing where it had always lived.

She could not deny him. She also couldn't agree, *yes, go ahead and die for me, again.* Reeling from his confession, caught between two instincts, she was left with the compulsion to say nothing at all, the desire to simply rise up on her toes and press silent lips to his.

The floor throbbed with the footfalls of a thousand dancers. Lava skimmed over dark mirrors.

Before she dared to act on the urge, the music shifted.

With the faster tune, the surrounding monsters whirled apart, grabbing for new partners. One reached between Alesta and Kyr.

Alesta stumbled back in surprise. The monster took hold of Kyr, and another pulled her into the dance, stepping and spinning and passing her to a new partner, and another, and back again to Kyr, reaching for her hand like a lifeline.

He leaned close. "If it hadn't been you, if that flier had never crashed, I would have let some other youth go, as I did all those other times. That's why this must fall to me now."

The dance broke them apart, wheeling them away to three new partners. Alesta couldn't think what to argue, before they returned to each other's arms. What refusal he might accept. Two thoughts thrummed through her like a heartbeat: Kyr wanted her. Kyr wanted to die for her.

Well, she didn't need words. She had a crossbow.

She was simply going to have to beat him to Teras. Taunting her with this answered wish and forcing her to leave Kyr like this might be hell's last, best torment, but protecting him was more important than any goodbye.

Before Alesta could slip through the rotating couples toward the archway, a pale hand with copper claws wrapped around her wrist.

The monster girl. She arched a brow and flashed a grin like a small, sharp blade. "Hello, human."

Chapter Twenty-One

BLACK HORIZON

The monster wove her fingers through Alesta's, wound her arm around her waist, and pulled her into the dance. "You're bigger than most."

Through her flare of panic, Alesta felt a familiar white-hot pinch. Typical that in the lowest depths of hell, before facing and probably becoming an actual behemoth, she'd still be enduring comments about her body.

First, she had to convince the monster she'd made a mistake. Heart pounding, Alesta lowered her fringed lashes. "I'm not—"

The girl cut her off with her laughter, a wild vibrato. "*And* you're funny." She forced Alesta's arm down to her side, head tilting, gaze traveling down the paint and scales. "With such a darling costume." She ducked her head fast, prying off a spangle with a flick of her teeth. Alesta gasped as the girl unleashed another shriek of laughter.

The dancers turned to new partners, but the girl kept ahold of Alesta and dragged her back through them with startling strength. Alesta couldn't break away. Didn't want to call attention from all the other monsters. Tried to hide her eyes still, even as she sought out Kyr.

"I've made a study of humans," the monster girl told her, pausing for a moment as a wall of dancers blocked their retreat. A tangle of necklaces swung from her long, alabaster neck. "I'm sort of a collector." Her arm clenched around Alesta, hard enough to pin her in place while she let go of her hand to trace a copper-tipped finger along Alesta's jaw. "I even took one's name." Her claw's point pressed deeper, nudging Alesta to meet the monster's gaze. "So, you can call me Phoebe." Her pale eyes gleamed, their pupils sharp. Her nail dragged down Alesta's neck. "But my favorite, of course, is your hearts." Her finger drew a ring below Alesta's collarbone. "I've collected several of those." The circle tightened. The claw pierced deeper. A drop of blood bloomed, a match for Phoebe's skin and scales. "Right into myself."

Alesta's blood lashed in her ears. She ran through her options. Trapped by a hungry monster at the bottom of hell. Surrounded by hundreds more. Thousands of claws and teeth. The crossbow at her thigh she needed for Teras. She had knives at her wrists and belt—

Phoebe grabbed her again by the shoulder. "Let's go where I won't have to share you," she said with a scrunch of her nose, as if divulging a secret.

Alesta rooted her feet to the ground. Phoebe's fingers dug into her arm. No. She needed to reach Teras to save the kingdom, to save Kyr. She was willing to become a monster to do it.

So be a monster.

With that thought, the lightning she'd taken from the spider monster ripped through her. It sizzled over her disguised skin and burned on into Phoebe.

The girl shrieked now in agony. Whatever sort of monster she'd started as didn't share the same protection Kyr and the spider did. Or she'd eaten too many Soladisans to keep it. Her clawed hands fell away from Alesta just as the blazing pain overwhelmed her too.

Kyr caught her before she hit the ground, one arm behind her back. Blackness hedged in her vision. It threatened to swallow her down. Kyr looked so worried. His eyes flashed between her face and at something else, outside the dark collapsing rim of her sight. He hauled her upright. *"Run."*

Somehow, she did, legs thrashing, pumping, as Kyr towed her forward, through monsters turning—no longer dancing but staring. Pointing. Tilting heads. Baring teeth.

One lunged for her. Kyr knocked him back and barreled on. Another snapped her furred snout before him—Kyr swiped her away, but another was upon them, and another. Surrounding them.

Kyr clutched Alesta from behind, forearm wrapped across where Phoebe had cut her, hand clamped to her shoulder. He spun them around, slashing long claws at their attackers.

Alesta recovered enough to pull one of the hilts at her belt, from under skirts and hide. Kyr fought off a beast with flame erupting from its snarling mouth, and Alesta stabbed as her blade extended, in one motion, driving back the others.

Fire streamed toward them. Kyr ducked his head and slashed. His horns sent blood glittering through the air. The beast slumped back, throat spurting. Kyr kicked out at another devil and, half-carrying Alesta, leaped over it as it fell. They sprinted together for Teras' chamber, chased by monsters whipped to a frenzy. And by a word, shouted, passed on from fanged mouths and muzzles, growing into a strident siren—*human.*

Ahead, a wall of scales and fire writhed. Alesta concentrated on dodging surprised monsters and fighting off any that dove into their path, thanking Hektorus for all those hours Mico forced them to train, all the times Lor made her run through their sparring again. Kyr flung others to one side.

The doorway rose up before them, a line of more guards before it. She needed to ready the crossbow. She couldn't spare even a breath to do so. She looked over a shoulder to where a tide of monsters threatened to crash upon her and Kyr.

If she fell now, before reaching Teras, she'd be damning Mico and Lor and Vittore and his wife and daughters and Rina and Kyr's mother and every single person she knew. She dropped her sword and ran harder. If she could at least make it that far, at least count as this season's tithing—

All her desperate thoughts evaporated as they reached the doorway and the scarlet mass that was Teras blossomed to heights beyond comprehension. Wolf and leopard and lion curled against its radiant flesh like kittens. A sea of lava spread behind the devil's haunches, deep and shadowed and blazing, stretching to a distant black horizon. But near, the molten rock brewed brighter than Hektorus' blessed sun, shining through a tracery of crust at an infernal angle, painting the cavern walls in a wicked brilliance. Flowing all the way from the dread heart clenched deep in the earth, as far from true holy sky and air and light as possible. Lashing Teras to its power.

The devil squatted in the shallows, that power seeming to glare from within, muscles heaped and twisting over its towering form, spikes branching from its forearms, long fanged snout whiffing toward the commotion. The teeth that had threatened Alesta in her vision dazzled dangerously before her now.

The line of guards stood tensed before Teras, spears ready.

"I'm the tithing!" Alesta screamed. "Let me pass, I'm the tithing!"

But it didn't matter. The rush of monsters crashed against the waiting guards and Alesta and Kyr were caught in the melee. The great wolf leaped forward—to snatch a monster to one side of Kyr in its teeth. It worried the smaller creature back and forth before tossing it into the pit of lava.

Alesta and Kyr fought forward, broke from the crush, and crossed under the archway. The other two beasts sprang at once for them. Alesta hiked her skirt and reached for the bow. Kyr hurled himself in front of her.

Even with all his height, all his strength, he was not enough in the face of this. And she was too slow. Beasts before them. The mob behind. Murderous intention, closing in on them like all these monstrous jaws. Sharp as the teeth and claws it drove at them.

Teras shifted. Stone rumbled. Lava overspilled its trench, rushing toward them. Great clawed hands reached out.

Kyr's skin spiked. Teras swept him up, massive fingers crushing his scales. Alesta threw herself after him. Teras' other hand caught her mid-leap.

Air fled her lungs, like she'd been punched in the gut. The cavern floor fell away fast. Alesta's head felt too light. Black stars prickled across her vision.

Even worse, Teras' hold on her loosened.

"Alesta!" Kyr's cry chased her—the last thing she would hear, she was certain, before Teras dropped her into the lake of fire or the waiting horde of beasts or its own colossal maw.

When the devil dumped her out, instead, on a ledge of basalt, running under the high entrance to the Umbilicus, she was relieved for a whole breath—before the monster's long claws speared toward her.

They drove straight through her hides and skirts. Teras slashed.

Alesta's pulse and thoughts galloped wildly. This wasn't right; Kyr had said Teras only gave the tithings to the others—but Alesta had defied the devil. Disappeared from her chains. Invoked this punishment of Teras eviscerating her like she had done to the branzonos—

Teras didn't, though.

Instead, as Alesta gaped, it pincered the Lia pendant from Alesta's sliced-open pocket. *This* was what it was after? Lia was an affront to the devil, perhaps, or Teras had learned from Kyr's tithing not to let sacrifices bear any as protection. Snatching up the splinter, it brought its enormous snout near. The Lia vanished upon the devil's palm in a faint curl of smoke.

Teras roared.

Alesta thought her hair might actually catch fire in the beast's harsh breath. Her ears rang as Teras, still clutching Kyr in its other hand, tore away a ribbon of hide, and another, flinging them into the molten lake. It jabbed again at Alesta. The balm, crushed open between Teras' fingers, evaporated, and the seeds crackled and were incinerated. Teras poked and plucked, stripping Alesta piece by piece of kharis and costume. Burning away the scraps of holiness she'd carried here.

The devil displayed no satisfaction. Instead, Teras seemed to grow more furious, more frenzied, with each piece of kharis it destroyed. Alesta coughed in the haze of Lia smoke and tugged her ragged skirts over the bow and arrows and rope. She couldn't let Teras take them.

Kyr yelled for her and twisted within Teras' grip. The three beasts prowled below, fur bristling over their shoulders, teeth snapping, paws tracking, spines sinuous. As if writing some kind of deadly runes over the stone to ward off the mass of monsters pressing into the chamber. Some kind of monstrous language the devil might speak—and Teras did speak now, its voice like the churning of lava and the grinding of rocks, resounding painfully inside Alesta's head. Kyr crashed his one free hand to an ear, and the agonized look he'd been giving Alesta collapsed into a tight grimace.

Alesta tried to get to her feet, to give herself a chance to take the shot, but the devil's voice shook her so tremendously she thought she might fall over the side of the cliff. Scattered chips of stone bit at her shins and palms when she fell to her knees. Teras' speech surged around her as if she was inside one of the Towers' great bells—but it was discordant with anger and fractured by madness. Fragmented as the obsidian shards that skittered over the ledge. Alesta couldn't piece together what it was saying. What she did make out made no sense, as unclear as the choking fog of kharis smoke lingering.

Something about singing. Walking over green hills, under golden leaves. Something about a god noticing Teras.

But the devil had spawned right here. Teras had never walked where things grew, never trespassed itself upon Soladisa or any other god-blessed isle, only with its cursed breath and the smaller demons it unleashed on them. It had to be a trick, the devil enticing her with lies.

Or else there was more to the monster than what everyone saw, what every book said.

She'd studied Teras devoutly, and now Alesta's curiosity burned in her. Some part of her had been chasing her way here, for days, for a year, to look the devil in the face. To look her own failings in the face. To punish them both for their sins. Now thoughts of keeping to her proper place, to the path set by the Arbor and Mico and her own fear, crumbled away. She knew she should finish her mission, but she had to see how this all fit together, needed *to know*—

Alesta stretched toward the cloud of kharis and breathed in deeply, welcoming the vision that blossomed through her mind.

The pain and heat and noise fell away, muffled as if Alesta had plunged underwater.

Then Alesta Saw.

A handsome young woman, dark curls tangling across her terrified face. "Hurry," the girl pleaded. Teras' harsh voice seemed to echo distantly around her and the grove she stood in, its hulking form to shadow over her. The wind kicked up, setting the trees shuddering, and the whites of her eyes grew wide. "He's coming."

She grabbed Alesta's hand and pulled her through the trees.

"Who?" Alesta cried. Teras? Branches snapped under her feet. Leaves whipped across her face. Or what monster was after them?

The girl raced on. "Great Mother Cressa preserve me—" The rest of the girl's prayer was stolen by the raging wind. It howled somewhere high and far too close, crashed through the branches, tore at the girl's loose homespun dress. Alesta, determined to glean whatever the kharis wanted her to know, could only follow as the unseen horror, something burning at the edge of her vision, harried them.

"He's coming!" The girl's voice broke into a frightened scream as the wind wound about them like a lasso, and blasted wide, sending every tree around them falling to the ground.

The girl froze in the center of the trunks spread out like a nimbus. Her dread was a palpable thing Alesta could feel in her teeth. It strangled the girl's next words down to a rasp. "He's here."

The wind rushed in. A divinely furious blaze descended upon them, air igniting into fire—into a god.

A god Alesta had seen a thousand times, had stared at in chapel and the Arbor's central courtyard and Kyr's paintings. The god she'd prayed to, raged against, traveled through hell for.

Hektorus was golden-haired and muscular, all burnished as if by a light within. His tan skin and draping robes and sandaled feet, not quite touching the soil churned loose by uprooted trees, all seemed on the verge of erupting back out into ferocious blazing. He ignored Alesta, casting his gaze, burning with condemnation, at the trembling girl.

She screamed again and the vision fractured. Confused fragments flew through Alesta's mind—

The hazy shadow of Teras around the girl deepening into vivid red as it fell over her. As if consuming her.

That scream cutting across miles and miles, the god's furious will bearing the girl away to a world of eternal shade and flame.

Soft human skin erupting into scales.

The kharis smoke lifted, and the cliff's edge back in Orroccio's deepest pit seemed to tilt, searing into Alesta's cleared vision as she stared.

Teras had been a girl.

On Soladisa, once, forever ago. Before Hektorus threw her into this place, rooted her to the well of evil that transformed her into this, left her to burn and burn for centuries upon centuries.

Alesta stood, unsteady. A headache like death pulsed in her temples. "You—you were human." She shouted, as much to clear the cloying smoke and the reverberating voice and the confusion of its story from her pounding head as anything, "Then why throw away the tithings you demand?" Hundreds and hundreds of Soladisan lives could surely have turned even this abomination back to what it—she—had been.

The monstrous voice refused to be banished, words crashing like incessant waves. *It would never be enough. He tied me to the source. It flows into me forever. It would take something far greater to ever burn me free.*

"Then *why*—?"

Kyr howled at the same time. "Why the tithings?" He thrashed his hand.

Teras swung Kyr before her, angled her snout down at him, and roared.

I want what's mine. The devil thundered. *Stolen from me! Given to the island.* Smoke seethed from Teras' nostrils. *Mine! They refused. So I took what I could. Tokens to appease the monsters here, offerings to purchase their shoddy loyalty. I took and took and took. Allowed myself to be bought off. Stealing something precious. From those who had taken what was most precious to me.*

Kyr slumped in Teras' grip, clamping his palm again to his head.

"What?!" Alesta cried out. She should have drawn the crossbow, but couldn't think beyond pulling Teras' attention from Kyr. "What do you want?" And she did want to know—wanted to learn how to staunch the raw wound of this girl that threatened like a chasm of pain that would swallow everything up.

That this girl had been falling through for centuries. "A new bargain, then! Let me help you. Tell me what you need."

Teras opened and clenched her empty hand. Her claws scraping over her scaled palms were like swords singing on shields. *Lia.*

"You want us to bring you more?" They could do that. They could absolutely do that. She could fix this. Pull the lever and protect the kingdom. Teras would have to let her and Kyr go—Alesta glanced up the Umbilicus—in order to fetch what she wanted.

The tree.

The bubble of hope within Alesta's chest burst. "The—"

Lia is mine.

Her hope turned to acid. Her own voice hurt nearly as much as Teras' as she choked out, "The entire tree?"

Out of the earth. By the tithing date. Or Soladisa burns.

"No!" Kyr braced his free hand against Teras' claw, bearing himself up. "Don't make another deal with her. The tithing is bad enough."

The Lia tree. All of Soladisa's magic came from it, all of Soladisa's bounty.

"She's lying!" Kyr called.

Teras shook him. *I do not play tricks with my bargains, like some do.* Her claws wrapped around Alesta again, drawing her up until her toes barely touched the ledge. *Or I could take this season's offering now.*

The threat pressed into Alesta's head. Teras' fingers pressed into her flesh. Her chest. Her limbs. There was no escape. Like all the weight of all the levels of this maze was finally crushing her.

"No! I'll pay the tithing!" Kyr pleaded. "Let me pay it."

No. Not again.

They don't want what you are.

Kyr stilled as if he'd been struck.

Pain pays for pain. She was unhinged. And what girl wouldn't be, trapped in hell for an age, burdened with all its monstrosity? Alesta felt ready to rip her own skin inside out to escape the awful, unrelenting press of heat and muscle. The shame that coated the slivers of breath she stole down.

Black smoke huffed and curled from the devil's nostrils. Her gaze cut back to Kyr. *My beasties expect their gift.* The impatient crowd bellowed. *Won't be pleased. But I will hold them off, I will end the tithings, for my Lia.*

Kyr's voice was frantic. "How are we to even get out of here, get home, get a *tree*—?"

Up to you. Teras squeezed. Tighter.

Alesta rasped a silent, airless scream.

Lia. Or her life.

Kyr lifted his head, strands of lank hair like claw marks across his anguished face. "No. Please. *Alesta*—" His voice was longing raked with despair. His hand groped in her direction.

Teras' great head listed. Something zealous flashed through her vast eyes tracking from Kyr to Alesta. Something as trapped there as Teras in this pit. Something of despair and longing—and understanding. *No greater pain than to lose the girl you love.* Her grasp loosened, and she withdrew her hand from around Alesta, whose blood sang with the blessed release.

Teras let go of Kyr as well.

But he'd still been suspended over the full height of the cavern floor.

Teras batted him toward Alesta—not far enough. His clawed

toes merely scrabbled at the cliff's edge. His arms flailed, carving nothing but air. Alesta, struggling to pull breath back down into her lungs, lurched for him.

Her hand caught his. Kyr's wide eyes met hers. For a heartbeat, she did not know if they would tip to the safety of the ledge or a final, fast descent.

At least they'd fall together.

She strained and towed him back. Kyr staggered forward, running his hands up both her arms. His gaze was still locked on her face. His dark lips moved, but her ears rang with echoes of Teras' voice. Her offered deal. Kyr trying to trade his life for hers again.

And the shouting of hundreds of devils calling for Alesta's blood. Teras turned away to lean on one angled forearm and cast her fiery glare at the beasts. *Not yours yet.*

Alesta drank in a deep, scalding breath. Shouldering past Kyr, she pulled the loaded crossbow from her thigh. She dropped the stirrup to the ground, and with a stomp and a pull cocked it.

Teras swung back their way. *Can't deny them forever. Choose.*

Alesta lifted her weapon. "I have."

Beside her, Kyr grabbed for the crossbow. Alesta struggled to keep the arrow trained on her target. Kyr pulled harder. *No.* His finger warred with hers for the trigger. The bow veered into his possession.

Chapter Twenty-Two

WHAT DEVILS FEAR

She'd told him he could save her life. He was damn well trying. But even attempting to prevent her destruction, to ensure he was the one who would have to die before turning into an atrocity, Kyrian couldn't bring himself to be reckless with his claws this close to her.

Alesta wrestled the crossbow back.

Before he could stop her—beg—howl—she took the shot.

The arrow flew across the cavern. Kyrian's heart plummeted. She *missed*. It soared high, trailing the rope like a spider's filament above Teras' head, and lodged into the wall of the Umbilicus. The shaft splintered into vicious hooks, metal clutching to the rock.

Alesta shouted to the devil, "I accept." Her face turned to Kyrian, blazing. "Together. Just hold on."

On purpose. She'd missed on purpose. Aimed to let them both escape. This was all wrong, but in the face of her courage and resolve he could only throw his arms around her. She jabbed at her belt, and the rope pulled them after the arrow, into the heights of the pyroduct.

🦢 246 🦢

His claws fissured into the stone. Alesta released the rope, and he hauled them up, handhold by handhold, to where the tunnel angled enough to rest upon.

They collapsed into the gentler slope, warm air streaming over them. Kyrian fought the urge to shake Alesta. Or clasp her nearer for one last moment. "What did you do?"

She blinked. "I designed the arrows to work as grappling hooks to help me climb through Orroccio."

"Not *that*."

"I—I don't know." She ran her fingertips over his temple and down his cheek. "Found another solution."

She thought she could fix everything. He loved that about her. Except right now, when too much was falling apart at once and she would be left buried. "Only you could come all this way and try to *negotiate* with the *devil*." He grabbed the bow. "Give me another arrow. I'm finishing this."

Her voice became the kick of a stubborn mule. "You're not."

"We can't leave Teras to threaten everyone." He stood. He needed to go back. He needed to protect Alesta once and for all. He needed that arrow. But he couldn't *reach up her skirts for it.*

"I wasn't going to let her feed me to that horde, and I wasn't going to leave you alone here, or let you die—" Alesta stumbled to her feet. "Or shoot her. She's a Soladisan, in torment. The sea, all that poison, the tithings, the devil fever. Every way she's lashed out. It's all her hurting. All her pain." She shoved back her curls. "I don't know if it's right to deny the kingdom the Lia tree, its holiness and all it does, but if it really was Teras' and means you can actually go home, that no one has to come here ever again—?"

He drew upright. "Who's to say Teras doesn't mean to use

the Lia to do something even worse? Or free herself or——?" He whipped his hand as if he could throttle the air. "You can't trust that devil."

"That girl." Alesta's gaze seared into him. "Just like you or me. Punished by our god."

"For a reason!"

"Forced here and changed. We don't know——" Alesta's brows angled down together sharply. Her eyes darted from side to side. "Teras is supposed to be the curse made by the monsters' god, but she can't be. If the devil isn't what it seems, then what else have we been wrong about?"

Her glistening paint and scales had almost all been sweated off or lost. Not everyone could wipe them away so easily.

"A monster is still a monster." The edges of his words burned his throat.

"Kyr." Her face crumpled with sympathy.

Oh, gods, he'd told her how he felt. Out loud. And now she would wince and apologize and make clear how appalling she found it. Why couldn't she just let him die for her? Maybe there was still time to go back and throw himself into the lake of fire. "It's not worth the risk," he said.

She reached again for him. He held utterly still as she bracketed his face with her hands. "You are worth saving."

He couldn't bear her pity, couldn't stand to hear she would protect him only out of her misplaced guilt. She hadn't made him this. "I am a devil."

"You are not. You're Kyr——"

"He's gone, or should be."

"You did what you had to. You became what devils fear.

A legend in hell." She steered his face back to her when he tried to turn away. "That doesn't prove you're wicked. That means they could not smother the good in you. They could not douse your light. Look—" She stroked a hand down, running his hair between her fingers. His locks turned from pure shadow to something brighter at the bleached ends, harboring a faint glow in the red illumination feeding from Teras' lair, like metal in the forge fire. "You're right here. The same boy from home. Its sunlight still lives in you."

He swiped his hand between them. His claws cut away the ends of his hair and untethered him from Alesta. He didn't even know who that boy had been. If he'd ever possessed any goodness, or just the commands of the Arbor. "Sunlight *burns* me. What do you want me to do, return to Soladisa to be hated and hide away forever in dark rooms?" Acid drenched his words as his shoulders hunched. "You think my mother will welcome me back with open arms? When she could barely tolerate me as I was before?"

His traitor voice broke. His chest shuddered. Home was an illusion. It was Alesta who had made it anything like paradise to him. It was Alesta's imminent rejection he dreaded most. He hadn't expected to live long enough, after releasing his foolhardy words down on that dance floor, to have to endure waiting for her to tell him they were unwanted. He was unwanted.

Would the other possibility—shimmering, unthinkable, a mirage on the horizon—be any better, when he still had no option but to turn back and slay Teras? Or watch Alesta leave him behind on this rock?

His gaze traced the chiaroscuro of her, bright against the darkening tunnel. The striking lines of her face and solace in her softness. Every heart-twisting curve. All the abundance of her sparking keen want in him. What had she said? They were already in hell. Might as well sin.

The bow hung heavy from one hand. He ached for her to touch him again. It would kill him just as much as to hear no, with his end dark and near, yet his heart lurched after the one answer it truly hungered for.

Want me. Ruin me.

He couldn't read what waited in the still pools of her eyes staring back. Echoes sounded down the tunnel, and they both flinched.

Teras' sway over Orroccio's monsters seemed tenuous, and with another tithing lost, who was to say the beasts wouldn't breach her lair and follow them somehow? He told Alesta, "You have to get clear of here."

Her slack mouth tensed. "*We* do."

They didn't have time to argue. He scratched the scales along his forearm, turning his face back the way they'd come. "When I take down Teras, that will hopefully create enough chaos for you to slip away and wait for Mico—"

"Stop it, Kyr."

"Just give me the arrow and go."

"I already said I acce—"

He rounded on her. "Until the monsters chase you back! *That's* what you said! A thousand times." His voice scraped the bottom of his well of hurt and longing, betraying too much. "I sent for you." Alesta only gaped, and his next words came as a growl. "You didn't come then, but they're chasing you now. *I* am trying to chase you home."

"And I am not leaving without you!"

He opened his mouth again to argue that they had no more time to argue, but she waved her hands in that way of hers, when she was trying to draw the words out of herself.

"No one told me. And Nonnina fell so ill that week. I didn't know until after you were already gone."

Why did that knock the air from his lungs like when Teras had struck him? Why did any of it matter when they had no time and there was nothing to redeem, only evil to extinguish? "We still can't put our faith in a monster."

"I don't——" Her mouth twisted. "I was all mixed up, every-thing was floating and—and swooping." She blinked. "Maybe I'm wrong. I don't know what I believe. Or that I'm not damned and making a wicked choice." She scowled up at Kyrian. "But my faith in *you* is rock solid. And I'm not going without you."

"You need to. Trying to save myself only turned me into this—this horror." Clinging to a daydream of anything better, like she was with this new deal, would surely end as badly. Even as the idea of freeing Soladisa of the tithings tugged at him like a riptide. "You don't have to try just because you feel guilty."

Something ignited in her eyes, fervent and wild. "I feel a lot of things, but guilt is the last of them right now." Alesta thudded a fist into the smeared paint above her bodice. "I would let you eat the heart out of my chest to see you home safe. It's already yours."

Her words struck him like the arrow had finally found a worthy target in his own monstrous heart. "You——?" His breath choked off. Blood roared in his ears, louder than Teras.

Joy—unfamiliar, electric—jolted through him, and he reached for her hand. But the sight of his own—inhuman, clawed, a thing made to slash apart, not hold together—made him clench it back.

His elation collapsed. It was worse than he'd anticipated. Her feelings for him would doom her. He felt himself falling into the same misstep—leaving the kingdom at risk to ensure she lived. He was as damned as ever, irredeemably monstrous. But he couldn't be the reason she died here. Couldn't let his darkness extinguish her light. He'd have to see her to the surface. Only that far, though.

His grotesque fingers loosened on the bow. His chest felt as hollow as this tunnel. "I can't go home."

She set off up the Umbilicus. "We can argue about that later."

"There's not even a way off Orroccio. Nothing ever leaves." Not without turning itself into a sea monster.

"We'll figure it out." Over her shoulder, her lips pulled into a wry grin. "You think I can't find a way?"

Of course she could. She was Alesta. She was brilliant, and resourceful, and fierce.

He had been bent into being so many different things. He wasn't sure any longer what he might once have been meant to be. He only knew that he was the one who loved her.

He would follow her even to the sky that hated him, to the world that burned.

The Devil's Umbilicus cut a clean path through hell, delivering them quickly near the surface, where a cool draft warred with the uprushing heat of lava, but the journey was somehow so much worse than their descent. Ambition had always burned strong in Alesta, but for a full year, her one goal had been to reach Orroccio and destroy both Teras and herself. Now, hope for something more slipped under her skin like shards of broken glass. Glistening. Painful.

It didn't help that Kyr was upset and agitated the whole way, constantly looking over his shoulder when Teras set the island rumbling with her own moodiness and increasing impatience, worried something chased them even here—or probably still pondering whether to race back and try to finish her off. Repeating that they couldn't trust her not to have some dark plan for the Lia. While he grudgingly helped Alesta up a steep stretch of the tunnel, where it reared to finally reveal the night sky, he fumed, "First you insisted on going down there and killing Teras. Now you insist on believing her?"

"She agreed to the deal." The davinas' writings all told how demons always stuck to their bargains just as gods did. The alberos had used it to shame children during chapel, that if they broke faith with someone, they were worse than even devils. For some reason Teras believed the Lia belonged to her. Maybe being tied to the wellspring of monstrousness had driven her mad, and she thought the tree could still make her human again. "Fulfilling it will result in the end of the tithings. That's all that matters."

"If it were that simple, the kingdom would have handed over the tree from the start." Even as he said it, uncertainty creased Kyr's features. He scowled and clawed at the wall as they climbed.

This was what Alesta feared, having to speak up and be at odds with everyone, again. Putting herself out of harmony with Soladisans who had no reason to doubt the truth of what they knew of Teras, the necessity of the tithings.

She dragged her feet up the slope and pushed her hands over her hair. Guilt was so much easier. Responsibility carried such a weight of uncertainty. Who was she to question the Arbor or the king? Hektorus' divine fury from her vision blazed in her memory.

Maybe she was making yet another mistake. Maybe it *was* wrong to take the tree from the kingdom. Would Hektorus be glad his favored people were no longer beset by the devil—no longer paying the tribute Mico always said tarnished their devotion to the god—or affronted they'd sacrificed his gift to them? And they'd be giving up so many boons that made their home a paradise. Medicine. Fuel. Temperate weather. What if they freed Soladisa of the tithings only to doom everyone to widespread sickness and blighted crops and shivering winters? What if Alesta was bringing calamity to the entire kingdom like she once had to Kyr?

Turning back for home, up this winding, wide tunnel, she'd felt more lost than ever before, uncertain if all her studies with Mico and all the teachings of the Arbor that she'd lashed herself to like a ship steering through her year of grief were wrong. But something was rumbling up from deep within her, too—a belief maybe not quite in herself, but in what she'd recognized in Teras's eyes, beneath their fevered gleam. In the vision she'd claimed from the kharis. No malice lay there. Only anguish for what she'd lost, all too familiar. Maybe it wasn't the same despair and longing as Alesta had felt, for losing what she loved, for losing herself, to grief or the judgment of others. For clawing for whatever she could. But she knew the truth of that pain. Maybe it actually ended here, with this new bargain instead of vengeance.

They finally reached the lip where the tunnel met the surface, and Kyr pulled her against one side. She wondered if the starlight was making him wince, or only her plan. "They're never going to agree to this. Enzo, the alberos. They won't listen to what Teras wants." He rested one hand against the wall, under a tracery of luminescence. "They shouldn't."

They'd probably try to send her straight back to the tithing rock and watch safely from the ship to make sure she didn't slip her chains this time. And that wasn't good enough. Not anymore. Hope bred new fear, like the glowing lava at the bottom of hell spawned devils. She couldn't fail at this, couldn't bow to the Arbor, couldn't resign herself to racing back here without the Lia, to merely stave off Teras' wrath another season with her life.

There was too much she wanted for that life. She was worth saving too.

Right now, she couldn't even rush out into all that fresh air, under all those stars. Dark shadows of the flying monsters, out night hunting, cut across them. Ideas for how to reach that future she wanted darted as quickly through her mind, but she was exhausted and hungry and anxious. Trying to form words just for Kyr felt like hauling heavy rocks. The idea of making those at home listen—of making her voice as forceful as Teras'—of having to argue that her choice was right—made her want to hide in these caves forever.

But at least she wouldn't have to speak up alone. "Mico," she said. Kyr blinked, and she rushed on. "He can help. He's committed to freeing everyone from the threat of Teras. He's cultivated relationships among the davinas, the guilds, the university masters. He's all but named heir and has good standing with everybody. Everyone adores him."

If anything, Kyr's troubled look deepened, the golden sheen his cheekbones had taken on a few hours after he'd killed to buy her safe passage stark against his worry. But Alesta knew she could convince him. He always came around to her ideas eventually. "Mico can whip up pressure to accept the deal. And Rina's father should be back—the Arbor may not be happy, but so long as the king orders it, he can pilot a cargo ship with the tree in time." She didn't care if it was a half-thought-out, reckless course of action. All her careful plans blew up in her face anyway. Together they'd figure it out. She drew a deep breath. "We can do this."

The frown on Kyr's face eased. One side of his mouth lifted gently. "How did you carry hope all the way through this place?"

The last of that breath erupted from her in a snort. "It wasn't hope that drove me here." She stared out at the soaring beasts as she recalled all the times she'd shrugged off Rina's invitations, all of Vittore's offers to share a meal those last weeks after Nonnina's passing. Because she thought she needed only one thing. Only deserved one thing. Like Kyr nearly insisting on turning back and destroying himself.

For long months of grief, she'd gone as cold and still and hard as one of Mico's tools pulled from the forge, dying back into black. Now hell of all places was bringing her alive again, stirring her awake, setting her aglow with ardent feeling. She was done wallowing in guilt and anger like Teras in that lava. She had a choice.

She leveled her gaze at Kyr. "You were dead, and now you're not. You should hate me, but you don't. You make me hope."

Kyr's eyes were silvery in the luminescence, and at her words, emotion shimmered over them like moonlight over a wave. He breathed, "I wanted to hope." His dark lips twisted. "It was only, when you didn't come that day on the dock, I thought maybe I was the only one who hadn't understood that we weren't even—" His hand flexed against the stone. "I could never tell, with others. Everyone always wanted something."

Her hushed voice brushed its echo along the dark basalt. "I did want something."

His brow flicked up, quick as a prey animal's heartbeat. Firmly, she claimed his hand with hers. She wanted so much. For the kingdom. For Kyr. But also for herself. Maybe she didn't need to feel shame for that anymore.

Maybe she should remember Nonnina's words and not wait for a *later* she might not see. Take whatever sweetness she could.

The look Kyr gave her now was more than moonlight brushing along water. It was sunlight breaking through clouds. Lava cracking open rock. Incandescent. Experimentally, she swept her thumb over his wrist.

Something jutted from his hand. She tugged it nearer the trails of light. "What's this—?"

He jerked back, hiding his hand with the other, but a milky blister covered his last knuckle there, too. "You shouldn't—"

"Are you hurt?"

He shook his head, nostrils flared. "It's just—new."

She froze. Because he'd had to kill again. A kind of monster he'd killed plenty of before, if it had resulted in this noticeable a change now. She squinted at the pale bump. "I wonder what its function is . . ." She tilted her head to get a better view.

"It's poison," he sighed. Her gaze lifted, questioning. "They have these all over their hands, those ones that were among the mob down there. My first time fighting my way up, one landed a solid punch before I—before it died. My face swelled up twice its size."

"Venom, then," Alesta corrected absentmindedly, tracing a finger just above his skin. "Poison is a passive defense."

"Tell that to Ciro."

True enough. He'd been found on the beach, already dead, but the signs of branzono poisoning were clear. She wrinkled her nose.

"There's a stinger, here. Probably activates like your scales, when you're threatened." She straightened up, realizing she'd gotten distracted. She wanted to take his hand again, but Kyr was still clutching both away from her, so she knocked a fist gently into his shoulder, beneath the spikes. "Still hoarding all the most fascinating bits of monstrousness for yourself."

He gave her a *that isn't funny* look. "I thought it was going to *stay like that.* I didn't know it wasn't just another—like everything else." He fumbled his hands together. "Like this."

"Right. Well." She'd botched that about as well as she could have. And the friendship she'd only just repaired with Kyr, the something else between them she wanted—wanted more than that sky opening up above them—was not something she could stand to make a mistake with. *Be logical*, she told herself. Plenty of things changed all the time into something just as good—or better. Sand to glass. Caterpillars to butterflies. Like the swarm she was feeling in her stomach right now. "Clearly we need to get out of here before this place bestows any more gifts on you. We can scavenge what we need and make it home with enough time to travel back before the full moon."

"Alesta." He looked as if he were weighing whether to say whatever he was thinking. Probably that she was too awkward for words, and he was going to head back down to Teras just to get away from her. "I still think—since there's no way, for me at least—"

The stone around them shuddered.

Kyr braced his hand to the basalt again, shielding her from the grit that fell. A fissure snaked up the opposite wall. Outside the tunnel, clouds of ash spilled across the stars.

Teras.

The rumbling stopped as quickly as it had started. Kyr's expression turned from doubtful to grim. "It'll take more than hope to get you off this rock," he said.

"I know." She was doing it again. Her mind caught up in its thoughts so much she'd thought she'd said it already. "I'm going to build us wings."

Chapter Twenty-Three
STOLEN WINGS

The sky was a dark bruise when Alesta said it was clear of the flying beasts. They'd only have a short spell between their nesting and the sun rising to scavenge what she needed and make it back to the smaller caved-in entrance. To find someplace she could work and where Kyrian wouldn't start burning under Hektorus' righteous sunlight.

"You only need wings enough for yourself," he told her as she picked through dried-out carcasses, squinting in the gloom. The home they were desperately trying to save offered no refuge for him. There was no place both he and Alesta belonged. "Anything else is wasting time you might need to get the Lia tree back here."

She frowned over one dead monster with a wing shredded by claws or weather. "I've studied aerial mechanics nearly a year. I can replicate a design quickly. Plus, two sets will increase the chance at least one of us makes it back. That's safer for Soladisa." When they'd ventured out under the sky, Alesta's sloped shoulders had eased in a way Kyrian hadn't seen the entire time below, but now as she examined another corpse, she tensed. "And I really do need your help explaining everything and convincing them all."

Fine. He would say it. He'd been cast out of Hektorus' favor, whether he clawed his way off Orroccio or not. "I can't withstand more than an hour or two out here, under full sunlight." His scales were already itching in the nearing dawn. And no one would listen to him in this state anyway. Gods, Alesta couldn't even hold his hand, after the last killing he'd done. He'd known in that moment he needed to convince her to go without him.

She began fanning the wings of the next monster open. "We'll travel at night."

"What if it takes longer? Alesta, I can't *see*."

"Plenty of extra hides. These can stand the sun. I'll make you coverings." She bent the wing's joint back and forth experimentally. "And I'll use the Lia rope to guide you home."

It already felt as if a cord connected them, fate tying them together. But what if that only meant he would drag her down with him? "I'm not one of your sheep, I—"

"Even my sheep were never as stubborn as a royal heir," she muttered. She stood, the salt wind whipping her tangled hair across her cheeks. "My lord Kyrian, I will drag you from hell whether you like it or not. No more arguments," she ground between her teeth, "unless they're regarding whether we should utilize the heat venting from the Umbilicus to achieve lift or climb one of those obsidian towers to launch." All the severity and intensity she would direct at such a problem or apparatus she was puzzling over turned on him as she watched for any dissent.

Her keen gaze seemed to slice him open, and the words spilled out on a sigh. "Gods, you're brilliant. You're beautiful."

She released an exasperated snort, tossing her head in disgust.

"You only think I'm beautiful because you're surrounded by monsters." She scuffed a toe dismissively into the carcass at her feet.

"No." Beauty wasn't courtly features, the proportions taught by the art masters at the Towers. It wasn't surfaces, but what suffused them. The memory they stirred. All the fires of hell were nothing to the way the thought of her burned in him, a sun never lost to him, a bright star guiding him through a year's dark night. He closed the distance between them, to the edge of the spread wings. "I think you're beautiful because I'm surrounded by monsters and you came for me."

She fought to keep her mouth twisted in that disapproving scowl, but she was losing. He caught the flush of her cheeks before she bent over another carcass. "This specimen's still too fresh. Did you know these creatures have two stomachs?" He tried not to listen too carefully while she speculated about monsters' digestive systems, until she'd chosen which for him to carry inside.

Ashen clouds had hidden the rising sun, but as they made for the tunnel mouth, spears of its light broke through. Orroccio's black rock bleached away. He could barely see Alesta well enough to follow her to the entrance, down into the relief of shadows, furiously glad she couldn't see how his face twisted into an ugly grimace. Trying not to look at his own horned shadow the sun cast back into hell.

They found a cavern to stop in, not far above the territory he'd carved out for himself. A little light bled through the folds of stone to mix with plentiful luminescence chasing drips of water down the walls for Alesta to work by. Water plinked as she got settled, and he hung back near the cave entrance, watching as she drew a large knife from her belt and sawed the wings free.

Feeling just as torn up inside his own monstrous body.

She may have silenced the argument about his returning, but it warred on within him. He desperately wanted to help the kingdom. Maybe that didn't have to mean sacrificing himself to this place again. Maybe the real penance was in returning. Helping Alesta. Working with Mico. Seeing this final deal done and Soladisa made safe.

And living out a hell there of his own making.

He was fooling himself. It was too late for him to help anyone. He'd never inspire anything there but fear and disgust.

Alesta switched to a smaller knife to punch holes in the wings' hide, and Kyrian began pacing from one shadowy offshoot of the cavern to another, chasing away anything that might be nosing about as well as any thoughts of his beyond the present task.

The hours were marked only by the increasingly agitated rumblings of Teras and Alesta's progress. Unwinding a spool of thin wire from her pack. Bending it on the edge of her blade. Weaving it along the bones of the scavenged wings. Kyrian had always loved to watch her work. She was always so enthusiastic and curious, and her nose scrunched in this particular way when she was about to realize something. Like an adorable alarm before she began shouting. He'd always hoped, even if it was more likely to lead her off the island than to any position at the Towers, that her ambitions would succeed.

Now everything depended on it.

The ghost of sunlight had retreated the second day when she called him over to fit one set of nearly finished wings to him. Only an emerald glow brushed over her soft cheeks and coiled through the tresses she'd woven back into a coarse braid, as he forced himself to fold his arms and tell her, "Make yours first."

She waved the end of the Lia rope at him. "I can't construct it on myself, so help me out."

He suspected she was merely crafting a way to manipulate him into joining her return home, but he came and stood before her.

"I know not to let Lia interact with the hides this time," she said. "Not that Teras left me any of the more volatile forms." She wound the rope around his shoulders and chest, into a harness, and jerked her head at the wall where she'd been scratching out designs and equations with a chalky piece of stone. "I've done about a hundred calculations figuring the ideal center of gravity, but working with what we've got, we're aiming for good enough." She measured out another length of rope and exhaled thinly. "To not fall out of the sky. Which is agonizing to me."

"Can't imagine I'd find it pleasant plummeting into the poison sea, either."

"Not that." She tugged on the rope, a playful glower on her face, and for a brief moment he considered letting her pull him over. But no. Feelings were one thing. The one thing sustaining him when he considered what would be waiting for him on the far shore. Which was why he shouldn't go. There could be nothing more to this.

Alesta wove the rope from strap to strap, across his chest. "Not following the formula exactly," she explained. "Makes me itchy." She smoothed out her efforts, and he knew he could only be imagining that her hand lingered on his shoulder. "Do you think—" She glanced at where her work spread all over the floor nearest the wall's faint glow—wings and wire, the crossbow she'd considered scavenging for parts before declaring it useless, its quiver, odd knives and ribbons she'd pulled from the pack. "These wings are going to help save Soladisa. Albero Paolo would call them merely wicked. Nothing to the divine." Her hand rested now on the harness she'd fashioned, her nail dragging back and forth over the silken Lia. One of the last slivers of sacredness they yet held here. "Right and wrong. Sin or virtue. Monstrous and holy." Alesta let her fingers stray from the rope, skimming over his rough skin. Chasing his breath straight out of his chest. "We know now they destroy each other. What if somehow they're as connected as two islands, buried under all that poison?"

Yes. If Kyrian could find his voice, he would explain how she proved her theory with her touch, like heaven and fire at once.

The cavern rumbled. Teras' impatience shuddered through Orroccio like thunder.

Alesta's face contorted with empathy. Her grip anchored on the harness. "How could anyone deserve this? How could Hektorus make her a monster and leave us to face her?" She let go to shove her hands over her hair, making a wreath of worry before shaking them out in frustration. "And how am I supposed to account for the dynamic arcs of these wings when I don't have anything to help modulate between lift and gliding?"

Shit. Heat crept over his face. She wasn't a guiding star; she felt just as lost after wandering in this maze, the darkness eating away at all her certainty. He thought of all the times, back at home, when she'd confidently declared herself bound for the university. How fast that assurance had crumbled when her flier crashed. All the times she'd laughed at the idea of feeling more than friendship for him.

How much of the strength he admired in her was pure bluster, because no one else was going to make things any easier for her?

He wanted to hold her. He *couldn't*. Instead, he reminded her, "He left the tree as well. A living offshoot of his power." She dragged her lip through her teeth. He ducked his head to meet her eye. "Hey. Even if you can't do this——" Her face blanched with panic. "It's all right. We'll figure something else out." He had no idea what, but this was important she knew, that she didn't owe the world her success just to deserve the right to live in it. She wasn't a place at university or slaying Teras or even her remarkable inventions. "You are more than what you make. You are enough yourself."

She blinked at him. Her arms stilled and her lips pursed, maybe as if she were about to say something? The black of her pupils was blown, and she swayed forward a little before drawing a long breath. "The tree. Right. We have everything we need."

He nodded, knowing how tenaciously her focus stuck to a problem. "All you have to do is get it here."

She seemed to notice her arms lifted before her and stared a moment. Kyrian thought she might be worried about going home with the hint of monstrous skin there, but then a *V* etched itself over her nose and excitement kindled in her eyes. "The springs in my wrist guards! They'd work for the power mechanism if I rotate the pull crank." She grabbed him by the shoulders, hard, and shoved away, grinning.

Between Alesta running back over to her work, pulling wires from her wristbands and shouting about improved efficiency, and Teras' stony grumbling, he missed the other footfalls until they were already breaking from the shadows.

Several monsters. The flat-snouted band of them he'd rescued Alesta from. Running in from the tunnel behind him.

The cavern was too broad to block them all. Alesta had needed the room to work. So Kyrian launched himself at her, shoving her back toward the wall, half-carrying her when her feet stumbled. Rushing her to a position he could protect.

But there was no safe place in Orroccio, least of all in his arms.

Before he could turn on the chalky things and drive them away like he had a dozen times before, one was on him. It slammed into his back, driving him against Alesta, knocking his forearm into the stone. The beast jammed its claws under Kyrian's ribs, where his patchwork monstrousness left him vulnerable.

A sharp flare of pain. Alesta's eyes, wide and worried.

He'd tried to tell her. He was displaying a weakness now.

Her.

His scales reacted faster than he could. They slashed out—into Alesta. She gave a little gasp, in this place not made for anything so soft. Then her scream shattered everything.

A constellation of pain blazed across her front. So bright in the shadows.

Like Kyr's eyes, near and gleaming with anguish.

He threw himself backward, with enough force to knock two of the monsters to the ground. More were upon him at once.

The pain choked off her scream when Kyr's scales ripped away. Alesta slid down against the wall—until two of the beasts grabbed her. Her hands sparked faint traces of lightning and her cuts protested as they dragged her away. Only to the tunnel entrance, where something waited.

A red stain on the gloom. Blossoming. Like the blood Alesta could feel seeping across her front, dripping down her arm.

Phoebe's smile sliced through the shadows. "*There* you are." Her scales pricked the darkness. Her mismatched skirts brushed over the floor.

Her clawed hand wrapped around the hilt of Alesta's dropped blade, lost back outside Teras' lair.

It was retracted, but Phoebe kept her distance. She wouldn't come close enough for Alesta to shock her again. And these monsters holding her seemed as unaffected by her lightning as Kyr had been. "Hold her tight," Phoebe told them. Alesta tamped down the fire sizzling under her skin. She already wasn't sure she could have remained upright without their punishing grip about her shoulders. Calling up the full shock might not hurt the monsters but would definitely knock her out.

Across the cavern, the others fought Kyr. He rammed one monster into the wall, then barreled into another, knocking its head against the ground. Kyr had barely gotten to one knee when he caught sight of Alesta.

"Stop!" Phoebe ordered. She lifted the blade to point at Alesta's neck.

"No——" Kyr clapped a palm to the ground and began staggering up.

"Don't," Phoebe warned. "Or I'll see how powerful my new toy is." She flashed a grin at Alesta. "I was so excited to add it to my collection. Now——" Her voice sharpened as she turned back to Kyr, who had pulled into a ready crouch. "Where was the button to make the pointy bit spring out? Do you think it would go straight through her throat?"

Kyr dropped back to his knees. His muscles slackened and his chest heaved under the tangled rope, but his voice had a hard edge of menace. "Don't touch her."

Phoebe widened her pale eyes. "Oh, I won't. Not until she's dead." She scowled at Alesta. "I learned that the hard way." She bunched her shoulders, suddenly almost giddy. "That's what you humans say, isn't it?"

Alesta didn't answer. Her cuts throbbed. The monsters' iron hold had her arms going numb. And a fierce itch had set in where the damn page from the *Codex* had slipped from between the fabric of her breastband and bodice.

Phoebe's tongue flicked over her lip. "She's still mostly human. I couldn't let her go. I'll eat her heart once she's dead."

Alesta let her head fall so she could see the beast holding her on one side. Her voice scratched in her throat. "Don't you have anything to say about that? Don't you think you deserve my heart?" If she could get them fighting over her again—

"Oh no," Phoebe said, shaking her head. "We have a deal. I claim the human, in exchange for helping my new friends kill him"—she jerked her head at Kyr—"and get their territory back." She patted the cheek of the monster between her and Alesta. "They simply needed some better leadership. Someone to explain how he won't put up a fight, as long as we have you." Phoebe cocked her head, gaze traveling between Alesta and Kyr. "Anyone could see that, at the revels. Humans are so fascinating together." She wrinkled her nose at Kyr. "Even if you're not much of one anymore."

Kyr clutched a hand to his side. His old stammer broke through. "I will. I will kill you. If you hurt her."

"It looks like you've already done that yourself." Phoebe's trill of a laugh echoed through the cavern, as all but the one fallen monster and those holding Alesta surrounded a wincing Kyr. "Besides. You'll be dead first."

"Wait—" Alesta's hands prickled with fire.

Kyr's gaze cut to her. "I'm sorry." He wasn't only saying sorry— he was saying goodbye. There was no fighting their way out of this, not when he refused to sacrifice her first, not when her death meant he couldn't reach Soladisa to save it anyway.

One of the circle swept his claws fast, catching Kyr across the cheek.

Alesta scrabbled her feet uselessly as Kyr's scales flared again. "Get away from him." Laughter from the beasts now, and *how dare they?* Her vision pulsed, echoing the repeating thought in her head. *Mine. Mine. Mine.* Kyr—falling over as another monster landed a kick to his gut—he was *hers.* She'd walked through hell and back to claim him. She'd made a deal with Teras. This little devil and these brutes were nothing in comparison. Easier to manipulate than the weapon Phoebe was holding wrong.

As long as Alesta didn't pass out from blood loss first.

"You want more human things?" she asked Phoebe. Her voice wavered and she schooled it to sound enticing, not desperate. "Do you have any books?" Alesta didn't need to see Phoebe's brow furrow with neat little lines to know she didn't. Tithings were sent with fine clothes and precious jewelry, like the pendants hanging around the monster's neck. And books wouldn't last long among hellfire. "Humans love books. They love reading them."

Phoebe's tongue ran over her lips again. "What's reading?"

"I have a piece of one," Alesta told her, pointing with her chin to where the page peeked out. "Here in my bodice. It's yours if you let him go."

The monsters' hands tightened on her. They didn't like this idea.

Neither did Kyr. He barely moved from where he'd hunched over one forearm, but Alesta saw his claws scrape the stone floor as his hands clenched. *Don't get upset*, Alesta wanted to tell him. *Get ready.*

"We have a deal," one monster barked, as they all shuffled away from Kyr to loom over Phoebe.

The monster girl sucked her teeth. "We do. And anything on the human is mine anyway. I don't need to make another." She leaned closer, blade still aimed at Alesta's throat, reaching with her empty hand. Her lip curled with faint disappointment. "You're not as clever as most humans, are you?" Her bronze claws extended, carefully pincering the folded page from Alesta's bosom without touching her skin.

Alesta squeezed her eyes closed.

This was going to hurt.

Chapter Twenty-Four

UNDER A MONSTROUS SKY

A monster's touch might have been enough. But Alesta had to be sure. Before Phoebe plucked the *Codex* page away, Alesta let the stinging in her arms blaze into lightning.

Kharis and monster skin. Holy and infernal. Connected, perhaps—but mutually destructive, certainly.

Especially when you set them both on fire.

The Lia parchment ignited. Phoebe startled back, orange flames between her claws. The other monsters still held tight—until the holy smoke blooming from the vanishing page set everyone coughing. Phoebe fumbled with the blade's handle, finger failing to engage the button she was meant to have turned to her thumb, mouth twisted in fury and pain. Alesta tried to run forward, to Kyr, but the lightning left her limbs heavy and fumbling.

Then a vision powered by the potent Lia overtook everything.

Alesta fell, but never hit stone. She fell across stars, constellations bursting open like fireworks at a festival, like sharp white monster's teeth yawning wide and swallowing her whole. She fell through air, stroking over her skin, cradling her limbs, rushing like water past her cheeks, drawing infinite tears from her eyes. She fell into waves, sweeping currents, depths within depths, where secrets no one even knew to look for sheltered in an abyss beyond the reach of light or breath.

Alesta's chest ached for them. It ached for air. Her lungs collapsed under the weight of water, the force of augury. Her eyes burned, seeing nothing but black.

She was lost.

Her mind reached for Rina, thinking she would be able to make better sense of what the Lia showed her, with all her study and attendance at the Sight-summonings. That she ought to be the one having these visions. Alesta wanted Rina to take this one, or at least take her hand. To guide her through this dark place.

As Alesta had never allowed her to for all those dark months.

Then in her vision, Rina appeared, guiding another girl. She was racing down a hall at the Towers, Lor in tow. "But what can it *mean?*"

Lor's long legs easily matched Rina's steps. "Obviously Teras is angry."

"We must speak with Mico. What could have happened to—" Rina broke off as they rounded into Mico's chambers. Her mother, Davina Bianca, stood beside him.

"Mother!" Rina dropped Lor's hand. "We were—we were worried—" Her hands fluttered before brushing at her voluminous lavender skirts. She shrugged and said simply, "The sky."

"I was just inquiring of the davina if this has ever happened before," Mico said smoothly.

"And has it?" Lor asked. "The western horizon is all dark with some unnatural storm."

Davina Bianca addressed her answer to only Mico and Rina. "In the first days of the kingdom and tithings, it is written that ash blocked out the sun. The Arbor's records show it occurred once again, years later, when a tithing ship was delayed by a storm out of the north. But every time the offering was accepted, and the devil settled again." She came and stood before her daughter. "Just as it will be well this time. The Lia will protect us. The tithing has been sent—"

"But—"

Bianca swept back Rina's loose curls, hanging from under a wreath of braids, and gave her shoulders a squeeze. "You needn't worry. Only about betrothal season, which will be here before you know it."

Lor shifted her weight to one side, arms wrapped around the bodice of her simple frock. "What of the reports from the farmers?"

Mico began saying something about branzonos, as Bianca turned to listen, but Rina, and Alesta's Sight with her, drifted nearer the open window.

Her face lit blue with a flash of lightning. A real storm was passing over Soladisa. Rina blinked, and ran out onto the balcony, until she braced her hands upon the balustrade. As if listening for something through the roar of the wind. As if searching for something.

Bianca shouted for Rina to come back inside, and Lor strode out after her. But for a moment, Alesta could have sworn Rina—dark eyes startled wide, before a sky full of lightning—looked down at her, still lost in the black void.

Alesta wanted to cry out, to tell Rina to have them send the Lia, but there was only the crash of thunder—and then, in her vision, another girl, willowy, wheat-haired, with a haunted stare that seemed to fall like an axe between Alesta and Rina.

She beckoned, and Alesta could only follow as she led her out of the darkness, as she walked over the green, rolling hills of Soladisa on a sunny day, feet skimming above the ground like Hektorus. A goddess. Graziela's guide.

Alesta chased after her, feeling the girl drawn to something—someone. Someone Alesta had seen now in three visions, monster and prey and here—a carefree girl with dark curls blown back by a sweet breeze off the sea. *Aria*, Alesta knew, the name alighting in her mind like a lost bird finding home. Who Teras was before.

Aria sang as she worked, pulling wild fruit into a woven basket at her hip, and Alesta felt happiness well up inside herself, brimming over, full and sweet as honey.

A dark frown on a face like King Enzo's flashed through the vision. The rising feeling within Alesta arrested. She felt her blood clogging. She felt roots tying her to the ground, gone suddenly muddy and rocky—a sharp, wet, devouring mouth. Boughs pushed up through her, wove about her ribs, burst from between her lips. Leaves erupted from her eyes, from every orifice—like blades, every one—and a great terrible weight broke her away from the sky where she walked, pulled her down down down—

Kyr stopped her fall, catching her in his arms. Shook her. Shouted. "We have to go!" He yanked her to her feet—thank the gods, she had feet and not tangled roots—feet that tripped over a monster, gone still on the ground. Kyr hauled her away from the clearing smoke.

She stumbled again. Orroccio was rumbling worse than ever. Her head throbbed. Alesta's hand clutched for her work, for the wings. Their escape from this place.

"No time!" Kyr kept one arm wrapped about her waist, bearing her up, as he grabbed only the crossbow and quiver and swept them out of the cavern. "Are you all right?"

Was she? She wasn't burning in the stars or buried in the sea, but she was trapped here at the top of Orroccio, Kyr rushing them upward like there was anywhere left to go. The kharis smoke down in the cavern had probably damaged the hides she'd worked for days on, there was no way to let Mico and Rina and Lor know what needed to be done—

Kyr's voice frayed on sharpening concern. "Are you bleeding?"

Right. After the wild vision of the Lia, all the confusion of what she'd Seen, it felt calming to consider a practical, immediate question. No balm to heal her this time. She groped a trembling hand—so she wasn't completely calm—to her injured arm. The skin was sticky. The cuts ached. But the bleeding had at least slowed. "I think the lightning cauterized the cuts."

"Gods. Shit. I'm sorry."

"Are *you* all right?" She could see his cheek was bleeding, and she knew he must have other injuries.

His only answer was to mutter, "We'll be all right."

They erupted from the tunnel. It was dark, but the emerging stars shone like beacons. The moon was far too close to full. Kyr grimaced but didn't stop until they reached the nearest tower of obsidian. He dropped the bow to guide Alesta to a low rock nestled between its jagged walls.

It was too dark. The winged monsters would be out hunting, and this little crevice wouldn't protect them. "The beasts—"

Kyr let go of her and grabbed a tall slab broken off the tower's side. "They won't reach you." He heaved the glassy stone between them. "I'm so sorry."

"Wait—" Alesta lurched to her feet. She might not be bleeding much, but everything hurt. She doubled over, too late to stop Kyr from lodging the slab tightly between the tower's close walls and trapping her. Her palm slapped stone. Kyr was a dark blur through the glass. "What are you doing?"

"There's no time now." He sounded strange, as if he were under-water. "Not to remake the wings. Not to make it back in time." He stooped for the crossbow, tucked its quiver into the rope still wind-ing around his shoulders, and strode several paces away. Ignoring Alesta's shouts to come back, he lifted the weapon and fired.

A shadow fell out of the sky.

The other flying monsters shrieked. Some reeled away, some dove for Kyr. Alesta's shouting turned to screams. Kyr reloaded and shot another monster, and another, knocking beasts from the sky and drawing the others to him. When they reached him, he caught them across the neck with his claws, fired the last arrows into their bellies, smashed the bow into their heads.

"No!" Alesta beat her fist against the wall he'd trapped her behind. "Kyr, don't do this!" The monsters thudded to the ground, heavy as her pounding heart. How many before the killing worked a new metamorphosis? Before it bred deeper hatred for himself within Kyr? "Stop!"

Dark blood slashed across the glass. Alesta stared at it as Kyr wrought more violence under the waxing moon like a great mon-ster's eye, the stars its cold scales. He didn't stop. He gouged the creatures with his horns, wrenched their wings apart with his bare hands, speared his claws through muscle and sinew and blood and screams and darkness.

Alesta sank low, fingertips to the glass, chest hollow. Strong trails of smoke streamed from where arrows spiked fallen beasts' haunches. The amber-tipped arrowheads buried in monstrous flesh burned on and on. Like Kyr's rampage. More beasts left their hunts or nests to plunge through the darkness and attack.

Kyr slaughtered them all.

Alesta yelled herself hoarse, pleading with him to stop, before at last there was nothing left to kill. Kyr fell to his knees amid the smoke and starlight. His back spasmed, and he pitched forward, catching himself on his knuckles, crying out. Blood and glass smeared Alesta's view of him bowed over into a dark nightmare. The silver light tracing his arched back broke—shattered—as something erupted from his shoulders.

It unfurled above him, devouring the faint stars. Kyr rose, two powerful black wings spreading wide.

No vision from the Lia, no thunder yet roaring up through Orroccio had shaken Alesta as deeply as this.

Kyr took a few staggering steps. The wings flapped, sails in a frenzied breeze. For a moment, Alesta thought he would disappear into the black sky, as deep and terrible as any hell, forgetting her, forgetting himself, like the other sacrifices had extinguished their human selves in monstrousness.

Then his treads crunched nearer. His face was lost behind the spill of his hair, the shadowed glass. But it was more than that—his pale skin had nearly glowed in the moonlight when he'd looked up to the stars and monsters and made his choice. How much of that boy was he still? How much had he paid to buy Soladisa another chance?

Fury and despair and wonder swarmed in her belly as he pulled the slab away.

What Alesta did know was she would never again let him go

alone into any darkness. She dove into the night of him. His arms wound around her. His wings beating were like the sky breaking, and then he lifted her into it.

Alesta was flying at last. This brought Kyrian no joy.

There was only the horrifying sense of the wings behind him, strange and prying at his shoulders, inescapable, no matter how fast he pushed forward over the poison waves. The tightness over his face he fought the urge to claw off. The prickles of gods knew whatever had happened to his teeth, too full in his mouth.

The knowledge of what he'd done to gain these wings. No matter how far they bore him from Orroccio, he would carry that with him.

Those creatures had only been trying to survive. Same as Teras, whatever her real plans for the Lia. Same as Kyrian when he'd been dropped in hell, abandoned, and abandoning the edicts of the Arbor. He'd begun to feel a little more like himself, near Alesta again, but he was the same vile thing that had crawled from Orroccio's depths, broken with every virtue he'd been taught mattered. Broken.

He clung to Alesta and kept his eyes on the First Tear, the brightest star in the constellation honoring Hektorus' lost daughter, where it hung over the eastern horizon. He let it burn into his vision, let the pain guide him to a home he could no longer avoid.

But darkness engulfed darkness—a storm brewed up from the sea and blotted out the stars. Rain pelted his wings. Winds whipped the waves below high, threatening to catch at them.

Lightning lit the storm clouds like a vast lantern. Its flash illuminated massive dark shapes within the water—leviathans or sharp rocks, smaller monsters writhing between them. Kyrian squinted against the stinging droplets and strained upward, struggling to stay on course.

He was faster this time when danger struck. Even with his monstrous protection, real lightning scorched worse than Alesta's. He had already flung her from him when a tremendous crash rang down over them and his scales spiked.

She tumbled through the storm, arms reaching, mouth a silent shout in the tumult. Another bolt sizzled down to where poison fire burned among the wild waves, silhouetting murky horrors beneath the surface awaiting her splash.

He grabbed for her. Caught her by one hand. Wrenched her upward.

Then, as if ill fate hunted Kyrian for his latest sins, lightning lashed over his back again, and they both were falling.

Chapter Twenty-Five

†EMPEST

Alesta's hands scrabbled at an invisible ladder. Hektorus' blessed air merely rushed between her fingers.

Kyr dropped fast and twisted, catching her and cradling them both with his wings wrapped about them as they hit the water. She cringed against his chest, telling herself the flying monsters must have protection against the waters they fed in, waiting to see if the poison fire devoured Kyr's new wings, if the sea dragged them both down to become two more lost secrets hidden in its depths.

Kyr hissed, jaw taut, as a wave breaking into flame splashed toward them and licked up one wing and the corded muscles of his neck. His arms pressed Alesta more tightly to him, tucked under his chin, within the cocoon of his wings. She shut her eyes against the burning spray as the waves tossed them violently.

They must have drifted away from the worst of it, through the fire, to where the poison was less concentrated, because Kyr let go of where he held her against him to dredge them from the water, through the drenching rain, up onto a larger thrust of earth—a rock just large and flat enough for them both to collapse upon, hip beside hip. Kyr braced one arm over her, sheltering wings bowed about them both and lit up from behind with lightning.

The same new skin of the wings leathered over his face, leaving him unrecognizable, even as Alesta rubbed at her watery eyes and her blurred vision cleared. He stared back with eyes like the storm, pale as the waves whipped white. It was still Kyr, she told herself, as they caught their breath together. It had to still be Kyr.

Determining to act as if it was, she blurted, "You didn't know you'd get wings."

He blinked. A cloudy film swept sideways over his eyes, faster than his bruised-looking lids closed and opened.

Well, that was certainly a useful adaptation against caustic spindrift. She carried on, ignoring how it felt for that moment like she was looking into the inhuman face of Orroccio itself—coarse, forbidding. "What if you'd merely developed a taste for sea beasts? Grown a second stomach?"

His mouth dropped open a little. See, that was Kyr. Even with teeth grown spinier. She fought the urge to feel along his throat, to see if he wasn't speaking because he couldn't, like the branzonos. "You shouldn't have done it. It's too much." Too much to take on himself. His stony skin may have withstood the sea's fire, his wings may have borne them safely here, but still it was like he'd drowned at last—she'd let him fall fully into monstrousness. After he'd held on so long, she'd watched him slip under. She clutched the rope he yet wore, as if she could somehow still save him.

And then he did speak, the added roughness to his voice nothing to the wildness in his eyes that caught fire at her admonishment and swept through his words. "For you, I'd do more. I'd write it in the blood of a thousand monsters. Their blood or mine. I'd burn it into the sky with my own charring body."

A thrill chased through her. Alesta's own voice was barely a whisper above the tempest. "Write what?"

He bit his lip as if to trap the words there. But that sent her gaze to his mouth, and then his fell to hers. His face drifted nearer—till his breath caught. "It's too dangerous." It was. The moment was charged with it, more than any back at home when she'd feared betraying her feelings. Something scraped beside her ear. Kyr's claws digging into the rock. Going tense with restraint. They were balanced on this moment, between Orroccio and Soladisa, about to tip into something new beyond the horizon. "We'll have to wait out the storm."

She threaded her fingers up through his dripping hair. "We have time." Her hand trembled. She'd buried how she felt so long. What if she didn't know how to say it? How to show it?

"I can't." Kyr's throat bobbed as she tucked his jagged hair behind his ear, along the ruff there. "I never could, all the times I wanted, not if it might damn you, and what would damn you more than being promised to me now? I can't stay on Soladisa."

She tugged gently on the coil of hair. "Always such a stickler." The rules that had shaped her life seemed so small and far away now. The alberos and all their talk of pledges and covenants and virtues could leap into this boiling sea for all she cared.

But how could Alesta ask Kyr to return where she knew herself the cruelty he'd face, after he'd twisted himself up like this only trying to protect others? Where someone—the first king, a davina, *someone*—must have known the price they were paying was not inevitable, but a choice. Lightning flashed behind Kyr's wings, illuminating falling rain like dark stars, silhouetting the same fine structure she'd studied all day, branching now from his body. Like the spreading boughs in her vision. Alesta didn't understand all she'd Seen, but one thing was clear. The kingdom had let its children die. Why should Kyr force himself back to save such a place that hadn't tried to save him?

She lifted her voice above the roar of the vicious sea. "Then let's go somewhere else! Where they haven't been taught to hate monsters." There had to be some place. The world was so much more than she had known. So much bigger, so much stranger. She wanted more. No glory in lofty towers or hell's depths. She wanted to break for the horizon and find someplace free of it all. "We can go as soon as it clears."

Kyr shook his head, though he let his cheek graze against her knuckles. His lashes fell closed a moment. "You're shaking. I made myself into this. However you may feel—you don't deserve a nightmare."

As if she of all people would judge someone by appearance rather than the heart at their center, the engine of their spirit. She lifted her other hand and cradled his face. "I am not afraid of you. Only of losing you." Kyr's exhalation was soft on her face. Relief and yearning shone in his strange eyes. "Let them go on tithing if they think that's right. I don't know what is anymore."

He swallowed again. "But we could make it safe for everyone."

"Everyone?" Her thumbs stroked over his rough cheekbones flecked with gold, the cuts old and new there. *What about you?* her touch said.

It was a moment with no answer. There was no rule to follow to ensure success. No safe shore to seek. Nowhere to find home.

There was no place they belonged but with one another.

Lightning crashed out over the sea, whips of fire ready to cut them apart. Waves around them frothed white and sharp like monsters' teeth. *May as well sin*, Alesta thought, and she lifted herself to meet Kyr's lips with hers.

She pressed softly, her kiss not a pledge but a question. Wondering, when Kyr sucked a breath, if he would pull away.

Instead he dropped to his forearm and captured her mouth with his.

He kissed as if starving for the feel of their lips together. For her. The kiss broke open into a startling intimacy. It was a little strange, the shared softness, the scratch of his scruff and coarse skin, their faces so near. But as Kyr's keen teeth scraped gently against her lower lip and her hands traced down his biceps, scales running under her palms like coins, Alesta found herself curious to explore the possibilities it all hinted at. If only they were given the chance, someplace beyond this rock—she chased the thought away with another urgent drive of her mouth against Kyr's.

He angled his horns aside and seared the heat of his lips and tingle of his teeth down her jaw, along her throat, lighting her up inside like the burning sky. His hand skimmed her shoulder and brushed over the line of her hip, claws pursuing fingertips like the crisp bite with a first sip of wine. Her entire body ached to grow drunk with it.

Alesta had never before wanted the stark hunger in a monster's eyes to break free, but now she sought it. "Kyr," she breathed, because she did not want to hide anymore, "I love you," and that seemed to snap something within him, like the crossbow engaging.

"Alesta." He caught her mouth with another kiss. "It's always only ever been you."

Alesta's kiss pulled Kyrian from the deeper hell of his transformation straight to the heavenly fields. Her mouth parted again under his, and somehow the monster was gone, replaced by only a flood of want and rush of joy. *She loved him*, and so, for the first time in a year, he was glad to be himself. Maybe his entire life. Alesta's hand claimed the small of his back, tugging him against her, and he could see the stars. Their sweet light shooting through him chased away the lingering burn of the poison they'd escaped. Kyrian buried his face in the crook of her neck, his own hand searching out her other curves, giving in to this gentler sin. If he could only keep kissing her, he could hide from all the things he'd become. He could stay within the circle of her grace, the sanctuary of her softness, and never have to bear the judgment of anyone looking upon the grievous sins he'd written over himself.

He let his lips fall to hers again and sinned a little more.

Even when he told her she should probably try to rest before they journeyed on, he pressed light kisses to her temple as her eyes drooped shut. But while the wings he'd bought with yet more violence shielded them from the rain and lightning for a few hours longer, they could not block out the dying storm, the creeping flush of light.

They could not bar the truth of what he had to do. But Alesta loved him, so he could face it.

Resting his forehead against Alesta's, Kyrian found her hand

and wove his fingers through hers. Her breath was warm on his face. He closed his eyes before saying, "We have to go."

She gave a little moan from her throat, and for a moment Kyrian considered abandoning the entire world to fire just to stay here and see if he could get her to make that sound again.

Instead, as she drew a deep wakeful breath, he raised their hands and twisted them so he could see the tail of serpentine shimmer peek out from under her wristband. "When we get back," he told her, "be sure to hide this. We don't know how they're going to react to what's happened." This was true in that he didn't know the exact extent of horror and condemnation that would greet him. Dread poured through him at the thought. But if Alesta could still feel for him what she did, maybe it wouldn't be as bad as he feared.

She sat up roughly. "We don't have to."

He brushed a stray curl from her forehead. "You don't owe that place anything, but I do. I was selfish. I failed to act when others needed help." And just as he'd done nothing about the tithings he knew were wrong, his family—all those kings with his face—at some point long ago must have known what they'd stolen. What they'd cost the kingdom. Whether Teras had truly been wronged or deserved her punishment, it had entailed so many more deaths of the people his family were meant to protect. Like Alesta had said, maybe it would take one of them as damned as he was to finally make it right.

"I have to try to make up for it," he said. "Even in an imperfect way. It's the best I can expect of myself, as I am. But I have to try." He steered Alesta's hand to his lips and kissed her knuckles. "You make me hope." She bit down on a small smile. She was wind-wild, like she always looked on the headland at home. Hair tousled, cheeks pink. Like she'd already been flying. He tugged a loose lace on her wristband tight. If his hope was wrong, no need for her to endanger herself. "And you can still make a home on Soladisa." Maybe, his reckless hope whispered, he could too.

She stiffened. "I don't want to talk about anything beyond Teras' deadline. Let's just focus on getting the Lia." She began unwinding the rope from where she'd tied it and drew loops about both of their waists instead. In case of any more lightning, she told him. They pulled together to make the knots secure, as if that would promise the world they left for wouldn't tear them apart.

So he took her up in his arms and set off again, unable to say for certain if he flew away from or toward hell.

Alesta hunted for Soladisa on a tilting horizon. They'd started again well before dawn, and thick clouds veiled the rising sun for most of the flight, but now burned away. Anxious to reach the island's protection before Kyr's skin reached its limit enduring full daylight, she let her head hang and squinted into the east, checking for any sign of home, ready to call directions to him.

He'd closed his eyes, flying toward the sun's burn, and she let him know when he needed to adjust his flight higher, or was drifting too far above the waves.

The sky behind him was still a charcoal gray. The storm squatted over the west, even seeming to grow. Ominous plumes stretched after them as if ready to draw them back to Orroccio. Aria's impatience was mounting.

Soladisa at last appeared like a smudge painted beneath the sea, its hills and towers dripping into the sky. Alesta shouted and lifted her head, her cheek against Kyr's, to tell him. She was glad they'd come to make things right, but her aching fingers tightened on the rope binding her to him. "Almost home." They'd go to the villa first. Kyr would at least be safe there. Then someone could be sent to the Towers for Mico. She returned to her watch, twisting for a better view, and shouted to Kyr to bank south.

The island grew. Its beach stretched wide—littered with figures. Alesta peered at them, trying to understand what she was seeing. Those weren't shadows, but bodies laid out on the sand, scattered over the long grasses above. And others standing above them.

She shouted again to Kyr. "Higher!" He jolted at her tone but strained to gain height as they rushed toward their home shore—bristling with armed farmers. "Higher! Now! Bank north!"

Arrows whistled past.

Alesta gaped. "Those are *my* crossbows!" Kyr swore in her ear and her stomach dipped as he pulled them higher yet.

She'd made those weapons to help the farmers protect against encroaching monsters—*Oh.*

Another volley of arrows. Her design allowed farmers to fend off branzonos from up the slope of shore, and the next arrows sank in their arcs before they could strike Kyr or her. But the farmers chased them inland and would soon adjust their aim.

"Alesta?" Kyr's eyes opened to slits.

"Um, faster?"

He exhaled through his teeth, but his wings sped.

They left the farmers behind. "We're clear," she told Kyr. "Don't descend yet. We need to head north." They could go straight to Mico.

"Do they always guard the coast now?"

"Not like this." Those were branzonos on the beach. So many dead monsters. Or Soladisans who looked like monsters. She couldn't think about that now. "Let's get you someplace safe."

His arm tightened around her. "You're my someplace safe."

"That's nice," Alesta told him, "but won't help when the sun starts charring your skin." His wings and face were likely fine, but they didn't know just how much exposure the rest of him could stand. They needed to get him inside before finding out.

"Just tell me if there are more crossbows."

She kept a wary eye as they flew up the island, over the familiar fields, to the Towers. Everything was so orderly, the patches of grape vines and trees, the soft grains spread like dropped handkerchiefs over the hills, their furrows even stitches. When they passed over the city's streets, people pointed, shouted. If only they knew it was Kyr, they'd be so glad. For now, Alesta watched for armed attendants and guided Kyr to remain high until they neared the royal tower. "There's Mico's balcony!"

"Are you sure?"

"Of course. I've been there plenty." She couldn't exactly talk out design issues for devil-killing arrows with her professors. "Left! Too far—"

They hadn't actually landed before. They didn't exactly land now.

"Lower! Slow down!" Far faster than she expected, they crashed into the large balcony outside Mico's apartments.

She was tangled up with Kyr and the Lia rope. She was pretty sure she'd hurt her ankle. She was aching, and hungry, and exhausted, but all she could feel for the moment was a thrill like molten gold running through her veins. She had done it. She'd brought Kyr home.

"All right?" His hand swept over half her face and shoulder.

"Here—" She held the Lia taut and drew it across his claws. "Cut this."

Once she could stand, she pulled him to the corner of the balcony just around the curve of the tower from the sun. "Better?"

He nodded, though he held one hand before his eyes. "So much." His wings folded so he could press farther into the shadow.

"Lessie?"

She spun. Mico stood beside the sweep of brocade curtain at the back of the balcony. She rushed forward, heedless of her ankle or the fact she wore only breeches and bodice, eager to explain everything.

Mico's jaw fell. "It *is* you." He gripped her shoulders. "You're back! You're back safe!" He exhaled like he'd been kicked in the chest. "God's breath! How did you get here? Did you do it? Did you kill Teras?"

"No, I—"

His fingers tightened on her arms. "You didn't?"

"I have to explain—"

He let go of her and ran a hand over his forehead and hair. "We all agreed, finish the job, or make sure the tithing is paid."

She waved her hands, trying to get the right words out. "I know, and I would have, but—"

He glanced out at the city and shook his head just a little. Disbelieving. "Lessie, we're all in danger now. Everyone."

"Mico!" She knew there was still danger, still so much to fix, but she couldn't help the smile that spread wide across her face. Beaming, she told him, "I didn't come back alone."

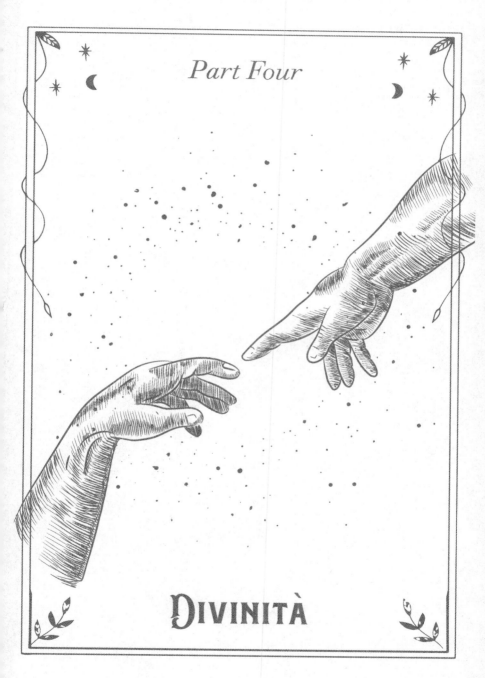

Part Four

DIVINITÀ

Chapter Twenty-Six

Truth Beauty

I t smelled like home. An assault of strawberries and fennel and the honey wax the attendants used in the royal tower. Kyrian almost slipped on the perfectly even, polished floor. Whatever killing the flying beasts had done to his eyes meant he could bear a little daylight. But not much.

A clatter behind him. Alesta must have pulled the heavy curtains shut, after guiding him inside, because Mico's chamber resolved from a hot yellow blur into uncertain forms, still bleary and bleached with the overpotent light—a divan piled with cushions, a desk with a shut journal atop it. A chair with a small table laden with shining plates and a steaming drink.

Everything so normal. Just as it was. And then him.

And Mico, backing away.

Alesta rushed past Kyrian with an uneven stride and fell upon his cousin's breakfast. "Thank Hektorus, I'm thirsty." She downed the tea.

"Lessie," Mico said from where he practically leaned against a giant wall tapestry, "are you sure—?"

"It's Kyr," she repeated, around a mouthful of food. "Turn down the lamp, for heaven's sake." She loomed nearer, pressing a small cake dotted with fruit into Kyrian's hand.

"But he's . . . It's—" Mico was an unsettled smudge across the room, under a kharis lamp that barely dimmed. "Is he on fire?"

"Don't be ridiculous." Alesta patted the skin of Kyrian's upper arm, still aching from the sun, and, Kyrian was mortified to see, smoking slightly. "He's fine now in the shade." She tilted her face up to him and murmured, "You are, right?"

He absolutely was not. "Yes."

Mico drew a few steps nearer, tugging his tunic straight. His hazy face, its shock still more than clear, was almost like looking at his own face he'd lost. "Kyrian. It's a miracle."

Kyrian did not feel like one.

Mico turned to Alesta and swept forward. Why was he grabbing her arm? Had he seen her skin there? Kyrian tensed, ready to intervene.

Mico merely ran his hand up to Alesta's elbow. "I didn't know what had happened to you. There have been ominous signs from Orroccio. Storms and clouds of ash. Earthquakes and unwieldy tides. So many sea monsters. We've had to set guards along the coast."

Alesta bit her lip. "We saw."

Mico leaned closer, voice dropping to a velvet murmur. "I'm so glad you're safe." He exhaled a rough breath. "Stunned. But Teras is clearly angry we haven't paid the tithing. We must protect the kingdom."

Alesta raised her hands in that emphatic way she had. Did she *want* Mico to see her arms? Did she want him to look at her like he had Kyrian, with horror? Instead of the conflicted amazement and concern on his face now? "The tithing isn't the only way," Alesta said. "That deal was because Soladisa stole something from her."

"Her?"

Alesta nodded. "We just have to give it back. The hardest part will be enough workers to dig its roots out, but—"

Mico's fingers slid off Alesta's arm. "You mean—the Lia?"

"That's the price. No more tithings."

Mico took a step back. "But to give it to the devil—" He sounded appalled, his lip pulling up with distaste.

Alesta reached out and clapped his arm. "The hard thing is worth it. Ending the tithings is what's most important."

Mico's shoulders dropped. "We must fetch Enzo, then. Let him know Kyrian is back."

The cake crumbled in Kyrian's fist. "Don't."

Mico jerked his gaze his way.

He wasn't back. Not the Kyrian he'd been here. He could walk the same halls at the Towers, through the same fields that had all seemed a vanished dream while he was gone, and never find what he'd lost. "I'm not staying," he said. "No one else needs to know I'm here."

Alesta took a quick, deep breath, but said nothing. Mico nodded slowly, reminding Kyrian unpleasantly of how placating he had always been with their tiniest cousins. Kyrian found himself drawing to his full height as Mico said, "I'll have the attendants tell Enzo Lessie is back, then. Between that and Orroccio's bad temper, he'll come at once." He disappeared into the burn of kharis before returning and telling Kyrian, "You can wait in my bedchamber if you want—" He gestured to the other doorway.

"I promise not to pin you down—you remember the way out the back stairs from its balcony." He gave a short bark of a laugh. "Not that you need them, I suppose." His voice turned serious. "But Enzo needs to know. You can't imagine how broken he was after you were lost. As bad as when Ciro was killed. He hasn't even named an heir still, despite the kingdom growing more impatient." Mico's lips pressed in a line.

Kyrian could imagine, because he wanted so badly to have himself back. Somehow. But that boy was gone. Enzo would find no balm for his grief in what Kyrian was now.

Alesta asked, "Do you think Kyr could convince him?" She glanced his way and back quickly. "If King Enzo doesn't agree, then you must speak with everyone you can." She told Mico all her ideas for calling on the king and Arbor to fulfill Teras' offered deal. "Maybe get those in our movement to talk to their families and neighbors. If enough demand their children no longer face the risk of tithing—"

But Mico warned they could just as likely protest giving the Lia to the devil. Kyrian simply stood awkwardly scraping crumbs from his palm, making a mess of this pristine room, feeling utterly out of place. Even more than he had growing up in this tower. When he'd had a home here, he would have been amazed to learn that was possible.

A knock came at the door. Mico looked to Kyrian before moving. "Come, cousin. Think of what's best for the kingdom. We can suggest his attendants wait outside."

Kyrian forced his shoulders down from where they'd crept. He hadn't come all this way not to help however he could. He nodded to Mico. "Fine." Though what he was even supposed to say, he still didn't know. None of the careful speeches he'd always recited at court seemed like they'd fit in this tooth-crammed mouth. He didn't know how to be here anymore. He never had, but like this, he didn't know how to fake it; he couldn't even put on the role expected of him. He felt more lost than ever.

Mico nodded. "I'll prepare him." He spoke at the door a moment before standing aside to let Enzo enter, alone.

The king strode into the room. Whatever warning Mico had given, Enzo's footsteps abruptly halted and his mouth fell open, amid his beard gone grayer. He stared at Kyrian.

Alesta, standing halfway between them, tugged at her bodice and took an awkward step forward. Kyrian couldn't tell if she was attempting to curtsy despite wearing no skirts, or had hurt herself. She scrubbed a fist down the side of her breeches. "I—" She cleared her throat. "I have returned with our lord Kyrian, my king."

Kyrian wished he could be as brave as her, speaking when it was so hard. But enduring another inspection boring into what he'd become, the shame and guilt it churned up, was all he managed while Enzo's eyes widened at his monstrousness.

Everyone could see it now. Alesta would see them seeing it, see how anyone who hadn't encountered what he was surrounded by greater horrors would never be able to see past it. His chest tightened with panic.

Enzo's hand drifted to his own chest, just as much shame in his eyes. "Is it really you?"

Hadn't Alesta already told him? Yes, Kyrian was a monster. He was one when he let youths like Alesta live under the threat of tithing without speaking up. But there was one thing he could do to make it better now. No courtly tones or bowing. He could show Soladisa what it had done to him. Why it needed to be the one to change this time. He let a deep breath swell his chest and said, "We need the Lia tree dug out and transported on a ship to Orroccio at once."

Enzo's brow furrowed. "What—?"

"It's how we end all this. No more tithings." Kyrian stopped his hand straying to his scales. His voice dug low. "Did you know what she was?"

Enzo exhaled, eyes falling closed a moment as he answered. "Yes." His eyes pleaded now. "But we needed her."

Kyrian's cold posture collapsed. "How could anyone need the monster?" He glanced to Alesta, who looked at just as great a loss.

"That isn't what I—" Enzo's eyes narrowed. "You mean Teras?"

Who else? "She was like us once."

Enzo only stared a moment, before shaking his head. "There's so much I was going to tell you. Once you were heir." He brushed his hair back, beneath his crown. "I tried to let you escape it as long as possible. It is a burden to be passed. Borne by every king of Soladisa."

Kyrian spread his arms. "Do I look unburdened?" He'd found his own load to carry, new and impossible to escape.

Alesta let out a little dismayed sound, sympathy twisting in her throat.

Kyrian's claws drew into slow fists. "The tithings. We don't have to bear it anymore, if only we make it right. Deliver justice to Teras."

Enzo raised his palms out to him. "There's more you still don't know or understand."

That's what everyone had always said in this place, trying to get him to follow along, to simply imitate their ways even if they made no sense to Kyrian. And he'd believed that was right. But he was weary of being placated by people who hadn't endured what he had, by this king he'd been so anxious to be enough for, who wasn't living up to what he should be at all. "I've learned enough."

"It will anger Hektorus."

"If he abides this injustice, he doesn't deserve our worship anyway." Kyrian's words seemed to burn all the air out of the room. Mico shifted behind Enzo, near the door and the tapestry.

Enzo's hand squeezed into an emphatic fist. "Life will be harder for the kingdom without the Lia. It's our duty to see our people are protected and cared for—"

He sounded like he was reciting from a book or a tutor. Was this how Kyrian sounded when reminding Alesta of the rules he'd always clung to? "We sent our people to die. Is it really protecting them if it costs their lives?"

Enzo dropped his fist into his other hand, punctuating each word. "More might without it."

"We all might have to give things up and work harder." Kyrian took an earnest step nearer his uncle. "We should. Starting with the king."

A thrum, and pain erupted through Kyrian's torso. His scales flared. His hands fumbled at his stomach, at something jutting from under his ribs.

At the fletching of the arrow buried deep into his gut.

Fire rushed through him, like the hell he knew he carried inside coming to life, reaching out to drag him down. He saw three things as he fell into its flames.

Enzo startling forward toward him.

Alesta's face drawing up with confusion.

Mico standing behind the king, a small crossbow like Alesta's in his hands.

Chapter Twenty-Seven

ALL IN THE FIRE

Kyrian looked up at Alesta from hell, to where she knelt over him. Her hair spilled around them. Her hands shook against his side. *"What did you do?"*

But Kyrian hadn't done anything. He tried to tell her.

Mistake. His middle screamed with more pain when he tried to draw breath.

"You'll be all right." Alesta nodded quickly. "It'll be all right. He heals fast." But her eyes widened as his shallow pants turned to violent shivers.

Enzo took another step nearer. "What has happened?"

His uncle didn't even realize. "He was attacking," Mico said, still behind the king. The tapestry was flung back, revealing more weapons hanging on wall hooks.

Alesta pressed her hands to where fire raged on in Kyrian's side, reckless of his scales too near. "Attacking! He wasn't! He wouldn't!"

Mico dropped the bow and drew a dagger from his belt. Kyrian breathed in to shout, even through another wall of agony—

Mico struck. Enzo staggered forward, royal medallion swinging from his neck. Mico didn't stop but slashed again, and again, as Enzo whirled on him. The king's throat spurted. Even as Enzo fell, Mico slashed across his face. Quick parallel cuts. Like claw marks. "He attacked the king."

Alesta lurched to her feet, bloody hands hovering over Enzo. Before she could reach him, Mico tossed the blade near Kyrian and caught her by the shoulders.

Kyrian shouted now. He slapped his hand to the floor, trying to rise. *"Don't—"*

Mico ignored him. "Together we can still kill Teras and liberate Soladisa," he told Alesta. "You've been to Orroccio. Survived it. You can help us finish off the beast." Mico's next words became lost to the crackle of fire in Kyrian's head that he wasn't sure was real or not, devoured by the relentless pain. He only half-heard Mico's insistent argument to Alesta. "The kingdom will rally around you, returned and uncorrupted." He cast a pointed gaze to Kyrian. Alesta followed it, and her jaw trembled. Mico shook her and pulled her nearer. "A hero. Too holy for the evil to consume. Marry me and secure my ascension to the throne. The kingdom needs to belong to those who reject the thrall of these monsters. Enzo let Teras take us, one by one."

The king was still; only his blood seeped nearer across the gleaming floor toward Kyrian like a slow, dark tide.

Some part of Kyrian's mind remained clear enough to know this was not another hallucination, not like the fire his pain seemed to make blossom all around him. A deeper pain clenched his heart. His uncle was dead.

"But—" Alesta's voice trailed upward, shock running up

against confusion. "Did you use the amber arrows? You'd made more?"

"We had to be ready to stand against the monsters." Mico flashed a smile. "You've said as much a hundred times." The smile slackened. "Surely you don't actually care about them? They are lost to evil." He grappled Alesta around. "Just *look* at them. That's not Kyrian."

She was shaking her head. Shaking her hands. "Kyrian. The splinter mechanism triggered—the arrow will break off. We can't heal him with Lia."

Mico murmured in her ear. "See how fast you turn to its goodness? We can rid ourselves of them all without giving up the Lia's power. Secure the kingdom. Finally make Soladisa a fair one that sees the value in all people. In us."

Alesta stared at Kyrian, like he was falling farther and farther away from her. She should agree. He was down here in hell, and she needed a safe place. A home. There was none here for Kyrian. Mico hated him. Of course he did. Kyrian was a monster—a threat to the kingdom. Like those farmers had seen. He fought to find his voice as hellfire rampaged through him. Consuming him. Alesta should have everything she wanted. Everything she'd striven for. A place of status and security. But Kyrian's head was so muddled, he couldn't seem to form the words to tell her.

Mico dropped his hands from Alesta and strode to the desk. "We need to send someone at once to hold off Teras."

"But you're against the tithings—"

"You've forced the matter." His hands gripped the back of the chair. "Sometimes the hard thing is giving up someone for the greater good. If you don't want that to be you again, then you'll help me." He flipped open the journal and lifted a pencil. "Tell me everything you learned on the rock. How you were stopped. How the ones we send next won't be." He waited, pencil poised, words laced with threat. "I imagine you don't want to go back."

Unthinkable. Kyrian wasn't going to die twice just for Alesta to end up back in hell with him.

Alesta seemed to panic at the thought too. "No!" She turned away from Kyrian. "I can't go back there."

"I don't want to make you," Mico said through a smile. "I've always said you were useful—it's why I invested so much in you. Bribed the artificers to let you into the university. You were too smart to listen to devils, like Enzo and the Arbor did. Don't start now."

Alesta's brow rippled. "They confused me, the monsters." She raised a shaking hand to her temple.

The daub of blood she left looked like when Kyrian had painted her disguise. He would never touch her again. Flames lapped all around him where he lay.

Alesta stepped past Enzo. She *was* limping. "You—you can't imagine what it's like there. It sinks into your mind."

Kyrian couldn't tell over the roar of fire in his head if she was earnest or pretending. It made his heart ache either way. But she would be all right. He'd pretended for so long. He let his head rest against the cold floor.

"But after I was chased away from Teras' lair, the only thing that kept me sane—" Alesta took another uneven step toward Mico. "That kept me going—" She stood before him. "Was the thought of you."

Mico rolled his shoulders back and grinned. Alesta lifted a hand out to him. Kyrian let his eyes fall closed.

"You make me hope."

He opened them in time to see Alesta sparking all over with the spider's sharp blue burning. She and Mico fell to the floor.

Now they were all in the fire. Mico spasmed and sprawled back over the shining tile. Alesta cringed down into a ball and seemed to shake the electric flames from her hands. She half-crawled to Kyrian. "The arrow's Lia." She braced a palm against his side, away from the scales. A sickening tug and a mountain of agony exploded through Kyrian's body, a thousand sharp diamonds grinding and glittering. In their glare he only heard Alesta say, "That'll help but the spikes will—they'll keep burning you. Why did I *make* this?"

Why was she still here? Any moment now they'd drag her away to take her back. His heart lurched at the idea. He cracked open an eye. "'Lesta—" Gods, his throat. It was like trying to talk through hot sand. "Get the Lia."

"I can't." She shook her head fast. "Not by myself. I can't leave you here."

"Have to. You're the cleverest. You'll figure it out." A shudder tore through him, under her hands fluttering above his scales. "Only way to stop Teras killing everyone. Without sending a tithing. I won't. Won't be part of that again." His tongue was heavy. The poison was quickly stealing his ability to speak. But he could see in her eyes that Alesta understood the importance of this to him. This was the one thing that might still make him worthy or human in some final way.

Mico groaned and thrashed one arm. They were out of time.

Kyrian told Alesta, "Could always stay and marry him."

Alesta released a quavering laugh, eyes bright with unshed tears. "Gods, you're so ridiculous, and I love you so much."

He seized her words to hold tight and fast, a talisman against the dark abyss he was tipping back into. She'd rescued him from it for a little while. Long enough to change everything. The quick kiss she pressed to his forehead sent him plummeting.

Her footsteps traveled away across the room, to Mico's bed-chamber. Mico began yelling. More footsteps. Shouting at the door. "A monster killed the king!"

Boots surrounding Kyrian. How were they here if Kyrian was back in hell?

Mico's voice above him now. "I've incapacitated it."

"Shall we slay it, and go be absolved?"

Kyrian's head began to clear and he realized Alesta had been right; removing the arrow helped. Some. The fire receded. His scales calmed. His belly still burned. He still couldn't speak.

He wasn't in hell. Just Soladisa. At Mico's feet.

"This monster is a king-killer," Mico said. "The kingdom deserves to see its righteous death and know the threat is gone. Tie it up to deal with later. I'll keep watch. For now, bear the king's body to his bedchamber and lay him out. Ring the bells."

Kyrian almost managed to make his limbs obey him before the attendants tied them together, and his wings, using the very rope Alesta had bound herself to him with. His head slumped again to the floor that seemed to tilt. He could only watch as they carried Enzo's limp body across the room.

Mico, alone with Kyrian, dropped the authoritative voice he'd been using. "My perfect cousin," he said, strolling past to the balcony. "Everyone's favorite." He whipped the curtains open, and the room flooded with light. Cringing, Kyrian struggled to turn away. "And now they'll cheer as they watch you die. It's perfectly justified. Hektorus will only be grateful. You are a monster, after all."

Mico crouched in front of where Kyrian had rolled, a few paces away. The sun turned him into a glowing blur like Hektorus' nimbus. An acrid burning—Kyrian's skin—ate away at the smell of honey wax and blood. "Those men wanted to steal the glory for themselves," Mico said, "but the people need to see what we're up against. And I think, if I take you outside, the sun will do the job, where everyone can witness how Hektorus wants all monsters treated. And how they need me to protect them from the threat." His grin was a sharp, white crescent. "I'm right, aren't I?" He listed his head, smile fading. "It was harder with Ciro. He was a good man."

Kyrian, cowering from the sun, fell still.

"And collecting that much branzono poison was dangerous. Sacrifice isn't easy. But at least I make mine to better honor Hektorus. Ciro would have followed his father's ways." He gave a heavy sigh. "I'm the only one ready to stand up for what's right. And now you're all out of my way. Luckily for the kingdom, with how Enzo was ready to hand everything to you, just as he handed his people to Teras. He told me at the ball that night of the festival he was only delaying the announcement, until your accident blew over." Mico's voice tightened. "He looked right at me but couldn't see the better option before him, only the future with you as king. We both know what a disaster that would have been." Mico stood. "Stop trying to get away," he said softly. His kick landed before Kyrian could twist to protect his stomach. The fire in Kyrian's side screamed back to life as the Towers' great bells began tolling.

Mico wandered over to his bedchamber. Eyes still on Kyrian, he shed his stained jacket and shrugged on a fresh one, its fine fabric just as bright as their uncle's blood.

Light, hurried footsteps. A dark purple hem beside Mico's boots, back near Kyrian. "What have you done?" An urgent voice Kyrian recognized easily even after a year. One who had condemned so many children to Orroccio. Davina Bianca.

"What had to be done."

"The king——"

"Was about to give up the power of the Lia. The shepherdess came back ranting about needing to give it to Teras to stop the tithings. The whole point of sending her was to stop paying any tribute to the beast." Mico's boots shuffled, toes pointing at Bianca. "I know you don't want your daughter to be queen of a powerless kingdom, or beholden to a devil. This was the perfect excuse to blame Enzo's death on a monster. You'll still get what we agreed: your daughter made queen, and much sooner."

"All the youths you and Rina were working with——they'll be expecting you to end the tithings. They could tell everyone what you've been doing, if you just try to take the crown."

"I'll fulfill that promise. Let them tell everyone. We can do more now; there's no reason to hold back any longer. I will be known as the king who finally brought Soladisa into perfect harmony with Hektorus' virtues. And I have no intention of being second in my own kingdom to Teras. I'll get Lessie to help one way or another." He nudged a toe into Kyrian's side, and the pain flared again. "She's not as bad as this, but she's infected with some kind of monstrousness. If we threaten to expose her, she might agree to help as we take the fight to Orroccio." He shrugged. "Or we'll toss her back on the rock after we glean everything useful she's learned. Once we have everyone on our side, they'll only take whatever she claims as madness. Corruption by the devil. They all know she's always been peculiar."

Kyrian writhed on the floor. The Lia rope burned into his wrists as he strained for Mico. He tried to shout that they couldn't send Alesta back, but something in that poison still running through his blood or the Lia still in his gut made him forget all the words, leaving him only to roar. The returning attendants rushed to Mico's side. Everything was exclamations and orders. They dragged Kyrian by the rope, through Enzo's blood, out the corridor, into the Towers.

Staring. Shouting. People drawing away in terror, people rushing forward to see. Echoes through the great hall, chasing the condemnation back to him. Rina, peering from behind a column, eyes wide with horror. "So it is true, then." Her lids sank closed. She couldn't bear to look upon him.

Mico had the attendants stop. He addressed the gathered crowd of courtiers, a bright mass through Kyrian's lashes as even the filtered light here became too much. "Yes, it is true. The offering to Teras has returned, chased by this demon who killed King Enzo." He held both palms to his chest, then raised them to the increasing questions. "We don't know how or why yet. The monster appears to have been trying to steal the holy Lia tree. It took our beloved king from us, but we will not allow it to rip away Hektorus' great blessing." Mico set his shoulders. "The devils will receive from us not the tree, but an army."

The declaration rang through the hall like horror resounded through Kyrian. He tried to tell them no, tell them why they couldn't send more Soladisans to their damnation there like him, but all his growls earned were sharp tugs at his bindings and a chorus of gasps from those nearest.

"Once the trade ships return," Mico continued, "I will have them carry an army to defeat the threat of Orroccio at last. I know many Soladisans are ready to protect our home, as they have the coastline from these foul beasts, or as attendants here, or offering themselves every season as potential tithings. Soon they will have the opportunity to protect us once and for all. But we must send a new tithing immediately." His voice was laden with the perfect moderation and resolve for a king. Kyrian wondered that he ever thought he was the only one putting on a performance at the Towers.

Now all Kyrian was to this place, just as in Orroccio, was scales and claws. His monstrous face.

Bianca stepped forward. "The king directed me to select a new sacrifice, before he was killed. His final wish was to ensure the safety of the kingdom." She folded her arms, sleeves draping. "The holy kharis has appointed the tailor's girl Lor."

"But——" The blood drained from Rina's face. Her mother shot her a look, and Rina snapped her mouth shut.

"She will be taken at once to stave off our destruction," Mico announced. "Go collect the shepherdess Lessie, as well. She's upset after the horrors of Orroccio. She ran off in the Towers, confused, ranting."

Rina drew up straight. "I'll help find her."

"Thank you, my lady." Mico inclined his head to Rina and

gestured to several attendants to follow her. "She needs tending to before she hurts someone, or herself." Mico's voice turned stern. "And take this thing to the game court. Let Hektorus protect us, and his holy sun destroy the monster."

The attendants followed Mico's directions. Courtiers murmured thanks for his taking quick action. Everyone already saw him as a king, as they saw Kyrian as a monster.

He was one. He'd failed Alesta. He couldn't help make even her safe, let alone everyone. He despaired now of the slight sliver of hope she'd given him, which only sliced him up inside worse than any arrows or claws.

Chapter Twenty-Eight
VISIONS

A lesta crouched behind a balustrade, watching Rina loudly direct a group of attendants to search for her. When they'd set off, Rina trailing behind in her sweeping gown, Alesta hauled herself up, palms slick on the stone, and hurried, best she could, the other way.

Despite the pain in her leg, she cut the long way around to avoid the searchers and rushed down another flight of stairs. She was filthy and barely dressed and had exposed her monstrousness. How was she going to get anyone to help return the Lia to Aria? Who was she going to convince, on her own, with Mico set against her? She tamped down her hurt at Rina having clearly taken his side. If she could reach the Arbor before him, before he convinced everyone she was mad, get the alberos to agree . . . They were the custodians of the tree; they might be able to make it happen. Mico had no true authority, had never been named heir. After a year of perfect devotion, she might have some standing with the alberos she could call upon. Maybe they *would* see her return as a miracle.

Her sore ankle gave out, and she tumbled down the last

few steps. The heels of her hands slammed into the carved flagstones.

Alesta leveraged herself to sitting with her elbow and bit back a sob. The alberos despised her. And Mico had bribed her way into university. Why did she think she could do *any* of this? She was a *shepherdess*. A field hand with a kind friend with a big library, who'd taken the time to teach her until she could teach herself and eventually design the arrow that was currently *killing him*.

She cradled her hands against her chest. Her breath was mere hiccups, like when she'd felt the weight of being under Orroccio. Everything she'd done had been to take control of her life. To prevent others using it as a sacrifice. But when she thought she was making her own choice, Mico had just been using her, like the alberos and king had wanted to. It was *ridiculous* to send her to kill Teras. She'd been so consumed with grief she hadn't seen it. She'd never have gotten close without Kyr's help. Mico probably figured he'd see if she got lucky or learn from her failure and keep sending gullible youths until someone managed it. She'd thought she was taking charge by joining Mico's movement, but he was only manipulating her. Just like with his pathetic attempt to make her think he'd marry her. Because he wanted to be on top of the hill she'd been trying to climb her whole life.

Her anger with him was just enough to get her moving again. She shoved herself back to her feet and rubbed her sore palms over her face. Pushing back her hair, she limped across a sunny courtyard toward a cloister festooned with wisteria.

Rina emerged from the shadows, her lilac skirts swishing.

Alesta eyed her for a weapon. They were always pretty evenly matched when sparring, but Alesta was injured and exhausted.

Rina's eyes—smeared with colorful paint—widened. "Oh, thank Hektorus!" She grabbed Alesta's stinging hands and pulled her under the wisteria. "Lessie!" She flung her arms around Alesta and sobbed.

Alesta had no idea what was happening, but without thinking she hugged Rina back. The solid warmth of Rina was such a relief, such a reassurance, she let herself lean into it, and found herself crying, too. Chin on Rina's satin puff sleeve, she said, "I thought you were looking for me."

Rina's hands clutched Alesta's shoulders. "I *was*." She leaned back, blinking away tears. Her eyes were bloodshot, her hair frizzy over a tired-looking crown of braids. "And thank the gods I found you."

"I meant, to take me back to Mico."

Rina sniffled and shook her head. "He's having Lor taken to Teras!" Words spilled from her quickly. "My mother faked the selection to help him because she wants me to be queen." By the boughs, just how many girls had he tried to promise himself to? "And he's going to send an army to kill Teras once my father returns—"

"He can't!" Alesta almost sat back down in shock. They'd all turn to monsters. How many more had to be lost to that island? To the war still raging between the gods' children, no matter how they tried to dress it up as peace or a neat bargain?

"And he's having Kyrian taken to be left in the sun—"

Alesta's stomach lurched. "The court's letting Mico do that to him?" What had she done, ever asking Kyr to return here?

Rina held up her palms. "They don't know it's Kyrian!"

"But then—how do you?"

Rina swallowed, taking hold of Alesta's hand again. Her dark eyes gleamed. "Lessie, I Saw you, last night."

"What?"

"I was watching the ash clouds and the storm, like everyone, and then I could hear you calling to me. I Saw your face. You looked lost. And then you were gone, but—"

The vision. When Alesta had knocked out the monsters with the burning Lia. When she'd reached out for Rina.

Rina rushed on. "It turns out my mother knew about all our plans. She's been helping Mico this whole time. To secure me a place because of my lack of visions—" Rina's grip tightened. "But, Lessie, I *have* been having visions, ever since last night. Vision after vision. My mother helping Mico, getting him all that kharis. Kyrian saying he'd come back to help everyone, even though he knew they'd be horrible to him—and they were, gods. And you, just now, heading for the Arbor. So I told everyone to look for you at the university tower, where you spent all your time."

"And shouted your instructions," Alesta said, catching on, "so I would know how to avoid them." Her heart clenched and felt lighter at once. She wasn't alone. Rina was her friend, a better friend than she deserved.

"But now—" Rina's chin wobbled. "All I See is Lor being taken to the rock and dying." Her voice broke. "I love her so much and she's going to die because of—because of me—" Rina burst into sobs once more.

Alesta could only hold Rina again. She knew too well how she felt.

Rina sounded utterly wretched when she managed to say, "I tried to hide it, even when I knew that holding back was why the

Sight wouldn't work for me when my mother called me to it. But I think she chose Lor because she suspects—she suspects how I feel about her."

Alesta pulled Rina along, an arm still around her. "We have to get to the Arbor. Now. If we can get them to dig up the tree and take it to Teras, Lor will be safe." And all the others Mico would doom with his war. She couldn't think about how long Kyr might have. A stone-like weight crushed her chest again. She wanted to run and find him, save him from the sun, but the arrow's spikes would keep burning him from the inside, too. She had to do what she'd promised him.

"If Bianca faked Lor's selection," she told Rina, as they rushed past the tithing chamber, "maybe the alberos and other davinas will be upset enough to stand against what Mico wants—"

"Lessie." Rina stopped short. "They're all fake."

Alesta wrinkled her nose. "What's fake?"

"I Saw. My mother's been helping Mico, but even before that, she always directed the smoke where she wanted. All the davinas and the alberos, they've always sent who they chose."

That was why it was poor field hands. Orphans. Molissans. Girls. Never nobles. Unless they wanted to get rid of them. Alesta stared at the forest of little Lia branches set out so carefully. Her own was gone now, like Kyr's had been for a whole year. "That's why the Lia chose Kyr after the festival," she whispered. "It wasn't his fault, but it looked like it was. It was an excuse for Mico to get rid of him without arousing suspicion." She hadn't damned Kyr at all. It had been Mico.

And then he'd gone to work on Alesta, taking her up in her grief, molding her into a weapon to aim at Teras. At Aria.

Beside her, Rina murmured, "A vision showed me my mother manipulating the others into choosing him."

All those people who'd demanded so much of Kyr, turning so easily on him to protect themselves. "The king too?"

Rina shook her head. "The Arbor kept the truth even from the kings, used tithing to send a message to bow to its teachings and maintain its power. That's how my mother convinced them, despite Kyrian's position, with Albero Paolo all worked up about the flier." She tilted her head, as if listening to something distant. "Otherwise they'd use people's confessions to help determine who to send. Or just select whoever they felt would be missed least." She suddenly swayed, eyelids falling closed. Alesta wasn't sure anymore who was holding up whom. Eyes still closed, Rina said, "Another one. I'm not even using kharis to spark them."

"I think they're my fault," Alesta said. "I've had visions, too. With the smoke from burning the *Codex*, and I think I called out to you—"

Rina opened her eyes. Fear shone in them. "Maybe, but after that first vision of you, I Saw another girl. And she saw me, reached out to me. Her stare was—" Rina's shoulders trembled. "I feel— opened up. In some wild way. She wants me to See something. To understand something. Fix something." She shook her head. "Never mind. This vision—most of the alberos have gone."

"Gone?"

"The bells. They've gone to King Enzo's side. Or they're already with Mico. Only a few are left keeping the Perpetual Adoration."

Alesta pulled her along until they could peek from the archway out at the Arbor's great courtyard. Two alberos yet knelt at the stone kneeler across from the tree.

Rina hissed, eyes shut and practically swooning against the doorway. "Lor. On the ship. They're leaving." She clutched at her chest. Like her heart hurt so much she'd rather tear it out.

Alesta stared at the alberos. There was hardly anyone left to convince. No one to start digging. Mico would soon have everyone in the Towers under his sway. Kyr would die. Lor would die. And then so many more would die, or be lost to monstrousness, sent to fight Aria.

Alesta's ankle throbbed. A pulse of pain started up in her temples. *Think.* Find the right lever to pull to get the tree to Orroccio. Its silvery-green leaves shivered in a divine breeze. Alesta felt almost as if they shook the air back, sending waves like a fever through her. Rattling her until something slid into place in her mind. A dread certainty prickled over her skin. "I have a terrible idea."

Rina raised a questioning look to her, under tear-soaked lashes.

There was no doubt about it now. Alesta was as damned as a girl could be. She wasn't thinking of pulling a lever so much as breaking it right off the apparatus.

She was going to cut down the Lia.

Forget digging it out of the earth, keeping the tree whole, keeping it alive. Aria couldn't argue the deal wasn't kept because of some missing roots, not when the alberos collected leaves and berries and branches all the time. The Lia would likely burn up the moment Aria touched it anyway. But once it was cut down, there would be no reason for Mico, the Arbor, or anyone else to stop its being taken to her.

"We need to get the last of them away from the Lia," she whispered to Rina. "Or knock them out." She reached to her belt and remembered she'd lost her last knives back in Orroccio.

Rina held out an arm before her. "You're moving slow. And if they see you, they'll only have a hundred questions and could alert the others. Let me." She wiped a finger under her eye, streaking yellow paint to her temple. She gave a pained smile. "Lor's always telling me I'm excellent at distracting people from their work."

She drew a long breath, then rushed forward, lifting her skirts, crying out to the alberos in the courtyard. "My lord Mico sends for any kharis you have! King Enzo is gravely hurt and needs a miracle cure."

One gave Rina a bewildered look, drawing his chin to his chest. "The others took kharis already."

At the same time, the other shook his head. "But the Adoration—"

"The king needs *more!* He's dying; you have to hurry!" The alberos' shocked gazes followed Rina as she made for the doors to the sacristy, where the kharis was kept.

One stumbled to his feet to stop her. Ignoring the pain in her ankle, Alesta emerged and sneaked up behind the one still kneeling, bending to grab a rake some hurried albero must have dropped when the bells started. She swung the handle across the back of the man's head and knocked him out.

Outside the sacristy, Rina was keeping up a constant chatter, prying at the door while the other albero pressed it shut. "Absolutely all you can carry!" But he still must have heard the whack of the rake or Alesta's footsteps, and turned on her before she was within striking distance. Eyes widening, the man caught the rake as she came at him and tossed it aside, then lunged for her. Rina flung the door open, knocking him sideways. With a cry of pain, Alesta landed a strike to his temple, and he hit the ground in a heap.

Rina sagged back against the sacristy wall while Alesta hobbled to the glass shed near the atrium. She needed an axe.

Somewhat thinly but with satisfaction, Rina said, "That must have been three or four sins at least."

Alesta searched through the well-oiled tools. The albéros used these because anything else would have no effect on the immortal tree. Its divinity protected it from most injury, but shears covered in its own oil could cut it. Alesta hefted the little axe they used for trimming tithing boughs and made for the tree at the center of the yard.

The pounding in her head increased. Like the footfalls of something even greater than Teras. Alesta felt as if she walked against a crushing tide. The scars on her arms began burning. Her monstrousness and the holiness of the Lia were like opposing poles of two lodestones. The tree was pushing her away.

Rina also seemed to be struggling, as she straightened and staggered nearer. "The tree——" She extended her arms before her, but Alesta couldn't tell if she was reaching for the Lia or attempting to shield herself from it. Rina's shoulders shuddered. She grimaced, but her eyes seemed frozen open. Alesta was torn between fighting on toward the tree or to Rina, to help her—there was no monster in her like there was in Alesta, but being near the tree was affecting her somehow.

Alesta dropped the axe and stumbled to her friend, just as Rina's pupils and irises sharpened to pinpoints, her entire eyes filling with white. "Hektorus placed a living piece of his divinity into the island," Rina pronounced. "Tied it there forever by rooting it to the earth. Limiting its power. Oh——*Oh. Oh, no.*" The unnatural white drifted like smoke from her eyes, like burning kharis, lit in the sunlight like molten gold coursing through the air.

"*They knew*. They all knew—it was her. Rooted there. Not taken. Not lost. Trapped. Forever." The smoke wound about the Lia tree, like a great tithing bough. Rina's chest heaved, faster and faster, as her words broke into sobs. "They all knew. They knew. The kings. The Arbor. They all knew—"

Alesta caught Rina as she pitched forward, cries crescendoing to screams. Her ankle pinched and she eased Rina to the ground, eyes blessedly closed. Alesta's gaze wrenched to the tree, where gleaming smoke still ringed its trunk.

Chapter Twenty-Nine

BOTH OF US BURNING

A lesta picked up the axe and threw herself back toward the Lia. She had to finish this. She didn't know what Rina's vision meant. Aria had been tied to the source of monstrousness, trapped there for an age. But what was that about Hektorus' divinity?

"What are you doing!" someone shouted behind her. "What are you doing here?"

She whirled. Nausea nearly as bad as what the tree was doing to her drenched through her insides. Perfect. Not every albero had left the Arbor. Albero Paolo must have been keeping vigil in the sanctuary. Now he took in the fallen men and rushed to crouch beside Rina. "What did you do to them? You wicked girl." His gaze fell to the axe in Alesta's grip. He flapped his hands at her, the billowing sleeves of his robes snapping. "Get away from the Lia!"

She tried to ignore him, making again for the tree. But she still felt like she was trying to run in a dream, through deep water, and Albero Paolo moved to her side without impediment. He grabbed her shoulder.

She did not have time for this. "I was too wicked even to feed

Teras," she said, turning to the albero. "Hell choked on me and spat me out." She drew back a fist and punched Albero Paolo across the jaw.

His head knocked against the flagstones.

Alesta stared at him, shocked by her own violence here, Rina's cries still ringing in her ears. What did Albero Paolo know inside that battered head of his? That the sacrifices were chosen not by the Lia but him and his brethren, for certain. That the devil was in truth a Soladisan girl punished and trapped? But why would King Enzo—gods, *the king*—say they needed Aria?

A wisping trail of smoke pulled her gaze again to the tree. Branches stretching for the sky. Roots plunging into the rich earth of Soladisa. Like in her vision.

What if King Enzo hadn't been speaking of Aria at all?

The wheat-haired maiden. Guiding Graziela down through hell—to where Aria was trapped. Finding Alesta in the darkness wrought by the Lia parchment and showing her who Aria had been. Starting visions in Rina to try to reveal—what?

Rina had mentioned a living piece of Hektorus' divinity. The alberos always called the tree that. An offshoot of his power. But what if it meant more? What if there was a reason the maiden had walked skimming in the air just as Hektorus did—like a child taking after her father?

Alesta watched one finger of smoke trace a path into the corner of the yard, toward the silent statue with golden hair upon the altar of Hektorus' lost daughter.

Stolen by monsters. Lost to history. Her story abbreviated. And only told by her father and the very people who had lied about the Lia, the tithings, from the very start.

Aria said she'd been noticed by a god. Alesta had assumed that meant Hektorus, throwing her into hell and punishing her for some unknown transgression. But in her vision, Alesta had Seen the maiden find Aria working. Felt how her song filled her with happiness.

Aria's frantic search for the Lia among Alesta's things. Her howl when it dissipated.

No greater pain than losing the girl you love.

Alesta's fingers clenched the axe handle so hard it shook. She still didn't understand everything. But for once, she did not feel compelled to search out all the answers. She knew enough. She lifted her gaze to the Lia's glorious trunk, its lofty boughs, stretching across the sublime sky. Like the slats of an animal's pen. Like Rina's screams rising through the air.

The Lia wasn't a tree at all. She was a girl—a demigoddess—transformed and trapped. Pieces of her cut off, taken and taken and taken. Leaves plucked and fruit pulled and bark scraped, all used by Soladisa. For centuries.

This was who Aria was desperate for. She wasn't waiting for a tree but the girl she loved.

Alesta had to free her.

She launched herself forward, the force of the Lia's holiness driving against her. Alesta dragged her feet across the flagstones, her ankle protesting. She climbed the low wall surrounding the heart of the courtyard, across the soil snaked over by the Lia's roots. The earth Rina said had trapped Hektorus' divinity here.

So all Alesta had to do to break it free was sever its tie to the earth.

When she reached the Lia, Alesta braced a hand against its trunk, then pulled away fast. Her palm was red, welts already springing up. She hissed, but raised the axe.

The moment metal met bark, the axehead dissolved into nothing but a splash of molten iron.

Alesta stared at the empty handle in her hand. Fine. This prison of a tree protected itself, even against the prepared tools when used in an attempt to destroy it. The axe was metal and Lia oil. What else might be able to work its way through the slender trunk and its holiness?

Alesta scrunched her nose at the imprint of her hand burned into the bark. Her gaze drifted to her inflamed palm. Holiness and monstrousness consumed each other. It wasn't good and evil, simply a reaction between the two. The Lia had burned away monstrousness before it could take root, all the times Alesta had been absolved. But now it had taken hold deep within her. The balm had burned away in a moment. Only Lia magically forged into metal itself endured. Like the pieces slowly killing Kyr right now.

But wood burned fast.

If she was right, and this tree harnessed a goddess to the land, Alesta didn't need to match all her holy power. Just the earthly form that trapped her. Just bark and wood and sap. Look at her wrist guards, turned worn in moments. The seeds evaporating in Aria's hand. The trunk was more substantial, but Alesta could withstand that much. There was plenty of her to burn.

She'd tried to free Kyr from hell, and feared she'd only failed him. She could still save all the others Mico intended to send, before they went to the same fate. She could still help Lor and Rina. She could help the wheat-haired maiden and Aria. She took a deep, steeling breath.

Her hand trembled.

She never wanted to be a sacrifice. She'd only wanted to be thought worthy of having a place here or to at least preserve it for others. Scrabbling for status, she'd driven herself to attain glory in others' eyes one way or another.

But the Arbor and its rules were false. Everything that propped some people up and shamed others. They were lies, or truths twisted to make people like her follow like sheep, believing they had no worth otherwise.

People cared about her anyway. They loved her. Alesta ached with the want to be with Kyr, here or on Orroccio or wherever would give them a second chance at what they'd lost.

But what mattered most was that she cared about herself. Enough to know she needed to do the right thing now. Not to prove herself. Not because anyone else said it was virtuous. Most would probably say it was wicked.

Only because she knew for herself it was right, and necessary, and would help those who'd had everything taken for too long. It would stop it happening again. She was no weapon in Mico's hand now, no arrow flying where he aimed. Even if she'd never completed them, she felt empowered as if she wore her wings, pumping her own way through the sky.

"If I don't survive this," she told the tree, too scared to feel ridiculous, "it's your job to try to rescue Kyr, and Lor, and Aria, and everyone."

Alesta flung the axe handle aside and wrapped her arms around the Lia's trunk.

It burned against her skin, even more reactive than the *Codex* page had been. Instinct drove her back, dredging her hands across the bark. It charred and flaked away as she pressed herself again to the tree. She knotted her hands together to prevent her retreating.

Heat and smoke kindled underneath her. It ate into the tree. It ate into her.

She wanted to let go. She pushed into the fire, cutting through the wood faster. When it became too much, she fought simply to cling to the tree, practically hanging from it where her hands sparked with blue lightning.

The tree crackled. Flames ripped into the air. In the glass of the atrium, Alesta could see their reflection shine, could see how she burned. She blazed. She was becoming light, like the stars so sharp, like rainbows that couldn't last. Like the gleam in Kyr's eyes when he looked at her.

Skin and bark burned. Blood and sap. Wood and bone.

Alesta unleashed a scream loud enough to banish a thousand monsters as everything went white.

The Lia seared into Kyrian's wrists.

He was in another nightmare, everyone accusing and shouting. They'd dragged him to the game court—covered in fine stone latticework and closed in on all sides by high balconies, protected by nets for when courtiers would come watch his cousins and him play. Filled now with Soladisans gasping at the sight of him. Calling him devil. Monster.

Kyrian couldn't see any of this. He huddled in a corner of shadow as the sun angled down into the yard, glaring off surfaces, soon to drown him in its light.

The fire in his belly had turned into a dull ache that throbbed through his entire wretched body. Through his head. The poison and the bells and the sun made it impossible to think. To even remember, in that way of nightmares, how he had come here. Where was Alesta? They'd stolen her away from him. Everything was a bright blur and a pandemonium of cries and jeers. Doubled over, Kyrian strained again against the rope. It cut through the skin of his ankles and wings, too, burning once it met his blood.

Mico's voice rang out, in place of the bells that had finally paused. "We shall let Hektorus' holy sky deliver justice upon this beast. As he protected us from monsters long ago, his sun will burn this devil away." Shouts. Cheering.

The noise. The roaring in his head. The sulfur in the air warning him he was close to giving Mico the show he wanted. Driving away every thought but escape.

They couldn't hold him. Thin rope and fragile stone? He'd fought his way out of the bowels of hell, off the devil's rock itself. No one left Orroccio, but he had.

He could even free himself from the monstrousness that caged him yet—he could break out and break necks and reclaim his human form, even if it meant forsaking the last scraps of his humanity. Even if it would make him what they all believed him to be.

The Kyrian who lived on this island had tried so hard to hide, to be what they wanted, to do things the way they said was right. Returning, he'd hoped to make things better for them all, to finally be better, himself, and they answered with only abuse and derision. He could sit here and die like they all wanted. But the sun marched nearer across the courtyard floor, and he had learned to survive, doing whatever it took. Wasn't that what his kingdom had taught him above all? It was only what Soladisa had done for itself, ensuring its survival by sending its youths to die. Sending him to that place. Making him a part of it, making him see they were no different underneath all their artifice from Orroccio. Why not visit its horrors back upon them? Paint in beautiful, shining blood that truth?

He was the nightmare.

The singed and bloody Lia rope snapped. Kyrian drew his claws free. The exclamations around him turned to screams as he slashed the last strands of holiness holding him back.

His skin threatening to ignite was his only catechism now. He could once again let his death purchase the lie of peace. Or he could be the monster they all saw.

Either way, he would burn.

Chapter Thirty
JUBILEE

In the echoes of Alesta's screams, the glass of the atrium melted and shattered, its pieces a thousand burning stars, and another girl was bleeding beside her.

Her limbs were a bloody, mangled mess. Her long fair hair stuck to her brow with sweat. Alesta, falling to the soil next to where the girl lay without touching the earth, was sure she'd made a cosmic error, blundered far worse than ever before. The pain of knowing that hurt even more than the all-consuming pain ravaging what was left of her body.

The girl inhaled.

Alesta wasn't entirely sure she was still breathing.

The girl exhaled, and was whole.

At least Alesta could witness this before she died—something beyond mechanics, beyond the kingdom's magic. Beyond judgments and bargains and any boundaries. Her dying heart staggered at this grace, filling the hollow feeling left by the alberos' speeches, expanding every smallness she'd ever felt reduced to. This was the greatness she'd sought, always just beyond her reach. Until this moment.

And then that greatness turned to her, the goddess' green eyes brimming with a kindness like springtime. A whisper of a touch. A breath like a caress, over skin suddenly healed.

"It's her." Alesta sat up to see Rina, hands splayed against the low wall ringing where the tree had stood. Her friend's face pulled into a wide smile. "It's you. Lia!" Rina dropped into a deep curtsy.

"Yes." The word upon the goddess' mouth was a gentle smile, a voice silvery and full. Lia rose in one fluid movement, wheaten hair swinging past her slender hips. She was naked but stood as regally as the first king and queen of Soladisa in the mural across the courtyard.

Alesta scrambled to her feet, feeling her unharmed skin where her breeches were shredded across her thighs, her chest where one strap of her bodice was charred away. Her entire beautiful, abundant, unburnt body.

She lifted her hands, staring at her unblistered palms. Her arms, where the wrist guards had burned away, free of lightning scars. She shivered in a breath. "You can heal monstrousness even when it's taken hold?"

"Yes," the goddess said again. The silver in her voice forged into something fierce. "I intend to save Aria this way."

Alesta didn't know the proper intercession like a davina or albero might. She simply blurted, "Kyr first! Please." Her eyes widened at her own audaciousness. "Please. I never could have made it to Aria without him, or back to free you—"

"Yes."

Alesta's chest heaved a little gasp, as if she could drink in Lia's answer. No bargaining when all was given freely. No accounting sins when all forgiven. The goddess blurred and multiplied in

Alesta's vision as tears sprang to her eyes.

Rina had rushed to grab something from the ruins of the shed and now shook it free of glass and dirt as she approached again, holding out one of the white smocks the alberos wore while gardening. "May I offer you something to clothe yourself with, my most exalted lady?" She always knew just what to say.

Lia nodded, and Alesta helped her into the smock. Rina held out a hand to help Lia step down.

"We have to hurry," Alesta said, battered boots smacking into the flagstones. Her ankle felt better. She winced only because she was berating a goddess—who stumbled against Rina.

"Apologies!" gasped Rina. "My head is still ringing."

Lia took a few faltering steps and sank onto the nearest bench. "I also need a moment. Before I can walk or perform another blessing. It can be taxing, holding divinity in a mortal form. And this one is much smaller than the tree was."

"Of course," Alesta said, trying not to scream that they needed to get moving. "Thank you for helping," she hastened to add. "You're very generous—" Especially after what the kingdom had done to her.

"Not particularly," Lia said, a little dazed, "among all the gods."

"Oh?" Rina asked, as the goddess looked upon the mural of the tree she had been.

"It's just that my father loves bargains." Lia stared at where Hektorus rode the sky, shimmering and fragmented. "He loves feeling his power over others." With a sigh, she explained, "My father is known in the heavenly fields as something of a trickster. He made me a bargain—" She broke off, a pained look on her lovely face.

"The betrothal covenant!" Rina nodded. "The promise to choose who you married."

Lia pursed her lips. "He swore I could marry whoever I bestowed my kiss upon. Then, when I fell in love with Aria, before I could seal the bargain, he planted her in the source of monstrousness and me in this island." The brightness in her eyes dimmed. "He made my sweet Aria a monster, and me a sacred tree, used by this kingdom, but unable to draw upon my full power."

"How *dreadful*," Rina breathed.

Alesta, still piecing together that Hektorus and the trickster god were one and the same, let out a quiet huff. "You couldn't even touch in those opposing forms, without destroying each other."

"He thought it was a clever joke. The monsters' god had made his own curse, as my father slew him, that humans and monsters would become what they killed."

"*That* was his curse?"

Lia nodded. "And for monsters to grow stronger, too, if they did turn more human. They'd all either learn to leave each other in peace, or meld until indistinguishable. But it would be impossible for the humans to erase his children from the earth."

Alesta rubbed her arms where her scars had disappeared, thinking of Kyr, of Phoebe. No peace had come of any of these deals. But so much hatred. Against each other and themselves. "So it's not Hektorus blighting us for our sins, like the Arbor says." With monstrousness, or plain ugliness. "He didn't make me this way because I'm——" Her voice cracked.

Lia leveled her gaze at Alesta. "He did not make you at all. Great Mother Cressa gives all humans life. And she loves each of her children."

Alesta couldn't swallow down another revelation, not when every fiber of her was busy agonizing over Kyr. Her eyes, suddenly wet again with tears, turned impatiently toward the archway out of the courtyard.

Thank the entire mysterious pantheon, Lia tentatively stood. "What my father primarily makes," she said darkly, "is trouble. Starting the war against one of the oldest members of the pantheon."

Rina stepped forward and offered her arm again. "But why? If it wasn't over you?"

Lia let her guide the way across the yard. "The underworld god and his monsters were ancient among ancients. Declining in power, the god no longer attending the pantheon's court. My father decided they offended him and to claim more of the earth for his favored humans, who worshiped him for it. He was tired and injured afterward. I found him on this island, where the humans who had barely survived before were founding a kingdom. He'd promised to give me to their king, who wanted a bride, to be bound to him and help, in exchange for the king taking care of him when he was weak." Lia shook her head, her smock ruffling behind her as they rushed down a long staircase. "He only liked the man because of how he fawned over him so much. But he'd already made the covenant with me, and I spoiled his plans for playing the benevolent patron when I met Aria. So, he taught me a lesson." Her voice grew thick. "His bargains are traps, more often than not." She cocked one eyebrow at Alesta, who was trying not to break into a sprint beside her. "He played a trick on that king, too. He got me to help strengthen his new kingdom, but not as he expected."

They reached a lower courtyard and Lia dropped Rina's arm. "I think I can manage on my own now." And she followed quickly as Rina led them on, shortcutting through a tower.

Alesta's hands clenched and opened like dual heartbeats as they raced past chamber after chamber. "Are you certain you can restore Aria to what she was? She's seeped in so much monstrousness." Could Lia even really save Kyr? Would there be anything left of him to save when they reached him? Her stomach flipped and she sped her feet.

"The source of monstrousness is a deep well," Lia said, "but it does have its limit. It's merely the remains of the dead god's power. Even as a demigoddess, I can draw upon the full force of all living divinity, which is infinite."

Lia's breath hitched at this. Alesta frowned. That sounded like an awful lot to pull through her mortal form, like she'd said. "Is that dangerous for you?"

Lia didn't answer as they hurried on under the arching ceiling and globes lit by her own stolen magic. Only as they reached the far end of the hall did she murmur, "What good is my power if I do not use it to free her?"

They emerged to a cloister echoing with shouts as people streamed away from the direction of the game court. The three of them had to work their way against a crowd of fearful faces, even as others lingered and pressed to get nearer and see, like fighting through a brackish tide.

The shouts turned to outright screams as they shoved their way nearer the yard. Rina elbowed escaping courtiers to one side and Alesta rushed forward, to the lowest level's nets. Her fingers clutched at the fibers, and she leaned forward to see Kyr, another net tangled over one widespread wing, ramming a shoulder into the latticework ceiling covering the court.

He fell back as pieces of the stone cracked off and dropped to the court's floor. He crashed into a balcony—the nets barely protecting the courtiers, screaming and shoving to get away—and rushed again upward, flying wildly, hitting another spot on the lattice.

Rina sucked a breath. "What is he—"

Alesta tugged at the net and shouted, "Kyr!" But he wouldn't hear her among the multitude of cries. She ran along the side of the court, until she found a section of damaged net, where Kyr must have slashed at it trying to get out. Yanking hard, she called out to him again. "Kyr! We can heal you!" She turned to Rina. "Help me!"

Rina's eyes were round as she followed. "Are you sure? Even if it *was* Kyrian, he seems—not himself anymore."

"He can't see! He's hurt and panicking—"

Rina still looked uncertain as she pulled opposite her. The frayed ropes came apart just enough. Rina held them back as Alesta squeezed through.

Kyr barreled into another balcony of courtiers, slashing with his horns. This time he growled and stabbed a hand through the netting. Alesta saw Mico throw himself backward, barely avoiding his claws, but Kyr punched out again and his knuckles caught his cousin across the face.

Alesta whirled to Lia, fingers tight on the net. "Can you heal him from here? Can you fly?"

Lia shook her head, tense concern on her face. "I am not my father."

Kyr bellowed and flew upward, haphazardly striking at the lattice. The skin on his arms smoked. If he got out, he'd fly away heedlessly, and the sun would surely kill him. It would turn him into one of those charred figures she'd seen laid out on Orroccio. "Then I'll call him down."

Rina wrung her hands. "What if he hurts you?"

Alesta looked to where Kyr thrashed between her and the sky. "That's not who he is." She took several steps forward into the center of the court, swiping her palms down her ragged breeches. "Kyr!" He still didn't seem to hear her, though a few of the crowd cast bewildered looks her way. Again she called his name. Another piece of lattice broke away and the sun slashed across Kyr's skin. Any more and he'd slip out into the burning sky. She nearly choked on his name, on her regret for bringing him here. People were pointing at her now, squinting, mystified. She drew a long breath. Then she lifted her chin and shouted, "My lord Kyrian, stop being so over-dramatic and get down here at once!"

Kyr wheeled about the heights of the court. Cries of confusion added to the cacophony. Mico, a gash across his cheek, pointed down at her. "Take hold of that one! Orroccio has driven her mad!" Alesta ignored him, yelling again to help Kyr find his way to her. If Lia could save him, everyone would see what Orroccio would do to anyone else they sent. They'd see they needed to end this war, not with more killing, but by fixing what had been broken.

A rush of wind over his wings echoed by gasps through the courtyard, and Kyr swept down toward her.

Her voice died in her throat. When he landed, he collapsed to his knees, wings outstretched to their full span, a hand clutching his side. He bounded up at once, coming at Alesta fast as rising screams raked through the air.

She caught him as his arms went around her shoulders and he sagged against her. *"Kyr."* He folded his wings and dropped his forehead to hers. "It's all right." Alesta looked to where Lia was following through the netting. When Alesta shifted, Kyr tightened his hold on her. The sun boring through the latticework set spots all along his arms burning. Tears trailed over the leathery skin of his face. She pulled Kyr's hands from her shoulders and guided him to where Lia outstretched her own. "She's going to help you." Kyr seemed to struggle, as Alesta had when trying to reach the tree. She tugged him forward, step by step. At last Lia wrapped her hands around Kyr's.

Someone exclaimed something about the girl's feet not touching the ground, and then a charge of light and air flew out from where Lia held Kyr. Alesta blinked against the brightness and the wind and staggered back.

Kyr fell to his knees before Lia. She cupped his face in her hands. The light grew, but his monstrousness did not burn away so much as melt, scales and wings and horns, leaving Kyr as he was and not as he was one year ago.

When it faded, Kyr knelt on the ground in rags, human once more.

Chapter Thirty-One
SKIN AND SALT

lesta could only stare as the crowd reacted. "Goddess!" People in the balconies dropped to their knees, just like Kyr. Some wept. More cried out to Lia, who looked a little pale but smiled down at Kyr. Courtiers rushed back from where they'd pushed to get away. "Our lady!"

Lia stepped back, hands spreading wide. Kyr rose, unsteady. The spikes from the arrow littered the ground beside him. Shards of sunlight scattered over his smooth skin. Some of the changes Alesta had seen in him back on Orroccio were still evident—sharpened cheekbones, marked now only with sun-gilt streaks of tears. The shadow along his jaw and black hair falling past his shoulders.

But everyone recognized him. They began calling out his name as well.

Alesta wanted to run to him. She wanted to run away, suddenly feeling exposed and off-balance—then she realized the ground *was* actually shaking. Distant booms sounded.

Rina was yelling. She grabbed Alesta by the arm. "We have to go! Now!"

Lia's palms pressed to her chest. "Aria." She swept to Alesta's side. "I must reach her."

"That's what I've been saying!" Rina shouted. "Before the ship reaches her first!"

Kyr lifted his gaze from his trembling hands, finding Alesta between the two other girls, the wild look in his dark eyes striking her like an arrow hitting dead center.

Without turning from Kyr, feeling as if something was lodged in her throat, Alesta told Lia, "We'll get you to her." If Lia could do for her what she'd done for Kyr, there would be no more tithings, no more losses.

Kyr took a step toward her, only for Mico to block the way. "I'm amazed," Mico said, loud enough to steer the court's attention in his direction. "Shocked. That it was you."

Alesta noticed the gash along Mico's cheek was already an angry red from where Kyr's stinger must have struck. If the world didn't end, and she survived, she was going to enjoy seeing his face swell twice its size for a few days. It would make a good start toward the justice he owed them all.

For now, Mico wore a mask of troubled concern, as he turned to the crowd. "That it was our lord Kyrian who killed the king."

Kyrian sucked his teeth, feeling out his mouth. Deciding what to say.

As always, Mico had no trouble talking. "Thankfully," his cousin went on, "we have been blessed and visited by this goddess, who has revealed the truth." He bowed low to the goddess.

"Allow me to extend you welcome, our most exalted lady, on behalf of my kingdom—"

His words were swallowed up by a new outcry. Gold turned gray as the sky rapidly darkened. Ash spread over the fragmented sky. Shouts came now about Orroccio. Teras' wrath.

Rina pleaded, hands twisting her skirts into wrinkles. "We have to go! *Lor!*"

Mico raised his hands, turning from one side of the court to the other. "I've taken care of it. The new tithing has been sent."

Alesta burst out, "It won't matter. Orroccio offered to take me, or allow us to bring Lia. We don't know another tithing will be accepted."

Anxiety pulsed down Kyrian's spine. They still needed Soladisa's help to keep their end of the bargain. But maybe this goddess Alesta had somehow called upon would aid them further.

"I've already told you—" Mico turned on Alesta, sticking his face in hers. "You are not taking the Lia to the devil."

Worries about Orroccio evaporated for the moment. Kyr dove forward, bearing uncertain, but he wedged his remade body between Mico and Alesta.

"You know, cousin—" His own voice sounded strange in his head, and he found himself stumbling over his words. He pressed on, speaking low as he told Mico, "I might have eaten you to help myself become human again." The memory of what Mico had done to him—how he had sent Alesta after him into hell—flooded Kyrian, and his hands threshed the air. "I would have been justified. You are a monster, after all."

Mico's lip curled. Then he ducked back, as if afraid of Kyrian. As if Kyrian had been reaching for him.

Kyrian's hands clenched at his sides. He'd eaten many repulsive things in Orroccio, but none as sickening as Mico. "I'll leave you to your own judgment," Kyrian said. His nostrils flared. "Well. And everyone else's." He raised his voice to match the one Mico had been using for their audience. "They deserve to know it was you who killed Enzo." Pain having nothing to do with kharis arrows pierced through him. "And Ciro."

The noise from the balconies quieted, then rumbles grew, like a wave sucking out to sea and rushing back. Kyrian caught sight of Bianca, not coming to stand beside Mico, but keeping her watchful eyes on the people.

Mico scoffed. "He's lying. He killed our king!" Gesturing at the slash on his face, he turned to another side of the court. "You saw him." Another. "You saw what he was."

They had. Mico had the respect of every part of Soladisan society. In his embroidered jacket and shining boots, he looked like a king. Kyrian was barefoot, barely dressed, in rags. Minutes ago everyone here had witnessed him flailing like a trapped animal.

He felt like that animal was still clawing inside his chest as attendants and advisers ran onto the court.

"What he is!" Mico shouted, aping Kyrian's hands.

So much shouting. People yelling at both of them, at each other. As much discord as at Orroccio's revels. Courtiers and tradespeople called out, some of them following into the yard. "Our lord Kyrian would never hurt the king!" Many declared times he'd helped them, or been kind, in small ways he didn't even remember. Their shouting drowned out the few protests.

The people ringed them. The confidence drained from his cousin's face. "Don't let appearances deceive you! She's one, too!"

Mico pointed to Alesta. "She turned monster in Orroccio!"

A few in the crowd answered that this was visibly not true. Others demanded Mico's accusation be heard.

"Show them!" Mico darted past Kyrian, who for a fleeting moment missed being huge and hulking. Mico shoved Alesta. Shouted. "Show them all the fire you attacked me with." Kyrian hauled Mico back, but his cousin unsheathed a knife. Pointed it at Alesta. "Let's draw the monster out."

Vision going as red as the deepest stratum of hell, Kyrian locked his hand around Mico's wrist. *"Enough."* He dragged Mico's arm away from Alesta.

She had her hands splayed defensively but lunged forward. "No!"

Kyrian followed her horrified gaze to where Mico's other hand pulled another dagger from his belt to slash at Kyrian's exposed torso—at Alesta, unarmed and moving into the way.

The three of them crashed together. Kyrian watched Alesta's face, sure any sign of pain there would destroy him as hell had not. She stared back at him, and he suddenly knew exactly how dread must have painted her features that day she'd learned he'd been tithed.

Then Mico staggered back, his own bright blood staining his jacket now.

He coughed. The bloodied knife clattered to the ground. The first blade he'd aimed at Alesta fell from his hand. She fumbled it before sliding it into her belt. Mico clutched his side. "See the sin yet sticking to them!" he wheezed. "The violence!"

Rina, who'd pulled the goddess from the fray, made an indignant sound. *"You* attacked *them."*

People were rushing around Mico again, bearing him up, staunching his wound with someone's scarf.

Enough, Kyrian told himself this time. He'd waited too long to tell them all the full truth. "What everyone can see," he declared loudly, "is what going to Orroccio did to me." He swallowed, but raised his voice again. "Because I killed there. Which is what will happen to anyone who tries the same. We cannot send an army against them."

Mico protested, "We cannot serve the wishes of the devil."

"She's not a devil," Alesta cried. "She's a Soladisan, only sent there for trying to pledge to another girl."

Mico's lip curled. "An abomination indeed." He sagged against the courtier at his side. "And my lord Kyrian admits he's a killer."

Another who'd been defending Kyrian earlier clamped his hand to Mico's shoulder. "You're the one everyone here saw attempting murder." Yelling started up again, quickly growing into an accusatory rumble, as insistent as the wordless one venting from Orroccio. *He wants to send us all to die there. He'd make us all into monsters. Our lord Mico killed the king.*

"I think you need to go rest, cousin," Kyrian told him.

Mico's brows darted together, his face gone pallid, but he didn't waver. "You can't let them take the Lia!" he ordered weakly. "Don't let them take it to Orroccio!"

The goddess granted Mico a sweet smile. "But I want to go."

Mico's lips pursed in confusion as more courtiers helped him, whether he was willing or not, from the yard. Rina started saying something about Lor again, but Kyrian could only stare at the goddess she spoke to—at her long hair, almost silvery under the ashy sky. At the albero's smock she wore.

It was too much—the arguments and the truth hitting him and the thousand questions it invited. He knew they had to get moving, but he just needed a moment. He turned to Alesta. Her own clothes were burned, he realized. Her cheeks were ruddy. Was she all right? He leaned in—he no longer had to stoop to meet her eye. "Hey."

"Hello." Her voice was small.

"You're not hurt?"

She shook her head. "Never better."

She'd just faced down an out-of-his-mind devil and apparently freed a goddess, not to mention surviving his murderous cousin, but he knew how her strength didn't mean she didn't struggle. Still, she'd done it. Somehow managed beyond his wildest hopes when he'd lain dying on Mico's floor. "So, Lia?"

Alesta gave a little shrug. "Not a tree. How do you feel?"

He felt like his throat was going to close up as he swallowed back tears. He couldn't say how she was the reason he'd hung on to himself even as he'd burned. That her faith in him was how he'd clung, through all his confusion, to the goodness she somehow still saw in him. So, he simply took her hand in his. Wondering at the sight and feel of his own skin against hers, he swept his thumb over her knuckles. He didn't deserve it, any of it—the unexpected reprieve from monstrosity, the faith his people apparently had in him, or her hand in his. He blinked, but the tears still didn't stop.

"But the cargo ships aren't returned yet!" Rina's voice penetrated the daze he was in.

Lia was asking, "How then may we reach Orroccio?"

Panic rose in Rina's voice. "And catch up to Lor in time?"

She gave Alesta a little shake. "Alesta? What are we going to do?" To Kyrian, she added, "I am glad you didn't burn alive, but a pair of wings would be incredibly useful right now."

Wiping his eyes with the back of one hand, Kyrian released a gentle huff. He'd missed Rina.

Alesta looked around at them. "Lia can't fly like her father. Kyr's wings are gone." She stared down at where his hand still held hers. He wasn't entirely sure he was capable of letting go. "All we have are each other." She lifted her face again, and *gods* there was that glint in her eyes that always made his heart clench the same, no matter how the rest of him might transform. "I think I might have a way."

The stark red sun was still high as they set out to the old barn, its light blotted in ash spewed from Orroccio.

Courtiers and others had swarmed Lia and Kyr, and attendants and advisers insisted they'd help with whatever was needed, so a crowd followed them down the island. Lia was quietly kind to the Soladisans angling to get near to her, even as some begged her to save them from *that beast* or *the devil*. Alesta supposed patience that had endured centuries was no weak thing.

Kyr was less concerned with politeness. When some important-looking adviser had called to him about needing to discuss vital matters and offering to take him to the royal tower, Kyr had replied with only a curt, "Later," and offered his arm to Rina, who'd begun crying again. He'd towed Alesta along with his other hand, setting a pace out of the Towers the entourage could only trail after.

He paused once, to accept a pair of boots from an out-of-breath attendant. He squeezed Alesta's hand harder as they passed the villa, but they spoke only of what Rina had learned in her visions and what Lia had told them, under a darkening sky, until they crested the last hill and the barn stood before the gray-blue sea.

Another boom shook the ground, and Rina loosed a little shriek, clinging to Kyr. Everyone looked to where the western horizon darkened. But Kyr peered down the slope the other way. "It's wrong. Isn't it?"

Alesta followed his gaze. "What is?"

He shook his head. "It's been so long, but——" He angled his head, and nodded. "There's a light coming from the east?"

Alesta squinted at the unexpected light riding over the waves. The false twilight Aria had created lightened with faint gold on that side of the world. "There *is*. What is that?"

Rina gave another moan, and Alesta tried to think how a friend should reassure her. "Lor can't be in danger, yet," she told Rina. "The ship's still in the middle of the poison sea." Rina shut her eyes, dragging them all to a stop. Alesta gritted her teeth at herself for upsetting Rina more, but they really did need to keep moving.

Rina remained still, eyes closed. "It's him." Her whisper barely carried over the breeze whipping from the east. That couldn't be right—when had the wind changed? The ash had carried here from Orroccio.

"Who?" Kyr asked her.

People began pointing at the strange light. Some ran ahead toward the bluffs. Some stopped and pulled back fearfully.

Rina said again, *"It's him!"*

Lia drew nearer, threading through the exclaiming people, strands of hair blowing across her uneasy face. "It's my father. He knows I'm free." She tucked a lock of hair behind her ear and pressed her lips in a line. "He's coming."

Chapter Thirty-Two

OVER THE WIND

A lesta stiffened as Rina drifted away from them, lifting one hand before her. "Hektorus. He's speeding across the world. Wind and light—" The crowd hummed with this news, the god's name a susurrus spreading through it.

Alesta's throat went dry. She did not feel the wonder some of the courtiers and attendants clearly did. Was Hektorus angry she had freed his daughter? She'd never thought their god would judge her well on his shiny pair of scales, but now panic clawed in her belly. She couldn't seem to swallow.

Rina pivoted to Lia. "He wants to prevent your reaching Aria."

The demigoddess nodded somberly. "He'll trap me again. Aria will remain what she is, and if we don't want your island to burn, Alesta will have to—"

"No." Kyr pulled their hands to his chest.

"Right." Alesta finally swallowed. "Don't want that. So let's get Lia over there." She'd worry about the other possibility when they saw if Lia could in fact free Aria. Even if the tithing ceremonies had been fake, Hektorus might yet see Alesta end up a sacrifice to

Orroccio. "The wind should only help us."

Some people were falling to their knees again, exclaiming about Hektorus returning at last. A few broke out in ecstatic prayer. "Grant me, oh Hektorus—"

Lia snapped her gaze to them and darted over, looking truly angry for the first time, hands clenched, muscles in her arms tensed into cords. "Do not ever utter those words." The people gaped up at her. "That will invoke my father if he is near enough by."

"But that's how we always pray," a man objected.

A woman asked, brows drawn together, "Why shouldn't we invoke our heavenly patron—?"

Lia lifted her head and explained to everyone, eyes wide but filled with conviction, "When invoked, he must stand before you while you make your petition. It's how his power works. But it is a trap. Once you enter into negotiations, he will tempt you into a dreadful bargain."

"Got it." Alesta nodded. "No more bargains, no letting Hektorus catch us before we reach Aria. Let's go." She tugged Kyr along. One or two of those on their knees stared uncertainly at Lia, or murmured to one another, but most followed. They raced the rest of the way to the barn.

When Alesta and Kyr began shoving the barn doors open, the people clamored to help, and soon everyone could see her improved flier spreading its silk wings wide. Alesta glanced nervously at Rina and Kyr. Her last flier had hurt them both.

Rina was already hiking her skirts and climbing up into the craft. Kyr turned to Alesta, mouth open, eyes bright with wonder. "And it flies?"

She ran to grab one of his old paint shirts and offered it to him. It had been cold up high when they'd flown before. "Want to find out?"

A ghost of a smile curled the corner of his mouth as he took in the shirt and all his things behind her, just as he'd left them. But then a shadow passed over his face. "We can't lose anyone else to that rock," he said, accepting the shirt. He pulled it over his head, muscles rippling under his torso's smooth skin.

"Come *on*," Rina called down to them, "let's get going!"

An argument erupted over who should actually go on the flier, which Alesta hazarded could carry as many as four. Alesta and Lia, obviously, but the royal advisers and attendants finally grew insistent enough to object to Kyr's coming with them. "You are most likely king—"

"If I am," Kyr said, already moving one of the craft's blocks away from in front of one wheel, "it's only all the more reason for me to do this."

"But—"

Kyr hefted the block into the protesting adviser's arms and went for the next. Then the advisers demanded one of them accompany him, at least—in place of Rina.

Rina's alarmed face looked over the craft's frame. Alesta recalled how much she'd wished she had her flier to chase after Kyr when he was tithed. "Sorry," Alesta told the advisers. "My flier, my crew." She wasn't going to leave Rina behind and didn't think she could stomach returning to Orroccio without Kyr. Hektorus might have been coming, but until he arrived, they'd be doing things their way. She had Lia climb up with Rina, drew a deep breath, and began directing the attendants and everyone else eager to help. Soon they were pushing the craft out the doors and lining it up to face the bluffs.

It was strange having an audience for the launch of another flier. This was definitely as reckless as her previous attempt. But they were desperate. This time, Alesta didn't care about soaring to glory or impressing anyone. She felt a pinch in her gut thinking of how much she really had in common with Mico, vying for a place atop everyone else at the Towers. Her success had always meant someone else's loss. Just like Kyr's survival on Orroccio. Everything had a cost. But Lia had broken that equation open. Alesta planted her hands against the flier's frame and set her jaw. They were charting their own fate now.

She checked the craft over, shouting instructions, and finally followed Kyr up into its body. This flier was built for three to power, bowing wider in the middle like a small fishing boat. She ducked under the wires and workings, pointing everyone to a sling seat, calculating wildly. They could do this. Lia, tucked into the sharp angle at their tail, didn't really count—she might not fly but she didn't quite walk upon the earth—or the cypress floorboards. Good enough, Alesta told herself. To not fall out of the sky.

Which brightened more and more with Hektorus' approaching glory.

Rina was swimming in a bundle of satin. "Ugh!" She straightened, unfastened her skirts, and tossed them over the side. She settled into her seat in her slimmest petticoat and clamped her slippers onto the pedals.

Alesta took her place in the seat by the steering controls, shouted again, and they began. Wings and wheels stirred to life. The craft rumbled down the hill.

Alesta's hands were clammy where she gripped the tiller. They jolted over a bump, and Kyr locked eyes with her. They pedaled furiously. The flier gained speed and they descended the slope faster.

The grass pulled back and the sea rose up before them. With wings arcing through the air at full speed, they shot out over the rocks and water and wind.

The sky took them up into itself. Kyrian hadn't been able to see much at all the last time he'd flown. The waves spreading beneath them were like a field but painted slate, in rougher brushstrokes than when viewed from shore or ship, and each pared off a sliver of the golden glow out of the east. Still, this was similar to before—relying on Alesta to guide them through the air.

Rina let out a whoop that the wind carried off fast. Alesta pulled a rope and the wheels fell away from the craft, and they flew higher. Over their splash, Kyrian asked, "How do we land?"

She angled a control upward and winced at him. "We're supposed to glide to a landing. On the soft fields of Soladisa."

He reached forward and clapped his hand over hers. "Just hold on." It still felt a little strange, the unfamiliarity of himself—but her hand in his felt true. As long as they got Lia to Aria, everything would be all right.

He told himself this as the wind grew fiercer and the waves wilder. Alesta steered them high, beyond the reach of anything lurking in the water, where the breeze carried them fast and allowed them to take turns working the wings—even Lia, who stretched between two of the sets of pedals and gears and set them running with her magic for a while.

Kyrian attempted an awkward apology on behalf of Soladisa for how much power had been taken from her, which she was blessedly gracious about, and he resolved to think of how to make true reparation once they'd saved Aria and he could think more clearly. Rina fretted about catching up to the ship as hours passed. They were well out over the sea when a sudden gold spilled across the waves. Kyrian turned backward to see something bright erupting over the horizon.

Lia met his gaze. "He's getting closer."

Hektorus. Still only a gleam like bronze through clouds driven before him. Sending a biting wind ahead.

In the force of its gust, Alesta struggled with the controls. Kyrian was reaching to help her when Rina cried out. "The ship!"

Good. They'd overtake it, and Lor would be safe once they reached Orroccio ahead of her.

It took him a moment to understand Rina's cry had not been one of relief or excitement. The wind from Hektorus' approach had tossed the sea into such frothing, the tithing ship had been driven from its safe course. It listed into waters white with wind and writhing with monsters.

"*Oh no, oh no——*" Rina's face was as ashen as the sky.

Alesta yelled, "They're taking on water!"

"Can you get lower?" Kyrian yelled back.

Alesta looked to Lia. "If you pedal!" The demigoddess slipped closer to the front of the craft, stretched out her hand, and took over, while Alesta leaned into the tiller with her whole body. They banked hard. In a few moments, they rounded back toward the ship, darting low.

Rina shouted for Lor. A giant wave reached high, threatening to catch and drag them all down. Alesta pulled up, sending Kyrian's gut lurching, then drove the flier back toward the ship. Something thumped against the craft's floorboards. Kyrian leaped to the side, bracing himself against the wing frame, watching for when they got near enough. He leaned as far as he could—but Lor was still chained to the ship's bulwark just as he'd been on his journey. The alberos were in a panic. Red tentacles threw themselves over the side of the ship. He wrenched himself back upright. "It's too far. We can't pull them up."

"We can't carry them all anyway!" Alesta shouted, steering the craft back around.

Kyrian's hand tightened on the wood frame. His stomach had pitched about a dozen times as they'd flown, but a certainty like a heavy rock settled in its pit now. "One more time. Fly low."

"What can we do?" Alesta shook her head, wind drawing her curls straight across her brow and cheeks. "Hektorus is coming—"

"You can get Lia to Aria. I have to help them." Until the sea calmed, which he had to hope would happen once either Aria or Hektorus got what they wanted.

Alesta scowled but pushed the craft low again. Kyrian swung himself up on the side of the frame. "If he takes her before—" He swallowed. "Don't do anything ridiculous," he told her, knowing if there was no other option left, she absolutely would.

Alesta nodded, eyes wide. "Like jumping out of the flier into the poison sea."

They were coming back upon the ship fast. No time. He took what he hoped wasn't one last look of her, grim and vivid and wind tousled. "I love you."

"I love you!" she yelled back.

Then he threw himself from the flier.

Chapter Thirty-Three

AN UNCHARTED SEA

lesta had banked, trying to get Kyr as close to the tithing ship as possible, so she could see him go over the side, seeming to hang in the air an instant—then he was falling fast.

Rina shouted and vaulted over the craft's side. "I'm coming too!"

Wide-eyed, Alesta watched her plummet after Kyr. "Keep the workings going!" she pleaded to Lia, throwing herself back into pedaling. And then the ship was behind them. Nothing but choppy waves and poison fires and billowing ash clouds ahead. Lia shifted to keep both of the others turning. "I'll get you there."

She dared a look back, but the ship was already a dot on the sea made dark before the brightening tower of clouds on the horizon. Turning back to the controls, Alesta tried not to think of the power behind its glow. She tried not to think of Kyr in a sinking ship surrounded by monsters. She tried to gauge their course by the weak sun and keep her eyes on the horizon before her. But it was lost in shadowing smoke, lit through with Hektorus' brilliance and brewing an unearthly orange.

Kyrian landed with a splash into a storm of waves and tentacles and screaming. A rush of water the ship had taken on drove him into its dangerously low bulwark. He hauled himself up to see Rina emerge from a roll at the far end of the deck and struggle to her feet. Kyrian's heart skipped, but he reminded himself Alesta and Lia could manage.

Lor was pulling away as far as she could from where the rising water and red tentacles threatened. Kyrian grabbed an oar from the bulwark, half submerged already, and swung hard at a reaching branch of sucker-covered arms. He squinted against the stinging spindrift and batted the monster away while Rina sloshed nearer to check on Lor. The alberos were busy losing their minds and fighting off branzonos swarming onto the deck. This wasn't a poisonous current they'd veered into, but they'd never right the ship at this rate.

"Lorenza!" Rina fell against Lor, who half-hugged her back with her shackled arms. "Are you all right? Where's the key?"

"He's got it!" Lor pointed to an albero being dragged over the side of the ship.

Shit. Kyrian dove for the man, whacking at the tentacles winding around him. When they loosened, he flung the oar at Rina and heaved the wide-eyed albero back to the deck. The beast's tentacles whipped against Kyrian's back and arm, pricking through his thin shirt. He swiped back before recalling he no longer had claws.

The beast towed him back. His legs hit the ship's wall. He yelled to Rina, who was fending off a branzono who'd gotten too near Lor. "Get the key!"

The albero was crawling from the waterlogged side of the deck. He huddled away from the monsters and chaos. Rina fell upon him, digging into his robes, yanking open his collar.

The sea monster jerked Kyrian backward, and he almost toppled into the water. That morning he might have dealt with such a beast easily, but he was his old self again—through no virtue or deed of his own—and what power did he have to offer? But he was not letting himself be pulled down into monstrousness again. He pried at the tentacles like strangling vines. Freeing one from across his neck, he bit down hard on it, which made the rest release and give him up. He sputtered and barreled over to Lor just as a wave slammed into her. She flailed, tangled in her chains. Kyrian ducked underwater and lifted her by the shoulders just enough for her to gasp a breath.

Rina was back with the key. She fumbled with it while Kyrian bore Lor up. A wave caught them all, and Kyrian was choking when the first shackle fell open. As soon as Rina had the other, he scrambled to his feet and ran for where a branzono had an albero pinned against the mast. "Stay alive!" he shouted back to the girls. It was an absurd order. Especially for his first, if he really was to be king. But he'd be damned to hell a thousand times before he let anyone die being tithed for the kingdom again.

He hauled over the branzono and punched it, knocking it out against the flooding deck. He found more oars and pressed them into alberos' hands. Shouted for them to fight off the tentacled sea monster together.

Thoughts of humans turning to monsters—those attacking or protecting this ship—flashed through his mind. But they only had to hold on a little longer. Once Hektorus saw Lia had completed their covenant—Kyrian could not bear to think if the god snatched his daughter from the flier first, and Alesta was left to go on alone—the windstorm would cease. Aria would be saved, and the rage of the poison sea would calm. They just needed to stay alive until Alesta returned what had been lost. She'd done it already for Kyrian—found him when he was lost even to himself, his spirit trapped in a dark mirror-maze stretching past Orroccio back through his last years at home. Lia may have restored his body to what it had been, but Alesta had returned Kyrian to himself.

For now, what he could do with that second chance was keep everyone in one piece until they could steer the ship back to safety. With Lor and Rina and the others attacking at once, the sea monster let go of the ship, and Kyrian called everyone into a ring around the men trying to right the vessel, to protect them from the rest of the branzonos.

The wind was still dragging the ship westward, and an albero cried out, pointing. Ahead of them, the sea was in turns foamy and slick. Here and there oily waves lit from beneath seethed into flame. A field of poison—which the tithing ship had no protection against, no Lia tar slathered over its hull. They had to steer around it. They had to *be able* to steer. Kyrian shoved a branzono over the bulwark and shouted for everyone to begin bailing water.

He and Rina and Lor guarded their backs as they worked, but a branzono climbed up over the ship's side and swiped its claws at an albero dumping out a bucket. Kyrian rammed the branzono's gut with an oar as the man stumbled back behind him. The sea mist around them turned suddenly scarlet. Kyrian spun. The albero clutched at his neck. Kyrian reached out. He pressed a hand over where blood gushed from the albero's throat. The ship pitched wildly, and time seemed to slow as green leathery arms snaked from behind Kyrian, encircled him, and drew him back. He wrenched himself around, ready to knock the monster into the sea. The ship rolled hard. Their legs tangled and cracked into the bulwark as it tipped low.

Kyrian and monster dropped into the sea together.

Alesta flew on between two furious horizons, not sure which might swallow her up first. She fought with the tiller, catching blasts of wind to carry her and Lia on faster, cutting through the sky. She wasn't about to give up now.

Lia and Aria deserved to be together, just as Rina and Lor did. Like herself and Kyr. Even if people in power said no, said they were wicked, said they must follow the plan set for their lives, the plan set for the world. Hektorus had made Lia a promise, and then tried to twist her into doing what he wanted anyway. They'd all been playing a rigged game with the tithings. They all deserved to find their own fates, to go after whatever they wanted, without asking anyone's permission. Alesta's feet pounded the pedals she'd made as if they could grind up every cutting remark, every warning glance trying to fill them with shame for who they were. Every time she'd bowed to them.

Smash the lists of sins and virtues, tear down the names of hell and monster. She was getting Lia to Orroccio before Hektorus caught them. That was the final lever, the last gear, the lost key to remaking everything.

The sky behind blazed. The sky ahead curdled with smoke.

It pulled them into its murk. Alesta tried not to cough. Tried to maintain her bearings. There—amid the ash lit red—Orroccio. "Hold on!" she yelled to Lia. Alesta threw herself upon the controls, driving the flier down toward the rock. Her stomach climbed into her throat. There was no way off this craft but to crash onto the island—or whipped off course by the enraged wind, into the churning sea waiting to devour their last chance.

The water muted the howling of wind and monster, the slap of waves and cries of alberos. Light filtered through here beneath the tumult, illuminating the poison sea where Kyrian fell headfirst, and all that filled it—the branzono cutting through the water away from him fast. Rocks like shards. The cloud of burning poison bleeding strangely from the distance. A long bulbous monster trailing tentacles. A hundred smaller beasts with vicious teeth and sharp fins.

All fleeing something larger.

A hulking shadow deep below slipped nearer. Kyrian fought not to lose the small breath he'd captured before hitting the water as the leviathan swept beneath him and the ship. He struggled about and kicked wildly for the surface—where something else large loomed, a brightness above, driving its light deep as it passed, until the sea glowed green as life and the sky through the water became a shining gold. Hektorus would soon be upon Alesta. A need greater than the ache in Kyrian's lungs bloomed through his chest, to be at her side.

Monster below and god above and poison surrounding all, Kyrian fought his way to their little ship caught between.

Chapter Thirty-Four
CHAINS

They'd chained her to the rock. Sacrificed her for their paradise. Tied her with roots and soil to the land where they made their kingdom and took what they wanted.

But now Lia was free, waiting on another rock for the monster whose hunger for her reached across centuries and shores.

Alesta followed Lia as she walked barefoot but unflinching, skimming above Orroccio's bitter stone, heading from where they'd crashed toward the Umbilicus. Aria must have sensed Lia's approach, like she had the fragments of kharis Alesta had carried. Steam vented from high on the flying beasts' towers of stone, and the ground shook and bucked more wildly than ever, compelling Alesta to fall to a crouch on her raw knees and palms, but Lia moved on, untroubled amid the falling ash, a determined set to her shoulders.

The three beasts shot from the Umbilicus, ahead of a spill of vibrant lava. Alesta bolted forward, thinking maybe she and Lia could climb atop the rock where the alberos had chained her, and so many others—but the beasts ran wide away from Lia. Still driven off by her divinity, in any form.

On their heels the ground shuddered again, and cracked, the Umbilicus breaking open as more lava and Aria's monstrous form erupted from within Orroccio.

Lava washed around her tremendous body, radiating over the ground, filling the little hollows in the stone. Aria clawed at the rock, as if she'd barely managed to drag herself this far, stretching herself and the wellspring of lava as far as she might.

Alesta fought down a breath, choking on the steam that clotted the ash in midair. Choking on the thought that Aria had endured as Kyr had, and far longer. All that rage. All that pain. All that waiting. All that shame.

And as Kyr had on the other side of that obsidian wall, Aria stared at Lia. She seethed.

She stilled.

Lia knelt outside the pool of lava. She clamped her hands to the stone before her.

Alesta wished she could record the details of what miracle Lia performed next, to help her understand it. But simply watching, somehow she could see Lia reach into the workings of nature like they were mere gears needing setting right. Lia drew divinity from the world around her, and through her. It flowed into Orroccio's stone. The lava cooled, calming to beautiful, shimmering black. It carried on, through the island Aria was tied to, and through the monstrosity she had been hidden away in.

Aria roared.

The three beasts loped back their way, stirred to protectiveness, whining and bounding over the solid lava. They skirted the divinity pooling around their master, and ran on, still avoiding Lia—which left Alesta as a target.

She ran now for the tithing stone, though she didn't imagine she'd make it in time, or that these creatures who'd climbed the Umbilicus with their claws and muscle couldn't follow anywhere she fled.

Lia's divinity burned on through her and Aria. Smoke rose directly off Aria's monstrous body now. It wrapped around her, like a ghostly hand tightening its hold.

Lia frowned with concentration. The power around her intensified, bleaching the air and rock around her white.

Monstrous and divine clashed, and an explosion punched through the air like a volcanic blast.

Alesta was blown into the tithing rock, shoulder cracking against it. The lion and leopard fell limp, knocked against the stone. The wolf whimpered and stumbled to its feet. Alesta rolled her back to the wall, gasping each breath, embers stinging her skin and catching in her hair.

Lia was all keen focus, channeling more divinity like Nonnina drawing more thread through her spinning wheel. The force of it set her glowing, her bones within her illuminating. Her chest heaved. Her sure shoulders trembled now. And on and on she poured what power she could, onward to Aria.

The wolf darted forward. Alesta stooped and grabbed a fallen chain, broken free of the stone from the blast. She whipped it at the beast. It snapped its teeth back.

Aria's skin became a tracery of scale and radiance. She was tied to the source of monstrousness. But Lia's divinity was infinite. If she could survive it.

The wolf lunged for Alesta. She slung the chain over its neck, leaped upon it, and pulled. As she struggled, the air burned red around Aria, a flood of anger and pain. The rock underfoot both Aria and Lia began to melt down again. Aria's roar broke into a wailing howl thundering through the gray sky growing brighter— any second Hektorus would descend upon them—and Lia howled back.

The wolf drooped to the ground. Alesta's grip on the chain didn't loosen until it went limp. The links fell from her battered fingers when she saw, sweeping down toward the island, a piece of the sky tearing open to let the light of another world—maybe a thousand worlds—rush through.

Hektorus was here.

Chapter Thirty-Five
CALAMITY

No time to think. Alesta drew one breath, looking to Lia—her face still carved into a fierce grimace—and used that same breath to shout as loud as she could, the prayer ripping from her throat, "Grant me, O Hektorus, your divine concession!"

The light snarled together like a knot into the form of a man. The god stood before Alesta.

Hektorus appeared as he had in her vision, hair golden as a nimbus, a sheen of light over handsome features and muscular figure, feet skimming a breath above Orroccio's rock.

Alesta had never heard him speak, though, till now. His voice was thunder threaded with the threat of lightning's sting. "I have no time to bargain, girl."

The force of Hektorus' attention, the scrutiny of a god, was more dreadful than any time kneeling before the alberos or enduring stares at the Towers. "But—" Alesta slumped off the wolf and forced the words out, the taste of metal suddenly on her tongue. "You must allow me to make my petition."

The air around them crackled with static, as if also about to kindle into an inferno. Ash hung heavy like dark stars in a burning sky.

Alesta was sure Hektorus was a moment from flicking her into the sun and stealing Lia away for good, leaving Aria a monster and the rest of Soladisa at her mercy.

But Lia had been right. The sparks in the air wove themselves into golden circles around them both, the god and Alesta, as if they stood on two halves of his gleaming scales. His power demanded he listen. Hektorus jerked his chin down in a sharp nod. "Quickly, then."

Alesta opened and closed her mouth. A trap. She'd entered it to buy Lia the time she needed—and the roar of her fight continued—but now one wrong move would make it snap shut upon Alesta.

Hektorus clenched a hand and the golden ring around her tightened. "Every moment you waste risks my losing my daughter. What do you seek?" The static stung against Alesta's arms, orbiting faster into a whirlwind that pulled her from the ground. Her toes scraped only air, just like the gods.

Any deal she made, no matter how carefully she examined its conditions, was sure to entail her doom. She could take time to negotiate at least, ensure Lia could finish saving Aria first.

Suddenly Hektorus smiled, his teeth like pearls. "I will give it freely, if you make the covenant without delay." Almost as if he'd guessed her plan to drag this out. He tugged Alesta nearer with a small gesture of his arm, letting the golden rings around them press close together, and reached out to stroke a meaty hand down the side of her face. His touch made her head feel at once as if she'd drunk an entire bottle of wine. "What do you desire?

Not every transformation I enact is to create a monster." His grin cut wide. "Beauty. A figure envied by all."

Alesta blinked, fighting away the intoxication. This body had gotten her through hell. It had brought Kyr back. It had freed Lia. This was the body that Kyr had held, the face he'd kissed, and who knew if he was drowning right then and never would again? "No."

That smile didn't shrink at all as Hektorus said, "Will that young king really want more kisses from you now he's back to his old self?"

Anxiety swirled through Alesta's belly, like the wind speeding around her. Stealing her breath. Leaving her lightheaded. In the rush from the Towers, she'd ignored this exact worry pricking under her skin. Hektorus was delving into her mind and emotions, preying on them to trick her into damning herself. But Kyr had gone to his death for her once upon a time, and her faith was strong not only in him but in herself. She'd ask no bargain that would only poison every future moment she might get with him. "That's not what—" she gasped into the vortex around her. *"No."*

Hektorus' fingers trailed back up to her temple. "Ah, of course. Your difficulty stating your wish has a reason right here. Your spirit is a different shape than most. It fits strangely under my magic. I could smooth it out for you. Make everything so much easier."

Dizzy, seeing stars sloshing like the waves that could be sinking the tithing ship and drowning all her friends that moment, Alesta shook her head.

Hektorus' voice sounded as if it came from inside it, its soothing tones snuffing out the stars one by one. "Not even for the sake of your young king? Do you really want to stand up with him before the entire kingdom the way you are? Wouldn't that be a shame?

Won't you seem ridiculous?" His eyes stayed trained on her, but through her confusion Alesta could feel him fully aware of his daughter shouting behind her, and how every word of bargaining brought Lia that much closer to defying him or dying in the attempt. "Come now," Hektorus murmured. "You're more than clever enough to work out a deal you'll be happy with, to help him." He released a concerned sigh. "If he even survives to take the throne. Perhaps you'd like to bargain for his life?"

And no doubt somehow ruin it again as she once had, if she made one mistake in the wording of the deal. She had to choose something to ask, but it was so hard to think, with divinity brushing against her mind and metal tasting on her tongue and Lia screaming and Kyr probably drowning in poison and monsters— Alesta practically choked on her next *no*.

Hektorus' handsome face drew into an impatient frown like the knitting of thunderclouds. "Then make some request, or our negotiations are finished." The rings around them wobbled. Weakened. However his godly power worked, he wasn't bound to stand forever listening to nothing. "Speak, or get out of my way."

Alesta's head pounded in the face of godly conviction. Aria was roaring louder than ever behind her. Either Lia had failed, or she needed more time. Maybe Alesta *could* think of something simple to ask of Hektorus—something to ensure everyone's safety— She *was* clever—Kyr had said so—*Kyr*.

Hektorus turned coaxing again. "Just make one prayer to me, and I will bathe you in my grace, bear you up with my favor."

Yes, she'd always yearned for that. She could find the right trick to render the trap harmless. Her body relaxed, as the golden circle loosened around her. Her mind went almost liquid in the wash of

Hektorus' persuasion. It would be all right; Hektorus was the kingdom's patron and benefactor—he only wanted to help. He would
bless her at last. All would be well.

"Say yes," Hektorus commanded, "and you will no longer be a
sinner, out of harmony with everything good."

Words she once would have given everything to hear. Now they
snagged on the last barb left within her head. Harmony didn't
mean breaking yourself to be the same, silencing yourself to go
along with others. The world needed her just as she was, standing
before this god, speaking up for all Soladisans.

Alesta clenched her hands, hoping the bite of her nails would
help sharpen her thinking. It wasn't enough. Her fingers brushed
against the dagger at her belt. Mico's dagger. She drove her palm
against it. The pain cut through her tangled thoughts, keen as
Mico's blade forged of Lia that would never be lost—delivering a
beautiful, dangerous solution.

"I do . . ." She had to drag every word up out of herself like
water from a well. Speaking to Hektorus made her voice want to
hide within herself more than it ever had. "I do have a boon to
ask."

She glanced over her shoulder, at liquid rock pulsing into the
air with the reverberations of the devil's screams and divine power.
At Lia, limbs trembling, hair stuck slick to her pale brow with
sweat. At Aria, massive claws furrowing into the lava.

Alesta turned to Hektorus. "You'll take your daughter back,"
she began, talking around to her request, "and we won't have any
magic left." Her voice was halting. "I had some kharis, but it all
burned up. I turned—a little bit monster."

Hektorus made a sympathetic purring. "The corrupt cannot

hold the holy. But with one prayer—"

It tumbled out of her. "I pray you return the holy magic—a thousandfold over. To help the kingdom you pledged your daughter to help." Displeasure shadowed the glowing god's face at this reminder of his untidy bargains. His nostrils widened with restrained annoyance. Alesta chose her clever, careful words. "But no tricks. I don't want it returned where I lost it, deep in Orroccio, or hidden in the poison sea, or anywhere else I could never—"

"Yes, yes." A line of frustration carved deep between Hektorus' brows. "Make the bargain."

"I want it given right into the same hand where it burned away."

Hektorus beamed magnificently. "I accept your bargain as stated and grant this sacred covenant by my divine power."

The trap slammed shut.

Quick and determined, brilliant eyes already back on his daughter as he eased away from Alesta, Hektorus pulled magic from the air like darts of power, and forged it between his hands into an orb, glimmering and pulsing and almost alive.

He held it out, and a thread of the gold ring around him poured forth, bearing the ball of power forward. Hektorus' muscles coiled, ready to grab Lia the moment Alesta took the boon. But the gold static carried it past her, drove it on farther—

To Aria. Whose hand had clutched for the Lia she longed for, when Alesta met her deep in hell's abyss, and burned it instantly to smoke.

The holy magic broke open against Aria's claws, washed over her monstrous, incandescent body, and burned away the last ribbons of lava tying Aria to Orroccio.

Alesta blinked against the scorching rush of air. She'd sprung the trap, but it wasn't for her.

Fury shattered Hektorus' restraint. Rays of sunlight shot from the creases of his glower. Fear shot down Alesta's spine. Faster than she could wonder what he would do, Hektorus broke the gold chains around them and flung her away, before erupting back into a formless dazzling force charging upward.

As she fell to the ground, Alesta twisted to see, emerging from the massive blaze of scarlet that had been the monster Teras, the figure of a girl. Dark-haired and beautiful, like in Alesta's vision. Lia rose in one fluid motion, speeding forward like an arrow shot true, and raised her hands to the girl. They pushed aside the final shreds of monstrousness melting away from Aria, who, as the sky turned a sublime and burning white, grasped Lia and kissed her hard.

Thunder clapped across that sky, resounding wordless admonition through Alesta's head. The brightness grew until Alesta had to throw an arm before her eyes, until her skin screamed, then the light evaporated. The clouds darkened and dissolved, pummeling the water around Orroccio.

Hektorus vanished beyond the downpour.

The relief from all the blazing, the chasing, the undiluted divine attention—the lack of any divine retribution—left Alesta limp. They'd done it. She turned her cheeks to the raindrops as Lia and Aria collapsed together and kissed and talked and cried and kissed again. Eventually they walked over to her, roughspun dress and smock sticking to their legs, hair hanging in wet ropes. Rising to her feet, clutching her bloody palm to her side, Alesta couldn't help smiling at how they held hands, even as her relief shifted to worry for Kyr and everyone else on the ship. "Hektorus kept his end of his bargain with you, then?"

"Gone off in a huff." Lia's lips twisted. "As he does. But he doesn't break his covenants. He'll leave us in peace."

Alesta rubbed her arms gingerly, where the golden light had traced thin welts over her skin, where Hektorus' departing fury had cast a pink sunburn in moments. "I expected him to take out his frustration where he could."

Lia sighed. "He prefers to entice people into hurting themselves. Touching that much holy magic yourself would have burned you up in a heartbeat. And he doesn't stick around when he loses face, not when there are plenty of places to be worshiped. Why do you think he never came back to Soladisa, after they saw him weakened from war, and barely able to keep his word?" Lia's mouth spread into a smile, broader than any she'd given that day. "Speaking of that bargain, I would like for you to meet, properly, Aria."

Alesta noted how Aria's hand kneaded Lia's. The woman nodded a wary hello, dark eyes reflecting the rain. The divinity Lia had used to free her was powerful, but Alesta knew everything she'd been through couldn't be solved in a flash of magic. She'd have Lia by her side, though, at least, her presence more powerful than any kharis balm. The two of them wandered a little ways off, to talk or probably kiss some more.

Alesta kept her face turned toward the sea.

The clouds wrung themselves out and the rain ceased, having washed the ash from the sky. Puddles and waves sparkled in the late afternoon sun. The worry in Alesta's chest built to a painful bubble of pressure as she watched for any signs of the ship.

The idea that she might have bargained for its safety towed regret through her insides. Had anyone at all survived?

She sat on the rocky beach, hugging her knees to herself. She'd thought she'd lost Kyr once. She'd stared across this sea, bereft. Even as tears ran down her face, she didn't think she would ever give up waiting now. She'd become another of the dried-out corpses scattering the coast.

The sun was low when she saw the ship and leaped to her feet. As it grew closer, within the safe passage yet parted through the waters, she could see some of its sails were tattered. Nearer still and her eyes roved its deck for her friends.

The ship drew up to where the alberos had dropped their dinghy when they'd brought her here, and there was Rina—clinging to Lor's side. Waving and shouting.

Pointing.

With a great stutter of her heart, Alesta realized something splashed in the water between the ship and herself. He must have dived before they'd even stopped.

Kyr. Legs dredging through the shallow water, shirt drenched and clinging against his torso and arms. Long hair slicked back and shining in the setting sun. Anxious face breaking into a smile with that dimple that made Alesta's heart feel as if it now stopped completely. It really wasn't fair. Her clothes were half-burned off and stuck over with wet wolf hairs. She was sunburned and scratched. Thanks to the rain, her own hair wasn't actually on fire, but she was still covered with the acrid tinge.

Kyr stalked up the shore, over the last stretch of rocky beach, closing the space between them. When he reached her, he lifted his hands to cup Alesta's face. "You—" He planted a kiss to one of her tear-stained cheeks. "*Perfect*—" He kissed her other cheek. "Calamity." He pressed his lips to hers, and they lost themselves in a kiss unburdened with care of claws and unbound from worry of the future, that made Alesta believe everything was in fact absolutely perfect, herself and the entire world around her.

THE SOFTEST SKY

They held the wedding at the villa.

The royal advisers fussed at Kyr, saying an event of such importance should take place in the great sanctuary and royal hall, but he insisted there was plenty of room for anyone willing to trek down the island. They were getting used to his ways. The attendants despaired over his new wardrobe as well, when, his first days back, Kyr rejected every woolen stiff-collared jacket they offered in favor of simple, soft shirts Lor made for him.

Alesta, though, felt he looked perfect in his white shirt and embroidered vest as he stood at the front of the crowd assembled in the villa's gardens and invited Lia and Aria to make their covenant with each other.

Enough of the nobility and common people had demanded Kyr's coronation that it had happened the same week of his return, and with the alberos disgraced and the davinas unable to spark visions once Kyr ordered all remaining kharis sequestered, he seemed the only suitable person left to perform the marriage. Lia and Aria had deferred to him and his mother for most of the planning, happy to cocoon themselves in the apartments they were given and spend most of their days walking Soladisa's fields and beaches together.

After the ceremony, there was wine and food and music in the cool autumn afternoon, with anyone who wanted to attend welcome, and almost everyone had. After being pulled into dancing with Rina and Lor until her feet hurt, Alesta found Kyr chatting with his mother near a table laden with casks of wine. He worried the shirt button at his wrist, but things had been getting better between them, since the first tense weeks when he'd decided to stay at the Towers. The wedding preparations had helped, Alesta was pretty sure. She waited until his mother moved off to talk with another guest before sidling up to Kyr and knocking her shoulder gently into his. "All right?"

He relaxed against her and nodded. "We will be." Somebody's child ran up to the table and grabbed handfuls of the flowers strewn about as decorations before turning to pelt Vittore's youngest with them. Kyr smiled at the other children stealing flowers off the decorations winding around the garden's columns and racing through the crowd, throwing petals at each other. Children who would never have their names carved in boughs or watch their friends sail for Orroccio.

They could still shriek as loud as anything, as they chased each other through the dancing. Alesta laughed at Kyr's wince. She grabbed a cask from the table. "Want to sneak away?"

He put on a shocked look. "What? And miss all the best screaming? Gods, yes." His hand slipped easily into hers and didn't let go.

He held on as wedding guests turned from dancing and conversation to bow to their new king. Kyr nodded back genially, and walked on with Alesta, swinging their hands between them, then lifting them to lightly kiss her knuckles. He was everyone's lord Kyrian again—but her Kyr always.

She led him out past the reaches of the celebration and behind a line of cypresses, to the wide-open field west of the villa. Rina and Lor had already arrived and were plucking food from the platters laid out among the blankets and pillows.

Kyr stopped and stared. "You two planned this?"

Lor shook her head, munching a grape. "It was all Alesta."

Alesta pulled him along. "I thought we could each use someplace to escape." Being the center of attention along with a demigoddess and the others who'd help save her, the focus of a hundred courtiers' questions every day, was as exhausting as Kyr had always said. And he was still having nightmares, less often, but persistent. She couldn't reach back and change what had happened—erase all the time fighting for survival, sleeping on jagged stone—but she could borrow a few dozen pillows from the villa and steal some of the wedding feast: cheeses and honeycomb, squash blossoms and roast garlic, soft breads and cake dusted with anise. She plopped down beside Rina. "And food that has never had legs or a face."

"I appreciate that." Kyr laughed, settling beside her and scooping up some honeycomb.

"Wait until we get to Molissa," Alesta told him, uncorking the wine. "They have this porridge that will make you swear off monster slime forever." At this, he threatened to wipe honey onto her nose. She snapped her teeth at his finger, and he popped the morsel in her mouth.

Rina, leaning back against Lor, gave Kyr a dubious look. "Molissans like their food well spiced." She shook her head, overly grave. "You might die."

Alesta snorted. "You'll die when you see the libraries," she said. "I thought the Towers' were impressive." She poured a little wine into the waiting goblets to pass around. She'd been to Molissa twice now and the smaller island of Lekos a bit farther once, and tomorrow she was taking Kyr on his first visit. While the sea to the east had especially calmed since Aria was saved, and the kingdom had hopes of sailing it even now they no longer had the help of the Lia, Alesta had focused these past months on remaking a flier so they could establish regular sharing of books and knowledge to help it rebuild itself, without relying on the sacred tree. The less isolated lands possessed treasures of research into topics of natural philosophy and medicine left unexplored by Soladisa under the strictures of the Arbor, even a name for the way Alesta and Kyr were different—*autistic*, the Lekonians called it—as well as promising agricultural techniques. Kyr was hoping to spend this visit convincing several scholars and experts to make plans to return with Alesta in the future. But she knew he was also going to lose at least a few days wandering the massive libraries, full of volumes Soladisa had never seen.

"You can't die——" Lor sighed.

"Hear! Hear!" Alesta said, raising her goblet.

Lor smirked as she finished her thought. "You need to come home with some new ideas to scandalize the nobility."

Rina turned to Lor. "Did you hear his latest? I think three courtiers passed right out at the mention."

Lor shrugged. "Talk in the streets is all supportive."

Kyr shoved back his hair, which was already almost long enough again to need cutting. "If everyone simply decided I was king, I see no reason it can't happen again—with every Soladisan having a chance to be considered."

"Except Mico," Lor added.

Rina and Alesta booed loudly. She hated when his name came up. It always made her feel unsteady and a little foolish, having to remember the person she took as her friend had turned out to be such a deceiver. No matter how many times Rina pointed out he'd tricked many more than her.

"Except Mico," Kyr amended, scrubbing a hand over his clean-shaven jaw. No one quite knew what to do with his cousin. Previously, any serious transgressions led their perpetrators to Orroccio. For now he was under watch in a smaller set of apartments in the Towers, still convalescing from the injury he'd given himself. The wound had festered, and it took rather longer to heal without Lia medicine. Kyr had been ready to have the remaining kharis and other pieces stolen from Lia during her imprisonment as a tree destroyed, but she'd refused, saying she preferred they serve a purpose. So he'd had it all locked away for only the greatest emergencies that might befall the kingdom or any of its people. Mico's slow recovery did not rank.

"I'll keep an eye on him for you," Rina said. She alone was still having visions—less frequently, after a few weeks—which had turned out helpful more than once already in this time of flux. Along with her catching Kyr up on a year's worth of court gossip. "Keep the kingdom safe until you get back."

"And I'll keep you safe," Lor told her, wrapping her arms around Rina and resting her chin on her shoulder.

Rina grinned at Alesta, a pleased glint in her eye. They'd spent a few evenings catching up on their own gossip.

Kyr gave his goblet a swirl. "One of my advisers suggested only landowners be part of the selection process, and I agreed"—he took a sip, ignoring the way Lor's thin brows drew sharply together—"it could be a good opportunity to declare everyone the owners of the land they work, or buildings they inhabit."

Everyone was still laughing at his perfect imitation of the adviser's reaction when Lia and Aria strolled up. Laughter turned to cheers for the couple.

"You made it." Alesta beamed, standing to help arrange pillows for them.

They toasted the brides and asked about their plans. They'd spent the first weeks after Aria's restoration seeking any others back on Orroccio or in the sea who had once been human tithings. That first day, one of the branzonos had followed the tithing ship to the rock, not attacking, just watching from the water, and Lia had restored a girl who remembered a life on Soladisa generations ago. She and the few others Lia and Aria had found had been given a home in the Towers, though Kyr had been working to find records of their tithings and any living family.

Alesta had been surprised that Aria was willing to return to the island where she'd been imprisoned so long, but Lia confided, one evening after a shared meal on Kyr's balcony, that Aria didn't feel able to move on, or wed, until they'd done all they could for any survivors. And the monsters of Orroccio, ordered by Kyr to be left alone by humans now, gave their former master and her demigoddess companion a wide berth—though the three beasts followed like tame pets all through their searching. Kyr was hopeful about true peace between the two islands, and Alesta had been making her own codex, a record of her travels through Orroccio and everything she'd observed there, everything that might benefit the people of Soladisa to know—to better understand their neighbors to the west and how they might avoid any future conflict, after the centuries of violence between them.

Alesta loved when Lia and Aria would join the rest of them for meals, although she understood why they'd want to seclude themselves together after so long. When Lia went out, or joined Kyr's assemblies discussing the kingdom's future, she had more questions from Soladisans than anyone. People were growing interested in the pantheon beyond Hektorus. Cressa and Fucina, Velio and Pelagia. As much as Alesta wanted to ask her own thousand questions about the different gods and goddesses they knew so little about, she had made it clear she'd take Lia and Aria wherever they wanted to go, if that was what they wished. So far, they seemed content to stay on the island that had been Aria's home, where they'd met.

Now Kyr offered Lia the use of some of the abandoned chambers of the Arbor, if she was interested in sharing her knowledge with larger groups. Lia tilted her head. "I think that's something I'd like to do."

It sounded like something Alesta wanted to be a part of too. Excited to attend when she got back, she felt a swell of gratitude inside her chest that Lia could offer teaching rather than any sort of bitterness against the people who had, knowingly or unknowingly, been part of her captivity.

Lia smiled at Aria. "After a decent honeymoon. A hundred years or so should be enough." She leaned over and murmured something in her new wife's ear. Aria was still quiet around people besides Lia, but now she nodded, and Lia asked everyone to indulge her request for a song.

Aria's voice was like wine and rich earth, smooth and smoky and stirring. As she sang, Alesta ate a seed cake and Kyr rested his head in her lap, draping an arm across her legs and claiming her hip with his hand. Rina walked her fingers along Lor's thigh until she batted them off her knee and captured Rina's hand in her own. The sky washed over with a dim purple, and rabbits and deer appeared in the distance as the group listened and talked and ate and laughed, until the brides slipped away together. Rina rose soon after, holding a hand out to Lor. Music still drifted from the main celebration. "Come dance with me?"

Lor stood and stretched and took her hand. "Only if you behave yourself. You've had too much wine."

Rina pouted. She tugged Lor closer and kissed her knuckles. "I haven't. I just love you and don't care who knows it."

Lor stared at their hands, a slow grin growing on her face, as if she wasn't quite sure how she'd ended up so fortunate. Alesta hugged a pillow against her chest. She knew how she felt.

"You did wonderfully today," Rina told Kyr as they picked their way off the blankets.

"Happy to do the same for you whenever you like," he told her.

"Hmm." Rina closed her eyes. She'd definitely had too much wine. "I'm having a vision of you performing a marriage ceremony for every last couple on this island."

Kyr scoffed. "No you're not."

Lor pulled Rina along. "You'll manage it anyway, at the rate you're offering," she called over her shoulder.

"I can't. Not at every wedding." Kyr's gaze cut to Alesta. She threw the pillow at him. He caught it, tucked it beside her, and laid his head upon it and one bent arm. "I am excited to join you tomorrow. Life-ending levels of seasoning aside."

Alesta was full of anticipation too. Even at the idea of someday standing up in front of a crowd as big as today's. Kyr wasn't the only one who could fluster the other, though. "They have entire halls of art at the Molissan capital, too," she told him. "A whole building full of works from artists across the great eastern continent. And visiting artists hosted by the queen." She'd been saving this as a surprise, but it was worth spoiling for the look on Kyr's face now as he sat halfway up, a little dazed.

"A whole——" He blinked. "How many——?"

Alesta laughed, leaning on one elbow and patting his cheek. "You can find out while I'm meeting with their artificers."

He grumbled, turning and kissing the palm of her hand. "I want to come with you."

"It will all be talk of aqueducts and aerial mechanics——" They had so much to re-engineer to function without the Lia. So much work before them. It filled her with the same feeling as when she launched her flier now. Like they might still horribly crash, but the potential for what they could accomplish was as big as a hundred skies.

He dropped back to the pillow. "Still."

She snorted and let her head hang back, taking in the twilight tipping into night. It would take a dozen visits to cover everything they'd talked of. Kyr had a chance to do some real good, and he was using it, though he didn't want to be tied to the throne forever. Sharing the power and ensuring it remained shared was why he was so interested in visiting other countries and talking with their people. And there was so much she wanted to see and learn. Her

mind turned again to the question of what to do now that no tithing lay before her. She wanted to travel more, but maybe she could
return to the university, help make it a place anyone who wanted
was welcome to come study. Find a way to make sure they could,
taking turns in the fields and workshops—

Kyr's hand slid over hers and gave it a gentle pulse. She released
the lip she'd been chewing.

"Come here and bite mine instead," he said, his voice barely
more than a rumble in his throat.

The wide sky before them had deepened into a velvet blue,
pricked with stars like pathways to something beyond. Their light
reflected in his eyes as he wove their fingers together. She pressed
him into the pillows and dropped a kiss to his lips that tasted of
honey and promises yet to be made. She'd figure out her future,
and theirs, tomorrow—and next month, and next year. She had all
the time in the world.

THE END

ACKNOWLEDGEMENTS

My high school's mascot was the Blue Devil, something that caused predictable controversy, especially when as students we made devil horns with our hands and chanted *Devil! Power!* to cheer on the homecoming parade and football team (right across the street from my Catholic church). I can't say if this book justifies the concern, but with all the demonizing of public schools and educators going on these days, I remain stoutly grateful not only for the inspiration of the devil that grinned down at me from the walls of Davis High, but to the teachers there who first introduced me to Dante's *Divine Comedy* and to a wide range of viewpoints and voices that helped me become the kind of person and writer I hoped to be.

In turn, I'm so thankful to every reader who picks up or downloads this book, who spends time with its characters, and who, I hope, finds something to inspire them to go rebel against the real monsters, whether they're taking the form of ableism, purity culture, oppressive beauty standards, xenophobia, fatphobia, homophobia, patriarchy, or whatever small-mindedness or systems are standing in the way. And my gratitude extends to all the current educators, librarians, and booksellers who continue to champion and share vital, diverse stories with young readers.

This story could not have found a better first champion than in my agent, Lee O'Brien, and has benefited hugely from his keen editorial eye. Thank you for guiding me through the dark wood of revision and of publishing, and for loving Kyrian and Alesta as much as I do. I'm tremendously grateful for our partnership.

I don't know how rare it may be to have an editor who not only supports your vision for a mythological-mashup, everything-and-the-kitchen-sink book like this, but also digs into nuanced discussions of the representation of characters' identities and asks for more on the page; I just know I am deeply grateful for mine. It is such a privilege to work with Tamara Grasty, and their efforts with this story have transformed it into a final form I am so proud of and hope resonates with readers.

Endless thanks to everyone at Page Street who has given my stories such a loving, enthusiastic home, including Lauren Knowles, Cas Jones, Krystal Green, Lauren Cepero, Elena Van Horn, Emma Hardy, Lizzy Mason, Shannon Dolley, and copy editor Heather Taylor. And a heartfelt thank you to designer Rosie G. Stewart and cover artist Flora Kirk for making this book beautiful on the inside and for crafting a stunning cover that declares so boldly that fat girls can be heroes, at the center of their own stories.

All the love to my widespread writing family, including *Shore*'s first reader, Loretta Chefchaouni, S.A. Simon for organizing the Trash Swap that lit a fire under my drafting, the rest of my wonderful Pitch Wars class and my mentors and friends Alechia Dow and Sheena Boekweg, and the inimitable Inklings. Immense thanks to everyone who read early versions of this book, including

Cate Baumer, Heidi Christopher, Samantha Elden, Jules Arbeaux, Jenny Howe, Courtney Kae, Leah Bauer, and Michelle Bui. Every one of you is a treasure and makes my writing better, and I know we like to joke about levels of publishing hell, but I'm so glad we're in it together.

Eternal thanks to my entire family, including my mother Leslie Kuss, for reading this and everything I write, sweet and beautiful Kaylene who always cheers me on, and Dan, for being an even bigger Italian nerd than all the rest of us. To my children Sophia and Nate, who are absolute angels, and not only for faithfully doing their pandemic homeschool so I could draft this book. And to my husband, David, for reading all my stories and encouraging my writing in tangible, everyday ways; for showing me autistic love is real and so, so beautiful and supporting me through my unmasking journey; and for being my best friend since we were just kids. I love you to hell and back.

About the Author

Leanne Schwartz has spent about half her life at either the library or the local theater, where she has played Lady Macbeth, Lady Capulet, Clytemnestra, and Hera—perhaps one reason she writes such vengeful, murderous girls. When she's not teaching English and poetry, she can be found baking pizzelle, directing scenes for the student Shakespeare festival, and singing along to show tunes. She lives in California with her family.